THE ___ ___ME

THE SHAME

Glasgow Southside Crime Series

Book 3

MAUREEN MYANT

This edition produced in Great Britain in 2024

by Hobeck Books Limited, 24 Brookside Business Park, Stone, Staffordshire ST15 0RZ

www.hobeck.net

A CIP catalogue for this book is available from the British Library.

ISBN 978-1-915-817-48-8 (pbk)

ISBN 978-1-915-817-47-1 (ebook)

Cover design by Jayne Mapp Design

Printed and bound in Great Britain

Are you a thriller seeker?

Hobeck Books is an independent publisher of crime, thrillers and suspense fiction and we have one aim – to bring you the books you want to read.

For more details about our books, our authors and our plans, plus the chance to download free novellas, sign up for our newsletter at **www.hobeck.net**.

You can also find us on Twitter **@hobeckbooks** or on Facebook **www.facebook.com/hobeckbooks10**.

To my children
Katherine, Kevin and Peter Myant

ONE

Glasgow

DS Mark Nicholson gazed at the raindrops weaving their way through the grit on the windowpane. It had to be a year or more since it was last cleaned. He pulled the mask away from his nose for a moment to take a deep breath. Masks were a necessary evil, but he wished he didn't have to wear one. Over the past month the number of Covid cases had fallen, so it wouldn't be for much longer, he hoped. He flinched as the door opened and the harsh tones of Alex Scrimgeour broke into his ruminations. 'Less of the daydreaming. Get in here. Now.'

Damn. He hated being caught out. 'Can it wait, sir?' he muttered. 'Five minutes and I'll have this report finished.'

'No, it can't fucking wait. Move.'

Bloody Scrimgeour. He was such a pain in the arse. Mark should be grateful – he'd been staying at Scrimgeour's flat since Karen had chucked him out – but fuck, it was hard at times. He followed the DI into his office.

Alex Scrimgeour sat back in his seat and barked out the information. 'Uniforms are out at a house in Crookston, a bungalow. Young couple moved in a year ago and they're doing an extension. Their builders started work in the cellar this morning and they've found skeletal remains.' He scratched the top of his head with a pencil. 'God knows what sort of state they'll be in. Took the stupid buggers some time to realise. They were using a jackhammer to break up a concrete floor, and from all accounts the skeleton is in more bits than a thousand-piece jigsaw.'

'Any indication of age?'

'Definitely an adult. Other than that, we'll have to wait to find out more.'

'Right,' said Mark, feeling a rush of adrenalin. At last something more interesting than the usual round of gang related stabbings and beatings.

'You need to get over there, pronto. Here's the address.' Scrimgeour handed Mark a piece of paper. 'We've no idea when the body dates from, although as it is a skeleton it'll be from years ago. I think you can rule out the couple who live there now. They only moved in last year. Don't go too easy on them though, in case they brought it with them.' He grinned, showing long, yellowing teeth.

'Are the uniforms there yet?'

'You got cloth ears? What did I say not two minutes ago?'

Fuck, he was a right idiot. 'Sorry, sir. I meant SOCO and the pathologist.'

'Aye, they're all there. Now, beat it. I want you there an hour ago.'

The house was in a long street of neat and well looked after bungalows. They all looked the same: pebbledashed, painted white or cream with PVC replacement windows and doors. Many of the front gardens had been paved over to create a parking space, though there were one or two that had a square of lawn surrounded by bedding plants. Number 253 was one of them, crime scene tape cordoning it off. A builder's van was parked in the road outside with three grumpy looking men leaning against it. One of them clocked Mark immediately.

'Here, big man. You polis? What's going on?'

Mark shrugged. 'Sorry, I can't say anything at the moment. Excuse me.'

'So, it's a human skeleton right enough? Callum here thought it was a dug.'

Mark gave them a wry grin. 'Sorry, guys, I can't comment.'

'You're a right numpty, Callum, so you are,' said the builder. 'Fancy thinking it was a dug.'

The youngest of the three, who looked about twelve, pouted. 'How would I know what it was? I'm not an expert.'

'Fuck's sake, Cal. That looked like a leg bone you drilled into. Ever seen a dug with legs that long?'

Mark left them to their argument. Poor Callum. He'd never be allowed to forget his mistake. He spoke to the nearest uniformed cop. 'DS Mark Nicholson. I'm in charge.'

'PC Joe Tynan. The pathologist's already here. I'll take you to her.'

They walked together to the back of the house, where there was a small door leading to the cellar. Another uniformed police officer handed him a white over-suit and he put it on.

PC Tynan lowered his voice. 'It's Doctor McEwan. She's been beefing about there being no officer in charge.'

Mark grimaced. Moira McEwan was known to be difficult. She should have retired years ago but refused to go, saying she'd only leave in a wooden overcoat. He stooped when he went into the cellar, as it was only about one metre seventy from the concrete floor to the joists. The pathologist was at the far end, kneeling on the ground, sifting through the dirt that had been dug up so far.

'What do we have here then?'

Dr McEwan lifted her head, 'Good to see you, too, DS Nicholson. I see the police continue to lead the way in polite conversation.'

She was a real stickler for etiquette; he should have remembered. But he wasn't in the mood to indulge her, and a devil prompted him to say, 'Sorry, Moira. Good to see you. Not for much longer though, I hear? Word is you're retiring soon. We'll be sorry to lose you.'

She glowered at him. 'Aye, right. They won't get rid of me that easily.' She pointed to what looked like a random pile of bones. 'Right, what we have here is an adult female skeleton. It's in several pieces, as the builders were using a jackhammer to get through the concrete. Fortunately, they didn't destroy the pelvis. I've examined this and it shows the remains are those of a female. Age unknown at present, but judging by the teeth she was quite old when she died. There's also clothing and a sheet that was used to wrap the body.'

'Any idea how long the body's been in the ground?'

Another look. 'You should know by now I'm not into guessing games.'

'Is there any possibility the current owners brought the body with them and used the building work as a cover?'

She gave him a wry grin. 'You've been reading too many crime novels. No, no chance.'

'What makes you so sure? Is there anything at all to help us narrow it down?'

'You don't give up, do you? OK, I'll give you this much. What I've seen of the clothing looks mid twentieth century in style. Fifties to sixties. Does that help?'

'Well, it'll help to rule out the new owners, but I'd all but done that anyway. What about whoever lived here before?'

The pathologist got to her feet with difficulty. She ignored the helping hand offered by Mark. 'It depends on how long they lived here. If it was a short time then you might be able to discount them, but then again vintage clothing has been popular with young women for a few years now, so you never know. Forget I mentioned it. Best wait and see.'

'Right, thanks.' For nothing, he added silently. 'I'll get the uniforms on to interviewing the neighbours, see if they've got anything to say about the people who lived here before.'

Mark gathered the team together and briefed them. 'Find out what you can about the ex-owners of this place. As far back as they can remember. Get details. Names, dates, any work done on the house or garden. What were the people like, anything strange about them? People love to gossip, so charm them into spilling the beans. And remember to keep socially distant. No popping in for a wee cup of tea.' That got a laugh. He looked at his watch. 'I'll see you back at the station. Briefing at four p.m. OK?'

There were enough officers here to get through a good part of the street in a couple of hours, so his time would be better used elsewhere. He'd find out where the last people had moved to and interview them himself with one of the

PCs. He knocked on the front door to speak to the new owners. A woman of around thirty answered. Her face was pale with shock. He introduced himself and she invited him in.

'I was wanting to ask you a few questions. Are you on your own here?' he said.

'My partner's at work. I was working from home today, to let the builders in and so on, but...' she trailed off.

'Well, we can wait until he gets home, if you like or—'

'She, my partner's a woman.'

Mark cursed himself for having made the assumption. 'My mistake, sorry. Do you want to wait until she gets here? Or someone can come back this evening, if you'd prefer.'

'It's fine. I can't settle down to do any work anyway, so if I can get this over at least then perhaps I'll catch up with things later. What do you need to know?'

'First of all, your name?'

'Sally Robinson and my partner is Emily Robertson. I know, I know.' She waved off the comment that was on the tip of his tongue. 'And if we ever get married, we'll both change our name to Robsdottir. The Icelandic way, you know.'

'Wouldn't it have to be Robertasdottir? I thought girls take their mother's name there.'

'Yes, of course. We should have thought of that. Both our mothers are called Anne. Maybe we'll go for Annesdottir.' Her voice was flat with exhaustion. She side-eyed him. 'But that's not why you're here.'

Mark returned to his questions. What was he thinking, getting diverted like that? 'When did you move in?'

Ms Robinson thought for a second before answering. 'We've been here a year. We moved in last August and the first thing we did was start the planning process. It was back and forwards for a few weeks. They had lots of questions for the structural engineer, you know because we were going to be excavating the cellar. We got planning permission in December and then of course we had to get builders' estimates. We'd just accepted one and then, wham, Covid struck.' She sighed. 'And now we have all this to deal with.'

'Yes, I'm sorry. It must be hard, I know. Do you happen to have the name of the people who sold the house to you at hand? No worries if you don't. We can easily access it.'

'It was a man, Ronnie Sanderson. His wife had died two years earlier and he said he found it too lonely living here. He moved to Newton Mearns, to a new apartment, to be nearer one of his daughters.'

'I don't suppose you have his address?'

'Yes, it's in the office.' She got up and left the room. Mark took the chance to have a good look at the room. It was clean and tidy, but the décor was dated. There was what looked like a reproduction fireplace with a living gas fire. The walls were papered, not plastered, and although the floor was wooden it was scuffed and tired looking. Ms Robinson came back in and handed him a piece of paper.

'Here you are. Is there anything else?'

'What were your impressions of Mr Sanderson?'

Ms Robinson frowned, concentrating. 'We only met him briefly. Twenty minutes or so when we looked round the house. My main impression was that he was sad. But he was a nice man, chatty. Talked about how he and his wife had been very happy here. They'd lived here for... oh, I'm not sure, more than twenty years anyway.' She paused. 'You can't suspect he has anything to do with...'

Mark didn't answer. He stood up. 'Thank you for your time, Ms Robinson.'

She walked him to the door. 'I don't know if I want to stay here now. We were hoping to make this our forever home. This... this discovery. It's horrible, like a curse.'

Privately, Mark agreed. No way would he want to stay in a house where a body had been found buried. He made an indeterminate sound and reminded her they'd be back later to interview her partner. As soon as he was outside, he pulled off his mask. It was good to be able to breathe again properly.

Mark glanced at his phone. There was enough time to go and see the ex-owner of the house, Ronnie Sanderson. Ms Robinson might be sure he hadn't done it, but Mark was ruling out nothing yet. He stopped the nearest PC and said, 'You're coming with me. Trip to Newton Mearns.'

The young woman officer looked pleased. She got into his car.

'I'm Emer O'Brien,' she said. 'Drafted in from the north.'

'Quiet up there, is it?'

'Put it this way; this makes a nice change.'

Mark laughed as he typed the post code into his satnav. 'Well, we're off to leafy East Renfrewshire to speak to the previous owner, find out if he knows anything. You'll be taking the notes. I've ruled out the current owners. The clothes worn by the deceased are from the fifties or sixties.'

'Last century? Wow.'

Mark tried not to roll his eyes. She made it sound so long ago. 'But I'm not ruling out the previous owners yet. Ms Robinson said she thought they'd lived there for over twenty years, but she wasn't sure. If that's the case, it's out with our time frame, but he might have information about whoever stayed there before.'

It only took fifteen minutes to get to the apartment block in Newton Mearns where Mr Sanderson lived. The man who came to the door was nothing like what Mark had imagined. From Ms Robinson's description he'd envisaged a small, thin man, deep in his own grief. This man, on the contrary, was well over six foot and wasn't fat exactly, but well built.

'I'm looking for Ronnie Sanderson,' said Mark.

The man's gaze flickered between Mark and Emer. 'That's me. How can I help you?'

Mark showed him his warrant card and introduced himself and Emer. 'Can we come in, please?'

Mr Sanderson's face dropped, a look of terror in his eyes. 'It isn't one of the girls, is it? Oh, please God, no.'

Mark hastened to reassure him. 'If by the girls you mean your daughters, no it's not about them. But we do need to speak to you.'

The apartment smelled of newbuild. It was neat and tidy inside and homely. There were photos on the wall and Mark looked over at them. 'This your family?'

'Yes.' Mr Sanderson's voice showed his stress. 'Please, tell me why you're here.'

Mark told him in as few words as possible, watching all the time for his reaction. Either the man was an excellent actor, or he was unaware there was a body in the cellar. His shock looked one hundred percent genuine.

'What will happen now?' Mr Sanderson asked.

'I can't say for sure, but it would be helpful to have a DNA sample from you. I have no idea whether it will be possible to extract DNA from the remains, but if it is we'll want to compare it with the DNA of everyone who has lived in the house.'

Mr Sanderson grimaced. 'Am I a suspect then?'

Mark didn't comment on this. 'We need to eliminate you from our enquiries. I understand your wife is deceased.'

Mr Sanderson's cheerful demeanour disappeared, and Mark saw for the first time the man described by Sally Robinson. He looked diminished, the light fading from his eyes. 'Yes. She had cancer. Bone cancer.' He sighed. 'It was a shock, I can tell you. I thought we had years ahead of us.'

'I'm sorry for your loss.'

'Thank you. Anyway, I'll do anything to help. You won't need to test the girls, will you?'

'I'm not sure. I imagine your DNA will be enough.'

'Ah. Well, actually, they're adopted. Will that make a difference?'

'It might. What age are they?'

'The twins are twenty-five and Ailish is twenty-one. They all left home to go to university in Aberdeen. Ailish lives there but Maisie and Cara came back to Glasgow. Maisie lives around the corner with her partner.'

Mark noted their names and ages. Unlikely as it was, if the remains turned out to be from less than ten years ago, any of them could be implicated. He stood up and Emer followed suit, putting her notebook away. 'Thank you again for your time, Mr Sanderson. We'll be in touch about DNA samples and we may need to take them from your daughters too, depending on how long the remains have been there.' He paused at the living room door. 'Before I go, you don't remember by any chance, who you bought the house from?'

Mr Sanderson raised his eyebrows. 'I certainly do. And now you mention it, there's something I need to tell you. You'd better sit down again.'

TWO

Glasgow 1991

ENID PUT the bungalow up for sale two days after her parents' funeral. The estate agent tried to talk her into 'tarting it up'.

'Nothing too drastic, a coat of paint here and there. New carpet in the lounge. Tidy up the garden.'

She ignored him. 'What will I get if I put it on the market like this?'

'You'll get more if you follow my suggestions.'

'I want a quick sale. How much?'

He hummed and hawed, asked about the roof, when the central heating had been installed, the double glazing. Eventually he came up with a figure that more than satisfied Enid.

'I want it on the market tomorrow. Fixed price.'

It sold within the week. A couple in their thirties bought it and professed themselves delighted. The woman visited her after their offer was accepted. 'I love this house,' she said. 'We're going to be so happy, here. I know it.' She lowered her voice. 'We're hoping to adopt. The garden will be perfect for children.'

Enid smiled. 'I'm sure you'll be very happy here.' Behind her back she crossed her fingers. They seemed like good people; they'd be great parents, she was sure. Better than hers had been.

And now it was a week before they were due to move in. Enid had cleared the house; she wanted nothing of her parents to remind her of them, nothing except their money. Money was impersonal. She was being foolish; the furniture was good quality, but she'd phoned up various charities, and bit by bit, it had gone. Enid's bed had been the last thing to go. The British Heart Foundation had collected it an hour ago. A narrow single bed, not the standard three feet wide but a miserable two foot six inches. A child's bed. She'd ordered a king size bed for her new home.

The bungalow was empty, only carpets and curtains remained, and she was sure they wouldn't be there for much longer. Mr and Mrs Sanderson, the couple who had bought the house, had been round earlier that month, measuring, taking notes in their matching Filofaxes. Enid had been surprised when the woman had phoned yesterday to request another visit. She didn't know why. There wasn't a space left to be measured in the house, but she agreed and now she was waiting for them to appear.

She walked through the house one last time. It was a small bungalow, four main rooms: living room, dining room and two bedrooms. She went into her bedroom first.

It had no personality. Devoid of her belongings, few as they were, it was not an attractive room. Not that it ever had been. Her parents had pinched space from it to make an en suite bathroom for their own much larger bedroom. It had left a tiny room, eight feet by nine feet. Once the bed and wardrobe were in, there was little space for anything else. The carpet was an indiscriminate shade of sludge, the colour washed out and faded by the sun over the years, although where the furniture had stood, there were patches of the sage green it had once been.

Enid closed her eyes, and unbidden, a memory crept in. She had been only seven years old. The scene played out in her mind: waking up in a wet bed, crying out, then lying in terror of having woken up her parents. She saw her seven-year-old self, curled up to avoid the wet patch, shivering with cold and apprehension. Unable to get back to sleep, she got up at six o'clock, praying her parents didn't hear her. She stripped the bed and took the sheets and her pyjamas along to the kitchen. The washing machine, a twin tub that needed hauling from one side of the kitchen to where the sink was because it had tubes that had to be attached to taps, was too difficult for her to use. No, she had washed them by hand. Of course, they were dripping wet and her hands were too small and weak to wring them out properly. She did her best, but in a matter of minutes the kitchen floor was covered with soapy water. No matter how hard she tried, she was unable to mop up the mess and she'd left it, hoping it would have dried by the time her parents got up. It hadn't. Now, over thirty years later, Enid touched the side of her head, convinced she was still able to feel the bump that had arisen when her mother, infuriated by the flooded kitchen, had hit her.

She banished the thoughts. This was no time to be thinking about her parents. She should be celebrating leaving them behind. She left the room, closing the door behind her.

This would doubtless be a child's bedroom soon. If so, she hoped he or she would be happier here than she had been.

In the hall, she paused before her parents' bedroom. She wouldn't go in. Clearing out their personal effects had made her physically sick. Touching their clothes, however briefly, had tested her strength to its limits. In the end she'd filled black bin bags with everything in the room, shoving things in any old how. She took them to the dump, wanting them gone like her parents. To do this she'd had to call a taxi because she didn't drive; her parents hadn't allowed her to learn. The taxi driver had been jocular, over friendly.

'Is that you getting rid of the evidence?' he'd said, winking at her in the rear screen view mirror.

'Something like that,' she replied. She didn't know why she added, 'They're my parents' personal belongings. I'm clearing out their house.'

She'd embarrassed him. 'Oh, I'm sorry. Me and my big mouth. Have they passed away, then?'

'Yes, in a car crash.'

He had nothing more to say, but at the rubbish tip he'd been helpful, telling her to stay where she was while he dealt with everything. Once back at the bungalow, he apologised again.

'I'm sorry for your loss. Such a terrible thing.'

'Is it?' she replied.

A frown passed over his amiable, chubby face, 'Oh, right. I see what you're getting at. Better that they both went together. For them of course, not for you. Devoted to each other, were they?'

She handed him a twenty-pound note to cover the fare. 'Keep the change,' she said. It wasn't his fault he was so clueless.

No, there was no need to go in that room again. She moved on to the kitchen, which was off the dining room. When she was a child, she had escaped the misery of her life through reading. Enid Blyton was her favourite author. She longed to be one of the Famous Five. Their adventures were impressive and exciting, far removed from her dull life, but more than anything it was the food she longed for. In every book, or so it seemed, there was a farmhouse with a rotund, jolly farmer's wife who would put on a spread for the hungry children. Huge hams, whole chickens, freshly made bread, massive cheeses. The kitchens in these farmhouses were large, warm, welcoming rooms, with a scrubbed pine table at their heart and filled with the smell of scones baking. Nothing like her mother's chilly kitchen and the dreary dining room with the small Formica table that helped to make her food look unappetising and unappealing. Pale blue did nothing to enhance the watery stews and thin mince that were regularly served up for dinner. They were bad enough, but nothing had prepared Enid for the tripe and onions served up to her one evening after school.

Years later, Enid read that the colour of food was an important factor in appetite. Blue was an obvious no-no, but beige food wasn't attractive to the stomach either. The sight of it in itself was off putting. The plateful of white tripe, surrounded by a watery liquid, half-cooked, hard boiled potatoes and mushy cauliflower was hard to beat. Enid knew better than to say anything. She steeled herself, sat down and tried to eat. It was beyond her though. She did her best with the potatoes and cauliflower, hoping it would be enough to appease her mother. She took tiny forkfuls of the tripe and swallowed it whole, praying she wouldn't gag. But it defeated her and at last she put down her cutlery.

'I'm feeling unwell. May I be excused?'

'Finish your meal.' Her father didn't look up.

'But—'

'I said, finish your meal. Now.'

Something snapped in Enid. 'I can't. It's disgusting.'

Her father put down his knife and fork. 'What did you say?'

Whatever demon had possessed her didn't hang around to defend her. 'Nothing.'

'Finish your meal, you ungrateful little bitch. Finish it or I'll cut out your tongue and make you eat it.'

Tears streamed down her face as she forced the food down. When it was over and her plate was clear, she didn't dare move until she was told she was free to.

What age had she been? Thirteen, fourteen? It was a guess. She hadn't remembered that incident until now. She hoped she'd never recall it again. She left the kitchen and went into the final room, the lounge as her parents called it.

This was the largest room in the bungalow, but it was small, perhaps fifteen feet by twelve feet. It was dominated by a tiled fireplace in a particularly dreary shade of tawny brown, and the wall behind it had been covered in the faux wood panelling that had been all the rage in the late sixties when the room had last been decorated. No doubt it would be the first thing the new owners would get rid of. It made an already dark room look gloomy in both winter and summer. For the life of her, Enid didn't understand why the couple were so enamoured with the bungalow. The only thing it had going for it was the price.

Every Sunday morning had been spent in that room for as long as Enid remembered. Since her parents had fallen out with the pastor of their church, they didn't attend services but instead held their own. They'd persuaded a few of the women and a man to join them, dragged them into whatever feud it was they had with the pastor.

Sundays were the worst days of the week. Sitting in that dreary room, the only child in a roomful of adults. Reading the bible aloud. Always the Old Testament with its vengeful God. Sometimes there was chanting, which would lead to what they called speaking in tongues. It sounded like nonsense to her. The worship lasted for three hours or more. And then when the others left, her parents would berate her, tell her she was a sinner, useless. She was stupid, ugly, too thin. She was ungrateful, thankless, sinful. She absorbed it all, believed everything she was told, all the while weeping into her pillow at night.

She looked round the room. They were gone now and were no longer able to hurt her. Was her life to be defined by her upbringing by two perverted human beings who were hypocrites and liars? No, she wouldn't allow it. It was time to make a clean break from the past, and the first thing she would do was change her name. Her life as Enid Cavendish was over. She hadn't chosen a new name yet. Next week she'd go to her lawyer and find out what to do.

A tapping on the window made her jump. She looked round. The new owners were standing there, smiles splitting their faces. In spite of her misery, Enid smiled back. She went to open the door.

'Miss Cavendish. Thank you so much for allowing us to come round again.' The woman started talking as soon as she saw Enid. 'You must think we're awful pests, but we can't wait – Ow! That hurt.' She glared at her husband, who frowned back and whispered, 'Linda! Think about what you're saying.'

Her hand flew to her mouth, 'Oh, gosh. I'm sorry. I didn't think. You must...' She tailed off, blushing.

Enid took pity on her. 'Don't apologise. You have no idea how much I'm looking forward to the move. Come in. What was it you wanted to see?'

'The cellar, if you don't mind. We thought we might extend down there, but I'm not sure there's enough head room.'

Enid repressed a shudder. She hated the cellar, had done since she was a child. It was used for storage, and she'd paid a firm to come and clear it out after her parents' death. It had been expensive but was preferable to going in there herself. 'I... I'm sure there isn't. Especially towards the front of the house.'

Mr Sanderson sensed her reluctance. 'No need to come with us; we'll let ourselves in if you'll give us the key.'

'Didn't the estate agent show you the cellar?' She had paid extra to get the estate agent to show people the house and had only met the Sandersons after they'd put in an offer.

'Yes, he did. But we didn't pay proper attention as we thought we'd be using it for storage. It was only when we were discussing plans with the architect that he mentioned we might be able to extend in there.'

Enid recovered herself. 'I don't think there would be enough room down there, but you can see for yourself. I'll show you.' Enid took them out into the back garden. Her hands trembled as she opened the door. How she hated this place. She'd be glad to see the back of it. She tried not to breathe in the stench of decay, of the always present damp. Sometimes she'd swear she smelled it in the garden, the stink overwhelming the scent of the flowers. There was a light switch on the left-hand side as they went in, and she pressed it so the space flooded with light. When they came into the room after her, the disappointment on their faces was clear.

'Oh. You can barely stand up.'

'Yes. It's fine for storing bits and pieces, but it would need to be excavated to ensure enough head room,' said Enid. She was shivering, her stomach churned.

'Are you feeling all right?' asked Mr Sanderson.

'I missed breakfast, silly of me.'

'Oh.' His eyes said he didn't believe her. His wife didn't notice the interaction.

'It sounds like a lot of work. We should stick to the original plan of converting the attic.' She turned to her husband. 'What do you think, Ronnie?'

'I think you're right, Linda. It's a shame though, but the architect said if it needed excavating it would add thousands to the price.'

'That's a pity,' Enid managed to say. The shaking had stopped.

The couple were subdued. 'I hope you're not too disappointed,' said Enid as they were leaving.

Mrs Sanderson smiled. 'To be honest I'm relieved. It would have been a lot of work. We hadn't thought of it at all, but the architect we've hired is keen on that as an option.' She laughed. 'To be honest I think he thought a loft conversion was too boring and wanted to do something different. But I'm more than happy not to do it. If we want to extend further at any time, there's always the garden.'

Enid waved them off and returned to the cellar to make sure she'd locked up properly. She stood inside, shivering. The cellar extended to the whole length of the house, but it was shallower at the front than the back. At the back it was about six feet high but at the other end it was more like five feet. It would be a hell of an excavation, and odds on it'd compromise the foundations. The floor was uneven too. The ground had been concreted over in the past, but it hadn't been smoothed out and there were bumps here and there. They were small except for one near the back of the space. It was large and unsightly. Enid closed over the cellar door and went back inside. She had nothing more to do. Now the house was completely empty she'd booked a room in a hotel for tonight. Tomorrow she would pick up the keys for her new home in Edinburgh, a small modern apartment in Newington, near Holyrood Park. It was less than ten years old. Bright and clean with nowhere for shadows to hide. There wasn't a private garden but the communal one was huge. She'd sit out there in the summer. Gaze at Arthur's Seat. It was perfect.

THREE

Glasgow

MARK HAD TAKEN SO LONG over Mr Sanderson's statement, he and Emer were late for the briefing at four o'clock. Scrimgeour frowned at them when they entered the room.

'You're late.'

'Sorry, sir. We went to see Mr Sanderson, who was the man who sold the house to the present owners. He had a lot to say for himself.'

'Let's begin there then. What did he say? Anything helpful?'

'Yes. We found out who lived there before them.'

'OK,' said Scrimgeour. 'Good. Saves us having to look at the land register. Who was it then?'

'They bought the house from a woman called Enid Cavendish. She'd lived there all her life with her parents. They had died and so she sold up.'

'When was this?'

'It was 1991. She was in her late thirties, according to Mr Sanderson, so she and her parents must have lived there since at least the nineteen fifties.'

'Good, good. Fits with the time frame we have so far,' said Scrimgeour. 'Anything else?'

'We were on the point of leaving when he told us this story of the day before they moved in.' Mark repeated what Mr Sanderson had told them. 'And then, right at the end, get this. He said, and I quote...' Mark opened his notebook. '"She was trembling as she showed us the cellar. Shaking like a leaf. We were disappointed that the cellar wasn't deep enough to give us the space we wanted. The architect had said it would add thousands to the building costs if we excavated it, so we decided there and then we wouldn't do it. And, looking back on it, Miss Cavendish looked so relieved when we said that." Do you think perhaps...' Mark looked up. 'He didn't finish his sentence, but I was thinking exactly the same thing. Was Enid Cavendish perhaps behind this? Or did she know something? If the body was put there in the fifties or sixties, her family definitely lived there at the time.'

Scrimgeour looked thoughtful. 'Do we have her full name and current address?' he said.

'I've asked DC Nugent to look into it. We have her name but no address. I did a quick Google search but came up with nothing, although her name, Enid Cavendish, is unusual. I asked Mr Sanderson if he remembered where she'd moved to but he had no idea.'

'She can't have disappeared,' said Scrimgeour. 'There must be a record of her; try the electoral register.'

'Well, as I said, Fiona Nugent is on it.'

'Good, she's like a terrier with things like this. If anyone can sniff Cavendish out, it's her.'

It was past eight o'clock when he got back to the flat that evening. Mark looked round his temporary lodgings with mixed emotions. His immediate feeling when Scrimgeour had offered him the use of one of his spare rooms had been relief. It had been a shock when Karen found out a month ago that his ex-lover, Suzanne Yates, had had a baby and was claiming it was his. He had no idea how Karen had found out. He wouldn't put it past Suzanne to have told her, although she had assured him she wanted nothing from him. After all, she had a history of telling Karen things. When they'd been having an affair, she'd written a letter to Karen pretending it was from him. That had been the beginning of the end for them. Karen had thrown him out then and now she'd chucked him again. She'd been livid – who wouldn't be? But he had nowhere to go.

'You can't do that,' had been his immediate reaction.

'Try me, you lying, cheating bastard.' Her voice was deadly quiet, always a danger sign.

'Where am I going to go? There's a pandemic on, in case you hadn't noticed.'

'I don't care.' Karen was rigid in front of him; a drop of spittle hit him in the eye.

He wiped it away. 'I didn't plan this. You think I want another wean? And anyway, it's over, she wants nothing from me.'

'Oh, she wants something all right. You wait and see. She won't be happy until her claws are well and truly sunk into you. You fucking idiot.'

I used a condom,' he tried. 'Even though she was on the pill.'

She gaped at him. 'For God's sake, Mark! In what damn universe do you think I want to know any details about what you did with her? Get out now. My lawyer will be in touch. Now fuck the fuck off.'

They'd been here before. But the terrible night on the Whangie when they almost lost their youngest child brought them together again. There was no way back from this. It didn't help that Karen wanted another baby and now he'd rubbed her face in it. It was worse than Karen thought, though. She didn't know the baby had been conceived after he'd broken up with Suzanne. God help him when she found out. As yet she hadn't asked when the baby was born. Eventually she would, though.

To his surprise, Scrimgeour came to his rescue. He must be going soft in his old age. The previous year, he'd been reunited with his daughter, who'd been stolen from him as an infant, and it had mellowed him. Mark told Alex about Karen turfing him out and Alex immediately offered to put him up. It was the last thing he expected.

'I have a huge flat, Mark,' said Alex. 'You're welcome to one of the rooms until you get on your feet. I don't want any rent from you, but a share of the utility bills would be welcome.'

It was a more than generous offer. Alex's flat was massive – on the second floor of a beautiful tenement near Queen's Park. Mark had been there a few times but only ever in the living room, which was a touch soulless in his view. It had nothing personal in it to hint at Scrimgeour's personality. A massive leather sofa, a huge television and an expensive stereo system dominated the room. Maybe that had changed now his daughter was back in the picture. Despite his misgivings – Scrimgeour had always been a notoriously grumpy man – Mark accepted. He had no other options. It worried him though. Scrimgeour liked him, had a soft spot for him, and they generally got on well, but living with someone was a whole different ball game. How would they get on? He hoped it would work. It had to.

Alex had given him the larger of the two spare bedrooms and sure, it was a pleasant room, large enough for his needs. But heavens, if he thought the living room was without a soul, this was another thing entirely. Wooden floors, white walls and no furniture. Not a stick. Alex had moved what furniture there was to the other spare room to be used by his daughter when she came to visit. Not that there had been much chance since the pandemic.

A trip to IKEA soon sorted out the room. He bought a sofa bed, reasoning he'd use the room as a living room as well as somewhere to sleep so he wasn't always in Alex's way. He also bought the biggest chest of drawers they had. A cheap rug made the room more comfortable, but it had a long way to go before he'd feel at home.

When he arrived at the flat, Alex wasn't at home. Mark went into the kitchen to see what was in the fridge. The first couple of weeks he'd been here they'd lived on takeaways, but Mark reckoned he'd never save up enough for a place on his own if they kept this up, so he'd suggested they stocked up on essentials.

'Whisky and beer?' said Scrimgeour.

'Very funny. No. I mean pasta, rice, things like that. A few jars of sauce, chicken and mince for the freezer. It'll cost a quarter of what we've been spending on takeaways.'

'Aye, fine. You're cooking, mind.'

Fair enough. Scrimgeour's culinary skills were limited to burnt toast and charred bacon. They soon settled into a routine of Mark making enough for two. It was basic stuff but Scrimgeour was appreciative, he'd give him that. Mark was

25

fed up with processed food though. Alex tended to buy things like ready-made jars of pasta sauce. It was time for a change. He took two chicken breasts out of the fridge and prepared to make a Jamie Oliver recipe he'd found on YouTube. It looked simple enough, chicken fillets topped with Parmesan cheese, grated lime zest and herbs, wrapped in Parma ham. He was going to serve it with new potatoes and broccoli. He texted Alex to see if he was on his way home, and as soon as he pressed send, Alex walked in through the door.

'Good timing!' called Mark from the kitchen. 'It'll be ready in half an hour; do you want a drink?'

'I'm going to have a shower first, but get a beer for me, will you?

Half an hour later they were at the kitchen table. Mark had bought a bottle of Sauvignon Blanc to go with it, but Scrimgeour waved it aside in favour of another beer. 'What's this then?'

'Chicken wrapped in Parma ham.'

'Nice. Marks and Spencer?'

'Nope. Made from scratch.'

It went down well, although Scrimgeour insisted Mark hadn't made it himself. 'I'm sure I've seen this in Markie's.'

Mark rolled his eyes. There was no point in arguing. Alex's reaction pleased him, though.

After their meal, Alex got another beer while Mark poured himself a glass of wine. 'What do you make of this case then? Do you reckon this Cavendish woman is behind it?'

'I don't know, Alex. Mr Sanderson was pretty adamant she was pretty shifty about the cellar. If the body's been there since the early sixties, it's possible she knows something even if she's not responsible for the death of whoever it is. We need to find her and talk to her.'

'What information do we have about her?'

'There isn't much. Fiona was working on it when I left. All she'd found was Enid's date and place of birth. She was illegitimate, it seems. No father named on the birth certificate.'

'Yeah, it's not much to go on, is it?' said Alex.

'No, but there was a father around, because Cavendish told the Sandersons her parents had recently died. He remembered it clearly because she didn't acknowledge their words of sympathy. He thought it was odd at the time, but his wife thought she was too upset to say anything.'

'Do we know how they died?'

'Not yet, but I'm sure Fiona will have something for us tomorrow.'

'I hope so. Because if the body has been there for a few years there's not going to be a lot of evidence for us to look at. Right, I'm off to bed.' Alex got up and left Mark to ponder on what he was going to do next.

FOUR

Edinburgh

EDITH DRUMMOND WAS WOKEN each morning by her own personal *reveille* of a long trumpeting fart. She had lived alone since her parents died, so she had no way of knowing whether this was normal or not. She thought not. There was a lot that wasn't normal about Edith. For one thing, she had celebrated her parents' demise by buying the most expensive bottle of champagne in the local Oddbins. She wasn't used to drink, so her head was loupin the next day. It had been worth it.

This particular August morning she woke at four thirty, farted and turned over to go back to her dreams. Sleep eluded her, and with a start, she remembered today was the first day back at work after the school holidays. A holiday that had been particularly long this year, as schools had shut in March because of the pandemic that had now killed 800,000 people worldwide. A pandemic that had been predicted for years and yet had taken the world by surprise.

It hadn't been a holiday at all, in fact. For weeks she'd worked at home, making videos for her primary one class to

28

support their learning. She needn't have bothered. There were teachers in her school who got by on producing a few worksheets. Worksheets. Huh. They had their use, but they were no substitute for a human being. Each week she took a fairy tale and subverted it. She wrote out her own version of it and read it to the camera, dressed up as one of the characters. After she'd read it, she encouraged the children to make their own props and act it out. She based maths lessons on it, always ensuring counting and adding and subtracting were built into the story. Writing too was easy; the children had to choose an ending for the story and write it. She loved reading their efforts and made sure to encourage them to have a go even if they weren't sure of the spelling. Geography was covered by basing her story in a different place each week. Her favourite was her version of *The Three Little Pigs* who were cowboy builders using cheap and flimsy materials. The wolf was a health and safety inspector and the hero of the story. It was hard work but fun, and the reward was in the feedback she'd received from parents and children.

It was a blow when one of the parents posted her video of *The Three Little Pigs* on YouTube. He meant well, but there was always the prospect of someone seeing it and recognising her. The chances were slim, but she wasn't taking the risk. She'd phoned him and asked him to take it down. He agreed to do it immediately, accepting without a murmur her story that she hoped to publish the alternative tales one day and didn't want anyone stealing her ideas. If he thought it strange that she would nonetheless share them with twenty-four sets of parents, he didn't say. Anyway, that put an end to it, but not before it had been viewed more than eight hundred times with more than a few pleasing comments.

At seven minutes past five she abandoned her attempts to

sleep and got up. It was too early to shower. The pump she'd had put in to make up for poor water pressure was noisy, and her neighbours objected if she used it before six thirty. Resigned to an early start, she padded through to the living room with her book in hand. First things first: she uncovered her parrot's cage. Charlie greeted her with a disrespectful, 'Fuck off, Edith.'

'Fuck off yourself, you mangy old bird.' Edith left him in his cage. From time to time she let him out to fly round the room, but not today. She wasn't in the mood to clean up bird droppings. She ignored his squawks and went through to the kitchen, where she made herself tea and toast.

At six o'clock she cleaned the kitchen thoroughly, making sure she wiped all the surfaces. Edith had no intention of catching the virus, not that anyone had been in her flat to leave germs. That done, she had her shower, got dressed and prepared to go to school.

She'd started to cycle to work several years ago. The primary school where she worked was in Portobello, a coastal suburb of Edinburgh and not far from where she lived. She'd never owned a car although she had learned to drive after her parents died. While they were living, they'd discouraged her. More than that, they'd forbidden it. Her father in particular thought women shouldn't be allowed behind a steering wheel. Something about that stayed with her, and although she passed her test first time, she decided not to buy a car and instead make use of public transport. Where she lived now, there was a perfectly adequate bus service. And as she was over sixty it was free, which was a bonus. Her bus pass was a well-kept secret. No one at school, or so she believed, was aware of her real age. It was within walking distance, but it took an hour each way. Cycling through Holyrood Park to Duddingston and onwards to Porty was a no brainer.

She took her e-bike out of the bike shelter in the grounds of the apartment block, slotted in the battery and hoisted herself onto it. God, she was stiff. She took care to exercise every day, but it never failed to surprise her when her joints didn't do what she wanted them to. Several years ago, she had tested out different routes to school before settling on one that seemed to her the safest. Hills didn't bother her. The electric engine ensured she sailed up them with ease. No, it was the traffic on the main roads that was her main worry. Cycle lanes had been installed all over Edinburgh, but a few drivers took pleasure in scaring the shit out of cyclists, over-taking them with only a few inches to spare, though by law they were supposed to leave one and a half metres. The lanes also petered out in odd places. She'd seen photos of one on social media that ended after about a metre. Not much point in that.

The run to school went well. Today was an in-service day. A chance to make sure everything was in place for the children coming back the day after next. No doubt some of the teachers would spend time in the socially distanced staff room catching up. This year the main topic would doubtless be who had had Covid 19 and not the usual exchange of holiday stories. She'd stay in her classroom as she always did. She wasn't at work to make friends.

It was lunch time by the time she'd arranged the class to her satisfaction. A knock at the door startled her and she dropped the pile of books she'd been carrying. The head teacher sidled in.

'I'm sorry. Did I startle you, Edith?'

Olivia's apology didn't fool Edith for a minute. The head teacher didn't like her, and the feeling was mutual. 'Yes,' she said, turning her back on the young woman.

'It's time for the staff meeting. And lunch. I've ordered in a buffet.'

'I've brought sandwiches,' said Edith.

Olivia's eyes narrowed. 'Five minutes. Hall.' She slammed the door behind her, and Edith smiled.

Edith wasn't sure why she disliked Olivia Waring, although she was honest enough to admit age was a factor. At twenty-nine, Olivia was far too young to run a school in Edith's opinion. Last year, Edith made the mistake of voicing this to one of her colleagues, who suggested to her she was jealous. 'You don't like Olivia because you want to be a head teacher yourself.'

Edith didn't let her off easily. Most jibes she ignored, but not this one. 'I love teaching too much to sit in an office all day. Please don't project your own insecurities on to me.' But it wasn't only Olivia's age that bothered her. Olivia was two-faced, smiling at you while she sharpened her knife. She smooched up to everyone she met, and most people were taken in. The parents loved her, or at least the majority did. Some of them saw through her, usually after they'd had a run-in with her about the homework policy or school uniform. The rest were charmed, as were their children.

She was the last to arrive in the hall. She slipped in and took a seat at the back of the room, moving it away from her nearest neighbour until there was two metres between them.

'You won't catch anything from me,' huffed the young woman, who had been a student teacher there the year before and was now a probationer.

'No, but you might catch something from me.' That shut her up.

Olivia got to her feet and the buzz of conversation faded away. 'I hope you all had a good holiday.' It got a laugh. Edith rolled her eyes. What a bunch of brown-nosers. 'First of all, as you know, Miss Chambers retired from her post last term, leaving a vacancy. I'd like to introduce our new depute head whose appointment was finalised only two days ago. We're most fortunate to have him at the start of term as his last school was reluctant to let him go.'

'Retired my arse,' muttered Edith. 'You hounded her out, made her life a misery.' But her grumbles went unheard. She studied the man. He looked familiar. He was in his fifties, she estimated, tall with dark hair that was surely dyed. It didn't look natural. He was handsome, in a smug, well-fed sort of way. But his face... Where did she know him from?

Olivia continued, 'This is David Cameron. No, not that one. He's busy elsewhere. Writing his memoirs in his shepherd's hut.' She paused for the laugh, which dutifully came. Edith stared straight ahead, frozen to her seat. It wasn't possible. Her heart beat faster and she swallowed to fight the rising nausea. It was a common name, as Olivia's joke had shown. But there was no getting away from it. She recognised both his face and his name. The two went together. The question was, would he recognise her?

Edith took her varifocals out of her handbag and put them on. Usually she avoided wearing them as she thought they made her look older. That was better; she saw more clearly now. She wasn't entirely sure it was him. It was many years since they'd met, and he had aged. If she remembered correctly, he had been twenty-five back then. He'd be in his mid-fifties now. She needed to get nearer to get a better look, but she'd done herself no favours by sitting at the back and it would only draw attention if she moved now. She put her spectacles away as he stood up to address them.

He beamed out at them. 'I can't tell you how happy I am to be your new depute head teacher, and I'm looking forward to getting to know you all and to working with you. I came to teaching late. First, I was a mechanic, then an electrical engineer, and finally in my forties I saw sense and retrained as a teacher. I've been teaching now for eleven years, and I'm delighted to see a few old friends here from the past...'

Edith held her breath. It was him; it was too much of a coincidence for it not to be. The same name, same trade – well, not any more, obviously; he'd been a mechanic when they met – same voice...

He continued, nodding towards the front row. 'John Latimer, good to see you. And you, Patsy, and who is that I see up at the back?'

This was it. Shit. Edith shrank into her seat. She hated being in the limelight and this was going to be difficult to explain. For goodness' sake, she'd changed her name.

'It isn't, is it? Yes, it is! Franny Simpson, from Gate Street Primary. It must be years since I saw you, Fran. I'll catch up with you all later.'

Edith breathed again. His talk continued but she wasn't listening, too engrossed in her own thoughts. Of course he didn't recognise her. She too was years older; her hair was short and grey now. Not long and dark brown as it had been then. She was safe. She'd moved to Edinburgh from Glasgow after her parents died. Her name was different. She'd changed it by deed poll. There was nothing to worry about. Why, then, was her mouth dry and her heart beating as if it was a trapped bird trying to flee her chest? As soon as he stopped speaking, Olivia stood up.

'Now, this afternoon we shall be doing our statutory child protection training, but first I'm delighted to offer you a delicious lunch ordered from no less than Marks and Spencer. We'll have it in here. Bear with me while we rearrange the seating.'

Edith took the opportunity to slip away in the ensuing muddle of staff repositioning tables and chairs. Back in her classroom, she sat at her desk with her head in her hands, unsure what to do next. She was in the same position several minutes later when her door opened and Olivia entered in a cloud of ghastly perfume. If she wasn't wrong, it was that new perfume, Amer. Edith's nostrils contracted in protest. She was sensitive to smell. The last time she'd been in John Lewis, before the pandemic, Amer had not long been released. There was a big promotion of it and the stench followed her round the store like a stalker.

Edith sat up straight. 'New perfume, Olivia? Amer, isn't it? It suits you.'

Olivia looked pleased at what she thought was a compliment and then launched into her little prepared speech. 'Come now, Edith. I won't have this. You need to socialise more. Have you eaten your lunch yet? As soon as you have, I want you back in the hall. Mr Cameron is keen to meet you.' She paused. 'As our oldest member of staff, you have a certain position in the school.'

There was no denying it; Edith was the oldest teacher, but did Olivia have to mention it at every opportunity?

'I'll be there. By the way, did you know Amer is French for bitter? Strange name for a perfume, don't you think?'

Olivia flushed. 'Five minutes, otherwise I'm coming to get you.'

It was like being a child again, being bullied by her parents. How had this happened, that a woman who was not yet thirty, who was less than half her age, had this effect on her? It was a dire situation to be in.

Olivia leaned towards her. 'There's something on your chin. An eyelash, I think.' She touched it with her finger. 'Oh, it's... oh well, never mind. See you in five.' She smiled showing small, even teeth that had definitely been professionally whitened. They probably glowed in the dark.

Edith looked around her classroom for something to throw at Olivia's retreating back. Fortunately, there was nothing to hand. She chucked her sandwich in the bin, her appetite gone. Had the bitch done it on purpose? Edith was sensitive about the hairs that sprouted on her face and neck from nowhere overnight and checked every two or three days for any rogues. She ran her fingers over the spot Olivia had touched. Nothing. It was as smooth as she'd hoped. Olivia was trying to wind her up. Well, she'd get her own back later.

David was speaking to two of her colleagues when she went into the hall. She took a couple of dog-eared sandwiches from the platter on a table. Hovering over the table gave her the opportunity to listen in on their conversation.

'So, a late entrant to teaching then?'

'Yes. I was sick of the rat race that engineering had become, and I wanted to give something back to the community, so at the ancient age of forty-three I applied to do a Post Graduate Certificate of Education at Moray House.'

Edith decided to take the plunge. She had to know whether he recognised her or not. 'Any regrets since?'

He smiled towards her. 'Not in the least. I love teaching.

Never a dull moment. You must be Edith?' He held out his hand before quickly snatching it back. 'Sorry, sorry. I keep forgetting. This damn virus.'

'What is it we're supposed to do? Bump elbows, kick each other's foot?'

He laughed. 'I might fall over if I do that.' He took a sip of his tea. 'Olivia tells me you've been teaching here a while.'

Edith tried not to think what Olivia might have said. It wouldn't be flattering. Something about coming in with the ark or dinosaurs. She didn't care. The children loved her and that was what mattered. She smiled at him. 'It'll be twenty-five years in October. I came to cover for a maternity leave and never left.'

Olivia joined them and put her hand on David's arm in a proprietary fashion. Edith coughed. 'Social distancing, Olivia?'

Olivia jumped back as if scalded. 'Of course, of course. Sorry, David. I see you've met the oldest member of our team.'

Another ageist comment. Edith was going to note them. She was sick of them.

'What age are you, Edith, I've forgotten?' Olivia said, tucking a strand of her shiny black hair behind her ear.

'Old enough to know that you don't ask a lady her age,' said Edith. She was sensitive about her age, which was sixty-nine, and prided herself on looking younger. Her posture was good, she was active, and above all she had good skin with only a few crow's feet. She might be getting jowly, and God, her joints gave her hell at times, but that was to be expected.

'Of course, you're right. We'll keep it a little secret between us.' Olivia smiled and Edith shivered. It was chilling, not a friendly smile. Olivia continued, 'We must have a chat, Edith, catch up on things. Come and see me first thing tomorrow.'

What the hell was that about? She hoped her dismay didn't show, but she was going to have the last word anyway. 'Of course, anything you say. By the way, I love your dress. Such a brave choice with your colouring.'

Olivia narrowed her eyes. 'Eight a.m. tomorrow.' She left without another word.

Edith had forgotten David was there. He raised an enquiring eyebrow. It was tempting to say something cutting, but instead she murmured an excuse and made her way to her seat at the back of the hall to await the presentation on child protection.

Truth be told, she took none of it in. The remark about her age stung. Surely Olivia wasn't about to try to get rid of her? That was illegal. She'd check on her rights as soon as she got home. But at least David hadn't recognised her. She was relieved, of course she was, but it was a little insulting. In her mind she hadn't changed that much. She was slim, her posture was good. Perhaps it had been a mistake to allow her hair to go grey, but during lockdown she had no recourse to a hairdresser, and it was the easiest thing to do. What was she thinking? She ought to be downright thankful he hadn't recognised her. How would she explain the change of name for one thing? And then there was the other... No, she wasn't going to think about that. She sneaked a look at her watch. Olivia was droning on more than usual, labouring each point. Edith had heard it all before. The probationers, two young women who looked no more than twelve, were taking copious notes, bent over their twee little journals with their bejewelled and gaudy-coloured covers. By contrast, Edith had her trusty Moleskine open, but she had added little to her notes from the previous years. She was nothing if not organised. This notebook with its red cover was for child protection. An identical one but with a lavender cover was for health and safety, while black was for the curriculum and sapphire blue was for miscellaneous matters. She looked again at her watch; only a minute had passed. Time went slowly when Olivia was talking. It was nearly four and Edith wanted to get back to her classroom before the cleaners came in. Olivia had made it clear they must not be a hindrance to the cleaners doing their job, therefore all teaching staff had to leave promptly by five p.m. If Olivia finished at quarter past four, she'd have forty-five minutes to get things done. But it was not to be. Once she'd finished, Olivia went straight on to outline what they'd be doing tomorrow, which was to go through the social bubbles and all the arrangements for the dropping off and picking up of children. She talked for so long about it she would have been better to tell them there and then what they were to do. Or put it in an email. Time management wasn't Olivia's forte.

At last, it was over. Edith made her way back to her classroom. In the twenty minutes of grace before she was chucked out, she continued to plan for the children's return. It flew by, and when she was ready to go, she put on her jacket and checked for the key to her bike lock. A noise at her door made her look up. It was David.

'It's been bugging me,' he said. 'I'm sure I recognise you. You look familiar.'

Edith was aware of the flush rising up from her chest. She hoped it wasn't too obvious. 'Oh, if I had a pound for each time I've heard that. I have one of those faces... you know, common.'

'No, no. It's more than your face. It's everything about

you. The way you walk, the way you speak. Are you sure we haven't met?'

She made herself smile at him. 'I'm sure I would have remembered you if I had. Now, if you'll excuse me.' She brushed past him on her way out, keeping her eyes averted. Damn, damn, damn.

FIVE

Edinburgh

HE HAD RECOGNISED HER IMMEDIATELY. There was no mistaking the way she held herself. Proud to be the best part of six feet tall, her back straight and head held high. David was over six feet himself and didn't understand those tall women who shrank into themselves, hunching their backs to make themselves look smaller. People underestimate posture and walk as a way to recognise people, but it was a dead give-away. Nonetheless, he wanted to make sure before he spoke to her and made an arse of himself, so he had turned to his new head teacher. 'The woman at the back there, the only one properly social distancing. Who is she?'

Olivia lowered her reading glasses to look over the top of them. 'Bane of my life,' she said, not missing a beat. 'Bloody Edith Drummond.'

Strange. When they'd met her name had been Enid Cavendish. Perhaps it wasn't her after all, but no, it was. He'd bet his daughter's life on it. Why would she have changed her name, though? He tucked that bit of info away to chew on later. 'Bane of your life? That's harsh. What's she done?'

'Apart from looking down her nose at me and judging everything I do? Nothing, really, but she's past retiral age. I want young blood in my school.'

David raised an eyebrow. 'I'm not exactly young, Olivia.'

Olivia laughed, a tinkling sound that irritated the crap out of him. 'Darling, you're perfect as you are.'

Bloody hell, surely she wasn't flirting? He brought the subject back to Enid... Edith. He'd have to be careful there. 'What age is she?' He already knew but wanted to be sure it was her.

'Nearly seventy.' Olivia's mouth turned down in a gesture of disgust at the thought of being old. 'Can you imagine wanting to work at that age? She should be at home knitting or whatever it is old women do.' Olivia sniffed loudly. David moved a little further away. If she had brought a cold back from her holiday in Spain, or worse, he didn't want to catch it. He changed the subject. He'd speak to Edith – why on earth had she changed her name? – as soon as possible.

The chance came at lunchtime. She was late to arrive; everyone else had been there for some time, and he thought perhaps she wasn't coming. Olivia had ignored his change of subject earlier and had ranted for a while about how anti-social Edith was, how she undermined everything she did.

'She won't use the staffroom. She stays in her classroom at break time. If I try to arrange a social evening to help with fundraising, she never joins in.' The complaints kept coming, Olivia's pretty face marred by her dislike of Edith. There was more to this story, he thought, but he wouldn't hear it from Olivia. He'd ask one of his new colleagues to fill him in.

He tried again to put an end to her rant. 'I think it's for the best if two or three teachers stay in their class. It'll be a squeeze to get them all in at the same time, what with the social distancing we have to do.'

'My staff need to be sociable,' said Olivia. 'I hope you agree, David.'

Shit, she was a piece of work. Perhaps it was stupid to assume this school would be a breeze. She didn't seem like she was going to be the easiest person to work with.

He was standing by the buffet table when Edith came in. She didn't hesitate when she saw him and came across to hover over the unappetising spread before picking up a couple of unsavoury looking sandwiches. No way had this buffet come from Marks and Spencer as Olivia claimed. It had council purvey stamped all over it. David watched Edith out of the corner of his eye. He was talking to two of the classroom assistants about how he'd come to be a teacher and it was clear to him Edith was listening in, clearly waiting for a chance to join in.

'Any regrets?' she'd asked him.

'Not in the least. I love teaching. Never a dull moment. You must be Edith?' Like an idiot he'd tried to shake her hand but remembered just in time and apologised.

They chatted for a minute or two before Olivia came to join them. The two classroom assistants melted away. He had the impression they were wary of Olivia. As for Edith, she was immediately on edge. The temperature dropped. David had never seen such animosity between two people. They were as bad as each other. Jibes about age, about clothes. It was all-out war. When Olivia left them, he gave Edith an opportunity to comment but – good for her – she didn't take it.

At the end of the day he went to her classroom. It was time they spoke properly. He dived straight in with the old *I'm sure I know you from somewhere* routine. He'd caught her off guard. This time there was no mistaking the panic in her eyes, and his immediate thought was *what the hell is she hiding?* She recovered well though, and murmured about having 'one of those faces'. Her face was far from common though. Those high cheekbones, those cats' eyes. She had a look of an elderly Cait Blanchett. Not in the least bit common. He pressed her a little and she clammed up, rushing past him, desperate to escape his scrutiny.

'You're hiding something, lady,' he whispered as she left him in her classroom, but she didn't hear him, or if she did, she didn't let on.

SIX

Edinburgh

EDITH MADE sure she was at school by seven a.m. She
wanted the psychological advantage of being there before
Olivia. Olivia prided herself on arriving early and leaving
late, and she encouraged it in others. It was presenteeism,
nothing more. Those staff who complied spent much of the
extra time chatting to each other. Edith wasn't one of them.
She stuck to a firm routine of arriving well before the children were due in and leaving at four thirty, her eight hours
done. She rarely took a lunch break and eschewed the staff
room. What was the point of staying until six if you spent
your time gossiping? What would they do, all those point
scorers, now they had to leave to let the cleaners in? They
wouldn't be in earlier to compensate, that was for sure.

She was the first to arrive; Tommy the janitor was
marking off areas in the playground with a can of yellow
spray paint. She stopped to say hello. Early in her career
she'd learned it was best to keep the janny on your side. It
was easy enough; he liked her and she liked him. He was one
of the few people she had any time for in the school.

'What's this, then?'

'Oh hello, Miss Drummond. Getting the playground ready for social distancing. How are you?'

She'd given up years ago trying to get him to call her Edith. He was a former pupil, and old habits... 'I'm well, Tommy, thank you. And you?'

'Not great, Miss Drummond. My old mum passed away this summer.'

She went to squeeze his arm before remembering about Covid restrictions. She drew back and said, 'Oh, Tommy. How awful. I'd give you a hug but you know... Was it Covid?'

'Cancer. We've all forgotten about all the other things that kill you.'

'I hadn't heard she was ill.'

'No, it was all very sudden. Leukaemia. Just before lockdown she'd been tired and weak. She thought of going to the GP but left it because of all the save the NHS stuff. I nagged and nagged her, but she left it too late and now she's gone. She was only sixty-seven, you know.' His voice was unsteady. He was in his thirties now, but he was the same little boy at heart.

Edith hadn't known. She'd thought her to be ten years older, but she said, 'Much too young to die.'

They chatted for a few more minutes before Edith excused herself and made her way to her classroom. It was tempting to stay, because Tommy was a nice chap and she sensed he needed to talk about his mum, but she was determined to make a point to Olivia.

The sight of her classroom depressed her. All those tables facing the front. It was as bad as when she had been at school herself. That had been an old Victorian building with classrooms that had raised platforms or steps going all the way to the back of the room. It ensured each child had a good view of the blackboard. At least in theory. At Scotland Street school museum in Glasgow there was a room set out in exactly that fashion. There were five platforms, each with five pairs of desks, giving seating for fifty children in all. The desks were little more than narrow shelves on which to write, and the chairs a shared bench. If the child beside you got up, you too had to stand. There was no limit to class sizes, and so there were times when three children had to share the space meant for two. No wonder there had been frequent outbreaks of head lice. Every time the school nurse came, several children would end up with shaved heads painted purple. Or was that for impetigo? The thought gave her an itch. Time to get to work.

They'd been told each child had to have their own desig-nated space, so Edith had made name plates that she was going to tape to each table. Only half the children would be allowed in at any one time. Hopefully that would change next week as planned and the children would be in full time. They had already missed too much school. She had the same class as last year so she knew which children to keep apart and which ones would be disconsolate without a friend within whispering reach. She'd spent hours planning the layout. She had finished the last one and was moving on to her next task when Olivia breezed into the room.

'Ah, there you are Edith. I thought I said eight, my room.'

'You didn't mention a place to meet, and it's...' she peered at her watch, 'seven fifty-six.'

Two red spots appeared high on Olivia's cheeks. 'I'll see you in my room.'

Edith stuck her tongue out at the head teacher's retreating back. She counted to sixty, picked up her handbag and walked along the corridor to see what Olivia had to say. She waited until it was eight a.m. precisely before going into Olivia's office.

'Sit down.' Olivia was behind her desk. For someone who purported to follow democratic leadership principles this was ominous. Worse, the chair she indicated was a low armchair. Edith looked for an upright chair, so she'd be at the same height as Olivia. She pulled one across to the front of Olivia's desk and sat down.

'Oh sorry,' said Olivia. 'I should have realised you wouldn't want to use a soft chair.'

Edith didn't reply.

Olivia grimaced in pretend sympathy 'Are your knees playing up?'

They were, but Edith would never admit that. She smiled at Olivia. 'My knees are great, thank you.' Olivia looked disappointed and brought out a file from the top drawer of her desk. 'I've been thinking, dear. It's time to talk about how we are going to manage your retirement. I expect you'll be putting in your notice soon.'

Dear? Where the hell had that come from? 'I have no intention of doing any such thing.'

Olivia studied her nails. 'You can't work forever, Edith.' She looked up and tilted her head. 'You're past sixty-five, why would you want to keep on working? Half the staff here would jump at the chance of retirement. Especially the probationers.' She laughed at her own joke.

'Well, that's my business and no one else's.' Edith stood up. 'If that's all?'

'Sit down please, Edith. I want you to think about this seriously. The pandemic has given us all a fright. Aren't you worried about catching Covid? The fact is that as an older person you are much more at risk from it. You might end up off for a long time, heaven forbid. Surely you wouldn't want to disrupt the children's education any more than it has been already.'

'My attendance is excellent, as you well know,' said Edith. 'I've worked here for twenty-five years and not once have I been off.'

'Maybe so, maybe so.' Olivia dropped her voice. 'I'm thinking about you too, dear. The risk of long Covid, general deterioration as you get older. Surely you want to enjoy your retirement years?'

'I love my job and I am in excellent health.' To her dismay, Edith's voice was trembling.

'Of course, dear.' Condescending bitch.

Olivia pushed her hair behind her ears before she continued. 'In that case, if you're sure you won't retire, it's time for a move. You'll do learning support and Kieran Winter will take over your class.'

Edith's mouth was dry. 'You're not serious. I've prepared a whole term's work—'

'Give it to Kieran. I'm sure he'll be grateful.'

It was the dismissive way she said it that got to Edith. She'd spent weeks preparing lessons. She didn't mind; her work was her life, and she adored those children. But *give it to Kieran?* She'd burn her carefully prepared plans before she'd give them to that lazy bastard. He was a favourite of the head's and took advantage of the fact that for whatever reason (his handsome face, his sculpted body, his superficial charm?) Olivia chose to ignore his frequent absences, late coming and overall laissez-faire attitude.

'I haven't had a day off sick in all my years of teaching. Kieran was off for nineteen days in total last year. And don't

49

forget, the school year ended on March the eighteenth, meaning it was short by approximately one third. It's not a good attendance record. Has he been referred to occupational health?'

Olivia was rattled. 'I... I can't discuss that with you.'

'In other words, no. Perhaps he has a long-term illness that means he can't come in on Mondays. A fair number of his days off were on Mondays or before a long weekend.' Edith walked to the door and opened it. 'I've been keeping a record,' she said from the doorway. 'Of lots of things. If I were you, Olivia, I'd think again about moving me.'

Back in her room she sat at her desk, shaking. She hated confrontation, but she was damned if she'd allow herself to be manipulated in this way. Employment law had changed, and if she wanted to work, there was nothing to stop her. Not coronavirus, not a petty head teacher. She would work on regardless. One thing was for sure though, war had been declared and she needed all her wits about her and all her allies. Parents would help. A dropped hint here and there should do it, and who better to drop the word to than Tommy. The janitor was popular with parents and chatted to them regularly. He'd never be able to resist passing it on to parents. She looked out of the window to where he continued to paint yellow social distancing dots.

The rest of the day passed without incident. For hours Edith expected Olivia to come and turf her out, but she didn't show up, and by three o'clock she was beginning to feel more relaxed. Perhaps Olivia had changed her mind after all. She looked at her list of instructions. There were twenty-three items on it. She'd ticked them as she completed them, and she was now down to the last one. *Please ensure any soft toys or anything that cannot be easily cleaned is removed from your classroom.* Well that was easy. She'd taken all the soft toys home at the beginning of the outbreak to wash them, and they were still there. She was ready to go.

The door to her room opened and David came in. He looked embarrassed. 'Olivia sent me,' he began.

'Oh?'

'Um, yes. Apparently, you had words earlier on?'

Edith said nothing. She was sorry for him, standing there like a child sent for a punishment. Picking up her bag and moving towards the door, she said, 'Is there anything else?'

'Look, I'm sorry. I don't agree with what she's proposed. From what I've heard you're an excellent teacher and... look, can we go for a coffee or something? Have a chat about all this?'

Edith didn't want coffee, and nor did she want to hear his platitudes. 'No thank you. Say what you have to. I need to get home.'

David gave an embarrassed laugh. 'It's... um, Olivia really thinks you should retire. She's sent me here to try to persuade you, but...'

Poor soul, he was so embarrassed about something she'd known from the moment Olivia had stepped inside the school as head teacher two years ago. She smiled at him. 'You think I don't already know? Olivia and I already had that conversation this morning.'

'Listen, if you don't, she can make life uncomfortable for you.' His eyes didn't meet hers as he said this. Coward.

Edith leaned forward and spoke slowly and clearly as if he might have difficulty understanding. 'If she does "make life uncomfortable for me" then you can tell her from me I'll be taking her to a tribunal for constructive dismissal. As she no doubt knows, the law changed in 2011, so you do not have to retire at the age of sixty-five.'

'I know, I know. But don't you think—'

Edith held up her hand. 'Stop right there. I am not going to retire and that's an end to it.'

She hadn't thought it was possible for him to look any more uncomfortable. He didn't look at her as he spoke. 'Oh well, in that case I have to inform you that you and Kieran will share the primary two class and support for learning. I'll be setting up a timetable starting from next week. You'll have your class as normal for the rest of the week.' He left without saying another word, leaving Edith standing by her desk, face red, heart racing. It wasn't as bad as she feared but it was unacceptable, nonetheless.

'We'll see about that,' she said. Time to see Tommy.

As she'd thought, Tommy was a sympathetic ear. She didn't lay it on thick. She didn't complain but simply dropped it into conversation.

'Change for me this year, Tommy. I'll be sharing my class with Mr Winter.'

'What? But you always have the infants. You and Mrs Baker.'

'I know, but it'll be fine. You'll see.'

'Mr Winter? Isn't he the one who's always absent?'

She ought to ignore this and move on, but it was too good an opportunity. She'd have to be careful though. 'Oh well, people are absent for all sorts of reasons. I'm sure his were all above board.' That should do it. Indirect but nonetheless to the point.

Tommy tutted. 'Aye right. I heard lots of the parents

weren't too happy about the work he provided during lock-down. Near enough nothing, from what they said.'

Edith smiled; the seed was planted. 'I must be off now, Tommy, lots of preparation to do for tomorrow.' She'd buy a nice sympathy card and a rose for him to plant in his garden in memory of his mum. He liked roses, did Tommy.

———

The next day as Edith cycled into the playground, Tommy called out to her. 'Miss Drummond?'

She stopped. He waved and ran towards her.

'You need to see this.' He held out his phone to her.

'You've got a new phone? Latest model, is it?' Why was he showing her this? She got ready to move off.

'No! It's the primary two parents' WhatsApp group.'

'Oh,' she said. 'And?'

'I think you should read it.'

'How did you come by it?'

He blushed. 'I'm friendly with Janine's mum.'

Janine Ferguson's mum was an attractive, single parent who was in her late twenties. She had a reputation as a man-eater. Edith hoped Tommy would be careful.

'She's admin on the group and added me to it last night.'

Word had spread faster in the little school community than Edith had hoped. She took the phone from Tommy and began to read.

Jason's mummy
Guys! Have you heard Miss Drummond is to be replaced in part by another teacher?
18.31

Helen Dunlop
Yes! Bumped into Jessica's mum and she told me. But what part? What does that even mean? Do we know what teacher? I'm not happy and Ellie will be devastated. She LOVES Miss D. Haven't told her yet.
18.33

Fractious Father of Four
I heard they're going to be sort of job-sharing, half the week each doing P2 and half the week doing support for learning. It'll be a good thing for those kids who need support, she's a cracking teacher.
18:34

Helen Dunlop
Well I don't give a fuck about support for learning. None of my children need it. All Ellie needs is a good teacher and that's what she was supposed to have in Miss Drummond. I'm not going to stand for it.
18:35

Fractious Father of Four
I thought we had agreed there was to be no swearing on this group.
18:38

Helen Dunlop
Oh, fuck off, Billy. You're such a prig.
18:41

Mariella Greene
Haven't heard what teacher but frankly I don't care either

way. Miss Drummond is a good teacher but there are plenty of other good teachers in the school so what's the problem? Anyway, she's pretty old so maybe she's retiring. I don't think we should assume it's a bad thing until we know more.
18:42

Jason's mummy
That's so ageist. And actually, I heard it was going to be Kieran Winter who'd share the class and I've also heard he's hardly ever there. Apparently, he was off for five months last year.
18:45

Mariella Greene
Kieran's a friend of mine and he certainly was not off for five months. That's libel. If you don't want him to sue you I suggest you cease and desist right away. Anyway, this group was set up to pass on vital information to each other not pieces of gossip. I'm leaving it as of now. If anyone wants to join me in an alternative 'just for information' group, text me.
18:47

Jason's mummy
Fuck right off, you stuck up cow.
18:48

Mariella Greene
Always right up there with the witty repartee, aren't you, Amanda?
18:50

Mariella Greene has left the group

Jason's mummy
What a cow!
18:50

Jason's mummy
Guys, guys are you there? Answer me. I need your support
right now.
19:04

Frances (admin)
Can I remind you all to keep things civil in this group?
Thank you!
19:08

Edith handed the phone back to Tommy. 'Thanks for letting me see these.' In truth she would prefer not to have seen them, but it was good to know the parents were mainly on her side. Mariella Greene though. She'd never liked her; there was something 'off' about her, and as for her husband...

'So, what do you think? Will I ask Frances to add you to the group?'

'Oh, I don't think that's a good idea, Tommy. But keep me informed, would you?'

He winked at her; he always had been a cheeky wee rascal. 'No problem, Miss Drummond, no problem.'

Edith decided there was no point in getting back on her bike for the last hundred metres. She was at the school door when she heard puffing behind her.

'Miss Drummond! Can I have a word?'

Edith turned round. 'It's Leon's dad, is that right? You shouldn't really be here, you know. Playground's off limits to parents for now.'

'Yes, sorry. I'm Doug and it'll only take a minute. Is it true you're going to be sharing the class with another teacher?'

'Yes, it is.' She'd pick her words with care.

'But why? You always take infants, primary one to primary two. We kept Leon back at nursery for a year because of it. Of course, we would have done that anyway, he's a February birthday, but the deciding factor was knowing you would be his teacher.'

'That's good to hear, er, Doug.'

'So why? What's going on?'

Edith didn't appreciate the belligerent tone of voice that was typical of one or two of the more middle-class parents. Entitled was the new term used for what used to be plain rudeness. 'I'm afraid I don't know what you mean.'

'Just tell me one thing. Did you want this?'

She wasn't going to fall into the trap of confiding in a parent, so she smiled and said, 'I love my class, but I'm sure Mr Winter will also love them.' That should ensure the parents grasped who the proposed other teacher was if they didn't already know.

'Mr Winter? But he always takes Primary 4. And wasn't he absent for most of last year? Oh, this won't do at all. I'll be talking to Ms Waring later.'

Edith gave a non-committal smile. 'I'm sure it will all work out fine. Now, you must excuse me.' She got out her bike lock and chained the bike to the pole in the shelter.

Overall, her little campaign was off to a good start. Leon's dad was a pain; shame as his children were lovely, but he himself was arrogant and self-important. Despite her dislike of the woman, Edith pitied Olivia as she thought of the onslaught of complaints that would come from the parents. How would she cope? Edith laughed to herself. Come on, what did she care? It wasn't her problem. She set to work, looking forward to the return of her charges.

There was a lot to get used to. First of all, each class was coming in and leaving the school at different times. All primary ones and twos had to arrive at eight forty-five, while the rest of the classes had different times. The infants had to come in through the south gate, whereas the older children came in through the main gate. No parents were allowed in the school playground and all children had to be handed over at the school gate. Edith doubted it would work. Especially with the primary ones. There were always one or two, usually boys, who howled at the forthcoming departure of their parents. She'd need to look out for Will, who had taken months to settle last year. This year hadn't been a normal summer break, and it wouldn't surprise her if several of her class were a little wary after five months of home schooling.

She needn't have worried though. When she went to the gate, they all came in like lambs, easier in fact, because they needed no herding. As she crossed the playground with them, she listened to their joyful chatter and rejoiced. It was all going to be OK.

Her smile left her face though, or at least her real smile did – she kept an imitation plastered on her face when she saw Olivia with Kieran at the door of her classroom.

'Good morning,' she said, wanting to put Olivia off balance. 'Lovely to see you, Kieran. It's a shame you weren't here for the two days in-service. Were you ill?' She said this in the full knowledge he'd 'forgotten' when the first day back was and had booked his holiday with a return date after the start of term.

He blushed. 'No, I um...'

'Never mind that,' interrupted Olivia. 'Edith, I assume Mr Cameron told you of my plans for primary two and support for learning?'

'Indeed.' Edith shooed the children into class. 'This isn't a good time to chat,' she said. 'As you can see, I have to settle the class.'

Olivia sniffed. 'I'll see you both at lunch break. In my office. Kieran, you stay with Edith until then.'

Edith ignored Kieran and saw to her class, directing them to their places while he hovered by her desk, unsure what to do. When they had settled, he whispered to her, 'I'm as pissed off as you. I don't want to teach infants or Support for Learning. I was supposed to have primary six this year.'

'Who said I was pissed off?' said Edith in a sharp voice, but secretly she was pleased to hear he too wasn't happy. It would make things easier when it came to thinking about how best to sabotage Olivia's plans.

'Sorry, my bad. I thought...' His voice tailed off. 'What can I do?'

The morning passed more smoothly than Edith would ever have imagined. It was almost – and she found this hard to admit – fun. Kieran was much nicer than she thought he would be, both to her and to her class. Soon they got into a rhythm and the children liked it too. As the bell rang for the first sitting of lunch at noon, Edith rounded up the children to take them to the dinner hall. Kieran stopped her as she was going out the door.

'Shall I see you at Ms Waring's room?'

Edith raised an eyebrow. 'Depends whether you want to

hear what she wants to say. Me, I think I'll sit and have lunch with my class. We are entitled to a break, you know.'

Kieran stared at her. 'You don't like our head teacher, do you?'

Edith laughed. 'There are very few people I like.'

He looked at her with admiration. 'This is going to be a fun year after all,' he said. 'I'll tell Ms Waring you'll be along in fifteen minutes.'

'You do that,' said Edith and called the class to attention before walking them to the dinner hall.

SEVEN

Glasgow

THE FOLLOWING day was taken up with more interviews of neighbours in between trying to avoid the journalists who crowded in the street desperate for any news. The builders had disappeared. Off to another job, according to Sally Robinson. 'God knows when they'll come back,' she said to Mark when she saw him. 'How long do you think all this will take?'

'I'm sorry,' said Mark. 'It will take as long as it takes. This is a crime scene.'

She turned away, fighting back tears. It was a shame, but honestly? Tears? Over builders? A woman had died. It might be a long time ago, but the police had to do their job and he hadn't factored in having to make time for people being upset about their builders disappearing.

The team met again at four to discuss what they'd found out to date. It was similar to the day before; none of the neighbours knew anything, a few of them remembered the Sandersons but hardly anyone was around when Mr and Mrs

Cavendish were alive. Only one had anything to say about them and that wasn't much.

'They were weird, apparently,' said the PC who'd interviewed the neighbour. 'But she didn't remember much else. Kept themselves to themselves. She did say she'd always had sympathy for the daughter though. Didn't have much of a life, she said.'

Fiona Nugent was up next. She reported back on what she'd found out about the daughter. 'I've drawn a blank. I've done searches for Enid Cavendish and E. Cavendish. She was registered to vote in Glasgow until 1991, but after that, nothing. I'm telling you, my eyes are bleeding from looking at Google all day.'

Scrimgeour scowled. A young woman in uniform raised her hand. 'Yes? What is it?'

She blushed like a child. What age was she? No more than sixteen by the look of her, though she had to be older than that. 'I... I just wanted to say, I... I mean...'

'For heaven's sake, girl. Get on with it.'

Her face was scarlet. 'Perhaps she changed her name. I mean, if she had something to hide...'

Scrimgeour cracked his finger joints, making most of the officers in the room wince. 'Good point. What's your name, Constable?'

Mark thought it wasn't possible for the young woman to be more embarrassed. There were beads of sweat on her forehead. She'd think twice before drawing attention to herself again. 'It's Megan, sir.'

'Well, Megan, let's see what *you* can find out about Enid Cavendish. See if she has indeed changed her name. Get back to me asap.'

Poor girl. Mark didn't think she was long out of Tulliallan

Police College. He hoped Fiona would give her a helping hand, but from the look on her face Fiona was pretty pissed off at being shown up by the newcomer. Tough. She should have thought of that possibility herself. As should he.

Several hours later, Scrimgeour came over to his desk. 'That wee lassie was right, you know?'

Mark looked up from the statements he was studying. 'Megan?'

'Aye, didn't take her long to find out our woman did indeed change her name. And, get this. It was right after she'd left Glasgow. If that's not suspicious I don't know what is.'

Mark leaned back in his seat. 'Interesting, very interesting. What's her new name?'

Alex looked down at the notes in his hand. 'Edith Drummond. Once Megan found that out it was easy enough to get more information on her.'

'Where did she go? Is she in Glasgow?'

'Nope. She moved to Edinburgh. Newington. Right beside Holyrood Park. She works as a primary school teacher, although by all rights she ought to be retired by now. She'll be seventy next year. I've got her address here and the address of the school. You need to get through there tomorrow and interview her. I'll leave it up to you whether to go to the school or see her at home. The main thing is to take her by surprise.' He got up to go. 'Take Megan with you. She deserves a wee day out after all the work she's done today. I've a feeling we're about to find out who is behind all of this. Be sure to take a DNA kit with you. If there are any results from the remains, we want to be able to compare them.'

Mark shifted uncomfortably in his car seat. Christ, he hated the drive through to Edinburgh. That dreary stretch of the M8 with nothing to enliven it save a few metal sculptures. And no matter what the weather was when you left Glasgow, it was always raining or worse by the time you got to Shotts. That place had its own microclimate. He and Megan left at two o'clock with the plan of getting to the school where Edith Drummond worked before she left for home. The plan was to catch her off guard, and Mark reckoned she'd be less comfortable in her working environment. By the time they hit the Newhouse roundabout on the outskirts of Edinburgh it was three o'clock and there was a way to go. With any luck she'd be one of those conscientious teachers and not a clock watcher like several of his own teachers had been. Not that he blamed them. The school he'd gone to was rougher than a badger's arse.

He discussed his plan for interviewing Drummond with Megan as they drove. 'I think we should go for a slow reveal. Don't let on why we want to talk to her. Keep it vague, no specifics. We want to talk to her about a current case we're investigating.'

'But if she reads the tabloids, she'll know why we're here,' said Megan.

'Yeah, but it's worth a shot. We need to keep it quiet that we know she's changed her name. We can start by asking her if she ever lived in Glasgow. A lie immediately marks her down as suspicious.' If she did lie about that, Mark thought he had grounds for bringing her through to Glasgow for a formal interview, but time would tell.

It was after three thirty by the time they reached the school. Mark had never been to Portobello before. Any trips to the seaside when he was a child had been to west coast resorts; Largs, Ayr, Troon. Not that there had been many such visits. His father had preferred drink over family days out. Any spare money he'd had went on beer. Mark closed his eyes for a second to rid himself of the images from his past. He didn't want dark thoughts of his father interfering with his work.

The satnav guided them to a new build primary on the outskirts of the town. Mark drove into the car park and sat for a minute with the engine idling for a last-minute briefing to ensure Megan was fully on board. But they'd been spotted. A youngish man bustled over to the car. 'Can I help you, sir?'

'I'm here to see one of the teachers.'

'Do you have an appointment? The head teacher said no one is to come into the school without one.'

Fuck, a jobsworth. Perhaps it hadn't been such a good idea to come unannounced after all. 'No, we don't.'

Well, if you give me the teacher's name and wait here, I'll let whoever it is know.'

'It's Miss Drummond.'

The man's face fell. 'Oh, no. Her flat hasn't been broken into again, has it?'

'I'm afraid I can't say. But it is necessary to speak to her. Please let her know we're here. DS Mark Nicholson and PC Megan Webster.'

A few minutes later, a tall woman who looked as though she was in her late fifties came up to the car. She held herself well. 'Can I see your identification, please?'

Mark and Megan got out of the car and showed her their warrant cards. 'Is there a quiet room where we can talk?' said Mark, nodding towards the janitor, who was lingering nearby.

'We can go to my classroom. Please put on masks when you enter the school and be sure to follow social distancing rules.' She set off at a brisk pace, taking them by surprise so they had to scurry to catch up with her.

Once inside her classroom she sat down at one of the children's tables and indicated to them to take a seat. Megan folded herself into the tiny child's chair, but Mark sat on the top of a nearby table instead.

'What is this about?'

'Can I check before we start? Your name and address, please.'

'You must have these already if you've found me.'

Mark frowned at the words. It sounded as though she had been expecting them. 'We do but we have to ensure we have the right details.'

'Edith Drummond, 54 East Parkside, Edinburgh.'

'And how long have you lived there?'

'Thirty years, give or take a few months. What is this about?'

Mark ignored the question. 'I see.' Before he had a chance to add anything, she asked another question. 'Is this about my parents?'

Her parents were dead. Why was she bringing them up?
'No,' he said.

'It's not about the car crash?'

'What car crash?'

'N... nothing,' she stuttered. 'I witnessed a bump at a roundabout. I thought...'

'No, it's nothing like that. As I said, we have a few questions for you. Have you ever lived in Glasgow?' He watched carefully to see her reaction.

Edith became very still. Her hands were flat on the table in front of her, fingernails cut short. She looked down at them as if she'd never seen them before. A muscle twitched under her right eye.

'Miss Drummond?'

She blinked. 'Why do you ask?'

For heaven's sake. She was an expert in answering a question with another question. 'Have you ever lived in Glasgow?'

She sighed. 'Yes, I was brought up in Glasgow. In Crookston.'

He was almost disappointed she didn't lie. 'I don't know whether you've been following the news or not, but two days ago a discovery was made in the house where you used to live.' Her body relaxed. Was that relief passing across her face?

'What discovery? I haven't had time to follow the news in the past week. I've been extremely busy with work.' She looked genuinely bewildered, as if she had not been expecting that. Either that or she was an excellent actor.

'During building work at your old house, the remains of a person were found. They had been there for a considerable time, meaning the current and previous occupants could be ruled out. The remains were almost certainly buried during the time you and your parents lived there.'

She stared at him; her eyes unblinking. 'They found a body in the garden?'

'No, in the cellar. Are you able to shed any light on this?'

'No. I'm afraid not.' She stood up. 'This has nothing to do with me. So, if you'll excuse me...'

Mark hadn't expected such abruptness. He looked at Megan, aware she was expecting him to speak. 'We don't know it has nothing to do with you. The remains were buried in the cellar when you lived there. I'd like to do a DNA test on you, please.'

'Why?'

'To rule you out of our enquiries and perhaps to help with identification of the remains.' He decided to push her. 'Do you have any reason not to give me your DNA? If it's of no relevance it will be destroyed, and no note will be kept of it.'

Her mouth was pursed. Shit, she was going to refuse.

He tried again. 'It would be very helpful.'

No response. It was time to call her bluff. 'Can you tell me your full name, please?'

She lowered her eyes. 'I told you not two minutes ago,' she said.

'You changed your name in 1991 from Enid Cavendish to Edith Drummond. Why?'

The bluntness of the question took her by surprise. She scratched her nose. 'I didn't get on with my parents.'

Mark decided to risk it. She was uneasy, fidgeting, her hands restless. 'Is that why you killed your mother?'

She laughed then. 'What? You think the remains are those of my mother?'

'Aren't they? You're not exactly being co-operative. It makes me think you're hiding something.'

She blushed. 'Both my parents died in a car crash. I won't deny it, Sergeant Nicholson, I wasn't unhappy when they died. They should never have had a child, and they made my life a misery. I left their house and decided to start again, make a new life for myself. When I did so, I changed my name. I wanted nothing to remind me of them and how unhappy they made me.'

Christ, she was cold. Barely a flicker of emotion on that haughty face. A twitch under her left eye told him she was rattled but keeping it well controlled. He understood where she was coming from. He too had wanted nothing to do with his abusive parent. His father had not been a good man. He was responsible for the terrible injuries that left Mark's sister in a vegetative state. Nonetheless, he'd never seen the need to change his name. Was she telling the truth or was there a more sinister reason behind the change? He'd have to check up on her parents' deaths. If she was lying about that...

'I'm asking you again. Can I take a sample of your DNA?'

'Go ahead, if you must.'

The testing took less than a minute. Mark put the swab in the tube provided.

Miss Drummond stood up. 'Have you finished, Sergeant? I have work to do. Primary two children are not exactly tidy, as you can see from the state of my classroom.'

Christ, were they back at school already? He'd thought it would be later. Had he missed Oscar's first day at school? Oh fuck, surely not. Perhaps he'd go along anyway...

'Sergeant?'

'Uh, yes.' He gathered his thoughts, aware Megan was staring at him. 'Yes, we're finished for the time being. I'll get back to you if there's anything else.' As he stood up, there was a knock at the door and a much younger woman came in.

'You have visitors, Edith? Have they signed in?'

Mark's ire rose at the woman's condescending tone.

'We're right here, you can ask me. No, we haven't signed in. Not Miss Drummond's fault. I accept full responsibility.'

'And why do the police want to speak to one of my teachers?'

The archness of her tone got to him. One of her teachers? What would the haughty Edith Drummond have to say about that? 'This has nothing to do with the school. Now, if you'll excuse us, we have to go.'

He and Megan got up and left then, but not before he heard Edith snap, 'It's none of your business what they were doing here, Olivia.' Good for her.

EIGHT

Edinburgh

EDITH HAD the dream again that night. It had been a shock when the police turned up at the school. Glasgow was in her past. She hadn't set foot in the city since leaving it all those years ago. Not once, and she hoped she'd never have to return. Alarm had turned to relief when he said what it was in connection with, but it didn't last long. It was clear Sergeant Nicholson thought the remains were to do with her.

She'd refused to enlighten Olivia as to why the police had come to see her. She didn't want her knowing anything about her life. Present or past. On her way home she'd spoken to Tommy, told him yes, unfortunately there had been a break-in at her flat, but no, nothing important had been taken. She didn't enjoy misleading him in this way, but she saw no alternative. This way the rumour would be in full flight by seven this evening, thanks to WhatsApp, and with luck it would get Olivia off her back.

She'd had the dream for the first time when she was in her teens. It was always the same. A hole in the ground, filled with clothes and rags to cover up what was hidden underneath. She didn't know what it was that lay there, but she understood it had to remain unfound. It had occurred off and on throughout her adult life, but it was years since it had troubled her. Now it was back in all its horror.

What had she been doing in the cellar that summer day? She didn't remember what age she'd been. No more than nine or ten. Her parents hadn't expressly forbidden her to go into the cellar, but she had never had the chance, as it was kept locked. When she found the door to it open one day, she didn't hesitate.

There was an electric light in there that she switched on, because even with the door open it looked scary inside. It was full of things; a few dining chairs lay scattered across the floor, in one corner there was a heap of old tiles. When she looked at them closely, she saw they were the same as the ones in their bathroom, white tiles with an orange and brown design. Old planks of wood lay across the floor joists and there were bits of old carpet everywhere that must have been the source of the musty smell. Or perhaps they had mice. She went in, determined to explore.

'What are you doing in there? Get out at once.' It was her father, in one of his rages.

'I wanted to see if there was a secret passage.'

He came into the cellar then and grabbed her, hauling her out into the garden. Enid stumbled and fell onto the gravel path but stifled the cry that came to her lips. She was relieved to see their next-door neighbour was out mowing the lawn. Her father wouldn't dare hit her in front of him. He put on the false smile she hated and called across the fence.

'Children, huh,' he said to Mr Gallagher. 'Always going into dangerous places. It's not safe in there.'

Mr Gallagher ignored him and spoke to Enid directly.

'You all right, pet? That looks like a nasty cut.' She looked down to see blood pouring down her leg. 'It's fine,' she whispered. She imagined the outcry if she said what she wanted to: *No actually, I'm frightened of both my parents. Did you see him push me? They hate me, both of them.*

He spoke to her father, 'Best get that seen to,' before he returned to mowing his lawn. Her father had taken her inside then. She saw the tension in his face and feared she was in for a beating, but he cleaned out the graze and sent her to her room. Their neighbour must have picked up that something was off, suspected her father of wrongdoing. Why else would he have spoken directly to her instead of ignoring her as adults tended to do? But it was too late to say anything by that time. She was locked in her room as a punishment for going into the cellar. It was hard to understand.

'I told you it was forbidden,' he'd shouted at her once he was sure Mr Gallagher wasn't in earshot.

'You didn't. You never said,' she sobbed in reply.

'Stupid girl. Why do you think we always keep it locked? It's to keep you safe from the devils who live there.'

Enid was young and impressionable. Devils and demons were part of the religion forced onto her. Every Sunday, adults told her hell awaited those who strayed from God. Such talk from her father ensured she stayed clear of the cellar from then on. Over the years her fear built up until it was a phobia. She got a firm to clear it out when she was moving house. Only when the new owners had asked to see it did she go in there again. She told herself it was stupid to be frightened. It was daylight and two other adults were with her, but she was shaking. She'd locked up when they left and wondered briefly about the mound at the back. She'd never imagined it concealed a body. If she'd thought about it at all she imagined it was a heap of coal covered over with cement left over from concreting the cellar floor.

Now, well over half a century later, she understood why they'd kept her away. But whose was the body, where had it come from? One person came to mind; it must be them, but could she tell anyone? She hadn't been arrested, although it was obvious the policeman thought she was guilty. At least he'd stood up to Olivia though. His terse reply pleased her. He didn't look as though he'd stand up to a mouse, but there he was, putting Olivia in her place. It would have been awful if he'd told Olivia why he was here. Be thankful for small mercies. Edith thought she'd seen a look of sympathy in his eyes as he'd left the room. Her imagination working overtime. He hadn't said it but he didn't need to: *Don't go anywhere without telling us, Miss Drummond.*

The upshot was now she had two things to worry about: her job and her liberty. Thank goodness for her savings. Unless she was mistaken, she might soon need a good lawyer.

NINE

Glasgow

IT WAS late by the time Mark got home. He hadn't wanted to drive back from Edinburgh during the rush hour. Two hours for that time in the afternoon wasn't unusual. After checking Megan wasn't in a rush, he had driven down to Portobello, where they walked along the beach. It wasn't the most beautiful beach he'd ever seen. For Mark, little compared with the Ayrshire coast, which had stunning views of the island of Arran. Bass Rock, impressive as it was, had nothing on it.

They found a chip shop near the seafront where he bought himself and Megan a fish supper each, and they sat on the wall bordering the beach to eat it. At least there wasn't the profusion of seagulls you got in Glasgow. Over the past few years they were everywhere, and it wasn't safe to eat fish out in the open. Only last week he'd bought a homeless man a replacement for the supper he'd had stolen by a greedy bird. It swept down from the sky to pinch the fish from the man, who was sitting on the steps outside the concert hall in Buchanan Street. The poor guy had dropped the rest of the food in his shock, and when he picked up and ate a chip from the dirty steps, Mark had intervened to stop him, offering to buy him another meal. He thought about it now as he licked his greasy fingers and shuddered. Mark understood these guys, the sort of life they'd had. It could've been him.

'So, what did you make of our Miss Drummond?' he asked.

Megan took her time replying. 'In my opinion, she wasn't being completely honest with us. Why did she ask if it was about her parents? I mean, they've been dead all that time. And what was that about a car crash? I'd say she made up that stuff on the hoof.'

'My thoughts exactly. I thought she didn't know about the body in the cellar, though.'

'Me too!' Megan sounded excited, pleased to be on the same wavelength as Mark. 'She was genuinely shocked. But she's not telling us everything.'

The drive back had been worse than the drive there. Sun in his eyes, he'd missed the turn-off to the M74 for Glasgow South and had to continue by the M8 instead. The queue from Charing Cross tailed back to Easterhouse. Then he had to drop Megan off at her home. He wasn't in the best mood when he got in.

'What's for tea, tonight?' asked Alex as he walked into the kitchen.

'I've had my tea, sorry.'

'Christ, it didn't take you long, did it?'

'What do you mean?'

'Half a day in Embra and you're already all *you'll have had your tea*.

Mark laughed at the old joke. 'Aye, right enough. I think there's leftover curry in the freezer. And one of those packets of rice you microwave.'

Scrimgeour busied himself with getting his meal together. 'How did you get on, anyway?'

Mark took a bottle of Pilsner Urquell out of the fridge and opened it. 'Yeah, difficult to say. She was a right old biddy. Cold as anything. But I don't think she was aware of the body.' The saltiness of the fish supper had left him with a thirst and he gulped down the refreshing lager.

'Did forensics say anything about whether they'd be able to get DNA?'

'They're hopeful. But we won't know for some time yet. To be honest, she was apprehensive when I showed her my warrant card, shaking and everything, but when I told her what we found, she looked relieved. I'm pretty sure she's in the clear re this, although why she looked as terrified as she did, I don't know.'

'And what about wee Megan? How's she shaping up?'

'She seems bright. She was telling me on the way back she wanted to be a detective.'

'Don't they all, Mark? At that stage in their career anyway. What do you think of her? Does she have potential?'

'Hard to say on the basis of a few hours. But she did reach the same conclusion as me regarding Drummond. I'd say she has good observational skills.'

'Mm. We'll keep an eye on her, see if she is detective material, but she's off to a reasonable start.' The microwave pinged and Alex took out the defrosted curry and spooned it onto a plate. 'Get us a beer, will you, son?'

Mark got out another two bottles and opened them. He passed one to Scrimgeour.

Alex took it and sat at the table with his curry. He ate for a few seconds without saying anything. 'Ah, this is all right, this is.' He burped. 'About Drummond – as far as I can see, her reaction doesn't mean she didn't know anything about it. I suspect she's good at keeping her emotions under control. She's the best we've got.'

'She's keeping stumm about something. I'll give you that.'

'Aye, the fact she killed a woman and hid her under the floorboards.'

'Under the concrete more like. You sound very sure that it was her who put it there. Any particular reason? After all, her parents lived there too.'

Alex had just taken a mouthful of food, so Mark had to wait until he finished chewing. 'Good point. Here, maybe the body is her mother's.'

'No chance. She was killed in a car crash along with her husband in 1991.'

'Check it out. Make sure both deaths are registered.'

'I will do, but I think it's more probable they killed and buried the woman. After all, Edith Drummond might only have been a child when the body was put there.'

Alex raised his bottle in acknowledgement. 'Well, we'll have to wait and see. What did she have to say about changing her name?'

Mark thought back; he should have been more forceful in questioning her. He'd been led astray when he realised he'd missed Oscar's first day at school. 'She was matter of fact about it. Said she changed it because her parents had made her life a misery when she was a child. She was detached and unemotional when talking about it, as if she wasn't speaking about herself.'

'What had they done to her, I wonder?'

Mark held his breath, angry with himself for not exploring the question further. Fortunately, Scrimgeour was more interested in getting himself another beer and dropped the subject.

The next morning Mark took a chance and mentioned to Alex about Oscar starting school. 'I missed his first day. Do you mind if I go along to see him? I'll make the time up later today.'

'No, that's fine, but have you mentioned it to Karen? She might not like you turning up unannounced.'

He had a point. Karen hadn't spoken to him directly since she'd thrown him out. All communication had been through her lawyer. God knows how she'd afforded it, what with the cost of a single letter. Perhaps her old man was subsidising her. 'I'll send her a text.'

Karen hadn't replied by the time he got into his car. He was nervous about seeing her, prayed she wouldn't cause a scene. He parked a few streets away from the school and walked round.

The street was full of parents. The majority were wearing masks but there were a few, mostly men, who didn't. Mark took his out of his pocket and put it on. Perhaps it would stop the more gossipy parents recognising him. He had no doubt he would have been tried, judged and condemned for his latest misdemeanour by the coterie of yummy mummies who used to linger at the school gates long after their children had gone in. Karen used to complain bitterly about them and how judgemental they were. He hoped they weren't nipping her ear about it. She found it hard enough fitting in as it was.

Mark leaned against a wall across the road from the school. Karen and the children would have to pass him.

There was no sign of her. On the other side of the road, he noticed a young woman staring at him. She was the mother of one of Sophie's friends. Out of habit, Mark raised his hand in greeting, but she ignored it and turned away from him. So, that was how it was. He was to be cold shouldered. Fuck them. He took out his mobile phone and scrolled through it to see if Karen had replied. Nothing.

'You've got a nerve coming here.' It was the woman who'd been staring at him plus two others he didn't recognise. 'Does Karen know you're here?'

'Mind your own business, Jenny,' said Mark.

She bridled. 'It's Jane, actually.'

Mark knew this. He was deliberately winding her up. 'Don't you have anything better to do?'

One of the others piped up. 'You're a disgrace, Mark. Karen's heartbroken.'

'More fool her then, to confide in you.' Mark's temper was rising. He didn't know this woman, had never seen her before, yet she was judging him. He was the first to admit he'd been a shit, but to have a stranger accost him in the street? It was too much. Out of the corner of his eye he spotted Karen at the bottom of the street. 'Excuse me, ladies.' The sarcastic emphasis on the last word was unmistakeable.

Karen stopped dead when she saw him coming towards her. 'What are you doing here?'

'I sent you a text. I wanted to wish Oscar good luck on his first day at school.'

'His first day was yesterday.'

'I know. I've been working on the murder case up the road. The body in the cellar.

Karen frowned at him, shooting a glance at the children,

who were very subdued for once. Luckily, they didn't seem to have heard him.

'When are you coming home, Daddy?' asked Sophie. Her bottom lip trembled.

'I don't know, pet. But all three of you can come and stay the night with me. If Mummy agrees.'

'Can we, Mummy? Can we?' All three of them spoke at once.

Karen was rigid with fury. 'Did you do this on purpose? How can I say no to them now?'

'I've only seen them once since I left, or since you chucked me out, I should say. I think we're well overdue an overnight stay.'

Neither of them had noticed the three witches creeping up on them. 'You OK, hun?' said Jane, rubbing Karen's arm in the irritating 'caring' way so many women used.

Karen moved away from her. 'I'm fine,' she said.

'Nothing to see here,' said Mark. 'Piss off.'

'We're over here if you need us, babe.'

'I'm fine,' hissed Karen.

'You heard her. Now go.'

Was that a look of relief Karen gave him as they sidled away, disappointed at being deprived of their daily dose of gossip? 'What made you confide in them?'

'I didn't. Anyway, what do you care? It's none of your business.'

He was getting nowhere with this. He bent down to speak to Oscar, who was hiding behind Karen's legs. 'How was your first day at school? I'm sorry I didn't see you yesterday. Are you the teacher's pet yet?'

'No, Daddy,' said Oscar. 'Miss Carr says we're all her favourites.'

'I'm glad to hear it, son. Be good for her, won't you? And for Mummy too.' Mark turned to go. 'She loves you all. We both do.'

'Soon,' said Karen. 'They can come to see you soon. I'll text you.'

Back at work, there were no DNA results as yet. Dr McEwan was optimistic about the prospect of getting DNA from the remains but warned him it might take a while. Meanwhile they continued to interview neighbours, but they were getting nowhere.

Mark was pissed off. Apart from what Ronnie Sanderson had said, they had no leads. He had hoped to find someone with a clear memory of Enid Cavendish and her parents, but so far, the only witnesses had a vague memory of a 'strange family' who lived in the street twenty or thirty years ago. They didn't remember the number of the house. Every fucking street in Glasgow would have had a 'strange family' at one time or another. So, when one of the uniforms came to him with a possible lead, he wanted to hug her. 'Tell me again what she said.'

'She said she'd been living there for twenty years, and she knows a man who lived next door to the Cavendish family for years. He's ninety-five but sharp as a tack, she claims. She visits him once a month. Here's the address of his care home.'

'Great work. Thanks, Emma.' He noted the address and asked Megan to come with him. They'd go there now and interview the man, a Mr Brian Gallagher.

The manager stood before them, arms folded across her

chest. 'You can't come in. Only close relatives allowed. You can set up a Zoom call.'

'This is a murder investigation. Mr Gallagher is the only lead we have.'

'Look, we've managed to stay relatively Covid free here. A member of staff will help him with the iPad.'

'What about if we interviewed him outside?'

After a few minutes of negotiation, the manager relented and agreed to them meeting outside if all her instructions were followed. She showed Mark and Megan to a quiet part of the garden where there was a large wooden table. Once she'd placed three of the chairs a good two metres apart, she went back inside and brought out protective clothing for them to put on. She then gave them hand sanitiser and sprayed the table with disinfectant. Several minutes later a care worker brought Brian Gallagher to them in a wheelchair. He was a shrunken shell of a man, but his eyes were lively with intelligence.

'I thought they weren't going to let me out,' he said. 'But here I am. She who must be obeyed said it's in connection with a murder. Well, it wisnae me.'

Mark laughed. 'No, it's about neighbours of yours from a long time ago.'

'Aye? Who'll that be then?'

'The Cavendish family. You lived next door to them in Crookston Way, is that right?'

'Right enough. I remember them well. Richard and Doris were about the same age as me and my wife. When they moved in I thought we'd become friends, but no chance. They were weird.'

'In what way?'

Mr Gallagher raised his index finger to the side of his head and twirled it. 'Fruit loops. Religious nutters.'

There were plenty of them in a city as bigoted as Glasgow. 'Do you know what religion they were?'

The old man thought for a moment before answering. 'I don't know for sure. They were fundamentalists of some sort. Like the Plymouth Brethren, I think? There was only a handful of them. They used to meet on Sundays in the Cavendish house. I once made the mistake of asking why they didn't have a church like any other religion.' He tutted. 'Got a mouthful of abuse for it.'

This was interesting, but Mark was struggling to see the relevance to this enquiry. 'What else do you remember? Do you remember the child?'

'Of course I remember the child! Enid. What a name to give a wean. It was old-fashioned back in the days of Adam. Me and the wife worried about her all the time. Such a melancholy wee thing. Never a smile on her face, jumped if you spoke to her. What's all this about then?' His face changed. 'Oh no, it's not Enid who's been murdered, is it?'

'You haven't heard? It's been all over the news this past few days.'

'I don't take much notice of the news. These bloody politicians, up to all sorts. It's not good for my blood pressure, you know.'

'Well, I'm sorry to have to tell you, but new people moved in into their old house, and during the renovation work, the builders dug up a skeleton.'

'Jesus Christ. In the garden?'

'No, the cellar.'

'But they've been dead for years. What makes you think it's to do with them?

'I can't reveal details, Mr Gallagher, but forensics suggest it's been there for between fifty and sixty years, which suggests it was concealed when the Cavendishes owned the house.

Brian Gallagher fell silent, lost in thought. Mark thought he was on the point of going to sleep when he said, 'Dear God. I suspected all wasn't right in that family. I should have done more. I always...' He stopped and wiped a hand across his eyes.

Mark gave him a second before asking, 'What do you mean?'

The old man's eyes were watery. 'They were always shouting at the child. Horrible things. Telling her she was a monster and should never have been born. Those houses weren't well soundproofed and you picked up a lot of what went on through the walls.'

'Did this go on for a long time?'

'Oh, yes. We did phone social work after a particularly bad evening, and they made a visit to the house, but they must have been satisfied at what they found because they never came back.' He rummaged in his trouser pocket and pulled out a pristine handkerchief to blow his nose. 'And now they've found human remains...' His face fell. 'Was it definitely the Cavendishes who did it?'

'I don't know, Mr Gallagher. And if I did, I wouldn't be able to say more at this point.'

'Of course, of course.'

They sat in silence for a few seconds, lost in thought. Megan continued to write. 'Do you remember anything else?' asked Mark.

'It was a long time ago. I didn't care for them, and I was

heart sorry for the wee lassie. It's a shame they didn't die earlier. I suspect they gave her a hell of a life.'

'What do you remember of their death?'

'Not much. We had moved away by then. It was in the early nineties, I think. A car crash. But I don't know anything more than that. I think we read about it in the paper.'

Mark indicated to Megan that they were finished and stood up. 'Thank you for your help, Mr Gallagher. No, don't get up. I'll see myself out. But if you do think of anything else, call this number.' He scribbled down his mobile number on a scrap of paper and handed it to Mr Gallagher.

TEN

Glasgow

KAREN KEPT her word and texted him to say she was willing to let the children stay over on Saturday night. This would be the first time they'd visited Alex's flat – his last access visit had been a disastrous one to McDonalds, combined with a trip to the park in the rain – and he was nervous. He borrowed a couple of lilos and sleeping bags from one of his colleagues and bought one of those all-in-one toddler blow-up beds for Emma. There was plenty of room on the floor in his room for them, and despite his worries that they might wreck Alex's immaculate flat, he was desperately looking forward to them staying.

'Are you sure you're OK about this?' he asked Alex for what must have been the twentieth time.

'Mark, how many times? I'm not going to be here. I told you I'm going down to London at the weekend to see Kate.'

Kate was Scrimgeour's daughter with whom he'd only been reunited last year. She'd had a positive effect on him, no doubt about it. Scrimgeour was still a grumpy old bastard the best part of the time, but he had definitely mellowed. 'What are you going to do with them? For God's sake don't take them to McDonalds again. Even I know that's sad.'

Mark had the whole weekend planned. He was to pick them up at ten thirty from the house. He'd bring them back to the flat, where they'd make a game of making up the beds. Indoor camping, he called it. Afterwards they'd have lunch and they'd have the afternoon to play in Queen's Park before going back to make tea, leek and bacon pasta, a family favourite, although he would have to pick out the leeks from Emma's as she didn't like 'green bits' in her food. But if they were involved in the cooking, with any luck that would keep them out of bother. Then a film with popcorn as a treat. Sunday was going to be wet, so he'd booked a visit to the Art Gallery and Museum in the west end before he dropped them off at Karen's later in the afternoon. It was going to be perfect.

Best laid plans. He should have known. They loved making up the lilos with the sleeping bags, and Emma was delighted with her all-in-one bed with a picture of Elsa from *Frozen* on it. In fact, she was so pleased with it she wanted to take an afternoon nap, and it took the promise of an ice-cream cone from Langside café to get her moving. It was a sunny afternoon and they played for hours at the swings in the park before coming back to make tea. It was all going well until he suggested watching a film. Emma wanted to see *Frozen* again, but Oscar rebelled. 'I want to see the *Paw Patrol* movie,' he shouted. 'We always watch *Frozen*.' From there it was all downhill. Mark managed to divert them a little with the popcorn and made them compromise with a cartoon film about the Mexican day of the dead, which Sophie had suggested. Mark wasn't sure it was the best thing to watch, what with all the skeletons, but they were happy enough and settled into their beds without too much trouble. Until the middle of the night. Three o'clock to be precise.

Emma woke up first, crying about the film they'd seen. 'The dead peoples is coming,' she cried over and over until first Oscar and then Sophie woke up. By three thirty all the children were asleep in Mark's bed and he was on one of the lilos trying to get back to sleep for what remained of the night. He dropped off minutes before Oscar woke at five thirty announcing, 'I have to poo right now, Daddy', and by six it was clear there was no chance of any more sleep that night. He got up, deflated all the lilos and looked longingly at his own double bed. It held the promise of a soft duvet and a peaceful sleep.

He allowed them to watch a film after breakfast. The thought of doing anything else to entertain them exhausted him so he signed up for a free trial of one of the streaming services and they settled down in front of the *Paw Patrol* movie. He hoped there was nothing in it to give Emma night-mares. He'd never hear the end of it from Karen if there was. One scary film was more than enough. It was a success though and calmed them down, even Sophie, who had declared she was 'too old to watch this baby stuff'. When it finished it was time to get them into the car to go across the city to Kelvingrove Art Gallery. The rain was pelting down as they came out of the close. Parking the car had been diffi-cult the day before – Christ, how he missed his own driveway – and it was a good five minutes' walk away. For a brief moment he considered staying at home for the day, but it would be a mistake. He hoisted Emma up on to his shoulders and told the others to stay by his side while they hunted down the car, which had decided to play hide and seek. 'Fifty pence to the first one who spots it,' he cried. The ploy worked and kept them from whining. Twenty minutes later they were at the car park for the Art Gallery in the west end. More problems. He'd forgotten there was a charge and he had no change on him. They all had to sit in the car while Mark rang up the parking company and then struggled to read the numbers from his debit card. Three attempts before he got it right.

Once the parking was dealt with, Mark decided they'd concentrate on the animals' section. The stuffed animals and birds were excellent, and Oscar especially was interested in wild life. That should keep them occupied until lunch time. If only. The glass cases filled with stuffed animals didn't impress them and the words *this is boring* were heard more than once. It was turning out to be a long day. By half past eleven, Emma was whining and saying she was hungry. She had to have hollow legs. Three bowls of Cheerios she'd eaten this morning and two slices of toast. With jam. Mark tried to negotiate leaving lunch for another half hour – he'd had to book a space in the café – but it was a losing battle as the others joined in. They were tired from their disturbed night but not half as exhausted as he was.

'Ten minutes, then we'll go for lunch.' With luck the staff would take pity on him and let them in early. 'Let's look at the animals until then.'

A tap on the shoulder made him turn round. His smile faded when he saw who it was. In front of him was a less polished version of the woman he'd fallen for two years ago. Suzanne Yates. Her roots were showing and her skin was dull. She'd put on weight. She had a baby in a pushchair. His child. Mark's face reddened. He was all too aware of his eldest child, Sophie, watching them with interest. Nothing escaped her. When he finally spoke, he kept his voice neutral. 'Suzanne. How are you?'

A shadow flickered across her eyes. She was hurt by the cool tone he used. 'I'm fine and you?'

'Fine, yes.' There was a silence broken only by Sophie's voice piping up, 'Is that a real baby? Can I see it?'

'Well, he's sleeping at the moment, but you can take a wee peek, Sophie.' Suzanne crouched down until she was at the same level as her.

'How do you know my name?'

Mark jumped in before Suzanne said anything. He didn't trust her to keep her mouth shut. 'Sophie, I work with this lady. Her name is Police Constable Melanie Brooks, and as you can see, she has a baby called...' He left a space for Suzanne to speak but Sophie got there first.

'But you called her Suzanne.'

'Mummy hates that name. I heard her tell Auntie Debby,' said Oscar.

Suzanne looked amused, more like her old self. 'The baby's name is Angus,' she said.

'Well, it's been nice seeing you.' Mark was desperate to get away. Karen always quizzed the children about what they'd done. If she thought they'd spent any time together with his ex-mistress she'd be withdrawing from the contact agreement. He indicated the children with his eyes, pleading with her to understand.

She gave a half laugh as she said, 'You always were a cowardly shit, Mark.' She lowered her voice and hissed, 'Your own son. Don't you want at least to see him?'

Thank God none of the children had heard. They had wandered over to the case with the tiger in it. 'I'm sorry, I have to go.'

'What's the matter? Scared Karen might be hiding somewhere and see us together?' Suzanne smiled but there was no friendliness behind it. 'She won't though, will she? Not now she's kicked you out.'

'What? I... I... How the fuck do you know?'

But she was already gone, leaving him red-faced and stuttering by a glass case full of predators.

Lunch was miserable; whining children and indifferent food. Later, he was horrified he'd allowed the children to have Coca-Cola. Not diet Coke. The full-fat, sugar-engorged stuff. Sophie was delirious with disbelief. 'I love this, Daddy. I love you, Daddy.' Christ, Karen would kill him when he took them home high on sugar.

He drove up to the small, terraced house he'd bought with Karen. The driveway needed weeding, and he thought he'd offer to come over one evening and deal with it. Karen came out of the house and up to the car as soon as they arrived. 'Did you miss me, sweethearts? What did you and Daddy do?'

Sophie unbuckled herself from her car seat and scrambled out of the car. 'We went to the park and we watched two films and Daddy let us have a Coke!'

Mark made a face. 'I'm sorry, Karen. They'd asked for it before I realised.'

'Oh well, one diet Coke won't kill them, I suppose.' He didn't enlighten her. She turned to go into the house. 'See you on Wednesday then?'

'What? Oh yes, of course.' Damn, it was hard to get time off at the moment with this ongoing enquiry, but it was best not to mention it now.

He heard the ping of messages coming in to his phone when he was driving home but forgot about them until he was ready for bed. His heart sank when he saw there were three, all from Karen.

SUN AT 17.54
You devious shit. How dare you let her anywhere near my children.

SUN AT 18.06
Nothing to say for yourself then?

SUN AT 21.30
You can forget about Wednesday. I'm contacting my lawyer.

Mark put the phone down with a sigh. He'd allowed himself to hope too soon. When Sophie hadn't mentioned meeting Suzanne, he assumed she'd forgotten. He wished now he'd mentioned it himself. It was typical of him to take the easiest way out, to avoid confrontation instead of taking Karen aside and explaining what had happened. Well, it was too late now.

His phone pinged with another message. If it was Karen he'd phone and speak to her. Try to explain. Before he got the chance though, the phone rang. Unknown number. Without checking who it was he pressed accept call.

'Mark, what a nice surprise. I didn't think you'd answer. Did you like the photo?'

Why the fuck hadn't he blocked her? He'd removed her from his contact list after she'd contacted him last year to tell him she was pregnant but hadn't bothered to block her. Alex had strongly advised him to, and yet here he was. He hadn't had a chance to look at the message. He did so now. A beaming baby looked up at him. His son.

'What do you want, Suzanne?'

'I want you to look at your son. Isn't he adorable?'

Mark didn't reply. His head was swimming. He hated this woman. She'd ruined his life. No, his conscience prompted him, he was being unfair. He'd been a willing participant in their folly. And now he was being drawn back in.

'When do you want to meet him? He'll be a year old next month. Time for you to get acquainted, I think."

'Suzanne, when you contacted me last year to drop your little bombshell, you said you wanted nothing from me but thought I should know. I didn't reply. Surely you got the message? I want nothing to do with you or your baby.' He sounded harsh, but if he gave her the tiniest leeway she'd be relentless in her attempts to get him onside. She had to be told once and for all. 'I have no interest in seeing you or your son. If you want child support, I'll be happy to take a paternity test and we can talk about money *if* it turns out I actually am the father. Do you understand?'

For a moment he thought she'd hung up. Then, 'I'll be in touch, Mark. You haven't heard the end of this.'

He'd helped himself to a good quarter of Alex's best whisky. It was after midnight when he heard the key in the lock. The London train must have been late. Mark hoped Alex was in the mood to chat, because he needed advice. Damn, it sounded as if he was going straight to bed. He got to his feet and went out into the hall, catching Alex as he came out of the bathroom. 'You want a drink?'

Alex looked at his watch and made a face. 'I'm on at eight

in the morning. I assume your shift starts later, judging by the amount you've had to drink. I can smell it from here.'

'No, I'm on at eight too. I'll be fine. Nothing a strong coffee won't sort out. Listen, Alex, I need advice.'

Alex rubbed his eyelids and yawned. 'Can't it wait?'

'One drink, please?'

'Oh, go on then.'

Once Mark had poured them a good measure of the fifteen-year-old Bowmore, he leaned back in his chair.

'So, what's Suzanne been up to now,' said Alex.

'How did you know?'

'Who else is there? Did she get in touch?'

Mark told him about what had happened. When he finished he waited, hoping Alex would come up with a solution. But the older man sat in his chair, eyes half closed. 'Well?' demanded Mark.

Alex sighed and balanced his glass on the arm of the chair. 'What are you going to do?'

'I don't know.'

'Do you want to get to know your son?'

'At this moment? No.'

Alex stared at him. 'Honestly Mark, I think you should. If you don't, you'll regret it.'

Mark didn't reply. Of course, Scrimgeour would say that. He'd spent more than half his life mourning his only child, the daughter who'd been stolen from him. He hadn't had years of being woken at five a.m. or lain awake worrying about how to support three children. It would be beyond tactless to say so though. 'Maybe.'

Alex covered his face with his hands. 'I'm sorry, Mark. I'm knackered. I need to get to bed. We'll discuss this another time.'

Mark sat on in his chair for another ten minutes, toying with the remains of his drink. For someone who'd drunk so much whisky he was remarkably sober. He'd hoped Alex would have been able to give him direction, some words of wisdom to help him sort out his problem. As it was, he was lost. What the fuck was he going to do? Why, why, why had he ever got involved with Suzanne Yates? Well, the answer was easy. Lust. But it didn't help him one little bit.

ELEVEN

Glasgow

MARK WOKE at five o'clock the next morning. Typical when he'd drunk so much. His mouth was dry and his head ached. He might have felt sober when he went to bed, but his body didn't agree. He needed a lie-in not an early rise. And first thing he was going to have to give a briefing. Shit. He reached out for the pint glass of water he kept on his bedside table for moments like these before remembering he wasn't at home and he hadn't yet bought a bedside table. He'd drop into IKEA after work and pick one up there. It was time he stopped living like a fucking student. He raised his head for a brief second before laying it back down again. Christ, it hurt. Paracetamol and a cup of coffee, that's what he needed. Gingerly he got out of bed and padded to the kitchen.

He switched on the kettle and ground a handful of coffee beans in the grinder. The noise brought a grumpy Scrimgeour to the kitchen.

'For fuck's sake. What are you doing?'

'Making coffee, do you want one?'

'What the fuck is that noise?'

Mark switched the grinder off and told him.

'What the fuck do you want one of those for?' Scrimgeour rarely drank coffee and Mark had had to buy a new grinder and cafetière when he moved in.

'Coffee tastes better if it's freshly ground.'

'OK, make me one too.'

Mark put two spoonfuls of the grounds into the cafetière then added a third. He needed this to be strong. He allowed the coffee to brew before pushing the plunger down. He took two mugs out of the cupboard.

Scrimgeour grimaced when he tasted it. 'Bit strong for me.'

Mark added sugar to his before gulping it down with the painkillers. 'Leave it and I'll drink it.'

'How much did you have last night?'

"Dunno.' Mark didn't want to admit he'd swallowed half a bottle of malt whisky that cost well over fifty quid a bottle. Jesus, all that money and he felt like shit. He'd have to try to replace the whisky without Alex realising. He'd buy a half bottle of supermarket blend to replace it. No, better not. Alex loved his whisky and he'd kill Mark if he didn't get the good stuff.

'Like that, is it? Well, we're up now so might as well go in early. Lots to be done. I'll drive. You are not, I repeat, not to take your car into work this morning. And have a shower and a shave. You look like shit.'

They were in work before seven. The painkillers and coffee did their work and Mark was feeling human again. He gathered the reports that had been left on his desk and read through them. There was nothing on the age of the remains. The forensic team were continuing their search of the cellar, but nothing interesting had come to light as yet. He'd check later how much longer it would take.

Megan had continued her research over the weekend and had left him a brief report on what she'd found. The Cavendishes had lived in the bungalow since 1946, and before them there had only been one family, who had bought it when it was first built in the 1930s. Didn't mean any of the Cavendishes were guilty though. They had no definite proof linking them to the remains. He thought back to Enid Cavendish as she'd been. She was an improbable criminal, and after his interview with their old next-door neighbour yesterday he was more inclined to think the parents were behind it. If the body had been there for sixty years then it wasn't anything to do with Enid. She would have been far too young to be a killer. From Gallagher's account it sounded as though her parents had at best been harsh with her, and at worst they had been abusive. Was there anyone alive who had known them? Was there anyone to corroborate what Brian Gallagher had said? Gallagher had mentioned a church or a sect. That was a possible lead. He decided to phone Edith Drummond. He needed to ask her more questions. She hadn't fully explained why she had changed her name. Just a vague statement about not liking her parents. That surely wasn't enough to cause her to take such drastic action.

She picked up immediately. 'Miss Drummond, it's DS Mark Nicholson here. Do you have a moment to answer a couple of questions?'

'I'm about to leave for work. Can it wait? I like to be in by eight o'clock.'

'Is that your official starting time? Early for a teacher, isn't it?'

'Sergeant Nicholson, it is a myth teachers work from nine until three. Our hours are actually much longer.'

Aye right, he thought, a sour look on his face. What was it they had? Three months holiday a year? 'I need to speak to you now,' he said. 'I'm sure you can be spared for fifteen minutes. It's not as if the children are there at eight o'clock, is it?'

'Very well. Fifteen minutes. I'll set the timer on my phone.'

Mark suppressed a sigh. 'I spoke to your old neighbour on Thursday. A Mr Brian Gallagher. Do you remember him?'

A short silence then, 'Yes, I do. I thought he'd be dead by now.'

'He's ninety-five and living in a care home. He's alert and his memory is good. He remembered your family well. Said he and his wife were always worried about you when you were a child. You mentioned to me the other day that you had an unhappy childhood, if I remember correctly your exact words were that your parents 'made your life a misery.' Were Mr and Mrs Gallagher right to be worried?' For a moment he thought they'd been cut off, the silence was so profound. 'Miss Drummond, are you there?'

'Yes.'

'Did your parents abuse you?'

'I'm sorry. I can't talk about this now.'

'Miss Drummond?'

There was no reply. This time she definitely had gone. Mark tried her number, but it went straight to voicemail.

He didn't leave a message. He sat at his desk ruminating over what had happened. She must have been abused by them. It was the only explanation for her behaviour. He'd have to tread softly, but if they were abusive to her it was possible they might also have abused and killed someone else.

TWELVE

Edinburgh

EDITH BRUSHED AWAY her tears and took a deep breath. This was no time to break down. She had to get to school. If she cycled fast she'd get there a little after eight. Not that it mattered. Her official start time was half past eight, but it was a matter of pride to her. She splashed cold water on her face and rushed down to the bike shelter.

The wind blew rain in her face as she entered Holyrood Park. It cleared her head. She'd have to speak to that damn policeman sooner or later but not on the phone. It would have to be done face to face. She cycled on, feeling calmer as she got nearer to the school.

Tommy waved to her as she came through the gates, but she didn't stop. She had no wish to see what the WhatsApp group were saying about her now. It was flattering that some parents were upset, but she hadn't liked the spiteful comments about the children who needed additional support. The most vociferous among them were those who supported her. They were mainly middle-class professionals who thought this meant they were entitled to run a school.

Edith didn't like Olivia, but she wouldn't wish the likes of Mariella Greene or Doug Palmerston on anyone. They squeezed everything out of the state system before taking their children out at late primary stage to send them to private school. That way they saved five or six years of fees and avoided their children having to sit competitive entrance exams. By the time she got to her classroom she was agitated. She was letting this get to her. It worsened when two minutes later, the head teacher came into her room.

'Ah, there you are, Edith. Running late today, are we? You're flushed. Perhaps all that cycling at your age is bad for you?'

'It's five past eight. As you know, clocking-on time is eight thirty.' Edith ignored the comment about her age. Olivia was trying to get a rise out of her. 'Anyway, can I help you? I have a lot to do.'

Olivia leaned in close. Too close. Edith took a step back, but Olivia moved in again. 'Have you recovered from your little visit from the police? Burglary, was it?'

Edith continued getting her classroom ready. 'I don't have time to chat, Olivia.'

'Mm. I'm afraid I have more bad news for you.'

What was it now? Edith refused to rise to Olivia's jibes. 'What is it you want to say?'

'There's been a parental complaint about you, dear.'

How dare she patronise her in this way? Edith ignored her.

Olivia raised her voice as if Edith hadn't heard her. 'As I was saying, there's been a complaint.'

'Has there?' Edith tried not to seem too surprised, but it was hard. In her twenty-five years of teaching, Edith had never had a parent complain about her. Her immediate

103

thought was that Olivia had engineered this in an attempt to get her to leave. 'And what is the complaint about?'

'It's the Greenes.'

'And?' Edith kept her poker face, although inside she was churning. This wouldn't be good. The Greenes were both lawyers, and Oliva bent over backwards where the professional parents were concerned.

'Apparently you've been questioning little Sophia.'

Edith put down the book she was holding and frowned. 'I don't know what you mean. Questioning her? Isn't it a teacher's job to question? Use the Socratic method? So yes, I do ask her questions.'

'Apparently you asked her what she was going to be doing at the weekend. The Greenes say this is an invasion of their privacy. They also said they're not the only ones who don't like it.'

'I don't believe you.'

'Olivia pursed her lips. Well, Edith, that is what they said. You need to stop questioning Sophia immediately.'

'This is a catch twenty-two situation, isn't it? I have to be able to question her. If I don't, I won't be able to give an accurate report of her progress, and if I can't do that then they will undoubtedly complain. Perhaps it should be discussed at the next staff meeting. How are we to assess when we can't question children?' She bared her teeth at Olivia in an approximation of a smile. 'It would be a good topic for an education dissertation, don't you think?'

'Just do as I say,' snapped Olivia. 'I don't have the time for all this soapistry.'

'I think you'll find the word is sophistry,' Edith said to Olivia's back, wishing her face was visible.

Olivia let the door slam behind her. Edith wasn't sure, but there was a hint of *fuck you* lingering in the air.

With Olivia out of the way, Edith mulled over her interactions with the children. Had she said anything that impinged on the Greene family's privacy? It was true she'd asked all of the children if they were doing anything fun at the weekend. But surely that wasn't it... ah *now* she remembered. Little Sophia had sat saying nothing. She'd looked unhappy, so Edith had asked her directly, 'What are you doing on Saturday and Sunday? Something nice, I hope.' The child had lowered her head and whispered, 'We never do anything nice.' Edith had dismissed it as moodiness and said, 'Oh I'm sure that's not true, Sophia,' and moved on. Perhaps she'd been wrong to dismiss it so quickly. And now she was powerless to ask Sophia anything about her home life. Olivia wouldn't support her; she'd made that clear. She would have to think of another plan.

Mariella Greene had stuck up for Kieran, claimed to be a friend of his. Did she dare ask him about the family or was that worse than asking Sophia? The short time they'd spent teaching together had gone better than she'd imagined. He was good company. She decided to leave it. Her suspicions were high though. Why on earth did the Greenes not like that question? From now on she was going to keep a close eye on that child.

Every adult working in a school had a duty of care when it came to a child's safety. That wasn't what spurred Edith on. No, this was personal. When Edith had been at primary school she'd had a teacher, Mrs Murray, who kept her behind at playtime once and asked her questions to which Edith had no reply. *What do you do at home, Enid? Do Mummy and Daddy play with you? Do you ever get into trouble?* Enid had remained mute, unable to tell her teacher of the rows she got, of how her parents would tell her she was the spawn of the devil, how – the dreadful shame of it – she wet her bed night after night although she was eight years old. The teacher had given up after a while, unable to get through to the silent child in front of her.

'You're a clever girl, Enid,' she'd said. 'The world's your oyster, but if you never say anything...' Her voice tailed off with a trace of exasperation.

A few weeks later she'd bumped into her teacher when she was out shopping with her parents. They were in Woolworths in Shawlands. Mrs Murray spotted them and rushed over.

'Ah, Enid's parents. What a fortunate coincidence. Can I have a word?'

'What's it about?' glowered her father.

The teacher raised her eyebrows at his rudeness. 'I'm a little worried about Enid. She's become very withdrawn in class recently.'

The heat of her parents' stares slammed into Enid. 'Is that so?' said her mother in a high, jolly voice Enid had never heard before. 'That's not like the chatterbox we have at home, is it sweetheart?'

No one had ever called her sweetheart. The hypocrisy of her mother calling her that made her sick. If only she had the courage to speak out, but instead, she looked down and scuffed her shoe along the floor.

'Don't do that, Enid.' Her mother struggled to keep the annoyance out of her voice, but when she noticed Mrs Murray looking at her, she smiled. 'Of course, I know what's been wrong with her. She's had toothache for the past couple of weeks. We have an appointment with the dentist on

Tuesday afternoon, four thirty. Didn't want her missing any school.'

Mrs Murray's shoulders dropped, and she smiled back. 'No, we certainly don't want her missing school. Enid's a clever girl. University for her, I think. But next time, Enid, if you have toothache, tell me. I was worried about you.'

She'd managed a smile and said, 'Yes, Miss.' Then they were alone by the record counter where they'd met. 'Time to go home,' said her father.

Not a word was said on the drive back to their house in Crookston. Over sixty years later, Edith remembered her mother's nails digging into her hand as she dragged her up the garden path, fury emanating from her like a devilish miasma. Once home, her mother slapped her face, the sting of it making Enid gasp. Her father caught her mother's wrist before she landed another blow. 'Leave it. You might mark her. And then that interfering cow would be on our case again.' To Enid he said, 'Get out of here. No dinner for you tonight. Don't you dare draw attention to yourself in future. If the teacher asks you questions, then you need to answer them. But I'm telling you, if she ever comes to us again whining about how worried she is, I'll...'

She'd never found out what it was he would do as her bladder gave way, and to her horror, a stream of pee made its way down her leg, ending in a large puddle on the carpet. To this day she didn't remember what happened next, and she had no desire to recall it. It was best forgotten.

She had to keep an eye on Sophia. What if she was being abused in the way she herself had been? No child should have to go through that. Her estimation of Olivia went down further. Had she asked what it was Edith had pried into? She doubted it. The woman was a disgrace. She accepted whatever parents said in order to have a quiet life.

Tommy came to the door of her classroom. 'Mr Winter asked me to change a light bulb.' He held one in his hand. 'Actually, that's not true. I thought you should see the latest WhatsApp messages. It's all kicking off.'

Edith was torn. She was already behind with her preparations for the day, but on the other hand... 'I'm busy, Tommy. Can you summarise it for me?'

'No. Best you read it for yourself.' He handed her his phone.

Fractious father of four
Isn't it time we changed the group name to Primary Two?
17.10

Frances (admin)
Good point, Billy. I'll do that right away.
17.12

Gillian and Julia
Guys, we're not happy about this sharing of the class between two teachers. This is a copy of what we've sent to the head teacher.

Olivia,
It has come to our attention that Primary Two will be a shared class this year.
We would like a meeting with you to discuss this as soon as possible.

Gillian Foster and Julia McKay, (parents of Summer Foster-McKay)
We thought we'd put it out there in case anyone else is thinking the same.
Will let you know what happens.
17:14

Jason's mummy
Right behind you, guys. Mr Winter should take support for learning and Ms Drummond should be our kids' fulltime teacher.
17:16

Fractious Father of Four
I don't agree, Amanda. Children who need support should get the best teachers and not those who are hardly ever at work. I'll be writing to Olivia to suggest that to her.
17:18

Helen Dunlop
I heard one of your children needs support, Billy? Is that right? You and Jenny must be so worried. Nobody wants their child to end up in special school.
17:23

Fractious Father of Four
Well, if it was best for them then of course we would take that option. However, he won't be needing a special school. We had Albie tested privately by an educational psychologist and she confirmed he's dyslexic with an IQ of 142. In the top centile, actually. It's what we suspected but the school has ignored our concerns.

17:25

Janine
And I'll be supporting Gillian and Julia.
17:27

Fractious Father of Four
Whatever. You do what you feel is right. I'm off. Have to collect Arabella from athletics. We should have some exciting news soon.
17:28

Edith handed the phone back to Tommy without saying anything. He put it away and then pulled out a very flashy i-Phone, which he fiddled with for a few seconds before giving it to her. 'There's more. This is Janine's phone. She said to show you these texts between her and Helen on Messenger.

Get him. Stuck up git. What's a centile anyway?

Dunno. Is it one of those Greek things? Half man, half horse?

Is it? That can't be right surely. Anyway, trust him to have a dyslexic child. You know what that means, right?

Dyslexia? Difficulty with reading and writing.

No, I mean yes that's the definition. But it means when it comes to Nat 5s and things they get extra time. Gives them an unfair advantage. It's cheating.

But surely if they're having difficulty reading, extra time

won't give them an advantage? All it does is put them on a more even basis with everyone else. No way is it cheating.

Yeah, I suppose. Anyway, did you hear Mariella Greene complained about Ms D?

No way!

Said she'd been prying into their private lives. But when I asked further she didn't have much to add. Said she'd asked what they were doing at the weekend.

Eh? That's her complaint?

I know! It's a bit off, isn't it? I mean we all ask each other what we're doing at the weekend.

Do we know what Olivia said? I hope she sent her away with her tail between her legs.

Not in the least. M said she was very nice about it, said she'd ensure it wouldn't happen again.

Edith gave Tommy the phone back without a word. No doubt the whole of P2 knew about her tiff with Olivia by now. Damn.

'I thought you ought to see it. Forewarned is forearmed.'

'Mm. Well, thank you.'

'Are you OK?'

She straightened up. 'Why wouldn't I be? Now, I must get on with things. See you later, Tommy.' She turned back to what she was doing, blinking back tears.

THIRTEEN

Edinburgh

DAVID WATCHED the interaction between Edith and the janitor from the window of his office. What was going on? It looked as though Tommy was showing her his mobile phone. Why? Edith looked agitated; should he mention it to Olivia? He dismissed the thought. The animosity between the two women was palpable – why give Olivia ammunition?

Later on, he was pleased he'd kept his counsel. Olivia called him into her room as he was leaving at half past five.

'Going home already? Never mind, this will only take a minute.'

He gritted his teeth. He'd been at work since half past seven this morning and he had a pile of policies in his bag to check through when he got home. Why he'd thought it might be easier being a DHT he'd never know. He sat down in the seat indicated and waited.

'How are you settling in, David?'

Oh dear, the settling in speech. 'Fine,' he said. 'No problems.'

'Good, good. I'm glad to hear it. Now what I wanted to know is: how are we going to get rid of Edith Drummond?'

No lead in, just a brash question. He frowned. 'Edith Drummond is the last person we need rid of. She's an excellent teacher; her attendance is first class. I've been looking through everyone's attendance record and she's never had a day off. If we need to cut back on staff, I suggest we take a look at Kieran Winter. Do you know how much he was off last year? And how many of those days off were tagged on to a weekend?'

Olivia held up a warning hand. 'We're not here to talk about Kieran. We're here to discuss a woman who will be seventy next year, who is at risk of serious illness—'

Time to interrupt. 'I don't think so, Olivia. Edith is as healthy an old bird as I've ever seen. Have you seen her move? In any case, you can't make people retire if they don't want to. And the children adore her. In my opinion it would be a serious loss to the school.'

A slow smile spread across Olivia's face. She rarely wore a mask when in her own room although it was mandatory. 'And what would you say if I told you there'd been a complaint? A serious complaint.'

David stared at her. He didn't believe a word of it. He'd only been in the school a couple of weeks, but he prided himself on being able to suss people out and he'd got Olivia's measure within a few days. She was ambitious, narcissistic. It was all about *her* school. Well, he wasn't going to be caught out by her. 'Tell me more,' he said, reaching into his briefcase for his notebook.

'What are you doing?'

'I thought I'd take notes. You know, if it's as serious as you say...'

That mollified her.

'Anyway, this complaint?' he prompted.

'It's from the Greenes.'

'Ah yes, Sophia is in Edith's class, isn't she?'

'Yes, and Miss Drummond has been questioning her. Asking her about what she does at home.'

He laughed. This was not a complaint to be taken seriously. 'And?'

'And what?'

'Well, what else did they have to say?'

Olivia flushed. 'I think that's more than enough. I can't have teachers overstepping the boundaries.'

Silence was the best course of action, he thought. He waited.

'What do you suggest we do to get rid of her? I need ideas, now.'

God, she was dim. Hadn't she picked up on the clues he was giving her? The lack of encouragement, his disbelief, his body language. He was going to have to spell it out to her. 'I think you should consider carefully what you're doing. This complaint. Was it in writing?'

'I, um, no.'

'Was it from both parents?'

'Just the mother.'

'What exactly did she say?'

'That Miss Drummond had asked Sophia if she was doing anything at the weekend. If she was doing anything nice, implying the Greenes don't do nice things with their children.'

'That's it?'

'She said she didn't want Miss Drummond asking Sophia any more questions.'

'And you then pointed out that questions are a part of education.'

Olivia frowned. 'Have you discussed this with Miss Drummond?'

'No. I haven't seen her today.'

'Well, I don't see any point in talking about this further with you. It's clear you're not taking this complaint seriously.'

'Let me be clear, Olivia. If a complaint is valid, I will take it very seriously indeed. But if it's like this, silly and with no substance, then yes, I will ignore it. Is there anything else?'

She waved him away, her face tight with anger.

What the hell had she been on about? Olivia had lost all sense of proportion if she thought Mrs Greene's complaint needed to be followed up. He hadn't liked her lack of response to the parents. Surely she didn't expect Edith not to ask a child any questions. It wasn't realistic. No, Olivia was out of order on this one, and as for a campaign to get rid of Edith, forget it.

It was unsettling. There were always clashes of personality in schools. It was inevitable. Other teachers found Edith difficult because she was different and didn't conform to the social norms of a primary school staff. But this campaign to get her out was vindictive and, he believed, illegal. If Olivia wasn't careful, she'd land the authority in all sorts of bother and end up costing them money. He was at a loss though as to what to do next.

FOURTEEN

Glasgow

THE INVESTIGATION WASN'T MOVING FORWARD in the way Mark had hoped. There wasn't much to go on. The forensic team had torn the cellar apart without finding anything else.

'What next?' said Alex. 'What do we have?'

'We don't have much,' said Mark. We have an approximate date for when the body was put there, no earlier than 1960. We have the name of the people who lived there at the time. It's suspicious that Edith Drummond changed her name but she would have been too young to have done this. If the murder was committed years later then she might be the killer, but I wouldn't bet on it.' He rubbed his eye, which was itchy. 'If they manage to get DNA we can compare it with Miss Drummond's. I'm unclear as to why she was so reluctant to have hers taken.'

'Some people are, Mark. They think we're going to keep it for nefarious purposes.'

'Hmm,' said Mark. He wasn't convinced. 'Anyway, that's about it for now.'

'Should we search the garden, do you think?'

'I think we should,' said Mark. 'We can't assume there's only one body here.'

'Wouldn't they have used the same place?'

'Mm, possibly, but I think we should do it. Imagine the furore if we don't and later on another body is uncovered.'

'OK, I'll see whether we can go ahead and do it. It'll be expensive though, so we might have to leave it.'

The next day Scrimgeour got back to Mark. It wasn't good news. 'Don't tell me. No money?'

'Nope. They won't countenance it. It's not in the public interest, apparently.' He shook his head. 'I suppose they've got a point. If Dr McEwan's right and the body is from sixty years ago, we won't get a conviction unless it was the Drummond woman that did it, and from what you've said, that doesn't seem likely. Unless Dr McEwan is wrong in her dating of it. But for now, we work on the hypothesis it was one or both of her parents.'

'What should I do next? I'm astonished they don't want to search the garden. What if the body has nothing to do with the Cavendish family and it's actually a victim of a serial killer from the sixties?'

'Mark, you've been watching too many crime series on telly. How would they get access to the cellar for a start? No, there has to be a connection.'

Mark protested, 'But—'

'Leave it, Mark. Go and tell the woman who owns the house she and her wife can move back in.'

Mark went to the hotel where the couple were staying. Neither of them was particularly happy at the news.

Sally Robinson was the most negative. 'I'm not sure I want to go back. It's just... you know, sleeping in that place when a body's been buried there all those years. What if there's another one?'

'We've been through the cellar with trowels and sieves. Believe me, there's nothing else there.'

'But how can you be sure?' said her partner. Perhaps there's another body in the house, in the chimney? That's a possibility. Or the garden.'

'There's nothing else in the house.' Mark was careful not to mention the garden. Fortunately, neither woman picked him up on it. If it all went pear shaped and there did turn out to be more remains in the garden, he was damned if he was going to be the one to tell them.

FIFTEEN

Edinburgh

EDITH WOKE WITH A START, her heart pounding. She leaned over and switched on her bedroom light to get rid of the darkness overwhelming her. It was the same dream as before. The earth open to reveal – what? All she had seen was bundles of clothes and what might have been old bedding. A pit full of rags but that wasn't all there was. Something was hidden beneath it all. Unseen but there all the same.

She looked at her watch. Two twenty-two. The worst time to wake up. She'd find it hard to get back to sleep now. Her heart rate slowed a little and she checked it. Seventy-six beats per minute, higher than normal. She took a deep breath – in for five seconds, out for six – and tried again. That was better, getting closer to her normal resting heart rate of sixty. Would she sleep again? Truth was, she was frightened to, in case the dream returned.

You didn't need to be a psychologist to know why the dream had reappeared now. The grave in the cellar. She went through to her living room, opened her laptop and did a search to find reports of the discovery at her old house.

Body found in bungalow

Police are investigating the discovery of a body in a bungalow in Crookston. The body, or what remained of it, was found in a shallow grave in the cellar of the building as workmen were excavating it in preparation for building work.

Police stop search of bungalow

Police Scotland announced today they were no longer looking for any more bodies in the bungalow in Crookston where the remains of what is thought to be a woman were found last week.

She continued with her search. A news report, this time on STV, the reporter standing in the street in front of the bungalow, trying to control her hair as it blew over her face in the wind.

'Police have yet to identify the person whose remains were found in a shallow grave in the cellar of this house.'

There it was again. Shallow grave. What she dreamed about wasn't a shallow grave. Did this mean there was another body hidden where she used to live? In the garden? Her stomach churned. She was going to be sick. Hand to mouth she dashed to the bathroom. Perhaps this was all it was, a dodgy supper giving her nightmares. At heart though, she suspected it was more than that.

There was to be no more sleep for her that night. Edith didn't bother going back to bed. Instead she paced the floor until six o'clock. Thank goodness it was the end of the week. For the first time in her life she was tempted to call in sick.

That would play into Olivia's hands though, and was the last thing she wanted. With a grim smile of resignation, she went to have her shower. It was time to get ready for work.

———

Outside, the wind took her by surprise. Edith was tall and slim and provided little resistance to the squall. It was a struggle to keep cycling. The rain was near horizontal, and when she reached the roundabout near the gate of the park, she thought she might go back home, leave her bike and get a bus to work. She had to work off her nervous energy though, so she continued on into Holyrood Park.

It was hellish; the wind got stronger and the rain heavier. She was soaked through by the time she reached the school. Her mind was in turmoil. The dream wouldn't let her go. What did it mean?

'Edith? My goodness, you're soaked through. Are you all right?' It was David, the depute head teacher.

'I'm fine.' She tried to get past him, but he blocked her way.

'You look terrible.'

Thanks for nothing, she thought. 'Bad night's sleep.'

'Better not let Olivia see you like that. You know what she's like.'

She gave him a non-committal smile. For all she knew, he might be trying to trap her into saying something unflattering about Olivia. 'I can hardly be held responsible for the weather.'

'No, but is it wise to cycle here?'

Was there an *at your age* lurking in there? Surely not. There was no need to be so paranoid. 'Yes, actually, I think it is. Three reasons. Firstly, it's far quicker than taking public transport; secondly, it helps to keep me fit, and finally, I wanted fresh air.' *Not that it's any of your business*, she thought.

'Right. Oh well, I won't keep you. Oh, by the way, I'm hearing great things about the support for learning you're providing. I've spoken to several parents who are delighted.'

Edith smiled in acknowledgment and made her way to her classroom. It was one of her days with primary two and she was thankful for the lively children who helped her forget her troubles for a few hours. Once back home, she cleaned the bathroom. It was already spotless, but the process of spraying on bathroom cleaner and wiping it off was soothing. Old habits die hard, and she had been brought up by a woman who saw dirt as a personal affront. Today she tackled the grout in the walk-in shower using an old toothbrush to scrub away any signs of dirt or – God forbid – mould. Mould was a particular hatred of hers. She didn't understand people who let those little black spots multiply into unsightly clusters of black mould in their bathrooms or around their kitchen sinks. A blast of her special mould destroyer got rid of them in no time. Whenever she saw it (never in her flat – there was little chance of it growing there) she had to fight an urge to grab a toothbrush and start scrubbing. Today, with half an hour's cleaning, she was satisfied no speck of dirt for mould to latch onto had gone unnoticed. But it didn't make her feel better.

Although her laptop was calling to her, she decided not to do any further searches for now. She had to relax and stop thinking about it.

It was useless. Nothing helped her forget the dream; it was determined to get her attention like one of the naughtier children at school. Worse was to come; unbidden, the memories came back.

She hadn't thought about it for years. It was there in the corner of her mind marked do not disturb, like other memories from her childhood. Now she had to disturb it, though. It had to be exposed. Her dirty linen would be washed in public.

She'd been thirteen at the time. Or fourteen. What did it matter now? Her nights were restless, her mother cross and tired, snapping at her. Something was happening but she didn't know what. Her parents spoke in whispers behind closed doors, shooing her away whenever she approached. She listened at walls, her ear pressed to an upturned tumbler. Snippets of conversation came back to her. Snippets she hadn't understood at the time. Perhaps she'd imagined them.

You should have stopped this.

Me? You're blaming this on me?

We need to get rid of it.

This can't happen again.

She hadn't been able to sleep. Her parents, never the best carers, had surpassed their neglect in recent days. Two days since she'd had a proper meal, she grazed on whatever she found in the kitchen. Crumbs from an old packet of digestive biscuits, a bowl of stale rice crispies, a handful of porridge oats washed down with a cupful of water. She cried with relief when she found a half-eaten Mars bar at the bottom of her schoolbag. It wasn't enough though, and all day she'd had griping pains. Before going to bed, she'd asked for supper but her parents hadn't answered. She went to bed frightened they were going to starve her. Unable to sleep, she waited until midnight before she crept out of her room into the kitchen to see if there was anything else to eat. There wasn't.

The back door was open. Her father was meticulous about locking it at night. Enid wasn't sure if it was to keep burglars out or her in. Her parents were in the garden, down by the apple tree. What were they doing? She wasn't sure but it looked as though they were digging. Were they planting flowers at this time of night? Edith had a bad feeling about this and stole away to her room. She mustn't let them see her. That would spell trouble for sure.

The next day when she came home from school, she wandered round the garden looking for clues. She found nothing. Perhaps the earth was disturbed at the bottom of the garden. Near the apple tree. But it wasn't much and nothing new was planted there. Perhaps she'd been hallucinating because of the hunger. Thank God there was a stew simmering on the cooker. She hated her mother's cooking, but that day she was so hungry it tasted delicious.

Edith never lost the feeling of apprehension and anxiety about what she'd seen, but over the years she'd managed to stop herself thinking about it. Had she seen something that had led to that dream? It was so vivid. She closed her eyes and saw the hole once more in front of her. There was dark earth piled up next to it. Why would they have been burying clothes? Oh God, what if they belonged to the woman who had been found in the cellar? She tried to remember anything else from that time, but the truth was she was so good at repressing memories, nothing came to mind other than that eerie night-time scene.

Edith spent the rest of the evening in turmoil. She'd have to tell the police, that young detective sergeant. She was a law-abiding citizen. Why then was she reluctant to call him? A feeling of dread enveloped her. A feeling she was uncovering more than she wanted to. A feeling that if she did call them, her secret would come out. She sat by the window watching children play on the grass outside, while she tried to decide what to do. She ought to contact him and tell him what she suspected about the garden. But she was wary of saying too much. By half past nine, she was exhausted and decided to go to bed. Perhaps a sleeping pill would help her have a dreamless sleep.

SIXTEEN

Glasgow

THERE WAS a lot going on when Mark got to work the next day. Concerns about work had been pushed aside by worries about his family life. Sleep eluded him as he agonised about what Karen was going to do. It was unbearable to think she might stop him from seeing his children. In the evening, he'd tried talking to Alex again but sensed his irritation – Alex had always warned him off Suzanne – and eventually changed the subject. Things were bad enough without Alex turning against him because he always cocked things up. It was a relief to get to work where there was no time to think about Suzanne.

He hoped they'd get the DNA results soon. It was now more than a week since the remains had been found. Forensics had had a lot of difficulty extracting DNA from the skeleton but last time he'd spoken to them they were more positive. He was certain that whoever it was in the cellar was linked to the Cavendish family, so they needed to get good, solid information on them and, if possible, the previous owners, as well as continuing with door to door enquiries. Mark's next priority was to ascertain which church or sect the Cavendishes had belonged to and to try to find one or two people who had known them to corroborate what Brian Gallagher had told him.

'Best place to start is that church of theirs, if you can call it that,' said Alex. 'By all accounts they had no friends outside of that. Brian Gallagher said there were services held in their living room every Sunday. See what you can find out.'

The one good thing about a task like he'd been given was that it left no room for any other thoughts. His problems with Karen and Suzanne were soon forgotten as he went through statements from neighbours to see if there were any clues to the sect the Cavendish family had belonged to. An hour later he was no further forward and was despairing when Megan stuck her head round the door and said, 'Brian Gallagher's been phoning for the past hour. I thought you were with DI Scrimgeour. He says can you go to see him? He's remembered something.'

'I'm busy. Can we set up a Zoom call?'

'He wants to meet you face to face. In the garden again. Good thing it's dry today. Do you want me to come again?'

What Mark wanted was to be left alone to carry on with what he was doing, but he'd have to get this out of the way. 'Yes, that's fine. Bring his original statement and we'll see if anything needs to be added. No doubt it'll be a waste of time.'

Fifteen minutes later, Mark parked his car outside the care home. Despite his initial pessimism he hoped this might be the breakthrough he needed. He and Megan walked up to the front door and rang the bell.

'They can't all be out,' he said to Megan when no one answered. He tried again. And again.

A surly looking young man came to the door, bringing with him a smell of gravy and over-boiled vegetables. 'It's lunch time. Visitors aren't meant to come when they're eating.'

'Police,' said Mark, showing him his warrant card. 'I'm here to see Mr Gallagher.'

'Wait here.' The youth pointed to a bench outside the front door. Two minutes later he appeared with protective clothing and hand sanitiser. 'Put this on, as well as a mask, and use the sanitiser.'

Once they were kitted up they were shown into the garden, where Brian Gallagher was waiting at a table. 'Make sure you stay two metres apart at all times,' said the carer.

It was probably nothing, Mark told himself. Best not get his hopes up. Brian looked paler than he had when Mark last saw him. 'Mr Gallagher, how are you?'

A feeble hand waved at him. 'I've been better.'

Damn, he sounded weaker than he had the other day. This was going to be a waste of time. 'I've been told you wanted to speak to me.'

A look of confusion crossed the old man's face and Mark's heart sank. Surely he hadn't forgotten? 'What's that?' he said.

'You remembered something... about the Cavendishes,' prompted Mark.

'Ah right. Yes.' Brian struggled to sit up straighter.

'You were saying,' said Mark.

'They belonged to this strict religious sect. It was like the Plymouth Brethren. You know, radios, television all banned.

They used to spend Sundays reading the bible. But it wasn't the Brethren. I heard say once they'd been members but had left because of a fall out and started their own wee cult.' He shook his head at the memory. 'Religion, eh? Are you a religious man, Mark?'

Mark had been brought up a Catholic. It meant Karen's father had never accepted him as her partner. Her old man was dyed-in-the-wool Orange Lodge. Karen had told him the living room in her childhood home had been adorned with portraits of King Billy and other regalia associated with the Lodge and Masons. The ironic thing was neither he nor Mark ever set foot in a church. Mark found it hard to stomach the fact that his own father had been responsible for severely injuring his sister when she was a young child, leaving her so badly brain damaged she was unable to smile. What sort of a God allowed that to happen? 'No, I'm not religious.'

The old man smiled. 'Me neither. Though, I have to admit that as I get older, I don't mind the thought of eternity in the afterlife. But only the good place, eh? Anyway, they used to meet every Sunday in the Cavendishes' house.'

This was all very well, but it was essentially what he'd said the last time. Poor old guy, he was getting confused in his old age. 'Mr Gallagher, do you remember anything else about them? The name of the sect? The names of any of the people who went there?' Mark had little hope but had to ask.

'Aye, I do. Get me a cup of tea, will you?'

Mark didn't move. 'The name?'

Mr Gallagher was impatient, waved the question away. 'I'm dying for a cup of tea.'

Mark raised his eyebrows at Megan. She went over to the

carer, who was standing several metres away watching that they didn't get too close to Brian. 'Any chance of a cup of tea? Brian's desperate.'

'I'm not meant to leave you alone.'

'We won't go anywhere near him. He's not my type. Cross my heart.' Megan's smile got an answering one from the carer. Mark was pleased he'd brought her. He wouldn't have had the patience to banter with the sulky teenager.

Five minutes later a cup of tea appeared, but only the one. Nothing for Mark and Megan. Brian had refused to speak while they were waiting. It took all Mark's patience not to get up and leave. He didn't have time for this. His leg was twitching; up and down it went, like a pile driver.

'That's better.' Brian put the cup on the table when he'd drained his tea. 'Now, what were we saying?'

'You were going to give me names of people who attended their services.'

'The Brotherhood of the Luminescence of the Lord.' He enunciated each word clearly. 'That's what they called themselves. Have you ever heard the like? Fucking nutters.' He looked at Megan. 'Excuse my language, pet, but that's what they were. Thought they had a phone line straight through to the big man. All sorts of weird ideas they had.'

'How many of them were there? Do you remember anyone else who came to the house?'

'It was a small number in total who visited, less than a dozen, but I'd say there were seven or so diehards. All women except for Cavendish and another man, though he stopped coming after a while. I thought it was odd at the time. My wife did too. We used to joke they were in there having a good old orgy. They weren't though. It was all chanting and stuff. And speaking in tongues.'

'Speaking in tongues,' repeated Mark, eyebrows raised.

'Aye, real bonkers stuff. Have you noticed it's never any recognisable language they come out with? None of them ever speak French or Spanish or any language I've ever heard. They're dialects spoken in heaven apparently.'

'Heaven?'

'Aye, Convenient that. And only believers can understand.'

'How do you know all this?' asked Mark. He had his notebook out now to jot down any useful pieces of information.

The old man looked away. 'My wife. She infiltrated them.'

'What?'

'She became obsessed with them. Was convinced they were up to no good. One day she cornered Mrs Cavendish and invited herself along to a service.'

'How did Mrs Cavendish react?'

'Agnes said Doris wasn't best pleased, and she certainly wasn't made welcome. She went three times, if I remember right. Came back with these stories about how they'd sit in a circle chanting "Blessed is the Lord, blessed is the Light, blessed is the Luminescence" over and over. Then there would be silence until one of them was struck to speak in tongues.' He picked up his cup and made a face when he realised it was empty. 'Agnes was a language teacher, taught French and German. She also spoke Italian and Spanish. She was adamant the 'speaking in tongues' was a load of rubbish. Gibberish she called it.'

'Why didn't you tell me about this when we spoke the other day?'

Mr Gallagher put up his hands in a gesture of apology.

'I'm ninety-five. Some days are clearer than others. I hadn't thought about them next door for years.'

'And what did your wife think about the other people who went to the services?'

'Well, there's the thing. Years later, long after the Cavendishes had died in that car accident and long after Enid moved away, Agnes bumped into one of them. Her name was Janet. Janet Maclean. And what she had to say was very interesting. Very interesting indeed.'

Mark glanced at his watch. This was taking much longer than he had expected. When he'd got the message about Gallagher wanting to speak to him, he'd thought he'd be in and out in five minutes. He reined in his impatience. Brian was wallowing in his moment of glory, and who was he to thwart him? 'What did she say, Brian?'

'She reckoned there was something not right about them. She didn't go into specifics, but whatever it was, she didn't like it.'

'Was there anything else?'

The old man's eyes were rheumy as they looked at him. 'Yes, there is. She said she heard a baby cry one time when they were in the house. The Cavendishes had been reluctant to hold the service that day and had tried to send people away. This woman I was talking to, she told me she refused to go, it was the Sabbath after all and they had to worship. She'd ignored their pleas and pushed her way into the house. Bloody cheek if you ask me.' A drip shivered at the end of his nose and he rummaged in his pocket before bringing out a hanky. He wiped his nose and continued. 'Anyway, they were doing whatever it was they did at these services, praying or gibbering in tongues, when they heard a baby crying. It went on and on, so much so this woman interrupted the service to ask if anyone was going to see to the baby. Mrs Cavendish muttered about it being her cousin's child and her cousin would see to it in a second. But nothing happened and the baby screamed so much they gave up and went home.'

Megan leaned forward. 'I don't suppose you know any more about this woman, what did you say her name was again?'

'Janet Maclean. And aye, as it happens, I do know more. She's a resident here in this home. That's what jogged my memory. When I saw her this morning at breakfast.'

After his sleepless night and all the frustration of the interview with Mr Gallagher, Mark was exhausted and didn't feel up to wrangling with another nonagenarian. But he was here now and ought to get on with it. He thanked Mr Gallagher and asked if it would be possible to speak to Janet. A meeting in the garden was quickly agreed and ten minutes later she was brought out in a wheelchair. She looked nothing like the age she claimed to be, which was ninety.

The interview didn't take long. She confirmed everything Brian Gallagher had said, adding she'd left the sect not long after.

'Did anything in particular prompt you to leave?'

'No, I just wanted out. It was like a cult with Cavendish as the leader. It didn't feel right.'

Mark chose his next words with care. 'You called it a cult. Things go on in cults that upset people. Did anything specific worry you? This man, Cavendish, he wasn't abusing anyone, was he?'

Her eyes were shrewd. 'Nothing specific, no. He liked to touch people, and by people, I mean women. No doubt you already know that only women were part of that operation. Apart from Cavendish and of course, Eagleston.'

Mark frowned. 'Eagleston?'

'Yes. He was originally in the church my parents attended but he left at the same time as Richard and Doris. There was an argument, but I don't know what it was about.'

'I don't suppose...'

'He's dead. Died years ago. Good riddance to him.'

'Why do you say that?'

'Sergeant Nicholson, he was a predator. Practised what would now be called grooming. He was always trying to get the young girls to go to his house to pray. I met one of them years later and she told me what he'd been up to. Thought he was Jesus Christ himself and believed the sun shone out of his fucking arse.'

Mark blinked at the profanity. It sounded worse coming from this tiny, aged woman He was being sexist and ageist but... She laughed at the expression on his face.

'Your face. You're not a poker player, are you?'

'Tell me more,' said Mark. 'The girl you spoke to, did he abuse her?'

'I prefer to forget it, thanks. It has nothing to do with this current case.'

'You don't know for sure.'

Janet looked down at her hands. They were liver-spotted and frail looking. 'She said no. She told her parents and they made sure she was never alone with him. Don't know why they didn't go to the police, but I suppose people didn't in those days.'

She was probably right. The chances were it had nothing to do with this case, anyway. Mark stood up, ready to go, but

Janet wasn't ready to let him leave yet. She indicated to him to sit down again.

'Cavendish. He was a sex pest too. Always trying to get me to come to the house for a special prayer service. Aye right.'

They were wandering off the point. Sex pests and cults went hand in hand. Disgraceful as it was, there was nothing to be done about this particular accusation, as the relevant parties were all dead. He returned to the matter in hand. 'This baby,' he said, 'did you ever see it?'

'It was only the once. I didn't see it nor did I hear it again.'

'But you were told it was Mrs Cavendish's cousin's child?'

'Well, that's the thing. We were all puzzled because Doris Cavendish had told us she had no living relatives. One way or another she was lying.'

'Perhaps it was a friend's child?'

'That couple never had any friends. We were the only people who visited them.'

'You can't know for sure,' said Megan. 'After all, you were only there once a week. Perhaps others visited at different times when you weren't there.'

Janet pursed her lips. 'I'm telling you, they had no friends. I remember Doris telling me that. She was quite proud of the fact, said it gave her more time to commune with the lord. I ask you!'

She had made her mind up; there was no point in trying to change it. Mark didn't know what to make of this. 'Do you remember when this was? Anything about it?' He wasn't hopeful; this had happened half a lifetime ago.

'Yes, I remember exactly when it was. It was the twenty-fourth of June 1964. I remember because it was my mother's seventieth birthday.'

Mark made sure that Megan had noted this down. Maybe Edith Drummond had useful information. After all she lived there. She'd have known if there was a baby. He continued to question Janet for another few minutes. After ascertaining there was nothing else for her to tell him, Mark stood up to go. He was dejected. He'd got little out of this interview. Gossip and supposition, that was all. 'One more thing,' he said. 'Do you remember whether the daughter was there that day?'

Janet frowned. 'Was she? I think... Wait a minute.' She closed her eyes, 'No, she wasn't. I think Doris said she was away for a few days. It struck me as strange at the time because she never seemed to be allowed to go anywhere without her parents.'

'Do you know where she was?'

'Sorry, no. I thought it was probably a school friend's house but as I say, they weren't a sociable family.'

Mark thanked her and he and Megan left. It was time to get back to work.

There were several messages waiting for him at the station, three of them from Edith Drummond asking him to call her. He looked at his watch. He'd try to catch her now before he went home.

She answered straight away as if she'd been sitting by the phone. 'DS Nicholson. I have information which I hope will be helpful to you.'

'Yes?'

'I realise this sounds strange but please, hear me out.'

'OK,' he said.

'I have recurring dreams,' she said. 'Bad dreams. I hadn't had them for years but they started again after you told me about what was found in the cellar.'

Was there anything worse than listening to someone else's dreams? 'Have you remembered anything that might be helpful?'

'Please don't interrupt. This is very difficult for me. In these dreams I am always standing by a hole in the garden.'

Oh, for fuck's sake. Bloody dreams! With difficulty Mark stopped himself from exploding at her. He supposed he'd have to hear her out.

'When I'm looking into the hole there's a terrible feeling of doom surrounding me. As though I'm about to uncover something dreadful.'

'Is there anything in the hole?'

'Clothes and rags, bedding, I think. I don't know. It's just a dream. I'm sorry, I can tell you think I'm wasting your time. It's... what if I saw something when I was a child? What if the clothes I saw belonged to the person who you found in the cellar?'

She had a point. 'Thank you very much for bringing this to our attention. We'll look into it as soon as possible.' This was enough to get the garden searched.

'There's one other thing.' There was a pause, so long that Mark thought she'd hung up.

'Are you there?'

'I... it's a memory, from a long time ago. I saw my parents in the garden, late one night. It was dark and they were by the apple tree at the bottom of the garden, digging. I thought they were planting flowers or vegetables, but when I looked the next day there weren't any new plants there.'

Mark's heart beat faster. 'Did the earth look as though it had been disturbed?'

'I think so.'

'Thank you, Miss Drummond. We will no doubt be back in touch with you.' Mark rang off. They should have searched the garden.

SEVENTEEN

Glasgow

ALEX CLICKED HIS PEN. 'Right, we'll get a couple of uniforms over there straight away. You say she mentioned an apple tree?'

'Yes, at the bottom of the garden.'

'Well, let's hope it hasn't been cut down. It'll make life a hell of a lot easier if it's still there. We'll need to put a tent up. Don't want to be providing fodder for the tabloids. I mean it's only clothes. Not as if it's another body.'

They were already digging by the time Mark got there. The apple tree was in place. One of the team called out to Mark as he joined them. 'I don't suppose she was specific about where?'

'She said she saw her parents from the house, so you can count out behind the tree to begin with. Anything yet?'

'No. Wild goose chase if you ask me.'

'I'm not,' said Mark.

'Eh?' But Mark had gone down to the house to explain to its owners what was going on.

'You gave us permission to come home.'

'I'm sorry, but we've received new information we have to act on. We'll be away as soon as possible.'

They weren't happy. Neither was he. It was seven o'clock and he was ravenous. Hopefully they'd get this done as soon as possible. There was a casserole waiting for him at home and a bottle of red ready for him to drink. His stomach rumbled thinking about it. He walked back down to the apple tree.

'There's something here. A canvas bag. Shall I get it out?'

'Yes, but carefully please. It's evidence.' Mark watched as they eased the bag from the ground. It was rotted away in places and he saw there was material in there. The rags and clothes from Edith Drummond's dream? 'OK, let forensics take it from here.' He indicated to the scientist to come forward. 'Take this back to the lab and let us know what's in the bag. It looks like clothes if anything.'

The woman agreed. 'We should know for sure once we get them back.'

'Will there be anything useful on them? We're assuming they belong to the woman whose body we found but they might be rubbish they were too lazy to take to the dump.'

'I can't say. It depends on how long they've been here—'

She was interrupted by a shout from the digging team.

'Mark, over here. We've found something else!'

'What? What is it?'

'Looks like a toolbox. A big one. Should I open it?'

'OK, you've got gloves on, right? Be careful not to damage anything.'

'Right, I'm opening it now. There's a plastic bag inside. In good condition by the looks of things. I'm opening it now. Oh, Jesus Christ almighty.' The officer swayed and nearly dropped the box. Mark managed to steady her.

'What is it?'

'It looks like a skeleton... of a baby.'

There was nothing left to do. They'd sent off the clothes for forensic testing. The baby's remains went to the pathologist. Next day they'd dig up the whole garden, but it would mean bringing in more equipment and they wouldn't get hold of it until morning. One unlucky PC was left to stand guard over the site. Mark knocked at the door of the house. He was like a guilty schoolboy standing in front of Sally Robinson. 'So, you see. We'll have to search the rest of the garden. In case there are any more bodies.'

'Oh, for heaven's sake,' muttered Ms Robinson. 'This is beyond a joke. We've arranged for the builders to come back on Monday. I assume they can go ahead.'

'I'm afraid not.'

'But surely now you're finished with the cellar they can start work there. We'll tell them not to go into the garden. We've waited months for this to start, and now they're off to another job and we'll be bottom of the list. It isn't good enough.' Her partner looked as though she was about to burst into tears.

'Access to the cellar is from the back garden, and as this will be dug up...'

'This is appalling. Is this what we pay our taxes for? And you already told us you were satisfied there was nothing in the garden.'

He hadn't, of course. He'd been careful not to say that, but Mark allowed her to vent her frustration. After all it wasn't her fault that someone had chosen to bury bodies in her cellar and garden.

'You can stay here. We'll keep you informed of our progress, of course.'

'See that you do.'

Another satisfied customer. Mark had no doubt that a letter would be winging its way to the chief constable pretty soon.

It was late when Mark got home. Alex came rushing out of the living room as he opened the door. 'Is it true? Have they found a baby's body there?'

His face was flushed. He'd been drinking. Mark cursed himself for not foreseeing this. Alex had been involved in a case many years before, where a baby had disappeared from her pram. He'd been instrumental in putting away the father, who'd later killed himself in prison. Rumour said Scrimgeour would never be at rest until Danielle's body was found.

'Yes, it's true. But we won't know anything else until tomorrow.'

'If this is Danielle, it'll give me the vindication I've needed.'

'But you've always been sure Robbie Taylor killed her.'

'Oh, aye. I've no doubts about that, but...'

He was lying, thought Mark. The incident with Taylor's son, Jamie, last year when Jamie and his partner had tried to kill Alex's mother, had shaken him. If the remains were Danielle's, forensic tests would be done that might help to show once and for all what had happened all those years ago. Alex had also been sure Danielle's mother Brenda was involved too.

Alex was rambling on. 'Did you see the body?'

'No. I'm sorry. I didn't. Look, you can't do anything about it here and now. Why don't you get some sleep?'

'Do you honestly think I'll sleep tonight? I've waited years for this day.' His voice trembled. He was too invested in Danielle's case. Always had been. There were those who said it was why he'd never risen further than DI, but Mark thought they were wrong. After the disappearance of his own daughter and his wife's suicide, Alex had lost motivation for years and there were others who said he was lucky to still have a job.

'Go to bed, Alex. Try to sleep. You'll find out what's what in the morning.' The look Alex gave him stopped him in his tracks. It was one of bleakness and despair. He searched his mind for words of comfort, but all he came up with was a feeble, 'It'll be fine, you wait and see.'

EIGHTEEN

Glasgow

No ONE WAS late for the next briefing. There was a sombre mood in the room, not helped by the overcast sky outside. Most of the officers present had children, and the thought of a baby being unceremoniously buried in a metal box in a garden hadn't gone down well. The briefing was short – everyone had to be interviewed again. The two bodies might be connected but they might not. They weren't going to take any chances. Mark opted to go to see Brian Gallagher and Ronnie Sanderson again and set off with Megan in the car. Their interviews didn't take long. Most of the time was taken up consoling the men about such a horrific discovery. Ronnie Sanderson, in particular, had been very upset.

'To think that all this time... Oh God, I never thought I'd say it, but I'm glad Linda isn't alive to hear it. She'd have been devastated to think of the poor wee soul under the ground in our garden.' There were tears in his eyes.

'What now?' asked Megan as they got back into his car. She was subdued and pale. She was too young to have to deal with this sort of thing.

'We'll go to the house, see how the dig is getting on. No point in going back to the station yet.'

The press had already got wind of the find and the street was full of reporters. Worried neighbours peered from their windows, wondering what had happened to their quiet street. A news van from STV was parked outside the bungalow. What with that and the cars parked on both sides of the road, it was hard to make his way up the street and harder to get a parking space. He found one in a neighbouring street and walked back to his destination. As he walked into the garden, several reporters rushed over, questions flying from their lips.

'Is it true a baby's body has been found in the garden? Is it Danielle Taylor? Are there more bodies? Are we looking at a serial killer here?'

Mark pushed past with no comment. He went through to the back garden, the newshounds baying at his back. There was a digger in place and several police officers were busy at work. He went over to the nearest officer. 'Anything else?'

The PC put down her spade. 'Nothing as yet. We've asked for a metal detector.'

'Yes, good thinking. Bet you get nothing more than a few coins though.'

Mark hung around for a few more minutes before deciding to leave. He needed to chase up forensics.

Back at the station he called them. The scientist who answered, Dr Chaudry, didn't have much to say. 'What we have is a large, metal box, possibly a toolbox. It appears to date from the middle of last century. Inside was a plastic bag containing the remains wrapped in newspaper. If we date that it will give us an indication of when the body was

145

buried. It's not in the best state but there is print on it so that might help.'

Mark thought of Danielle Taylor. 'Do we have any indication of the age of the baby?'

'I'll let you speak to Dr McEwan. Hold on, please.'

The pathologist came to the phone. 'DS Nicholson. Always on at me for answers. Well, you're in luck. I'm in a good mood. Normally, I wouldn't be saying anything at this stage, but no doubt you've got reporters on your back about the possibility of it being Danielle.' She paused, always one for dramatic effect. 'You can tell them from me, no. The remains are those of a newborn baby.'

'So, to be clear. There's no chance it's Danielle Taylor? She was four months old when she was taken.'

Dr McEwan tutted and sighed. Her exasperation was clear. 'What did I say? It's definitely not her. The skeleton is far too small.'

Mark went through to Scrimgeour's office and gave him the news. There was a long silence when he'd finished.

'Right,' said Alex eventually. 'Thanks for letting me know. Does the newspaper date tie in with the other body?'

'They're working on that, but they did say the toolbox was mid-century. It fits with the first body.'

Alex puffed out his cheeks. 'They have to prioritise this. Along with the DNA. Get back to them and find out how long both are going to take.'

They got back to him with a date for the newspaper later. Alex had been very quiet since getting the news that the body wasn't Danielle. Mark hoped this might cheer him up. He went through to speak to him.

'It was 1964, June the twenty-fourth.'

'What? What are you talking about?'

'It's the date on the newspaper the remains were wrapped in. And what's more I have a witness who told me she heard a baby cry in that house on that very day.'

Alex scoffed. 'Aw come on, man. You're not telling me some old biddy can remember a date from the best part of sixty years ago? That'll be a first.'

'It was her mother's seventieth birthday. It stuck in her mind.'

'OK,' he said. 'Remind me again what age the woman is. The one who lived there. What is her name anyway?'

It's Drummond now, Edith Drummond. She was born in 1951.'

Right.' Alex thought for a second. 'Could the baby be hers?'

'She'd have been too young. She was only thirteen.'

'It's been known to happen,' said Scrimgeour. 'Don't rule her out yet.'

'It's... well, she alerted us to the fact there might be another body in the garden. Would she so that if she was responsible?'

'Perhaps it's a bluff, an attempt to fool us in case we discovered it for ourselves. Check her out.'

'Will do.'

'Any update on the other body, how long it's been there for?'

'It's not clear. Her clothes have been dated to 1960 and 1961.'

Scrimgeour clicked his teeth. 'So, between 1960 and

147

1964 those two bodies were buried. Is it possible the baby belonged to our unknown woman?'

Mark sighed. 'No. The pathologist said the bone density showed she was post-menopausal.'

'Right, we can rule out that hypothesis. All we've got to go on then is the Drummond woman. She has to know something. For fuck's sake, she was living in that house at the right time. Would she have killed and buried the woman? I don't think so. We're looking at one or both of her parents for that. But she was old enough to have had a baby. Her parents were religious zealots who wouldn't want a daughter of theirs having a baby out of wedlock. If she did have a baby, she might have killed it out of fear.' He rubbed his eyes. 'Or her parents might have killed it. It might be the mother's child. No matter what, Drummond knows something.'

Mark thought back to his interview with her. The first thing she'd mentioned was the garden. And she'd been lying. Her surprise about a body being in the cellar was genuine, but other than that... 'Do you want me to see her again, probe a little further?'

'Let her stew. Monday's time enough to see her. You can have a good think about what you're going to say to her.'

NINETEEN

Edinburgh

EDITH LIKED to catch up on the news before leaving for work if she had time. She no longer bought newspapers and instead relied on internet sites, mainly the Guardian, because there was no pay wall, and the BBC. She had half an hour before she had to leave for school, so she made a strong espresso using the stove top coffee maker she'd had for years, opened her laptop and searched for BBC news.

Most of the headlines were Covid related. The Chancellor had put in place a scheme to help the hospitality sector, eat out to help out. It was a great success apparently. Edith was worried it would lead to more cases. She'd steered clear although she was desperate for a change from her normal diet. More worrying was a finding that domestic abuse had increased during lockdown. She clicked on the Scotland tab to see what was new here.

As she expected, it was all about the pandemic. Cases were rising now children were back at school. She was about to close the link when a headline caught her eye. Another body had been found during the police search of her old house. There was a link to the full story, which she clicked on.

Her mouth dried up. Her hands trembled as she read through the article.

Police have reported that a further body has been found during the search of a house in Glasgow. Last week, builders discovered the skeleton of what is thought to be a woman, in the cellar. Now, there are reports that another body was found yesterday in the garden of the house. Our reporter, Alice Gillespie, spoke to one of the current owners, Emily Robertson, late last night. Ms Robertson was visibly shaken when she was interviewed.

'We're digging out the cellar to make a huge basement room, which is going to be our kitchen. Towards the back of the cellar there was a mound covered with concrete. We thought nothing of it, just that it was one of the quirky things you always find in older houses. It had to go of course, and when the builders smashed through it they discovered the skeleton. We were devastated when we heard. And now they've found a second body.'

The police officer in overall charge of the investigation, DI Alex Scrimgeour, issued a short statement this morning.

'At this stage we have little information to add to what you already know. The first skeleton was a woman's. Preliminary findings suggest the skeleton has been there for a long time, for at least fifty, perhaps sixty years. The remains discovered two days ago are those of a baby, but until a full forensic examination has been carried out we will not know for certain how long it has been there or what age the baby was when buried, although the first indications are that it was a newborn infant. The current occupants of the house have lived here for less than a year, and we understand the house has changed occupancy only three times since nineteen forty-six. We have interviewed the two previous owners and would ask anyone with any information about the house and its previous occupants to contact me at the number below. Thank you.'

Older readers will remember the notorious case of Danielle Taylor, who went missing from her pram in 1991. Danielle was four months old at the time. Her father, Robert Taylor, was charged and found guilty of her murder. Her body was never uncovered. DI Scrimgeour was instrumental in his conviction. Although police seem to think the child was a neonate, locals are speculating that Danielle has been found at last, only a mile or two from where she went missing.

Edith closed the lid of her laptop. Her heart was beating fast and hard. It pulsed in her neck, ferocious beats. Her pulse was one hundred and twenty. Twice its normal rate. Way too fast for a woman of her age who was sitting down. She stood up and went over to look out of the window. The rowan trees were studded with red berries, the sign of a harsh winter to come. It was certainly going to be a hard winter for her. She should have kept her counsel and said nothing about her dreams. No, it was the right thing to have done. But what now? This was the end for her. It was all going to come out. Her background, the depravity of her parents. What they'd done. What she'd done. She should never have changed her name. It would cast suspicion on her. The detective who'd interviewed her hadn't been satisfied with her explanation of her name change. He'd be back to probe some more. Could she bear to tell him, have it all out in the open? God, no. Edith was a very private person and this, this would kill her. Rage swept through her – would she ever escape her past? And yet, the police hadn't contacted her. Why not? Were they playing games with her? She stood up. She needed to get out of the house, get out in the fresh air, let the wind blow her past away and the rain cleanse her.

She sleepwalked through the day at school and managed to get home in one piece, though she had a nasty encounter with an impatient driver. She ignored his profanities. When she turned into East Parkside, they were waiting for her, parked outside her block. They got out of the car as soon as they saw her. The same two who had interviewed her before.

'We need to speak to you. Can we come in?' said the woman. Edith had forgotten her name.

She gave a brief nod and opened the door to the common entrance. They followed her upstairs and into her flat. This was it then, she was finally going to have to admit what she'd been hiding for all these years. Thank goodness she was at home. The thought of going to a police station made her sick with fear. The idea she might have to reveal her secret – dear God, what was she going to say? She couldn't do it, speak the words aloud. She'd give them nothing more than they had already.

Charlie swore when he saw them. 'Fuck off, bum face.' Edith apologised, trying not to smirk as she remembered how hard she had to work to teach the African Grey parrot these profanities. Hours of patient rewarding; her behavioural psychology knowledge had served her well.

'That's some vocabulary he's got,' said the woman police officer.

'I am sorry.' She wasn't. 'I'm afraid I've forgotten your names.'

'DS Mark Nicholson and PC Megan Webster,' said the man. He got straight to the point. 'Did you know more remains have been found?'

'I read about it this morning.'

'The latest remains are those of a baby. You told me you had dreamed of something being buried in the garden. Did you know about this baby?'

'I've already told you what I know. I saw my parents late in the garden one night, digging, near the apple tree. Is that where you found it, the baby I mean?'

Mark didn't reply. 'Is there anything else you remember?'

'I have vague memories around that time of my parents being more tense than usual. They sniped at each other. I heard my mother say something like *we need to get rid of it*.'

'That's convenient.'

'What do you mean?'

'Strange you've only remembered now.' The detective stared at her. She glared back at him. He looked down at his notes. 'Why did you change your name, Miss Drummond? What is it you're hiding?'

'What? I... nothing. I'm hiding nothing.' Damn the blush that always appeared when she was agitated.

'The baby we found, is it yours?'

She gaped at him, unable to believe what she was hearing. 'No, of course not.'

'We're working on the hypothesis that the child was born on or around the twenty-fourth of June 1964. What is your date of birth?'

'If you've already been researching me, you'll know what it is.'

'Indulge me,' he smiled. It was more of a smirk.

'I was born on the seventh of March 1951.'

'So, old enough to have a child in 1964.' She opened her mouth to protest but he held up a warning hand. 'I put it to you, Miss Drummond, that you had a child and, scared of what your parents might do or say, you killed and buried it in the garden. Or perhaps it was born dead. Now is your chance to say.'

Her stomach plummeted. Here she was, worried about her secret coming out and this dumb policeman was on the wrong track. For a moment she was unable to say anything, then she managed a strangled 'no'.

'It would be better if you admitted it now. We do have your DNA and we will be testing it against the remains, just as we've tested it against the remains of the other body.'

Was there a veiled threat in there? Edith stood up. 'I have never had children. It is one of the greatest regrets of my life, but I never had the opportunity.'

She thought he'd at least have the grace to look ashamed but, if anything, he looked sceptical.

'You see, we have a witness who told us she heard a baby cry during one of the 'services' held by your parents. She's been able to tell us the exact date, twenty-fourth of June 1964.'

Edith was defiant. 'Well, it was nothing to do with me.'

'Mm. Apparently you weren't there that day.'

'You're talking about over fifty years ago. No one knows whether or not I was there. I certainly have no idea where I was then.'

'You'd be surprised at what people remember. Perhaps

your mother was keeping you and the baby hidden?' His eyes were on hers, searching.

Any thoughts she'd had about offloading part of her story to this man fled. She'd say as little as possible.

'You said last time we met that you remembered your next-door neighbour Mr Gallagher.'

'That is correct, yes.'

'How did your parents get on with him?'

Where was he going with this? 'My parents kept themselves to themselves. They didn't say much to the neighbours. We never had them in our house, nor did we ever visit them. My parents weren't sociable or friendly people.' The day when she'd stopped to pet Mr Gallagher's dog came to mind.

'Enid, come and see our new puppy.' She hadn't needed to be asked twice. She bounded up to the fence to see the gorgeous tiny dog he was holding out to her. 'Careful, now. He won't hurt you but he might nip you. He's a baby, doesn't know any better.'

She'd stroked the head of the little cocker spaniel. He hadn't bitten her, and she fell in love with him. 'Can I hold him, please?'

'Of course.' Mr Gallagher was handing over the dog when her mother called out, her voice sharp. 'Enid, it's time for tea. Get in here at once.'

Edith remembered how astonished Mr Gallagher looked. It was only three o'clock. Had he commented on this? She wasn't sure. What did it matter? His look said it all. 'You'd better go, but come and see Scout any time.'

Enid had dragged her feet going into the house. She loved the dog but there was no chance of her ever having one or of her parents allowing her to visit the dog next door.

When she got into the house her mother grabbed her arm and shoved her into the kitchen.

'What have I told you about talking to that man?'

'I wasn't talking to him. I only wanted to pat the dog.'

A slap on the side of her head. 'Don't you dare talk back to me.'

The policeman's voice brought her back into the present. 'Miss Drummond, would it surprise you to learn that Mr and Mrs Gallagher were so concerned about your welfare they called the social work department.'

She frowned. "He phoned social work about me? When was this?'

'Yes, he did. It would have been when you were a child of nine or ten. Mr Gallagher remembers you and your parents well.' He paused. 'I'm asking you again, does it surprise you?'

'What?' She fell silent for a moment. 'Does it surprise me? I'm not sure it does, looking back. They were always asking me if I was all right. Things like that.'

'Do you remember a visit from a social worker?'

Did she remember? Of course she did. It was engraved into her memory, every moment of it. From the ring at the doorbell and her parents' puzzled glances at each other, to the beating she received when the social worker had left. Her mother had been careful to hit her where clothes would cover the bruises. Her father's beating had been more of an emotional one. He towered over her, his face puffy and red with rage.

'If anyone ever comes to our door again asking about your welfare...' he spat, vitriol evident in every last word. 'If anyone ever comes here again. I'll kill you. I'll bury you...' He stopped when her mother nudged him, then continued. 'I'll bury you where no one will find you.'

'You won't get away with it!' Enid cried. 'They won't believe you.'

'Doris, get a pen and paper.'

They made her write a note then, one in which she explained she was running away. She'd hunted for it a few times, wanting to destroy it, but she never found it. They'd hidden it well. When she cleared out the house after they died, she discovered it in a box in the attic. Until then she hadn't believed they would carry out their threat. But why keep it, if they didn't intend to use it?

She forced herself back to the present. 'I remember a woman coming once. She asked me if everything was all right at home.'

'What did you say?'

She'd said yes, of course. Anything else was impossible. 'I don't remember, but she didn't come back.'

Naturally she hadn't come back. Enid had forced a smile and said she was fine. That whoever it was who had reported them was mistaken. Her parents had been charming to the social worker, had come up with an easy lie to explain the scream the neighbours had heard.

'Oh that? That was Enid being silly. She watched a horror film on her own. It terrified the living daylights out of her. She won't do that again in a hurry, will you, darling?'

Stupid social worker. If she'd done more digging... But no, she didn't ask for the name of the film, check the date she was supposed to have watched it. Nothing. Like the idiot she was, she accepted their story and left.

DS Nicholson nodded as if he wasn't surprised to hear of

the social worker's negligence. 'This church your parents belonged to, tell me about it.'

'The Brotherhood of the Luminescence of the Light of the Lord? It wasn't a church as such. It was more of a sect.'

'A sect or a cult?'

'I don't know. What's the difference?'

Mark had read up about this. 'Well, as far as I know, a sect is a deviant religious organisation with traditional beliefs and practices, whereas a cult is a deviant religious organisation with novel beliefs and practices.'

'We met every Sunday and prayed. There were bible readings and people spoke in tongues. Well three of the women did; not everyone was chosen in that way. I've never been to any other churches, so I don't know what they do there.'

'I'm no expert but it sounds more like a sect. I suppose cults have more extreme practices.'

She was comfortable enough talking about this. She'd keep her silence for more important things. 'What do you want to know about it?'

'Whatever you can remember. How many people were in the congregation? How did it start? What church or sect did it break away from and why? Who broke away? Was it your parents or were any other people involved?'

'The first one is easy. There were nine of us in total. My parents, me and six women. Oh, and for a time there was another man came along, but he and my father fell out, and he left.'

'That would be Mr Eagleston?'

A flashback. A man looming over her, his face shiny with sweat. She repressed a shudder. 'Yes, that's right. How do you know?'

He ignored the question. 'When did this breakaway sect start?'

'Before I was born. I certainly don't remember going to any other church.'

'You don't know who they broke away from or why?'

She had her thoughts about why they'd done it but she didn't know for sure. Too many difficult questions being asked, no doubt. She'd give the police nothing. Going down that road might lead her to say too much. 'I think it was strict, like the Plymouth Brethren, but I'm afraid I don't know why they left,' she said. 'We met on Sundays. The services were long and boring, but I got through them. I don't have anything else to tell you.' Please God, let him be finished with her now.

But he was far from finished. He looked up from his notebook, stared into her eyes. 'Miss Drummond. The bones we found are those of a newborn baby. Think about that for a moment. A child never given the chance to live. Of course, we don't know whether he or she was born alive or dead. But given another body was found at the property...' He paused as if to let his words sink in. 'The other body is that of an older woman in her sixties or perhaps fifties. Two vulnerable people. Think carefully. Do you have any idea who these people might be? Do you know anything about their deaths?'

'I've already said I don't.'

'You are the only person left alive now who was living at that house when they died or as is more likely, were killed. We know the baby wasn't buried before June 1964. You were thirteen then. Old enough to have a child.'

So, it was back to this ludicrous suggestion? That she had had a baby and killed and buried it. 'I've told you already, it's nothing to do with me.' A tell-tale blush rose from her chest.

Damn. She needed to get him out of her flat. What she knew, what was in her past, had to remain a secret. She would not reveal the contents of the letter, which had explained so much and which had left her with the dreadful sense of shame she'd had to live with for all these years. She'd hidden the letter. Why she hadn't burned it she didn't know. It was in a brown envelope in a drawer in her desk with the instruction on it *to be opened only after my death*. It also contained a confession to what she had done. When she'd put it away, she'd hoped she'd never have to think of those days again. Hope was now dead.

TWENTY

Glasgow

SHE WAS LYING. All the signs were there. Her nervousness, the glances to the right, which showed she was trying to think of a reply instead of accessing a memory. When she was genuinely remembering she looked up to the left, as when she talked about what they'd done in their weird services. Mark hadn't intended to challenge her, but now he had, he studied her closely to see her reaction. It wasn't what he expected. She was genuinely shocked, he'd swear to it. Her face was scarlet as she told him again that the baby wasn't hers. He stared at her until she was forced to elaborate.

'I was thirteen. A very young thirteen. My periods didn't start until I was two months off sixteen. Have you any idea how cruel girls are? When my so-called friends at school found out, they never stopped going on about it. I was asexual, a skinny freak. If you don't believe me, my medical records will show the tests I went through when I was a young teenager and not menstruating. We're finished here,' she said, standing up to emphasise her point. 'If you want any more from me you'll need to arrest me. Good evening, Detective.'

She'd blindsided him. Mark had hoped the accusation would shock her. It had, but not in the way he imagined. He didn't think she was bluffing. Well, he'd have the DNA results soon enough. He wouldn't arrest her until there was more proof. Then he'd be back. He indicated to Megan they should leave.

On the short distance back to his car, Megan chatted away, question after question. *What do you think? Is she guilty? It's hard to think of her having had a baby, don't you think?* His answers were terse.

In the car she was more subdued, giving him a chance to reflect on what had passed. He wasn't sure he'd done the right thing and he had a feeling Scrimgeour wasn't going to be happy. For one thing, he still hadn't discovered why Edith Drummond had changed her name. That explanation of not getting on with her parents didn't wash with him Thousands of people didn't like their parents but still kept their name. In his experience people who went to those lengths had something to hide. With any luck Alex would be in bed by the time he got home. It was a good thing Megan lived on the other side of the city. It meant he'd get back later to the flat. When Mark drew up outside Megan's flat she stayed in her seat.

'That's us, then,' said Mark. He didn't want any more post mortems. He just wanted his bed.

Megan blushed. 'It's been really great working with you like this.' She pulled at a lock of her hair and twirled it round her finger. 'Perhaps we could have a drink some time?'

Fuck! Was she asking him out? This was the last thing he

needed. Mark's response was brusque. 'That wouldn't be appropriate, PC Webster.'

Megan flushed and opened her mouth to speak before thinking better of it. She got out of the car without looking back. He hoped that would be the last of it. For fuck's sake, she was years younger than him. Or he was reading more into it than there was.

When he arrived home, he saw the living room light from the street. His luck was out. For a moment Mark considered sitting in his car until the room went dark, but he was exhausted after the long day, and the drive to and from Edinburgh hadn't helped. If he went into the flat quietly, he'd manage to get to his room without Alex hearing.

No chance. Alex was waiting for him at the door. He must have been on the lookout for his car. Shit.

'Where have you been?' hissed Alex.

'You know where I've been. Edinburgh. I'll tell you all about it in the morning, I'm fucking knackered.'

Alex was pushing him towards the kitchen. 'You need to get rid of her.'

'Get rid of who?' Had Karen come to see him? Why was Alex so hostile?

'Your fancy piece. She's in the living room. I found her sitting on the stairs outside when I got home.'

'Suzanne? How did she find me?'

Alex raised an eyebrow. 'Who else? And I have no idea how she got this address. Black magic, maybe? Mark, that woman has trouble etched into her soul. You'll never get back with Karen if Suzanne's on the scene.'

He hadn't realised until now how disappointed he was that it wasn't Karen. 'I don't think she'll have me back.'

'Whatever. Get in there and get rid of her. I don't want her in my flat.'

'You shouldn't have let her in then,' Mark muttered, but Alex was already out of the room. Oh Christ, this was the last thing he needed. He leaned against the worktop and took a deep breath.

She was sitting on the sofa. Mark's first thought was that she looked worse than she had when she bumped into him in the Art Gallery. Her face was tinged with grey, her hair had lost its lustre, and from a distance he noted her hands shaking. 'What do you want, Suzanne?'

'We need to talk.'

'Where's the baby?'

'Angus is with a babysitter. I've changed my mind, Mark. I need support. I can't do this on my own.'

'If you're talking about money, then I'm happy to pay child support, but I insist on a paternity test.'

'Not money, no. I need emotional support. I need help with bringing up this child.'

This was worse than he imagined. He had no intention of being involved with Suzanne or her baby. It would be the end for him and Karen. She'd stop him seeing his own children; well, not Emma and Oscar. They were his biological children, but Sophie, yes. He wasn't her father, although she called him Daddy and he'd been a father to her since he and Karen had met. He loved Sophie like his own. His imperative, though, was to get Suzanne out of here. He'd think about what to do tomorrow. For the moment he needed to sleep.

'I'm not going to talk about this now,' he said. 'You've sprung this on me without any warning. You told me you didn't want me in his life unless I wanted to be.'

'And you don't?'

'Do I need to spell it out to you? No, I don't want him or you in my life. I already have three children. I've had it with nappies and sleepless nights. I have a demanding job that is more than full time. I can't take on any more responsibility.' This was a disaster. There was silence for a few seconds before he continued. 'I don't understand. You said last year you were happy to raise the child yourself. What's changed?'

She looked down at her hands, which hadn't stopped moving since he came in. 'I have cancer.'

She was lying, she had to be. Suzanne was a disturbed woman. She had shown that when they'd had their brief affair. But she looked awful, so tired. Grey and worn out. Much older than when they'd been together. 'When did you find out?'

'The day after I saw you in the Art Gallery but I've suspected it for some time. I've been exhausted since Angus was born. At first I put it down to my age and having newly given birth. Nobody tells you how tiring it all is. And then there was the pain as well as bloating and a tender abdomen.' Her voice quivered. 'It's ovarian cancer, Mark. And it's not looking good.'

Mark sat down in one of the armchairs and put his head in his hands. 'What's the prognosis?'

'They're going to operate in three weeks' time. Bloody Covid means there's a backlog. Don't worry.' She raised a calming hand. 'I've already arranged care for Angus. A nanny. Nothing else to do. Social care wasn't an option.'

You'd put him in the care of a stranger though and think it was OK because you were paying lots of money for it. Mark didn't say the words aloud. He didn't know what to think. 'Treatment? What are they recommending?'

'Surgery then chemo.' She shrugged. 'Mark, all I ask is for

you think about it. I'm not asking for a relationship with you, but if I die...'

'You're not going to die.' He was cold all over. This wasn't happening. He wasn't going to let her die and leave him with a child to bring up on his own. 'Suzanne, I don't know what to say. It's late, I wasn't expecting this. I don't know for sure Angus is my child. Why don't we meet on Saturday and do the paternity test and take it from there?'

She got up from the sofa. 'Where?'

'Eh?'

'Where shall we meet?'

'Not here,' he said quickly. 'Alex would—'

'Never allow it.' She finished the sentence for him.

'No, he wouldn't.'

'My flat, then. Ten o'clock on Saturday morning.'

'OK.' That would give him a few days to think things through. He wasn't going to rush into anything.

It was after midnight before she left. He assured her over and over he would be there on Saturday, all the time hoping a miracle would happen to give him a cast-iron excuse. Once she'd gone he resisted the pull of the whisky bottle. Things were bad enough without a hangover to contend with. He collapsed into bed and into a dreamless sleep. At six o'clock Scrimgeour hammered on his door.

'Get up. We need to get in early this morning. You need to brief the team about what you found out in Edinburgh yesterday. What have you got for us?'

He'd give a thousand pounds for another half hour in bed. He had nothing from his trip yesterday. No doubt Alex was expecting great things from him, and all he had was a dodgy notion that Edith Drummond was both telling the truth and at the same time holding back.

'I'm up,' he mumbled. 'I'll see you in the office and speak to you then.'

Alex was away by the time he stumbled out of the shower. He dried himself quickly and shaved. Quarter to seven. Damn. No time for the cooked breakfast he craved. He'd have to make do with muesli. He was at work with two minutes to spare and no idea what to say about his interview with Edith Drummond the day before. But for once his luck was in. Alex stopped him on his way into the briefing room.

'Results of the DNA samples are in. The adult ones were ready and they fast-tracked the baby's.'

'Good. Took them a while for the adult ones though.' Mark had been getting frustrated at the length of time it was taking.

'I think from what they said it was quite hard to extract DNA from that skeleton.'

Mark frowned. 'But not the baby's?'

'It was in much better condition apparently. Anyway, we've got them now,'

'And what's the verdict?'

'It's interesting. Edith Drummond is not the mother of the baby. She is related though. She's a sibling. And what's more, she's related to the other body. It's her grandmother, though the report said there was more of a DNA share between Drummond and the corpse than would be expected.'

Mark tried to get his head round this, 'Right. So presumably Doris Cavendish had a child and for whatever reason she or her husband killed it when it was born? Who killed the grandmother?'

'Presumably Doris or Richard Cavendish,' said Alex. 'Or most likely, both. But of course, we have no idea what the motive was.'

'What now?' Mark asked Alex. The last thing he wanted was another trip to Edinburgh.

'What did you get from the Drummond woman yesterday?'

'Not much. She told the same story as before. She'd seen her parents digging in the garden late at night. It was clear from what she said that she didn't have a happy childhood. She denied being the baby's mother when I challenged her. Rightly as it turns out. I'd swear she was hiding something, though.'

'No doubt, no doubt. Well, we'll leave her for now. Phone her later about the DNA results. Right, let's get in and get this briefing over.' Scrimgeour moved towards the room, but stopped in the doorway, fixing Mark in his sights. 'Have you dealt with Suzanne?'

'Yes.' Mark wasn't going to say any more. This was his problem.

'What did she want, anyway?'

'Money, what else?' He didn't want to tell Alex the real reason. He needed to sort things out in his own head before he brought anyone else into this mess.

'Huh, typical...' Scrimgeour turned to go, then stopped. 'Wait a minute. She's loaded, if I remember right.'

Mark cursed himself. He'd forgotten Scrimgeour knew how well off she was. She'd been arrested at one point for the murders her sister committed, and her financial affairs had been studied in great depth. As well as her own money, she'd inherited her sister's estate, which after the sale of the house must have been worth a good few hundred thousand pounds.

Alex narrowed his eyes and studied Mark's face. 'She doesn't want money, does she? She wants you involved in the child's life.'

Mark found it impossible to deny.

Alex pushed him towards the door. 'We'll talk later. Come on, let's get on with it.'

The briefing didn't take long. Digging was ongoing but they hoped to have completed the garden soon. All the neighbours had been interviewed. Not much had been discovered from them. Brian Gallagher had been by far the most informative. No one else remembered the Cavendish family other than vaguely. Scrimgeour concluded by saying, 'It's pretty clear cut. I'll speak to the Procurator Fiscal later today. The baby is related to Edith Drummond; they were siblings. It means she's in the clear, and the only possible explanation is her mother had a further child who, for whatever reason, she decided to conceal. We have no evidence to show Richard Cavendish knew about the baby, but it's doubtful his wife would be able to keep such a thing hidden from him. The other body is either the paternal or maternal grandmother of Edith and the baby.' He stopped as Megan put up her hand. 'You have a question?'

Her face was scarlet. 'Um, it must be the maternal grand-mother. Edith's birth certificate didn't have the name of the father so if she's related to the corpse it must be her mother's mother.'

Alex studied her. 'Well,' he said. 'The father could still

be Richard Cavendish. Edith may well have been born out of wedlock but it doesn't mean he isn't her father.'

Poor Megan, thought Mark. It was a fair point but she shouldn't be so quick to try to outsmart Scrimgeour. Fiona Nugent was smirking; she'd be thrilled that the 'girl wonder' as she'd taken to calling Megan, had slipped up.

'Nice try,' said Alex to Megan, 'and I wish you were right. It would be great if we could rule out one grandparent but there's lots of digging to be done still in this case.' He held up his hands at the unintentional pun. 'Sorry, forget I said that. Forensics are going through the contents of the canvas bag found in the garden. It's mainly clothes from the same period as the ones worn by the dead body. Same size too. We're working on the hypothesis they belong to the deceased.' He looked down at his notes. 'What else? Oh, yes. The Cavendishes have been dead for twenty-nine years, so there will be no prosecution. We'll never know if the death of the baby was an accident or if he or she was stillborn or murdered. It's highly possible the latter is the case.' He tapped his pen on his notebook to emphasise the point. 'My gut says the woman was definitely murdered. Her skull was badly damaged, and no, not from the overenthusiastic builders. Why was she murdered? We'll never know. A family feud, perhaps? And as for the baby? Who knows? Their next-door neighbour from that time, Brian Gallagher, has told us Edith, or Enid as she was then, had a miserable childhood. He and his wife were concerned enough to report the couple to Social Work. One child seems to have been too much for them, so...'

The words were left hanging in the air. It was a highly unsatisfactory outcome. No one to charge. No justice for the baby or its grandmother.

TWENTY-ONE

Edinburgh

EDITH WAS SHAKEN. That policeman, he'd had the nerve to accuse her of having a child and killing it. The irony, when she would have loved more than anything to have had a child. She'd never had the opportunity, and it was the great sorrow of her life that she was childless. There were compensations, of course. The children she taught were dear to her. With the instincts of the very young, they recognised her genuine affection for them, and in turn they loved her. It hurt her to the core that he suspected her of killing a child. The bastard.

In truth, Edith had been a virgin until she was thirty-nine. She'd told only two people, the two friends she'd made at the Open University summer school all those years ago. It had been such a shock when David had turned up as Depute HT at her school. It was early days, but other than that initial 'I'm sure I recognise you' he'd said nothing else about it. Please God it would stay that way. Before she knew what she was doing, her thoughts wandered to the week when, at the age of thirty-nine, she tasted freedom for the first time.

. . .

She'd gone to the welcome reception with a mixture of anticipation and trepidation. It took all her courage to cross the threshold and go into the room, which was full to bursting with men and women out to have a good time. Over by the window, a couple was engaged in near pornographic activity. Enid had heard that OU summer schools were packed with middle-aged people looking for sex, and that suited her fine. She was wearing the best dress she'd ever owned, a deep blue cotton, which brought out the colour of her eyes. She'd bought it in C&A in Argyle Street before catching the train to summer school in Stirling, using money she'd stolen from her mother's purse. Taking a deep breath, she stepped into the room. There was a table with glasses of wine already poured. She picked up a glass of white, thinking it would give her courage. She wasn't accustomed to alcohol. She took a sip and grimaced. It was lukewarm, unsurprising given the summer heat. She turned back to the table, wondering how many people had already dumped their glasses there. Now she looked at it, the glass was smeared with lipstick. She wasn't wearing any. Gross. Why had she come here?

The answer to that was simple. Enid was after one thing. A suitable man to sleep with. At the age of thirty-nine she had only been kissed once (a horrible non-consensual experience with her lecherous boss) and she was still a virgin. She had no option but to live with her parents at home. Her disgusting filthy parents, whose secret she'd discovered the year before. She had yet to decide what to do about it. Confrontation was out of the question. Her father's temper was to be feared. But she wasn't going to let it go. The hypocrites.

For years they'd instilled in her the tenets of their warped faith. They were members of a fundamentalist Christian sect, a very small one, with few members but many rules. Every day they had drummed into her the need for chastity. 'You must keep yourself pure for your husband,' they'd say. Any attempt to buy fashionable clothes was thwarted by their control of her finances. How she'd pleaded with them to be allowed to wear clothes that didn't make her look like a refugee from an Amish settlement. Her schooldays were a misery because of it. But her entreaties were dismissed as vanity and the work of the devil. The work of the devil, no less. Now she'd discovered their secret, she was flabbergasted at their hypocrisy.

She had no recourse to the money she earned. At sixteen they had made her leave school, although her exam results had been excellent and the school wanted her to stay on and try for a university place. But her father told her in his unctuous voice that God had other plans for her; university was no place for girls. Enid didn't think much of God's planning when all it amounted to was a job in an office, that sort of thing being suitable for a girl. The office was run by a friend of her father, a Mr Eagleston who was a member of the same sect. He stopped attending their services on a Sunday when Enid threatened him. To her shock and disgust, he'd tried to kiss her once, putting his hand up her skirt at the same time. The man was twice her age. 'I'll tell my father,' Enid had said in a panic. She wouldn't have – he'd have blamed her for being a temptress – but fortunately Eagleston didn't know that. She only saw him at work after that. Her father was annoyed he no longer came to their services but didn't challenge him. Eagleston continued to pay her wages direct to her parents though, and they gave her a small allowance, holding on to the rest to pay for her 'keep' as they called it. For years she'd stolen money back from her parents, small amounts at a time, and saved hard until at last, she had enough to pay for an OU degree. It was expensive but cheaper than other universities, which would necessitate giving up her job.

It had taken a lot of planning to do this degree. The course materials were sent to a friendly colleague's house for Enid to pick up and take home, where she'd hidden them under her mattress. Fortunately, her parents were happy to let her spend time in her bedroom; they'd never wanted her company. It left her plenty of spare time to study. Marked assignments were sent to her friend's house. Summer school was a problem, and she would have preferred to do courses without them, but that was difficult. She'd had to lie about where she was going this week, settling on a week's coach trip with an old school friend. Frankly, all this subterfuge exhausted her. At the age of thirty-nine, Enid had finally had enough of her parents.

Once she knew she was definitely going to summer school, she'd been thrilled, looked forward to it for weeks, but now she was here she wasn't sure. She didn't belong here among all these confident, assured people. People were watching her. She sensed their appraisal, their gaze penetrating her skin; she was exposed, naked. With a shiver of repulsion, she scanned the room for hostile eyes, but it was too dark to see properly. Something – a finger? – stroked the back of her neck and she spun round, but there was no one near enough to touch her. As her eyes adjusted to the poor light, she saw students gathered in groups, laughing and talking, their faces friendly and open. No one took any notice of her; no one was staring at her. Imagination, she told herself, imagination and nerves. She took a deep breath and moved further into the common room.

Her foot slipped and she looked down; a discarded sandwich oozed its filling onto the already grubby floor. She rummaged in her bag for a tissue and wiped the slimy substance from the sole of her shoe. There was nowhere to put the tissue. She let it fall, her eyes fixed on a distant point, hoping no one would notice. No one did. They were too engrossed in fascinating, seductive conversations. It would take more than a piece of rubbish to divert them. Enid stared at the ceiling, wishing she was anywhere else but here. A few balloons floated in the air, out of reach; others were tied to the wooden arms of the soft chairs. A girl brushed the tip of her cigarette against one and it exploded. Startled, Enid jumped. Another drink, that's what she needed, but where were they? She scanned the room until she spotted the glasses of red and white wine laid out in neat rows on a table. Mumbling 'Excuse me, sorry,' to unhearing ears, she pushed her way through groups of entangled students, dodging their cigarettes and beer glasses. Enid picked up a glass of white wine and took a sip. It was warm and sweet – Liebfraumilch; she noted the label on the bottles too late. She put it back and picked up a glass of the red, a Corbières that cost less than three pounds in the supermarket, but at least it was drinkable.

She melted into the background. Everyone was chatting. Did they all know each other already? It looked like it, as they'd greeted each other with hugs and kisses. Enid had never done such a thing in her life. Her greetings were confined to a brief handshake, if anything. No, this was not for her; she had to get out of here. She finished her drink, put down her empty glass and made her way to the door, but as she reached it, a young woman dressed in a way Enid loved but would never be able to emulate, stopped her. Small, at least six inches shorter than Enid and with a wild head of curls all the more striking in a room full of demure Princess Diana bobs, she held out a drink to Enid.

'Here, take this.'

Enid panicked. 'I... I was about to leave.'

'Please don't leave. We only met a minute ago. I'm Maggie.'

Enid tried to give her back the drink, but Maggie stopped her. 'No, I've had enough already. You keep it.'

Enid glared at her. She had decided five minutes ago to leave and now this woman was getting in her way.

Maggie noted her glare. 'Oh, lighten up, for fuck's sake. Everyone here is at least ten years older than us. If you don't talk to me, what will I do?'

Despite her irritation, Enid smiled. 'I'm not sure I fit into your age category. I'm older than you think.'

'What? Thirty-one, thirty-two? I was thirty a week ago. How is that possible?'

Enid laughed. 'I'll be forty next year.'

That shut her up. Maggie looked her up and down, one eyebrow arched. 'No way. I'd swear you were in your twenties. Love the dress, by the way.'

Unused to compliments, Enid blushed. Thank goodness she'd bought new clothes before she came here. The stylish Maggie with her short tunic, leggings and Doc Martens would be horrified to see her usual drab wardrobe. 'C&A. In the sale.'

'Gosh. I haven't been in there for a while. Looks like they've upped their game. So, what are you studying?'

'Introduction to psychology. You?'

'Me too. Oh, that's good. Someone to sit beside in the labs. Have you looked at what we have to do yet?'

Enid had scrutinised the notes for the summer school on the train, but she didn't want to seem over keen. 'There's plenty of time to do that later.'

'You're right. What a boring subject. I'm sorry, I'm such a nerd.'

'No, no. Not at all.' She decided to tell the truth. 'Actually, I've read through them twice.'

'Have you? Bloody hell, you're worse than me.' Maggie laughed and put down her glass on a nearby table. 'Let's go and check out the talent. Oh, Christ, I don't believe it.'

'What, what is it?'

'That bloke, the old one coming towards us, I think he fancies me.'

Enid spotted a middle-aged man stumbling towards them.

'Well, hello ladies.' The man loomed over Maggie. 'I barely recognised you with your clothes on, dear.'

Maggie grimaced at Enid. 'He came into my room by mistake.' She added under her breath, 'Or so he says.'

'And a very pleasant error it was too, heh, heh. Can I get you a drink? I'm George, by the way.'

'We'll get our own drinks, thanks.' Maggie steered Enid off to the other side of the room, leaving George open-mouthed behind them. They pushed their way through groups of students until they found a quiet space near the door.

'What was that about?' asked Enid.

'Just another sexual predator. The place is full of them.'

'Oh.' Enid didn't know what to say. This woman might be ten years younger than her, but she was much more savvy.

Confidence oozed from her. 'Have you been to a summer school before?'

'Loads of times. This is my final year. I've been studying history up until now, but I fancied a different subject this time round.'

'Lucky you. This is my first one. I managed to get an exemption from summer school last year. Is it always like this?' Enid gestured towards a couple who were snogging in a corner.

Maggie laughed. 'Oh yes, you wait. You get propositioned all the time. I think half the men come just for the sex, and at least three quarters of the women. If you want to avoid it then you have to find a buddy and then stick together to fend off the likes of our friend George.'

Enid wasn't sure about this. On the one hand she was here with a purpose – she had to get a man; on the other, well, it was sordid. She drained her glass and said nothing as Maggie chattered on beside her.

Enid was drunk. No surprise there. She rarely drank alcohol. Her parents allowed her a small sherry on special occasions, but Maggie had insisted on leaving the dreary reception and going to the bar, where she proceeded to order shots. Edith had never heard of them, and they proved to be tiny glasses of vodka, tequila and rum. They went down easily, and within an hour Maggie was her best friend, and as for the young man who joined them? He was handsome and she told him so, over and over again, to his and Maggie's amusement.

The bar closed at twelve and Enid wasn't ready to go home. Neither were Maggie and David. 'Come back to my room, ladies, and I'll show you a good time,' he said in a mock seductive voice. Enid wasn't sure whether he was joking or serious, but she followed Maggie's example and laughed.

The three of them filled up the small room. It was typical student accommodation; a single bed, wardrobe and desk areas and a chair. No room to swing a cat, as her mother would say. Enid lay down on the bed. Her head was spinning. She sat up again, frightened she was going to be sick.

'Are you OK?' asked Maggie. She sounded worried.

Enid said nothing. She wasn't used to people asking her this, to looking as though they cared.

'Enid?'

'I'm a virgin,' she said. Dear God, where had that come from? She put her hand over her mouth, but it didn't stop the words from spilling out. 'I'm thirty-nine and never been kissed. Well, apart from my letch of a boss who slobbered over me once. I live at home with my parents, who control my every move. My pay goes straight to them, and they give me pocket money as if I'm a ten-year old child. An allowance, they call it.' Maggie and David were looking at her, their eyes wide. 'You said you liked my dress, Maggie. Well, I had to steal money from my mother's purse to pay for it and the other clothes I bought so I'd fit in. You should see how I normally dress, as if I lived eighty years ago. I thought changing my clothes would help, but I'll never fit in, I'm a weirdo. They said so at school and you think it too, I see it in your eyes. Oh God, I'm drunk.'

'No, shit. No, we don't think that, do we David?'

'Of course not.' There was a pause before he added, 'It doesn't sound like a good scene, with your parents, I mean.'

He had no idea. It wasn't his fault. His sympathetic voice unleashed something in her and out it spilled. The humiliation of going to school dressed as though she came from the earlier part of the twentieth century, the taunts she received about her waist length hair, which her parents had never allowed her to get cut. The whispered jibes in class. The petty rules of her parents, keeping her apart from her peers, making sure friends were kept at a distance. She must have talked for hours while Maggie and David listened, nodding, exclaiming in horror and finally holding her as she wept. She kept her counsel though about what she'd discovered not so long ago. She'd never be able to talk about that.

'I'm sorry. I shouldn't have told you all this.'

'Rubbish,' said Maggie. 'You should have talked about it years ago.' She took Enid's hand in hers. 'You need to get out of there.'

'Easier said than done. You've no idea what I've had to do to get here,' she said.

David laughed. 'You haven't murdered them, have you?'

'No, but it's a good idea.' They all laughed, and Enid had never been happier.

'You know, I'd kill them if I got the chance.' As soon as the words were out of her mouth, she wished them back. She had horrified her new friends. It was obvious from their glances at each other how dismayed they were. First, she'd shocked them by telling them she was a virgin, now she was making it worse by saying she'd kill her parents. They'd think she was a psychopath. Perhaps she was. She didn't feel normal. Never had. She didn't know what normal was. To go into a room and feel at ease. To wake up in the morning beside the man of her choice. To love. To hold a child close, to hug and be hugged.

In truth, she had no idea what love was. She knew from

school and television that families were supposed to love each other, but they didn't know her family. She had no sisters or brothers. No cousins, aunts or uncles. No loving grandparents. Only her father and mother and a grandmother who'd visited once. The woman had taken an instant dislike to Enid and had never come back. No, she wasn't going there. That woman had been vile. A game she'd played as a child came into her head. A variation of What's the time, Mr Wolf? One person called out 'Take a step forward if you have an Auntie Mary' (or cousin Gordon or whatever). The first person to get to the caller would in turn get to call out names. She detested the game because she was always left standing at the back. One day she decided to lie. Alone at the side of the road as usual she took a step when the caller shouted 'a cousin called Hector' and again when they called 'an uncle called Tristan' and again and again whenever any name was called until she was neck and neck with Jinty McGowan.

'How come we've never seen any of these cousins? I don't believe you have any. Nobody goes to your house. My ma says your family's weird.' Jinty's brown eyes locked with Enid's blue ones.

'It's none of your business. I do so have cousins. Loads of them.' Tears pricked behind her eyes and Jinty, sensing victory, went in for the kill.

'So, if I went to ask your ma about your cousin Hector, she'd know who you were talking about? I'll go and see her now, will I?'

She was calling her bluff, but Enid didn't dare face up to her. If Jinty did speak to her mother, there would be a beating in it for her. For drawing attention to herself. It wasn't worth it. Best to walk away. It was the last time she played with

Jinty. Or the others. They taunted her but gave up when she didn't react.

They spoke together. David to say, 'You don't mean that.' And Maggie, more sympathetic, interrupting with an indignant, 'I don't blame you.' Enid didn't know what to say to either of them.

David turned to Maggie. 'What do you mean, you don't blame her?'

'What do I mean?' Maggie looked baffled. 'Have you not heard what she's been saying for the past wee while?'

'I know, but murder? Nothing justifies that.'

Enid was surprised at how emphatic he sounded. How sure of himself, of right and wrong. Not much empathy there. Time to intervene. She rolled her eyes. 'I'm joking, you two. No need to get het up.'

They laughed. There was more than a hint of relief in their laughter. A little imp made Enid push it. 'I mean, how would I do it for a start?'

'Poison?' suggested Maggie.

'Too easy to catch. We don't want our new friend to end up in prison.'

'OK, then. Stage a break in, bash them with baseball bats, tie yourself up...'

'And how would she do that, smarty pants?'

'I don't know. Come on then, if you're so smart, David. What would you do?'

'Strangers on a train,' he said without a pause. 'Get talking to someone on a train; they do your murder and you get rid of whoever it is bothering them. Read Patricia Highsmith's novel. It's all in there.'

What a coincidence. Enid had fantasised about this after

seeing the film, but she'd never have the nerve. David turned to her. 'You're very quiet. Plotting, are you?'

She smiled. 'I'm sorry I said anything. It was a silly joke, that's all.'

'Seriously though,' said Maggie. 'You have to get out of there. It will ruin your life. You need to make sure you get a life before it's too late.'

She shouldn't have said anything. Even now people were telling her what to do. Did Maggie think she'd never thought of getting out before it was too late? Patronising cow. For a moment she hated her.

David rummaged in a suitcase under his bed. He brought out a bottle of whisky. 'Drink, anyone? The night is young, and we have yet to think of a way to rid Enid of her dastardly parents.'

'Not for me, thanks.' He was making fun of her, like every other so-called friend she'd tried to make. She'd also noted that over the past hour, he and Maggie had moved closer together. She was the unwanted gooseberry, the spectre at the feast, so she got up and yawned. 'I'm exhausted, time for my bed. See you in the morning.' She was tempted to ask Maggie if she was coming, make her brazen it out, but she left it.

'Oh don't go, Enid. We haven't finished plotting yet.' Maggie lay back on the bed and stretched her arms above her head, showing off her ample breasts, which flopped to either side of her. David's eyes, Enid noticed, were glued to them.

'Sorry, see you later.'

Outside she breathed in the fresh air. It would always be like this, she thought. As ever she was the outsider, the one left out. Damn them to hell. She was furious with herself for telling them too much. Worried they would use it against her. She made her way to her room. No doubt she made a sorry sight wandering about the university campus alone in the dead of night. She passed a pair of lovers who had their arms wrapped around each other and were gazing into each other's eyes. They were singing softly, a duet that Enid recognised as being from Don Giovanni, 'La Ci Darem La Mano'. *There, you will give me your hand; there, you will tell me yes.* The words of a seducer to an innocent girl, with the age-old promise of marriage. What Edith wouldn't do to have a man take her hand and lead her to bed. She didn't need the promise of marriage. It would be enough to be seduced. To be desired.

On she wandered, past the lake where a number of students had taken their life, or so David had told them earlier in the evening. She shivered as she walked, although the early morning air was warm. Melancholy hung in the air, an invisible miasma over the water, and she quickened her step. She was nearly at her hall of residence when she saw him. The scene came back to her in a flash. How had she forgotten? Her face burned at the memory.

She'd been drunk, up at the bar buying the last round of drinks for herself, David and Maggie. He stood beside her at the bar, ogling the barmaid, who was ignoring him. Emboldened by drink, she'd spoken to him.

'She's not interested. You're wasting your time.'

He'd smiled at her. It was a nice smile. God, he was handsome. 'She will be,' he said with the assurance of a man who rarely heard the word no.

'Well, if she does spurn you, I'm in Andrew Stewart Hall, room number 117.' She picked up her drinks and promptly forgot she'd spoken to him. And now here he was. She slowed her steps.

'No luck with Nell Gwyn?'

'Who?'

'Your buxom barmaid.'

He frowned. 'Is that her name then?'

Enid debated with herself whether to explain and decided against it. 'No, I made it up.'

'Oh.' He looked at the ground and kicked at it. 'The offer you made? Were you serious?'

This was it, her chance. What was she thinking? She ought to say no, she didn't know him. They'd exchanged a mere half dozen words; he was here only because his first choice turned him down, he looked to be in his early twenties. There were a dozen reasons why no was the obvious answer. 'Yes,' she said.

Half an hour later she lay in bed wide awake and sober. So this was what all the fuss was about. Ian, for that was his name, was snoring beside her, his arm heavy across her chest. It was suffocating. She nudged him. 'Wake up. It's time for you to go home.'

He groaned. From the smell of him, she wasn't the only one to have had too much to drink. 'Don't want to.'

'Too bad.' She made an effort and rolled him off the bed. The thump he made was answered by one from below and an irritated shout of 'for fuck's sake, it's three in the morning'. Ian looked up at her and smiled. 'Time for a quickie?'

'Wasn't that what we had?' It had been over in a few minutes. It was far from the romantic tryst she'd imagined for all these years.

He stood up. He was really good looking. Defined muscles in his arms and legs, a flat stomach and a face film stars would envy. It wasn't such a bad idea. She drew back the duvet.

185

'Is that blood?' He pointed at a stain on the sheet. Damn, she must have bled. It hadn't hurt, so she assumed she was all right, but there it was. 'Are you having your *period*?' The horror in his voice made her laugh.

She didn't tell him the truth. 'What if I am?' She was talking to his back. He was struggling to get his clothes on. By the looks of him, having periods was the most infectious thing since the great plague.

'I... um. I've just remembered...' His facility for invention was poor. Enid stared at him without mercy.

'What have you remembered? You haven't put the cat out? Your wife is waiting at home for you? Or should I say your mummy? What age are you?'

Poor bloke. He grabbed at the one question he had a ready answer for, 'Twenty-three.'

'Best get back to mum then. Close the door when you leave.'

After he'd gone, she got up and had a shower. As well as alcohol, he'd smelled of something else, musty and stale, and she wanted to be rid of it. After her shower she climbed into the narrow bed and lay for the rest of the night, wondering if this was it. If all she had ahead of her was loneliness and the constant, draining feeling of being an outsider.

TWENTY-TWO

Glasgow

MARK SLOWED DOWN as he approached Suzanne's flat. His heart was beating fast, his chest was tight and his breathing shallow. Christ, he wasn't going to have a panic attack, was he? It was years since the last one. He leaned against a wall and took several deep breaths until his chest loosened and he was breathing normally. For the past few days, he'd tried to think of an excuse not to see her but hadn't been able to come up with anything genuine sounding. He would have welcomed Alex's advice, but Alex had other things on his mind. His mother, who was in a nursing home, wasn't well. For a time, they'd thought it was Covid, but all the tests were negative. Alex wanted her to go into hospital, but the advice from her GP was to keep her in the nursing home. Two nights ago, over a few malts, Alex had confided how conflicted he felt. 'Should I be fighting more for her?' he asked. 'Perhaps I ought to have insisted on hospital treatment.' Mark hadn't known what to say. Things must be bad though, as his daughter had come up from down south for a few days. She'd arrived the night before, when Alex was at the nursing home.

'You must be Mark. I've heard all about you.'

Mark grimaced. He had his suspicions about what Scrimgeour might have said. *Thinks with his dick* for example.

'No need to worry. It was all positive.'

He hoped he hadn't shown his surprise too clearly. 'Would you like a coffee or a tea? Have you eaten?'

'I'll wait until Alex gets back before I eat. A glass of wine would be great though, if you have any.'

Mark went through to the kitchen and picked out a bottle of red. An Argentinian Malbec, which was his current favourite. 'Red OK with you?' he called.

She came into the kitchen and sat at the table. 'Lovely. Tell me, what do you know about my grandmother? How's she doing? Alex sounded worried when we spoke.'

Mark poured them both a glass and pushed one across to her. 'She's very weak and confused. She has pneumonia and they don't seem to be holding out much hope.'

'It's what I expected. Should I go over there now, do you think?'

'Alex said not to. He'll be home shortly.'

'Oh, OK.' She sighed. 'Just my luck. I lose my mother, gain a father and grandmother, and within a year one of them dies. Still, at least I have Conor and his family.'

Mark busied himself putting out snacks. He didn't know all that much about Alex's family life, but the little he had said was about Kate's friendship with the family of the woman who'd raised her, the woman who she'd called mother but who was, in fact, partly implicated in the kidnapping of Kate when she had been a baby. Alex tried hard not to show it but he resented their closeness. Kate had gelled with them immediately, while now, a year after they'd found out the truth, she and Alex were still not fully at ease with each other. It was getting better, Alex said, but wasn't as good as he'd hoped.

'I know what you're thinking,' said Kate.

'Do you?' He hoped she didn't. 'What am I thinking, then?' Damn it, he sounded flirtatious. Not appropriate. He tried again. 'I was wondering if you'd had a chance to meet your grandmother?'

'Yes, I managed to meet her a couple of times before lockdown. Not that she realised who I was.' For a brief moment, her face fell. 'She kept calling me Sandra.'

'Sandra?'

'Yes, that was my mother's name. My birth mother.' She pulled her cardigan tighter. 'It's cold, isn't it?' She didn't leave time for him to answer. 'Apparently, I look a lot like my mother. It must be hard for Alex. I assume you know the story?'

'Yes, Alex told me about it.' Impossible to imagine what it was like, to have a child stolen from you, only to have her return as a fully formed adult. 'It can't have been easy for you, either,' he ventured.

She sipped her wine. Either she hadn't heard his question or was ignoring it. He had just opened his mouth to ask if she wanted anything else when she said, 'You've no idea how hard it's been. Everyone knows how awful it's been for my father, but they think because I was a baby at the time it doesn't matter to me. I was brought up by a woman who... oh, you don't want to hear this.' She stopped.

'Go on,' said Mark. He was aching to go to bed, but Kate was fizzing with energy and needed to talk. Her hands never stopped moving, fiddling with her glass, her hair, delving in and out of her handbag.

'It was less hard for me. I do know that. I didn't have years of imagining what had happened. I was safe, loved, being brought up by a woman who adored me, while Alex imagined me dead, or worse.' Her face darkened. 'But I'm struggling all the same. I loved Mirren, my mother. We were very close. I want to talk about her to Alex, but he thinks she must have suspected there was something off and I don't believe she did.'

Mark didn't reply. Alex had spent hours one evening talking about it. Mirren's friend Josie had stolen his daughter and passed her off to Mirren as a Romanian orphan, claiming the papers had been lost. Mark was inclined to believe Mirren must have been suspicious of her friend's actions.

Kate eyed him. 'You didn't know my mother, please don't judge her.'

She was right, but he didn't want to let her go unchallenged. 'You're right, I didn't know her, but you have to admit—'

She waved his protests aside. 'As I said, you didn't know her. Mirren was other worldly. She was artistic, always thought the best of people. Naïve, you'd say. What Josie told her... she would have believed that totally. Why wouldn't she?'

'But surely, when Josie asked her for money?'

Kate turned her face away to hide her expression. 'You have to believe me. She didn't know. She left thousands to Romanian orphanages. She believed implicitly that was where I came from.'

Before Mark had a chance to answer, they heard Alex's

key in the lock. Mark used this as an opportunity to escape. 'There's Alex now,' he said. 'I'll leave you to it.'

Now, in the cold light of morning he rebuked himself. He should at least have spoken to Alex, found out how his mother was. Instead, he'd slunk off to bed. It was worse because there had been no sign of either of them when he got up. He left without seeing them, as he had to get over to the west end by ten o'clock. Well, it was done now.

He pressed the buzzer at the tenement entrance and waited. After a moment Suzanne answered and let him in. His steps were heavy going up the stairs and he remembered happier days when he'd run up the worn steps, desperate to see her. What a contrast.

The door to her flat was open and he went in, leaving his shoes at the entrance as he always used to do. The cries of a baby – his son – emanated from the bathroom. She must be changing him. He stood in the hall and waited. The flat was shabbier than he remembered. The cream carpet hadn't been hoovered for a while and there was a hint of over ripe bananas in the air. Suzanne came out of the bathroom and dumped the baby in his arms.

'Here, look after him for a second while I make coffee.'

'I don't want anything—'

'Well, I do. I need coffee to wake up. For goodness' sake, Mark, take him. He won't bite.'

With reluctance Mark took him. Christ, he was heavy. He went into the lounge and sat down, placing Angus beside him. The baby smiled at him and babbled.

No, son. You don't get me that way, thought Mark. He

hardened his heart against the child. He had no way of knowing yet whether Angus was his. The baby continued to babble. It sounded as though he was talking to him. He ignored it and got out his phone. Within seconds he was scrolling through it, lost in the realms of social media. Mark gave a cry as a chubby hand reached out and snatched the phone. He prised it out of the baby's hands and put it away. Angus yelled in protest and Mark looked for something to distract him with. Nothing. Where was Suzanne anyway? He picked up the baby and went through to the kitchen.

'Suits you,' said Suzanne.

'Do you have a toy or something? He's trying to get my phone.'

'I'll bring some through with the coffee.'

Mark was desperate to hand the squirming baby back, but she continued to busy herself with making coffee. 'I haven't had breakfast,' she said. 'No time. I'm going to make myself a bacon roll. Join me?'

Christ, how to get him onside. He wanted to say no, but what harm was there in it? 'Thank you,' he said.

Suzanne brought some toys through to the kitchen and placed the baby in a playpen. Immediately Angus settled to picking up the building blocks and throwing them over the side. The smell of frying bacon filled the air.

They ate at the kitchen table, neither of them saying anything. This was as awkward a meeting as he'd ever had. First Kate last night, now this. Would he ever be at ease with a woman again? He finished his roll and put the plate in the dishwasher.

'You haven't forgotten where it is then?'

Mark ignored this. There were to be no reminiscences,

he'd vowed to himself. No going over the good times they'd had.

'Let's get on with this. I have things to do today.'

Suzanne stood up. 'Don't we all? Let's go through to the sitting room. It's more comfortable there. I'll take Angus and you get the playpen and toys.' She let him walk in front of her. He dumped the toys and playpen in the middle of the room and sat down on the smaller of the sofas. She placed Angus in the playpen and sat down beside him, much too close. He moved away from her, but she moved nearer again until he was squashed up against the edge of the sofa.

'Stop this,' he said. 'I don't want to play your silly games.'

She reached a hand towards his face and he grabbed it. 'I mean it, Suzanne. Say what you have to say.'

She stood up and walked over to the window. 'There isn't much more to say. I have cancer, I will need help with Angus during treatment, and if the treatment doesn't work, then I want you to bring him up.'

Mark put his head in his hands. 'First of all, I don't know he's my son—'

'Oh, he's yours all right. Look at him. He has your eyes.'

Mark said nothing.

'You don't believe me. No matter, I have a paternity test here all ready to go.'

'Secondly, you're not going to die.'

She gave a bitter laugh. 'Funny how that wasn't first on your list.'

'Thirdly, how do I know you have cancer?'

He'd shocked her. He regretted it but wasn't going to apologise. She got up from the sofa and left the room. Should he go after her? He made himself wait. A few seconds later she returned with a letter and thrust it into his hands. He glanced at it – it was from the NHS. He read enough to see it was genuine.

Mark handed it back to her without reading the rest. 'I'm sorry,' he said.

She laid it down on the side table. 'Is there a fourthly?'

'There is actually. I can't take on a child. You must realise that. I have a demanding job. I haven't been there for my other children. This would push me over the edge.'

'It's always about you, isn't it?' Her face tightened. He noted the fine lines above her upper lip. They were new. 'Look, Mark. You know I have no family. I wish I had. What I would do for a loving mother right now, to help me through this. She'd ask me how I was; she'd love Angus as much as I do.' She swept her hair back from her face. 'If I die, which by the way I don't intend to do, he'll go into care if you don't take him.'

It wasn't true. He'd be adopted. Childless couples were desperate for babies, she must know this. But despite his doubts, his heart went out to her. 'Aren't we jumping the gun a little? Let's get the paternity test done and see what happens from there. I meant what I said, Suzanne. If he's mine, I will pay you child support.'

'And I meant what I said; I have plenty of money. I don't need yours.' She sighed. 'Come on, let's get this testing over.'

The results would not come through for at least a week. They used a DNA kit bought from a chemist. Mark had looked them up online. They cost a hundred pounds. Mark offered to pay half, but Suzanne ignored him and he didn't press it.

'Did you bring your passport?'

'I got your text, yes. Here it is.' Mark handed it over.

Now it was done and all he had to do was wait. He let

himself out of Suzanne's flat after declining her offer of more coffee. He was at a loss over what to do next. A full weekend ahead of him, and for once he wasn't looking forward to it. He was desperate to see his children. It was ironic. On the one hand he had free and easy access to the one child he wanted nothing to do with – in his heart he knew the baby was his – and on the other, he wasn't allowed access to the ones he did want to see.

He got into his car and sat there for a moment, unsure what to do. He'd gone from never having enough time to do all the small things that needed doing to having not enough to do. It wasn't as if there were odd jobs to do around Alex's house. The place was immaculate. Bare but immaculate. Damn it, he'd drive over to see his family. Maybe he'd get lucky and Karen would speak to him.

His luck was in. Sophie answered the door, and her cries of joy were so genuine Karen wouldn't have the heart to turn him away.

'I wanted to explain,' he said to her face, which was rigid with controlled fury.

'I don't want to hear it,' she said, brushing away Emma's hands, which were clinging to her skirt.

'Please. I... it's a lot more complicated than you think.' He lifted Sophie up to cuddle her. Jeez, she was getting heavy.

'Put me down, Daddy. I'm not a baby.' She wriggled out of his arms. Never one to miss an opportunity, Emma moved in. He lifted her up and she immediately announced she needed a poo. He saw his chance. 'Shall I take her?' he asked.

'Be my guest.'

When he came back downstairs, Karen was polite but chilly.

'Thank you. Now go.'

'I saw the bathroom lock's hanging off. Might as well fix it while I'm here.' He was on to a winner. Karen always complained about the children never leaving her alone in the toilet. It must be killing her to have them able to burst in on her at any moment.

She barely hesitated. 'You know where the tools are.'

One thing led to another. A ceiling spotlight in the kitchen was replaced, a curtain hanging off the rail in Oscar's room was put back up, the grass was cut, the weeds in the driveway were tackled and he put together a small Ikea book-case for the girls' bedroom. By the time he'd finished all the odd jobs he'd put off for so long, the thaw had set in.

'I suppose you want something to eat?' she said when he showed her the bookcase neatly stacked with the books that had been lying on the floor.

'I'll make it,' he said.

'No, let's go out. You can treat us to a McDonald's.'

She'd thawed further over their meal and invited him in for coffee when he dropped them off. Once inside he decided to tell her about Suzanne. Her mouth tightened when he mentioned Suzanne's name. 'Please,' he said. 'I don't know what to do.'

Karen stared at him. 'No lies, no fudging. This is your last chance, Mark.'

She listened without saying a word. Mark told her the whole story, leaving out nothing. From the day he'd bumped into Suzanne in town and stupidly gone back to her flat to the meeting he'd had today with her. He told her about the cancer and how Suzanne wanted him to look after the child if she died. When he'd finished, she stood up and left the room. Mark wanted to go after her but sensed she needed to be alone. The children had been playing quietly upstairs all this time, with only the occasional shout to let him know of their presence. He looked around the room, which was so familiar to him with its IKEA furniture and cheap laminate flooring. How scornful he'd been of it when he was with Suzanne, how he'd longed for proper furniture and floors made from real wood. What an idiot. Too late, he realised material things didn't matter, it was the love and the relationships you had that counted. If only it was two years ago. If only he'd never met Suzanne.

Karen came back into the room and sat down. 'Do you swear you've told me everything? You didn't sneak into bed and impregnate her again this morning? You haven't made up this story about ovarian cancer to get my sympathy?'

He deserved this. 'I swear it's true and I haven't left anything out.'

Karen sighed then. 'You know how I detest that woman and what she and her sister did to us. It's such a betrayal, Mark, for you to have slept with her again. What were you thinking? And to get her pregnant? I don't think I'll ever forgive you.'

What he'd done was indefensible. It was best to say nothing and wait.

'But ovarian cancer? That's horrible. I wouldn't wish it on my worst enemy. And she *is* my worst enemy. If the baby is yours, Mark, you need to step up.' She held up a hand as he opened his mouth to protest. 'I mean it, Mark. You cannot let your son go into care if Suzanne dies.'

'But...'

'But nothing. He's your responsibility.'

Mark looked at his hands and reflected on what he'd done. How he'd broken up his family for the sake of a quick fumble. Yes, he'd been drunk when he slept with Suzanne that one last time, but that wasn't an excuse. Karen was right. 'I'm sorry,' he said. 'Sorry for being an idiot and messing it all up.'

'Are you?' said Karen. 'Or, as my primary seven teacher used to say, *are you just sorry you've been caught?*'

It was a good point. After going back to her flat with Suzanne that evening, he'd never given it another thought, never imagined there would be consequences to his actions. 'I don't know,' he said.

'No more lies,' warned Karen.

'You're right. I think I am sorry I was caught. I never thought about what might happen, about what I was doing to you, to Suzanne and to the children. But now I see what I've done, I am sorry. Does that make sense?'

Karen half smiled. 'Oh, Mark. What a shame it's come to this. Yes, it does sort of make sense.' She stood up. 'Do you want a drink?'

Mark was tempted. This conversation had been great, but he was exhausted after all the emotion and he also was self-aware enough to know where a drink might lead. He'd done enough harm to his family. 'I'll take a rain check.'

Karen nodded, her eyes bright with tears. 'Of course. Come in for a drink when you drop them off next time.'

Mark drove back to Alex's flat feeling better than he had for months. He didn't deserve Karen. This was to be the beginning of him sorting his life out. If she gave him another chance, he swore he'd never betray her again. There was a long way to go but as the old Chinese proverb went, *A journey of a thousand miles begins with a single step.*

He let himself into the flat quietly, listening out for voices to indicate that Alex and Kate were in. But the flat was silent. He was pleased. He'd done enough talking for one day. A difficult time lay ahead for him. He wasn't sure when Suzanne would get the results of the paternity test, but she'd promised to text him as soon as they came. Nor did he know what he'd do if Angus turned out to be his son, but he hoped he'd find the strength to step up and do the right thing.

TWENTY-THREE

Glasgow

MARK FELT great when he awoke the following day. Was this what it was like to have a clear conscience, to have no secrets for once? Alex and Kate were already in the kitchen, Kate at the hob, frying sausages. 'Do you want a sausage sandwich?' she said.

'Haud me back.'

'I'm sorry?'

Alex was reading the newspaper, whistling under his breath. He put the newspaper down and laughed. 'You need a crash course in Scots, hen. He means nothing will stop him. Hold me back.'

Kate laughed in reply. Both of them were at ease. 'How's your mother?' Mark risked asking.

'You're not going to believe this. On the road to recovery, apparently. They gave her mega strength antibiotics and they've done the trick.'

'That's great news.'

'Isn't it?' agreed Kate. 'And I'm allowed to visit. Fully

kitted up, of course. I'm going over there later today to spend time with her. And with Alex of course.'

Mark sneaked a look at his boss. He'd never seen him look so relaxed. The frown line that was deeply engraved into the middle of his forehead had softened. 'I'm delighted to hear that,' he said. Perhaps the crisis with Alex's mother had brought them closer together. He hoped so.

Alex put down his newspaper. 'I've been meaning to ask you, Mark. How's that wee lassie shaping up?'

'Wee Megan? Aye, she's doing all right. Why do you ask?'

'Well, keep it to yourself, but there might be a vacancy coming up. The work she did finding the Drummond woman, that was impressive.'

Before Mark had a chance to answer, Kate interrupted. 'Do you always refer to younger female colleagues in this way, you two?'

Alex looked baffled. 'What are you talking about?'

'That wee lassie? Wee Megan? What sort of way is that to talk about a colleague?'

Shit, she was right. Mark apologised, but Alex was having none of it. 'What about it? She is wee, she's barely one metre sixty, and last time I looked she was a lassie. It's what we call girls up here, well, sometimes anyway,' he added when he saw Mark's look of scepticism.

'Listen to yourself. If she is a police officer then she certainly isn't a girl. You have to be eighteen or over, and last time I looked, that counts as an adult.'

'All right then, wee woman.'

'Oh, come on, Dad. You must know how demeaning and misogynistic that is.'

For a moment, Mark feared Alex might explode. His face

was bright red, his lips pursed, but he gathered himself together and gave Kate a wide smile. 'That's the first time you've called me Dad, you know. Perhaps we should fight more often.'

Kate too had looked furious, but when she heard this she grinned. 'Maybe you're right.' She poured herself another cup of coffee, then added, 'But any more sexism like that and I'll be back to calling you Mr Scrimgeour.'

Mark spent much of the rest of the day at IKEA. It was busier than he would have liked and he was glad mask wearing was mandatory. He bought a bedside table, a new duvet cover and sheets as well as two cushions. A small coffee table caught his eye and went onto his list. At the last minute he bought one of those photo frames that held several photos. He'd stop off at Tesco and get photos of his children printed off from his phone. He should have done that sooner. They would cheer up his room.

All in all, it had been a good couple of days, apart from the visit to Suzanne of course. But he wasn't going to think about that. Mark studied his room. The addition of the cushions and photographs softened it and the bedside table and last-minute buy of a coffee table made it look more homely. Yes, things were definitely looking up. He'd told Karen everything, he was seeing his children later in the week, he felt more at home in his temporary accommodation, and the Crookston Way case was nearing an end. He'd be happier if there was a good motive for the crime, but with the probable murderers dead and gone, he had to accept they might never know what lay behind the deaths. Edith Drummond though. What was she up to?

――――――――

Mark's first task the next day was to phone Edith Drummond to let her know she was in the clear about the baby's remains. He wasn't looking forward to it. It would be better to do this face to face, but Alex had made it clear to him he should get on with it. As soon as he reached work he phoned her.

'Yes?'

'Miss Drummond? It's DS Nicholson here. I need to talk to you about the DNA results.'

'This isn't a good time.' The tone of her voice was terse. Once again Mark sensed she was hiding something.

'It won't take long,' he said.

'All right then. Go ahead.'

'The results show the baby is your sibling and also that the baby is related to the other person found in the house. That person is the grandmother of the child and of course, your grandmother too.'

There was a pause, then, 'I see. Is that all?'

She sounded cold, unconcerned. 'I will need to interview you again,' said Mark.

A sigh. 'When?'

'Shall I come through to Edinburgh again? Or I'll set up a Zoom meeting later today.' Mark thought she'd say no to this – he doubted her IT skills would be up to it – although he hoped she'd agree.

'Fine, I'm free this evening after six p.m. Send me a Zoom link.'

It was as well she didn't see the look of surprise on Mark's face. It would please her, no doubt, to have flummoxed him in this way. 'Right. Your email address please. I'll set up a meeting for six thirty p.m. and send a link.'

Mark spent the remainder of the day working on a new case that had come in. The bungalow bodies' case, as it had come to be known, was pushed to one side. It was no longer urgent; the main suspects were dead and no other bodies had turned up. Everyone's view was that one or both of the Cavendishes was guilty. There were no other suspects. What continued to puzzle everyone though was motive. What had provoked this seemingly respectable if unconventional couple to kill a baby and an old woman? Edith Drummond held the answer. Mark was sure.

The new case was nowhere near as interesting as this one. It was a sad fact that a lot of murders were mundane. Stupid arguments that led to a fight, domestic quarrels, road rage, that sort of thing. This one was no different. There was little detecting to be done; it was simply a case of gathering evidence. There were numerous witnesses to the fight that had broken out outside a nightclub and there was CCTV evidence too. According to witnesses, including the deceased's girlfriend, he had attacked a guy who he wrongly suspected of ogling his 'bird'. Unfortunately for him, the man had been sober, ready to fight back. He was also a boxer. One punch and the victim had fallen over, striking his head at an awkward angle on the kerb. It looked like self-defence. All the witnesses said that's what it was, and the CCTV footage confirmed it. Mark had interviewed him.

The man was brought into the interview room, sobbing. They'd had to wait fifteen minutes for him to calm down before starting the interview. At last the man's lawyer had given him the nod.

'Your name and date of birth for the tape, please,' said Mark.

'Darren Gilmour, thirtieth of August, 1993.'

'What happened?'

Gilmour looked at him, face bleak and streaked with tears. 'I was out with a bunch of work colleagues. I'd gone outside for a fag and this guy comes out and attacks me. It was instinct, I swung at him and now he's dead.' His head went down onto the table.

'Had you been drinking, Mr Gilmour?'

A shake of the head. 'No, I'm a personal trainer and I had clients early the next day. I don't drink much at all to be honest, and that night I had nothing except diet Cokes.'

Mark looked down at his notes. 'I see you said he accused you of "being after his bird". Is that true?'

'No, I don't know who his girlfriend is and I don't know him. Didn't know him, I should say. Never seen either of them before.' He looked at his lawyer. 'I'm gay, I wasn't interested in her.'

'Were you interested in him?'

His lawyer made a move as if to object, but Gilmour held up a hand to stop him. 'It's OK. I see what you're getting at. You're thinking I made a pass at him, and he took offence.'

'Did you?'

'No. It came out of the blue. Fuck, I wish I'd never gone near the place.' More tears. The detective constable with Mark handed him a tissue.

How awful. The poor guy hadn't been ogling the dead

man's girlfriend, he was minding his own business, he hadn't been drunk and yet it had come to this.

After a few seconds Gilmour composed himself. 'What's going to happen to me, do you think?'

'That's up to the procurator fiscal,' said Mark. 'Our job is to gather the evidence.'

'You must have some idea.'

'I'm sorry,' said Mark. He wanted to give the man a crumb of comfort, to console him. If it was down to him, he wouldn't charge him. But it wasn't his decision.

Gilmour was allowed to go home not long after with the customary warning not to leave the area. He'd been terrified. Mark was sorry for him, but the law had to do what the law had to do. Laws were there for a reason.

Once Gilmour had gone, Mark looked over the witness statements. They varied a little but the gist was that Gilmour had been standing outside the pub, minding his own business when a man had attacked him. A couple of the witnesses hadn't heard anything but three said that the victim accused Gilmour of trying to steal his bird before attacking him. Gilmour had punched the victim, Lee Forrest, once. He'd gone down and he'd landed badly, seemingly killed by the way his head hit the kerb. It was enough to put you off a night out.

He looked at his watch. Shit, it was half past five and he hadn't set up the Zoom meeting yet. He rushed to his computer, but as he was about to send the link to Edith Drummond, Megan approached him, looking worried. He braced himself; they hadn't spoken since she'd tentatively asked him out. But he needn't have worried.

'You know how you asked me to check Mr and Mrs Cavendish were dead?'

Mark frowned; where was this going? 'Yes?'

'Their first names are definitely Richard and Doris?'

'Yes.' His fingers were poised over the keyboard. He needed to get on with his next task. 'Is there a problem?'

'It's probably a mistake. But it wasn't their daughter who registered them. It was their niece.'

Mark scratched his nose. 'So what? Perhaps their daughter was grief-stricken, asked a relative to take on the job. I mean to have both your parents die in a car crash like that...' Even as he was speaking, he wasn't convinced. Edith Drummond was a cold fish. She wasn't one to cry over her parents, who she clearly disliked.

'A relative with exactly the same name? Enid Cavendish.'

A twinge of unease. 'It happens.'

She raised an eyebrow. 'It's not exactly a common name. I did a quick search on people finder and only found one Enid Cavendish.'

Megan was right. It was an unusual name. What reason had she for lying to the registrar? 'Good point,' he said. 'I'll get on to it.' He'd cancel the Zoom meeting tonight and look into this before doing anything more. 'Thanks, Megan. That's excellent work.'

She didn't leave. 'There's more.'

'Go on then, what is it?'

'They're brother and sister.'

'Sorry, who are?'

'The Cavendishes.'

'What? Are you sure?'

Megan lifted an eyebrow in response. 'The names of their parents are on the death certificates. They're the same in both cases. That makes them siblings.' There was a sarcastic edge to her tone.

'Leave it with me. Get back to work now.'

A flash of annoyance crossed her face. Too bad. Mark was irritated at the way she'd spoken to him. He turned his back to Megan and typed a terse email to Edith Drummond to rearrange their meeting for the same time the next evening. It would piss her off, but this was a development he had to think about. Miss Drummond had questions to answer.

His research came up with little of importance. To register a death in Scotland you either had to be a relative, their executor, have been present at their death or own the property they lived in. What surprised him was that if you were a relative you were advised to take a driving licence or a passport to show who you were, but it wasn't obligatory. Theoretically, anyone might have pretended to be Enid. He doubted it though. He expected she'd lied. About this and about her parents. Never mind, he'd get to the bottom of it tomorrow.

At six thirty precisely the next day, Mark opened the Zoom meeting room. Edith was there but hadn't turned on her camera. 'Please turn on your camera,' he said. He envisaged her sitting there, debating with herself whether it was worth the hassle to defy him. But he'd insist if he had to. He wanted to see her face while he was interviewing her. To his relief she succumbed and her image came up on his screen. She was rattled. There was an edginess to her.

'Let's get this over with then.'

'I have a number of questions to ask you. About your parents.'

He'd swear she twitched. 'Go ahead,' she said.

'Their names were Richard and Doris Cavendish, is that correct?'

'Yes.'

'And they died in a car crash in 1991?'

'You already know this. I've told you before.'

'Just checking, making sure I have all the facts. You were the person to register their deaths?'

'Yes,' she said. But she sounded wary.

'Were they, in fact, your parents?'

She stared at him, her face drawn and pale. For once she looked her age. 'What do you mean?'

We've checked the NRS.'

'I don't understand.'

The National Register of Scotland. Their deaths were registered by you but not as their daughter. As their niece. Can you explain? And we can see from their death certificates they were brother and sister. On both certificates it states that their parents were Dorothy and John Cavendish. So, Miss Drummond. Which is it? Are you their daughter or their niece?'

TWENTY-FOUR

Edinburgh

EDITH WAS SPEECHLESS. She had never imagined her deception in registering their deaths would come out. She'd never considered the police would look at their death certificates. She paused for a second before answering. 'Both,' she said.

DS Nicholson turned down his mouth. 'I don't understand.'

'I was Richard's niece but Doris's daughter.'

DS Nicholson tapped a biro on the table. 'Why not say that then?'

'I was upset. I registered Richard's death first and the registrar put me down as my mother's niece before I noticed. It didn't seem worth changing it.'

'OK,' he said. 'But that doesn't explain why you've been referring to them as your parents. Why did you lie?'

Edith stared at the screen, wondering whether to cut herself off from the meeting. One press of the red *leave meeting* button and she'd be out. He was powerless to stop her, after all. He was more than fifty miles away. Her mouth was dry and she licked her lips. 'I didn't want anyone to know I was illegitimate,' she said at last.

The detective raised his eyebrows. 'They died in 1991. No one cared about illegitimacy by that time.'

She bridled at his assumption. 'I did,' she said. 'The members of my church did. I was brought up to be God fearing. I don't believe all that stuff now, but at the time...'

'Go on.' His voice was softer now, inviting confidences.

'My mother was very ashamed of having a child outside marriage,' she said. 'She lied by omission. People assumed they were married, and neither she nor my uncle disabused them. I was told to call them my parents. To save any embarrassment.'

'I see.'

Edith waited to see if he'd pursue it.

He was frowning, unconvinced. 'That's an odd thing to do, is it not? They didn't need to pretend to be married. She could have said she was a widow and it suited her to have her brother around.'

He didn't know the half of it if he thought that was the odd thing about her parents. Edith gave a half smile. 'I agree,' she said. 'But they were strange people.'

'Tell me more about them. You said they made your life a misery.'

'What do you want to know?'

'What made your life so miserable? Did they hit you?'

Was that the worst thing he could think of? *Did they hit you?* Dear God. If only that was all they'd done. Eventually she managed to blurt out. 'They were very religious.'

'Yes, you said that before. And how did this show itself?'

Edith put her hand up to her face, hoping to hide her anger. This man, this upstart had no idea what he was doing to her. Making her talk about her past. She'd already told him about the strange practices of her parents; what more did he need? 'We've been over this already. We spent every Sunday reading the bible,' she said at last.

'Like the wee Frees?'

She supposed it was ignorance, that he thought the Free Church of Scotland with its strict observance of the Sabbath was as religious as you could get. 'Not exactly, no.'

'Tell me more.'

'We didn't watch television or listen to the radio. They censored what I read. I was allowed to read the classics, but anything more modern was out of bounds.' Edith paused, remembering. She looked at her hands as she spoke. 'Once I brought an Enid Blyton book home from school. I had to. It was a book by someone who had the same first name as me. Even in the 1950s it was an old-fashioned name. It was a Famous Five book. *Five Go to Mystery Moor*. I was reading it in class and my teacher told me to take it home...'

Edith held a memory of the terror she'd experienced when her mother had gone through her school bag. 'What is this?' she'd said, holding up the tattered hardback.

'A book,' she had replied in all innocence, but her mother had taken it as cheek. She'd grabbed Enid by her plait and dragged her to the bathroom. There her mother had run cold water into the basin and forced Enid's face into the water. Enid was terrified she was going to drown. Even now, over sixty years later, she never filled up the basin when washing her face or hands but did it under the running taps.

'Miss Drummond?' The detective's voice brought her back into the present. 'Are you all right?'

She gasped. 'I... yes, sorry. What was I saying? Oh yes, the book. Well, suffice to say, they didn't like it. One of the girls pretended to be a boy. That went against God's word, apparently.'

'I see.'

Edith doubted it. She'd revealed little of her past to anyone, that night at the Open University summer school being a notable exception. 'Is there anything else you want to know?' Recalling her past had exhausted her, and more than anything she wanted to close down this meeting, pour herself a large gin and tonic and lose herself in a rubbishy programme on television. Anything to escape her memories.

'I can see this is distressing for you. Richard and Doris Cavendish sound...' He tailed off. 'It would be helpful if you could tell me anything that might shed light on the remains found in your old house. As I said to you on the phone yesterday, the adult remains were those of your grandmother. Do you remember her visiting?'

A hazy figure flickered in Edith's mind. Small, thin, dressed all in black. Her face a picture of disbelief when she saw Edith. What was it she'd said? *What is this?* Surely not, she must have said *who is this?* Was this when she'd first suspected she had no place in the world? The shame of her existence?

'I have a vague memory of meeting her,' she said. 'I was young, no more than ten years old. She wasn't the sort of grandmother you read about in picture books.' She grimaced, thinking about the stories she told her class where grandmothers were loving creatures who slipped bars of chocolate to their grandchildren when parents weren't watching, who spent time playing games and listening patiently to their young charges' stories. 'I only met her that one time. She didn't like me.' That was all he was going to get.

'That's unusual. Perhaps you were mistaken? You were very young after all.'

Edith sniffed. 'She called me an abomination, so no, I don't think I am mistaken.'

Another frown, deeper this time. 'Are you sure? It's a strange thing to call a child.'

'Believe me, Sergeant Nicholson, when someone looks at you with disgust the way my grandmother looked at me, you don't forget.'

'But why would she have said that?'

'I expect religion was behind my grandmother's abhorrence of me. The fact that I was illegitimate.'

'That's an extreme reaction for that time.'

'Not for some religions,' she said. 'Look at the Magdalen laundries in Ireland. The last one closed in 1996. They were for mothers of illegitimate babies.'

'Do you know of any reason why your grandmother might have been killed by either or both of them?'

Yes, but she wasn't going to tell him. 'There was a fight one evening. I heard shouting.' It was hard to forget. The noises coming from the living room, the indistinct words. Edith had always feared it was about her, and years later she found proof. But had they killed the old woman? They were worse than she thought.

DS Nicholson wrote down a few words. She'd love to see what they were.

'Anything else?' he asked.

'No.'

'OK. What about the baby? You said you saw your parents in the garden with a spade late at night. Have you remembered anything else about that?'

'I'm sorry, no.'

'The woman who gave the statement I told you about – she claimed your mother said it was her cousin's child.'

'She didn't have any cousins,' said Edith.

'So, your mother was lying.'

'She lied her entire life,' said Edith. The bitter words were out before she could stop them.

'I'm sorry, but I have to ask this. 'Do you believe she or your uncle was capable of murder?'

'Possibly.'

'To kill a baby? Your brother or sister. Why would they do that?'

'Will they be able to tell, you know, whether it was a boy or a girl? I would have loved a sibling.'

'I don't know. I'll see if I can find out for you.' His voice dropped. 'Miss Drummond, please think. Why would they have killed a child?'

She ought to tell him. But the words wouldn't come. 'I don't know. I was a nuisance to them. They didn't like me, so...' She tailed off. 'Perhaps my mother was unable to bear the shame of another illegitimate baby or didn't want the burden of raising another child. I don't know.'

'Does that seem likely to you? That they'd kill a child because it was illegitimate? After all, you were allowed to live.'

'I'm sorry. I have no idea why my parents would have killed a baby.'

'Your parents? Your mother and uncle, surely.'

After a pause she said, 'They always insisted on me calling them my parents. Said it avoided unnecessary questions.'

He frowned. 'So, to make this clear. They were brother

and sister, but pretended they were married and you had to go along with that? You must have found it hard.'

Understatement of the year. But Edith said nothing. She did not want to go into the details of her childhood with this man, with anyone.

A few more questions and they were done. Edith pressed the leave meeting button and it was over. For the time being.

TWENTY-FIVE

Edinburgh

It was useless. Edith couldn't settle to anything once the Zoom call ended. All those questions had upset her, brought back dark memories. She hadn't recalled that day, that shocking, terrible day, for years but now it came flooding back.

It had been a dark November day when Enid inadvertently began the process that led to her finding out the truth about Richard and Doris Cavendish. A Sunday, long and dreary as Sundays at home tended to be. After the service there was nothing to do, no television and the rain pouring down, or more accurately, swiping at the window in horizontal swathes.

'I need my birth certificate,' she said.

There was a stillness in the room as if it was holding its breath. Doris shot a look at Richard. Neither of them said anything.

Enid sat in her chair and carried on reading the passport application she held in her hand. 'And I need the signature of a professional person. Across the back of my photograph to verify that it's a true likeness. Will Dr Meikle do it, do you think?'

No reply. Enid was used to their silence when she spoke, so she thought nothing of it. It often took them a while before they responded to any request. Thinking up ways to avoid doing what she wanted, no doubt. Several minutes passed before her father reached out and poked the fire. Sparks flew out onto the hearth, narrowly missing the rug spread out in front of it. 'Why do you want a passport?'

'I'm going abroad in the spring. Two of the girls in the office are going to France, to Paris, and they've asked me to join them.'

And how can you afford it?'

'It's a cheap package deal.'

'Even so,' said her mother.

I've been saving my allowance for years.'

Her mother raised another objection. 'Do we know these girls?' Girls. They were in their thirties. Her mother said the final word as though it disgusted her.

'It's Jane and Fiona. I went to Scarborough with them last year.' Her parents wouldn't object to them because they were known to the sect that they'd been members of, and anyway, that was a battle she'd already won.

More silence. Enid waited.

'I'm not sure where our birth certificates are,' said her mother. 'I'll have a look when you're at work.'

Enid didn't look up. 'Thanks,' she said. Out of the corner of her eye she caught the worried glances they gave each other.

It was three weeks before she raised the subject again. 'Have you found my birth certificate yet?'

Her mother's answer was curt. 'No.'

Enid wasn't sure what to do. Confrontation was useless. She'd learned the hard way. But she needed the certificate. There was talk of possible strikes at the passport office, which were likely to lead to delays of weeks in processing applications. And there were Christmas holidays to come, which didn't help. She needed the birth certificate and soon. But she didn't dare argue with her mother. 'OK.'

'I'll look again, this week,' said her mother. 'Don't say anything to your father.'

Why not? Enid pushed the question away before it verbalised itself. It was best not to ask questions in this house. She'd been beaten many times in the past for her 'damned inquisitiveness'. She decided to look for it herself if her mother didn't come up with it soon.

The opportunity to search for the certificate came a few days later. Both her parents were out. Her father at work, her mother shopping. Enid had a bad cold and had not gone to work, her first day off in over ten years. When her mother left the house, Enid got up from her bed and went into the dining room, where there was an old wooden filing cabinet that held all the important papers. As she suspected, it was in a terrible mess. Enid's parents were clean but untidy. Her mother in particular was obsessive about housework. If a drop of tea fell on the worktop from the teapot, she'd spray it with Dettol; the sofa and armchairs were scrubbed every week without fail, so that the material was worn down in places although they were only a few years old. She dusted behind the radiators every few days. Bed linen was changed twice a week. In spite of all this cleanliness, however, the house was messy, and the messiest of all was the dining room.

Enid opened the top drawer. It was stuffed full of papers, bills from the looks of things. There was no attempt to put them in order, no manila folders with electricity or mortgage or gas written on them. Just piles of paper pushed into a crumpled heap. She grabbed a handful and flicked through them. It would be surprising if her birth certificate was here, so she stuffed them back into the drawer.

The next drawer down held bank statements. They went back a long way and were all in her father's name. It was no secret he controlled not only Enid's finances but those of her mother. What was interesting was that there appeared to be a large amount of money in various savings accounts. He worked in a bank but not as a manager or in any promoted post. He never spoke about his work though, so perhaps she was mistaken. It was a mystery how he'd managed to save up fifty thousand pounds. An inheritance? A woman had visited once who said she was her grandmother, but she hadn't liked Enid and Enid had been frightened of her. Fortunately, she hadn't stayed long. Enid regularly went to a friend's gran's house at lunchtime. Her parents hadn't known about it, of course. If they had, they would have stopped her going. But they didn't and Enid grew to love the elderly woman and wished she had someone like that in her life. Her friend talked about her gran reading her bedtime stories, teaching her to make scones and pastry. Things Enid had no experience of. Instead, she had parents who despised her. She never did anything right. Her very existence offended them.

She was getting nowhere and soon her mother would return. She looked at her watch. By any reckoning she had half an hour and she had a choice to make. She was certain the birth certificates weren't here. They must be in her parents' bedroom. She was barred from their bedroom. After closing the filing cabinet drawers and checking she hadn't made it obvious she'd been searching, she made her way to the room. It would be safest to lock the front door to ensure she wouldn't be disturbed, but she might as well hang a sign up saying *I'm up to no good*. Instead she put the sweeping brush behind the door so it would fall down and make a noise when her mother came in. That way she'd cover up what she'd been doing, pretend to be in the toilet, say, giving her time to get out of the bedroom.

She stood outside the bedroom door, breathing fast. The last time she'd been caught in here she'd been sixteen years old. Remembering the row that followed made her dizzy. They'd locked her in her room for two days. She didn't understand what she'd done wrong. Girls she was at school with talked all the time about their homes, about what their parents' bedroom was like, and she didn't know what was so bad about what she'd done. She'd been looking for sanitary towels as she had been caught with her period unexpectedly. But they refused to listen to any explanation. Even though it was years later and she was a grown woman, it was with trepidation she turned the door handle and went in.

The first thing that struck her was the smell. Unlike the rest of the house, which reeked of disinfectant, this room had a musty, stale smell cowering underneath a superficial shield of sickly sweetness. Enid sniffed and immediately sneezed. There was a vase containing half dead lilies on the windowsill. Lily pollen; she was allergic to it.

The room was as she remembered it. The old bed with the mahogany frame dominated the room along with a matching wardrobe, chest of drawers and dressing table. They were old-fashioned but not in a good way. Enid's work-mates scoured second hand and antique shops looking for old furniture, but it was pine and oak they were after, not the light-swallowing tones of 1930s' mahogany. The bed was made up with blankets and a faded green candlewick bedspread like Enid's own. Though she, of course, had a single bed and her bedcover was orange, a throwback to the late sixties over twenty years ago, when her room had last been decorated. There was a rug covering the middle of the floor, but the floorboards weren't sanded and waxed as was fashionable, but were stained with a varnish as thick and dark as treacle. And as sticky.

She stood in the middle of the room wondering where to start. She had a vague memory of boxes of papers being stored in the wardrobe drawer. That was a good place to start. The drawer opened easily; it didn't stick like many drawers did in this house. There were no papers there, however, just a stack of bed linen. Nonetheless, Enid rifled through it in case there was something hidden within. Under the bed was another possibility, but a quick look determined there was nothing there but dust clusters. She sneezed again. Next, she tried the chest of drawers, but it was full of clothes and moth balls. That left only the dressing table drawers.

The top two drawers were crammed full of underwear, her father's in the right drawer and her mother's in the left. With closed eyes she felt for paper, but again there was nothing. A quick search of the remaining drawers was equally unsuccessful. Enid was stumped. The only other place was in the attic, but there wasn't enough time to go up there and look. She'd need to drag the ladder up here, and for another thing, her mother would be home soon. Dejected, she moved to the door but as she did, she had an idea.

The top of the wardrobe had an ornate cornicing. It looked like a good hiding place. She rushed to her room, grabbed a chair and brought it through. It was high enough to enable her to feel around the wardrobe's top, and yes, here it was. A large shallow box, of the type that expensive shops placed clothes in. Had her mother ever bought anything from such a shop? It was unimaginable. Doris dressed with no style whatsoever. Enid took it and the chair back to her room, but as she was about to open the box, she heard a key in the front door and the clatter as the brush slammed to the floor. She caught sight of herself in the mirror. There was a smudge on her forehead and her face was flushed. Quickly she hid the box under her bed before wiping her face.

'Enid! What's going on? Why have you left this brush at the front door?'

She came out of her room, moving slowly as though she was ill. 'Sorry,' she mumbled. 'I was cleaning the hall and didn't feel well so I went back to bed.'

'The hall didn't need cleaning,' said her mother. 'I did it only yesterday.'

Enid put on her best pathetic face. 'Did you? I'm sorry, I didn't know. I was trying to help.'

It would have been nice if once, just once, her mother had shown some appreciation. Enid hated herself for needing her parents' approval. She'd read that children should get unconditional love from their parents. Chance would be a fine thing. As it was, she had never felt loved and any luke-warm approval she received was dependent on her doing something for them. But lately everything she did was wrong. Her mother stared at her and said in a brusque voice, 'You're flushed. Better go back to bed. You need to get back to work as soon as possible. You don't want to lose your job because you're never there.'

In over twenty years of working for that firm, Enid had only had three days off sick. Hardly a bad record. But she kept her sharp reply to herself and returned to her room. She was desperate to see whether her birth certificate was in the box.

First of all, she had to be sure she wouldn't be interrupted. Her mother watched the Australian soap opera, *Neighbours*, whenever she got an opportunity. It should be on soon. Although it lasted only for twenty-five minutes, it would give her time to go through the box. Getting it back on top of the wardrobe would have to wait, but she was prepared to take the risk that her parents rarely looked there as it was so inaccessible. There would be plenty of chances to put it back without them knowing. For fifteen minutes she listened carefully for the sound of the theme tune for *Neighbours*. When she heard the opening notes, she reached under her bed and pulled out the box. It was full of papers. There were letters, photos and what looked like birth, death and marriage certificates. Enid pulled one out and looked at it. It was yellow with age, a birth certificate. It was for a Dorothy Singleton, born 13th June 1887 in Dartmouth. It must be her grandmother's. But whether it was of her father's mother or her mother's mother she had no way of knowing. Enid had long ago given up trying to find out anything about any of her grandparents.

She put the certificate to one side and pulled out another. This was a marriage certificate between Dorothy and John Cavendish. Ah, so Dorothy was her paternal grandmother. Was she the woman who had visited? The woman who'd taken an instant dislike to her and who disappeared without saying a word? One morning Enid got up and the old woman was gone. She'd been happy not to see her at breakfast. Her parents never spoke of it and it had been as if the visit never happened.

Enid studied the piece of paper. John Cavendish had

been a tin miner and Dorothy a housemaid. They had
married in 1908 when Dorothy was twenty-one and John
was thirty-seven. Enid wished she knew more about them.
She hadn't realised they were from the south of England. A
tin miner. That sounded dangerous. Her grandmother had
been a housemaid. For a moment she allowed herself to
imagine a grandmother full of stories about the grand house
where she'd worked, but it was hard to think of the rancorous
old woman as ever being young. The next certificate was her
grandfather's death certificate. He'd died in 1927 of malnutrition. Enid looked at the word in shock. Malnutrition. How
awful. He'd been fifty-six. It was too young to die, even in
those days. It must have happened during the Great Depression. Enid remembered a little about it from history lessons in
school. It had been a hard time with many going hungry. Poor
man. Her father would have been little more than a teenager
at the time. That would help to explain how difficult he was,
if he'd had no father to guide him through those years. On
balance she thought not. Father was a hard man to like, and it
was impossible to think of him having been a vulnerable
teenager.

Enid looked at her watch. It was ten to six. The
programme finished in five minutes, and no doubt mother
would come looking for her at that time, badgering her to
help with the evening meal in spite of Enid being unwell.
She picked up the next bundle of papers, expecting to find
her grandmother's death certificate, but there was no sign of
it. Instead, she found her father's birth certificate, Richard
Cavendish. And beside them those of several siblings
together with their death certificates. There were five in total
and all of them had died before the age of three: Robert,
John, Mary, Elizabeth and William. It looked as though her

father had been the youngest child and the only one to survive. Tears stung Enid's eyes. Her poor grandmother, to lose five children. It must have been awful for her. And then on top of that for her husband to die. Poor, poor woman. No wonder she'd been so bitter.

She unfolded the next certificate. Ah, another branch of the family. It was her mother's, Doris Cavendish. No, she was mistaken. It must be another one of her father's siblings because of course her mother wasn't called Cavendish when she was born. What a coincidence for her mother to share a name with one of her husband's siblings. It was a good job Doris wasn't one of the dead children. If she had been, it would have been heart wrenching for Dorothy – to see her only surviving son wed to his sibling's namesake. She put the birth certificate aside. A couple of minutes left to find her own and then she'd put the box away. It should be easy enough; hers would surely not be this decaying yellow all the others were. She flicked through the remaining papers until she found it. This wasn't right. There was no father mentioned. In the space for father's name was written: *Father unknown.*

This was why her father hated her. He wasn't her birth father. And it accounted for her mother's dislike of her too. She must have been so ashamed to have a child out of wedlock. This explained a lot, but it was hard to process it. It was time for *Neighbours* to end. Enid stuffed all the papers back into the box. There was no time to deliberate on it now. She'd leave it until her parents were safely asleep in bed.

It was after eleven before Enid heard the distinctive snore of her father. Her mother was likely to be awake – how anyone slept next to that snorting pig she didn't know– but it didn't matter. She never left her bedroom once she had gone to bed and certainly not to check in on her daughter. Enid reached under her bed and pulled out the box. She had noticed letters in there and she shouldn't, but she was going to read them.

The handwriting was old-fashioned, cursive. Enid squinted at the paper. There was nothing to say who it was to. She turned to the end to see who had written it. It was signed Mother. She went back to the beginning.

I was shocked beyond belief when I found out what you had been hiding all these years. No wonder you left your home when you did. For all these years I was worried about what had happened to you and I was so happy when pastor Jeremiah told me he had found out where you were. I wish to God he hadn't and I could have lived out my remaining years in peace. Your father would have been horrified and he would have denounced you, as I must. Thank God he's dead and will never find out. Enid blinked. This must be from one of her grandmothers, but which one? She returned to the letter. *I will return home tomorrow, but I will not overlook your wickedness. What you have done is evil and must not go unpunished.*

Enid raised her eyebrows. This woman must be the root of her father's puritan beliefs. This letter was over the top. She laid it aside. It didn't make sense. Had her grandmother found out how cruel they were to her? But if she had, why had she been so nasty to Enid? The language used was extreme. Wickedness, evil. She read on. A few seconds later she had the answer. She sat on her bed, her hand covering her mouth. God, she was going to be sick. She ran to the bathroom and leaned over the toilet. The words in the letter kept coming back to her.

'What is all this noise? You'll waken your father.'

It was her mother. Enid wouldn't look at her. 'I'm ill,' she muttered into the toilet bowl.

'I see that. Have you been drinking?'

The injustice of being accused by this woman struck Enid, and she stood up to face her mother. 'No, I'm sickened by something.' It was too late to stop it; vomit spewed out of her all over her mother's front and down her nightdress. Her mother yelped in horror. Good, it was what she deserved.

TWENTY-SIX

Glasgow

MARK LEFT the Zoom meeting with a feeling of dissatisfaction. All that time spent talking to Edith Drummond and he had yet to get the bottom of things. He sat for a few moments thinking about what she had said about her parents. No, not her parents, her mother and uncle. They'd been physically and emotionally abusive towards Edith and he had little doubt they'd killed both their mother and that poor baby. Most unpleasant. He closed down his computer and left work. Within half an hour he was back at the flat. Alex and Kate were in the kitchen.

Kate got up. 'Good timing. I've made a vegan paella. You're feeding my father well, I have to admit, but there's too much meat in his diet. You're going to have to eat some vegetables for a change.'

Christ, not vegan food. Karen had gone through a phase a few months ago and he winced as he remembered the cauliflower steaks that had turned to mush in his mouth. 'Lovely,' he said and sat down, trying hard to hide his apprehension.

It was surprisingly good. Hardly any ingredients: rice obviously, onions, peppers, tomatoes, chickpeas, green beans and plenty of seasoning. It was far from bland. 'Delicious, thank you,' he said when he finished.

'I'll leave you the recipe,' said Kate.

Mark noticed Alex making faces behind her back and tried not to laugh.

'What is it?' Kate caught her father mid grimace. 'You bastard! You said you liked it.'

'Aye I did. But as a one-off. You're not going to begrudge me my steak now, are you?'

Kate put her hands on her hips. They were in for a lecture. 'It's not good for you. All that animal fat clogging up your arteries. All I ask is for you to eat more fish and vegetables. If you don't you'll be dead before you know it.'

'Haha. Careful now. You sound as if you care.'

'I do,' said Kate in a barely audible voice as she gathered the dishes together.

Alex blinked. 'Well, I'll speak to the chief cook here and see what he can do.'

There was an air of tension in the room. Mark got up from his seat, but before he left, Alex asked him about his interview with Edith. Mark told him. Alex didn't say much in response. Eventually he sighed. 'We're not getting to the bottom of this and it's possible we never will. Anyway, the murder of Lee Forrest? How's the investigation going?'

'Well, we've got the guy who did it, as you know. Darren Gilmour, out clubbing with work colleagues. I interviewed him yesterday. He's devastated. He's a personal trainer but has applied to do a university course to become a paramedic. He'll lose his job, his future. All because a numpty attacked him.'

'Careful,' warned Alex. 'You're not the judge and jury here. Your job is to gather the evidence for the Procurator Fiscal and you need to do so without prejudice.'

'All the evidence suggests the wee bugger attacked him for the thinnest of reasons. He was only defending himself.' Mark's reply came out sharper than he intended.

Alex held up a calming hand. 'All I'm saying is be wary. Some folk are very plausible. When are you interviewing him again?'

'We've got several statements to take. I'll see him again once we've done all of them and then the report will go to the PF.'

'Right, keep me informed and please, remember what I said. You're letting this guy get to you.'

'Yeah,' said Mark. 'It's just, you know. He was heartbroken. It's the randomness that gets me. An eejit accuses you of fancying their bird and attacks you. He was gutted, I'm telling you.'

The next day was Wednesday, and he was due to see his children. The weather was good, and he'd take them to Pollok Park before treating them to a burger. Oscar loved the flying fox in the play park, and Mark had promised to take him there. But first he had to get through the day. He decided to go through the witness statements about the pub murder again to see if he'd missed anything. Nothing much had changed except another two witnesses had come forward. They differed from the others as they said Gilmour had spoken first to Forrest and not the other way round. Unfortunately, they hadn't heard what Gilmour said although they had heard Forrest go on to accuse Gilmour of trying to steal his girlfriend. Forrest threw the first punch and Gilmour retaliated. Forrest landed badly. End of story. He'd check the CCTV later to see if that corroborated the statements.

'Sir, there's a woman downstairs wants to speak to you. About Darren Gilmour.'

'OK, tell her I'll be down in five minutes.' Mark wanted to grab a coffee first. When he got downstairs, the woman, who was in her fifties, was pacing up and down. Mark went over to her. 'DS Mark Nicholson. I understand you want to speak to me about Darren Gilmour, Ms...?'

'My name is Victoria Henderson. We need to speak in private.'

'Of course.' Mark led her into an interview room. 'Please take a seat.'

Once Mark had taken her details she said, 'I need to tell you what I know about Darren Gilmour.' The woman's voice was measured. She sounded authoritative, like a school teacher. Mark would bet his life on it that if she was, no one would dare give her cheek.

Mark got out his notebook. 'You wish to make a statement?'

'I do.'

'Go on.'

'Last week I was out for a meal with my husband. We'd gone over to the west end to the Chip. Gilmour was there, with a woman. I recognised them both when I saw the evening paper yesterday.'

Mark's antennae twitched. 'Go on.'

'They obviously knew each other very well, if you get my meaning. My husband was on the point of telling them to get a room when I realised that I recognised the woman.'

'Go on.'

'The woman was...' She paused, no doubt for dramatic effect. 'Tracy Daniels.'

Mark leaned forward. 'You're sure of this?' Tracy Daniels was the dead man's girlfriend. She'd sobbed her way through her statement, ostensibly heartbroken.

'One hundred percent sure. I was her Maths teacher for two years. I don't know Gilmour, but as I said already, I recognised him from the photo in the *Evening Times*. And there was no mistaking that horrible tattoo he's got of a spider on his neck.'

Christ, this changed everything. Mark asked a few more questions and then took a statement from her. First things first. He needed a warrant to search Gilmour's property.

Gilmour answered the door immediately. He had a smile on his face, which dropped when he saw the two uniformed officers beside Mark. He stood at the door, 'Yes?' he said.

Mark showed him the warrant. Gilmour's face paled. He evidently hadn't expected this. 'I'll phone my lawyer.'

'By all means,' said Mark, 'but I'm afraid your lawyer can do nothing about this. Please stand aside.'

For a moment Gilmour didn't move. This wasn't like the man they'd interviewed before. There was an air of belligerence about him. Mark repeated his request.

Once inside they set to work. Gilmour had two laptops and a top of the range iPad, which were immediately bagged along with his phone.

'You not taking those,' he blustered. 'I need them for my work.'

'You're a personal trainer,' said Mark. 'What do you need them for?'

'All of my training programmes are on there, appointments... that sort of thing. And my phone, what the fuck do you think I need that for?'

'No need to swear, Mr Gilmour. We'll get them back to you as soon as possible.' Not that he'd be needing them if the statement made by Victoria Henderson was true. And Mark had little doubt it was. Gilmour had guilt written all over him. Fuck, he was an idiot to have been fooled by him. They turned up little more of interest: a small amount of cannabis, which wasn't enough to worry them, and a pile of pornographic magazines. Mark showed them to Gilmour. 'These yours?'

He drew back his shoulders. 'Aye, what about it? There's no law against it, is there?'

Mark pretended to think. 'Let me see. No, there isn't. Not at all. Strangely enough though, in your statement you said you were gay. And these pictures, well, they're all women.'

'Aye well, I'm bi. So what?'

'Are you, aye?' Mark didn't give a damn about the man's sexuality, but there had to be a reason why he'd claimed to be gay. To put the police off his tracks, that's why. He returned to the search, aware of Gilmour fuming in the corner.

After another half hour he decided to call it a day. They were about to leave when one of the uniforms came through to Mark with a large container of protein powder.

'Look at this,' she said to Mark as she opened the lid. The container was full of pills, hundreds of them if not thousands. Mark looked at Gilmour. 'Any comment?'

'They're vitamins.'

'Well, the lab will soon tell us what they are, and they will of course be returned to you if they are vitamins.'

Back at the station he told Scrimgeour what they'd found. 'You were right. Looks like Gilmour and Daniels were in it together.'

'Mark, you don't know that as yet. Keep looking for evidence.'

Mark left, subdued. Alex was right. He kept jumping to conclusions. Ah well, time to go and fetch the weans.

Karen greeted him at the door, her face pinched. 'Mark, I'm so sorry. I've been trying to phone you all afternoon.'

'My fault, battery ran out. I forgot to charge it last night. Is everything all right?' He moved as though to go into the house.

Karen held a hand up. 'Better stay where you are. Oscar has Covid. He was sent home from school this morning. Apparently more than half his class have it. Less than two weeks back at school and here we are. And, of course, we have to quarantine too.'

'Is he OK?'

'Bit of a temperature and a cough. He's had worse colds. Thank goodness it doesn't affect children badly.'

'There must be something I can do.'

'Stay well, Mark. I might need your help if the others get it, or worse, if I get it.'

It was the sensible thing to do, but it didn't stop his guilt at being the one who was able to walk away and leave her to deal with it all. Poor Karen. He hoped she wouldn't get Covid, but if she did, he was determined to do anything to help.

TWENTY-SEVEN

Glasgow

It DIDN'T TAKE LONG for forensics to come up with evidence that Gilmour and Tracy Daniels were lovers. Gilmour's phone was full of explicit texts detailing what they'd like to do to each other. It was enough to make a brothel keeper blush. There was nothing else incriminating to be found immediately, but it was enough to get them both in for questioning. Mark interviewed Tracy first. She sat across the table from him, her face white. She put her hands on the table but then hid them when she saw him looking. They were shaking. She didn't look at the lawyer she'd requested.

After he'd cautioned her, Mark launched into his questions.

'How long have you known Darren Gilmour?'

She glanced at the lawyer who remained impassive. 'No comment.'

'Did you and Darren Gilmour plan the attack on your partner, Lee Forrest?'

'No comment.'

She responded the same way to the next few questions. They were getting nowhere. It was time to up the ante. He brought out the file of printed out texts. 'For the purpose of recording I am showing Ms Daniels print outs of texts between her and Mr Gilmour. Please read the first one aloud for the recorder.'

'Babes, that was some fuck last night. You are the best.' Her voice was barely audible.

'Babes, that was some fuck last night. What's that referring to?'

'No comment.' Her face was scarlet.

Mark put down the next sheet of paper. 'I am showing you a photo, printed off from Darren Gilmour's phone, of a naked woman. Do you recognise this woman?'

'No comment.'

'Short spiky blonde hair, slender figure. Looks a lot like you, don't you think?'

'No comment.'

'And this tattoo of a rose on her right forearm. Familiar, isn't it?' Unfortunately for Tracy it was a warm day and she was wearing a short-sleeved blouse. The tattoo was clearly visible.

'I fucking told him to delete those.'

Beside her, her lawyer sighed. 'I'd like to request a break, thank you.'

'No problem,' said Mark. He and the DC who was with him left the room. 'Fiver she changes her statement before tomorrow,' he said.

They got nothing else out of Daniels. Mark brought Gilmour back in for questioning.

'Mr Gilmour, were you lying in wait for Lee Forrest on Saturday night?'

'No comment.'

'You and Tracy Daniels conspired to bring about the death of Lee Forrest.'

'No comment.'

'For whatever reason he was in your way, so you killed him.'

'No comment.'

The rest of the interview went the same way. Gilmour was saying nothing.

Later that day, Scrimgeour updated him. 'There's been a development in the pub killing. Dr McEwan got back with the results of Lee Forrest's autopsy. It's not as we thought. There *is* a wound on his head from where he struck it on the kerb, but that's not what killed him. He died as a result of a blow to his throat. His trachea was broken.'

'Did anyone mention a blow to the throat? Any witnesses?'

'All of the witnesses were behind the accused when the punch was thrown. They didn't have a clear view. Same with the CCTV. The camera picks up the punch and shows Forrest falling to the ground, but you can't see where the punch lands.'

'Now you mention it, there was something odd about the interaction caught on CCTV. Gilmour was hanging around the door of the pub for half an hour or so although in his statement he said he'd just gone outside for a fag. None of the witnesses mentioned seeing him in the pub but we can check that again with them. Had he been waiting for Forrest to come out? It looks as though Gilmour said a couple of words to him as he came out, because Forrest didn't seem to notice him at first but then turned round and flew at him. Him speaking first fits with two of the witness statements.'

Scrimgeour tapped his pen on his desk. 'Fuck, this gets worse and worse. Looked like an open and shut case and now what've we got? Gilmour boxes, is that right? A punch like that from him would be a killer. Was it deliberate though?' He looked at Mark. 'If it was and we can prove it, then it's murder.'

'I was totally taken in by the bastard. He was so convincing when we first interviewed him, all tears and snotters and loads of contrition. And then yesterday, completely different. Full of pent up violence and aggression.'

'Tread carefully,' said Scrimgeour. 'See if you can get the girlfriend to talk. It would be helpful if forensics hurry up with the examination of the computers and phones. I'd be very interested in their search history.'

They agreed they'd send the pair back to their cells to cool off for the time being. Mark phoned forensics, who agreed to prioritise the case. When he'd finished, he went to see the two suspects and told them they were under arrest. Gilmour's reaction was completely different to Daniels'. He stared in front of him, face and body rigid. She burst into tears.

The next day they were back in the interview room. Forensics had come up trumps with further evidence. Tracy was to be interviewed first with Mark leading the interview and Alex observing. Her lawyer looked furious as they entered the room, a scowl marring her immaculately made-up face. 'What is the meaning of this?' she said. 'Why was my client not allowed to go home last night?'

'You know why. She and Darren Gilmour were arrested on suspicion of conspiracy to murder. Gilmour is also suspected of murder.

'Are you charging my client?'

Mark didn't reply. Instead, he spoke directly to Tracy. 'This is your chance,' he said. 'You have an opportunity to tell your side of the story. We've been examining your electronic devices. Your laptop has an interesting search history. Shall I go through it with you?'

She shot her lawyer an anxious glance. Mark brought out two sheets of paper. 'Well, starting on the fourth of June this year, we have several searches along the lines of *Ways to kill someone without being caught* followed by *untraceable poisons*. Several days later there's a search for *how to make a murder look like an accident.*' He looked at her. No reaction. 'Nothing to say for yourself? OK, I'll go on. You posted several questions on Quora and...'

'Hang on, what's Quora?' said the lawyer.

Mark looked at his notes. 'In their own words "It's a platform to ask questions and connect with people who contribute unique insights and quality answers." The questions you posed include *how easy is it to poison someone; could you die from falling downstairs; which method of murder is the easiest; how do you get away with murder.*' He folded his arms and sat back in his seat. 'Quite a collection, isn't it? One of the responders was concerned enough to ask why you wanted to know. *I'm writing a crime novel* was your reply. Funny, when there's no sign of it in your laptop. We sent a search team to your house last night and there's no notebooks, no notes, nothing to suggest you are in fact writing a crime novel.'

'It's at the planning stage.' Tracy's lower lip was in a pout worthy of a toddler's tantrum.

Mark didn't bother to respond. He carried on to his next question. 'The following day you sent an email to Darren Gilmour. Do you remember what it said?' When she didn't reply he carried on. 'Babe, I think I've found the ideal method. A punch to the throat will kill if it's hard enough. I'll get him riled up so he'll attack you. You then hit him in self-defence and bingo, we're shot of him.' He put his head on one side and looked her in the eye. 'Not what you'd expect a loving girlfriend to say of her partner.'

'But I...'

'But what? You deleted them. You certainly did. Poor Darren. He must have been shitting himself when he saw those words. They're very incriminating, don't you think? So incriminating that he shot right back at you. In his words, not quite Shakespeare I think, he said, "Fuck's sake, Trace. What the fuck you doing writing this stuff? Fucking delete it now and your search history too.' He took out the charge sheet. 'Tracy Elizabeth Daniels, you are hereby charged with conspiracy to murder Lee Kyle Forrest.' When he'd finished with the charge he added, 'It's over, Tracy. You've been found out. Darren will of course be charged with murder. That's a life sentence if found guilty. For both of you. And with all the evidence mounting up against you...' His phone rang and he glanced down at it. It was Karen. God, were the kids OK, was she?

'Why don't you take it, detective? It's obviously worrying you.' There was a sneer in the lawyer's voice.

Mark ignored her jibe. 'We're finished here. You'll be

remanded in custody until your trial, Ms Daniels.' This last comment provoked another burst of sobbing from Tracy. Her lawyer whispered to her that they'd get bail, but Mark thought that wasn't a foregone conclusion. Anyhow, that was their worry and he had plenty of his own. Gilmour next. He'd get him charged and then go to pick up the kids.

Gilmour swaggered into the interview room. His lawyer had a sheet of paper in front of him. 'Mr Gilmour has prepared a statement, which I have in front of me. I'm going to read it to you now. "I, Darren Gilmour, state that I was in a relationship with Tracy Daniels, who was the girlfriend of the deceased, Lee Forrest. Lee Forrest was an abusive partner to her. He was controlling and beat her if she didn't do as he asked. When he came out of the night club on Saturday, he was boasting about how he'd give her a doing when they got home. I punched him. I did not mean to kill him. It was bad luck that he fell onto the kerb in the way he did. I accept that I may be charged with manslaughter and I am very sorry I reacted in the way I did."' The lawyer stopped speaking and sat back in his chair with his arms folded.

Mark pursed his lips. 'Mm. That's interesting, very interesting.'

Gilmour was sneering. His lawyer leaned forward. 'Are you going to charge my client with manslaughter or not?'

Mark ignored him and looked Gilmour in the eye. 'The post-mortem results are in. Mr Forrest did not die from hitting his head on the kerb. That was a comparatively mild injury. His death was caused by a blow to the trachea. We have correspondence between you and Ms Daniels about ways to kill people without being caught. And what is one of these methods? A punch or blow to the trachea.'

Gilmour's smirk vanished along with the colour from his

face. Mark picked up his statement from the desk. Before leaving the room, he turned and spoke directly to the lawyer. 'I think that answers your question, don't you?'

Jeez, that comeback had been satisfying. Mark wanted to go and gloat about it to anyone who'd listen, but first he had to phone Karen. She picked up at once.

'Is everything OK?'

A sigh. 'Sophie's coughing and Emma too. They're fine but I think I'm going to have to get them tested.'

'I'll take them to the testing centre if you like.'

'No, I've already requested tests; they'll be here tomorrow. I can't leave the house, obviously. I need food and the next slot for delivery is tomorrow. Any chance of you picking up the essentials?'

Mark was delighted to be able to help. There was a definite softening in her voice. He daren't hope she'd forgiven him, but for now he'd settle for being on reasonable terms with her. 'Of course. Do you have a list? Hang on, I'll get a pen.'

When the call ended, he leaned back in his chair. All in all, not a bad day. He'd enjoy it while the going was good. It wouldn't be long now until the paternity test results were returned. Possibly by the weekend. He swallowed hard at the thought and then put it out of his mind, determined not to worry about it before he had to. Why then, did it feel as though he had a brace of live eels in his stomach?

TWENTY-EIGHT

Edinburgh

EDITH SUSPECTED she might burst with all the worries she had. It was days now since she'd heard from the police in Glasgow. They said they'd keep her informed, but there had been nothing from them. That wasn't the only thing bothering her. She was increasingly concerned about Sophia Greene. Always quiet and shy, the child was saying less and less each day. Edith took Kieran aside and asked if he had noticed anything.

'Not especially. She's always quiet, I haven't noticed if she's got worse.'

Typical Kieran. She wanted to shake him. It had been a risk to ask him anything, given he was a friend of the Greenes. She ought to have known better. She didn't think he'd say anything though. His mind was always on other things. He was pleasant enough, but he had not become any more diligent even though there had been no more absences after his two days off at the beginning of term. Dope, that's what she suspected. He had the dreamy, unfocused air of a pothead. She had no proof though. He wasn't daft enough to bring it into school, but it was the obvious explanation.

She was on her own when it came to Sophia. It was a risk, given the warning she'd had from Olivia, but it wasn't right to ignore the child's demeanour any longer. At playtime, she stood in front of the class and said, 'Boys! Girls! I'm looking for three responsible children to help me tidy the classroom. Do I have any volunteers?'

'What's a volunteer, Miss?' asked Alfie, who was always first to volunteer for anything.

'It's a person like you, Alfie. It means if I need help, you come and help me without being told to. You do it voluntarily.'

'Oh, OK. Is it all right if I don't volunteer this time as I want to play football?'

'Of course it is. But next time I won't take no for an answer.' Edith wagged her finger comically at him and the class laughed. She looked round; several arms waved in the air. Unfortunately, Sophia's wasn't one of them. No surprise there.

'Oh, look at all these helpful children. Thank you, thank you. Robbie, Anna and Sophia, will you stay behind please, and the rest of you, don't worry. There's plenty of work to be done.' She prayed none of them had noticed that Sophia's hand hadn't risen, but of course, that was too much to hope for.

A voice piped up. 'Miss, Miss, Sophia didn't volunteer.' Alfie of course.

'Oh dear. Didn't she? Sophia, are you happy to help?'

Sophia looked at her shoes before dipping her head, a movement so slight Edith would have missed it if she blinked.

'There you go, Alfie. Happy?' She ushered the rest of the

class outside before turning to her three helpers. 'Now, first things first. Snacks.' She went into the desk of her drawer and pulled out a selection of the permitted snacks. Olivia was a health fiend, and while Edith largely agreed with her, she was tempted now and again to slip in a packet of chocolate buttons or a tube of Smarties and see how they went down. They'd love it. As it was the three children looked with disappointment at the range on offer – fruit loops, raisins and a packet of sad looking carrot batons – before Robbie and Anna picked out the fruit loops while Sophia stood motionless.

'Sophia? What about you? Raisins?'

'No, thank you. Mummy says I mustn't.'

'Mummy says you mustn't what?'

'I can't have treats because I've been naughty.'

'I see.' Edith looked at her for a moment. 'Robbie and Anna, you go into the painting corner and gather all the paints together.'

Once they were settled, Edith turned her attention once more to Sophia. 'What did you do that was so naughty? That's not like you?'

'I didn't eat my dinner.'

Edith felt a flash of sympathy, remembering the horrible incident of the tripe when she was a child. 'Was it something you didn't like?'

'I do like it. It was chicken nuggets.'

'Oh, I see. Why didn't you eat them?'

'They falled on the floor and the cat licked them.'

For a moment Edith didn't know what to say. Finally she managed, 'Are you sure?'

A vigorous nodding. 'Yes. The cat licked them, then Mummy washed them and put them back on my plate.'

Dear God. 'When did this happen, Sophia?'

'Last night. She's going to give them to me again tonight.'

If she wasn't mistaken this was one for social work. 'You must be hungry.'

Sophia looked down at the floor. Edith checked that the other two children were engrossed in their task. She went into her rucksack and brought out her packed lunch. 'Do you like ham?' she asked.

'Yes, Miss.'

'Well here's a sandwich for you.' Edith handed it to Sophia.

'But Miss, what will you eat?'

'Oh, I have plenty more,' lied Edith. 'Go on.'

The poor mite was obviously starving. The sandwich disappeared, followed by another. Then Edith offered her a satsuma, which was also devoured. All the time she was eating, Sophia kept her head down, never once looking up at Edith. Once she'd finished, Edith told her to go and help the others. She was pleased to see that Sophia looked much happier than she'd done since coming back to school.

At lunch time, Edith looked through her notebook and policy documents to find the latest on child protection. Reading through it all she was satisfied she had enough to go on to talk to the head teacher about it. She wasn't looking forward to it but it had to be done.

Olivia's face was impassive as she listened. She tapped her biro on her desk, an irritating distraction that made Edith stumble over her words. She wasn't convinced Olivia was paying attention. When Edith finished, Olivia sighed heavily. 'Right, well. Leave it with me. Note down anything else of concern and get back to me. But no more questioning the child. I won't tell you again.'

Edith left the office. Her neck was stiff with tension, and she stopped in the corridor to stretch.

'Everything all right?' David came out of his office.

'What? Oh yes, a child protection issue I've had to report to Olivia.' She lowered her voice. 'Sophia Greene. You teach her older brother Maths, don't you? Have you noticed anything?'

David's mouth turned down. 'With Oliver? Can't say I have. What's the worry about Sophia?'

They went into his office and Edith told him. She noticed that, unlike Olivia, he paid close attention to everything she said, asking for clarification and getting her to be more articulate about her worries.

'She's been exceptionally quiet for the past few weeks. It's hard to put my finger on it; she's always been a passive child. She volunteers nothing and speaks in the quietest of voices when she has to. I'm worried.'

'I'm not surprised,' said David. 'If that story about the food is true, it's horrifying... and you say she was hungry this morning?'

'Definitely. I'll have to get lunch in the dining hall. She ate all of mine.'

David grinned. 'You'll survive. Have we any information on the family? How are they doing after the lockdown? Did either parent lose their job? Is it a financial thing?'

'Her father drives a BMW, and Mrs Greene has one of those massive four-wheel drive gas guzzling things some people seem to need to drive around the wilder reaches of the city.' The words were out before she remembered seeing

David getting out of one of the said vehicles, a Porsche if she wasn't mistaken. 'Ah, sorry. I forgot you were one of that tribe.'

David laughed. 'Yes, I am. But it sounds as though they're doing OK if that's what they're driving. Well, best leave it to Olivia. For all we know, she's on the phone to social work right now.'

Edith looked at him. Was he trustworthy? She'd take the risk. 'The thing is, David, Olivia had a complaint about me from the Greenes. Apparently, I was invading their privacy by asking Sophia if she was doing anything nice one weekend. She told me not to question her again.'

'Yes, I heard about that.'

'And what did you think? Was she right?'

'Edith, I won't discuss the head teacher with you.'

She should have known better. Stupid to expect any support. 'She wasn't best pleased when I told her my concerns today. To be honest I'm worried she didn't take me seriously.'

He sighed. 'You two hate each other, don't you?'

Her response was sharp. 'That's hardly the point. A child's safety is at risk. That's the important thing.'

'You've followed the procedure. Best leave it to Olivia now.' He walked away leaving Edith staring after him, wondering what she had to do before anyone took her concerns seriously.

Over the next few days Edith kept a close eye on Sophia. If anything, she was quieter than ever. Edith tried to get her to stay behind again but she insisted she wanted to go out to play. If Edith offered her anything to eat, Sophia looked away and whispered, 'Not hungry.' Edith wasn't convinced. She tried several times to speak to Olivia, wondering why social work hadn't been to speak to her, but Olivia fobbed her off each time. Eventually she managed to catch her towards the end of lunchtime.

'How did you get on with social work? Are they coming to speak to me, to Sophia?'

'What?' Olivia frowned at her. 'Oh that. Nothing to worry about there.'

'What do you mean? The child was ravenous. She was expected to eat food licked by the cat!'

Olivia smiled in the patronising way Edith hated. 'I've spoken to Mr Greene. Sophia is an imaginative child. Apparently, he has been reading a story to her about an ill-treated orphan and she enjoys playing out the role. The whole incident of the meal was taken straight from the book.'

'What book?' demanded Edith.

'Oh, I don't know. I didn't ask.'

Rage surged through Edith. 'I see. Did you speak to Sophia?'

'No need. I was happy with what her father said. They're a very respectable family, you know; Mrs Greene's brother is well placed in the City Council's Education department. You'd do well to remember that. Now, if you'll excuse me, I've got a busy day ahead of me.'

Edith's fists clenched and unclenched. She was being warned off. They were middle class and therefore immune from abusing their child. Just like her own parents had been. That stupid teacher of hers. If only she'd trusted her instincts. How different her life might have been. Now she was in front of another teacher like the one who'd let her down. The sort of teacher who would always take the side of the parent against a child, the easy path if you like. How many times had it happened over the years, in spite of all the child protection guidelines? How many children had been let down by adults who backed each other, instead of listening to the child?

'I think we should call social work.'

Olivia folded her arms and glared at Edith. 'On what basis, Edith? A feeling? You're not happy? We need evidence. Hard evidence. Come to me with that and yes, of course I'll contact social work.' The bell rang and Olivia relaxed. 'Time to go, dear. You have a class waiting for you.'

Towards the end of the day, Edith called over a little group including Sophia. She wanted the girl close to her, to get a sense of what was going on. She didn't believe the parents' story about the book they were reading to her, but she was going to try to find out.

'Now, listen up, children. I'm trying to think of a book to read to the whole class. Do you remember last year I read *Clever Polly and the Stupid Wolf* to you all? Did you enjoy it?'

Their faces lit up as they recalled the stories of the little girl who outwitted the wolf who wanted to eat her. 'Yes, yes, let's read them again? Please!'

'But we read all of them. No, I want a new story and I'd like you to think of any books you've read with your mummy or daddy you really enjoyed and would like to share with the rest of the class. Do any of you have stories read to you?'

There was a chorus of yes and nods all round. So that part of Sophia's parents' tale was true. Now she had to find out if they had in fact been reading a story about an orphan to her. 'And are there any you liked? Ahmed? What about you?'

'Harry Potter and the Phisopherer's Stone. My daddy's reading that to me.'

'Wow! That's fantastic. And do you like it?'

'I love it! It is the bestest book in the whole world.'

'Well, that is a recommendation. I'll note that one down. How about the rest of you? Jonah?'

Jonah put his hand down. 'I don't want to be read stories,' he announced. 'I want to read them. I read to my little sister before she goes to bed.'

'Oh well done, Jonah. What do you read to her?'

'Revolting Rhymes. I like them. They're rude.'

'But not too rude for us. What a brilliant idea. That's another great one for me to note down. Anyone else got any suggestions? What about you, Sophia?'

'My mummy and daddy don't read me books.'

Edith's chest was tight. Here was the proof she needed. The parents had lied to Olivia and she, the fool that she was, had believed them. 'Oh, that's a shame. Don't you like being read to?'

'My mummy makes up stories and tells them to me.'

Damn. She had to be careful here. 'That sounds interesting, tell me more.'

Sophia looked blank for a second. 'People. Children,' she said at last.

'What sort of children?'

'Last week it was a story about a little girl whose mummy and daddy died. It was sad.'

It was true after all. What an idiot she'd been. And to think she'd been thinking of going behind Olivia's back and reporting the situation to social work. What a close call. She'd followed her conscience, she'd been shown to be wrong and Sophia was fine. Her imagination was too vivid, that's what it was, and she was projecting her own childhood onto that little girl.

She carried on speaking to them for another few minutes until a fight between the class terror, Eliza, and one of her acolytes sprang up and she had to rush to deal with it.

At long last the bell rang. Time to get on her bike and go home to another evening of fretting about her worries.

TWENTY-NINE

Glasgow

IT WAS a miracle Karen hadn't caught Covid now all the children had it, Mark thought. Not that you'd know it. After a day or two of high temperatures they were all fine, but of course they were going to have to quarantine for two weeks. Karen was raging. All those months off school, and now within a couple of weeks, classes were decimated and parents were confined to the house with their children.

'At least they all got it at more or less the same time,' she said when he phoned to find out how things were going. 'Imagine if they'd got it two weeks apart. I'd be climbing the walls by now. As it is I have the feeling I'll never get out again.'

'Let me come and look after them. Give you a break.'

He sensed her hesitation and pushed her again. 'Go on, you know you want to.'

'No. You'd end up having to quarantine and you'd miss work. In any case, I have to stay in anyway so there's no point. But once we're over this, I'll take you at your word and you can have them for a weekend.'

They finished the call on better terms than they'd been for a while and Mark settled down to watch the telly. Alex was out and he had the place to himself. He opened a beer and a family size packet of crisps and switched on the TV. There was nothing on he fancied, so he switched to Netflix and found a film he hadn't seen. Fifteen minutes in, his phone rang. It was Suzanne.

Her voice was quiet. 'I've got the results of the paternity test.'

'And?'

'I haven't opened them yet.'

'Why not?'

'I thought perhaps you might like to be there. To check I don't change them. I know you don't trust me.' Her voice was bitter.

She had a point. But he had been drinking.

'No, I won't come over. I've been drinking, and no way am I taking the risk. You know how low the drink-drive limit is now.' He ought to go over, but he wanted a night in and the idea of getting a bus or the subway to Suzanne's flat was deeply unappealing. 'Go ahead and open them. I trust you.' He crossed his fingers.

There was the sound of an envelope opening. 'Well?' he demanded.

'Positive. It's not a surprise to me of course.'

Until she said those words, Mark didn't realise how much he'd been hoping for a negative result. He stifled a groan. 'What do you want to do?'

'I don't want money, Mark.'

He wished she did. He wished it was simply a case of signing off several hundred pounds a month to her. It was the responsibility he didn't want. What if she did die? The other night he'd googled ovarian cancer and had been horrified to read it was the deadliest of the gynaecological cancers. It had a 50% survival rate after five years compared to an 80% survival rate after ten years for breast cancer.

Her voice interrupted his ruminations. 'You know what I want, Mark. I want you to play a part in Angus's life. I want you to take care of him if I die.'

'Suzanne, I'm sorry. I already have three children. I... I don't know if I can.'

'You can and you will. I've arranged a meeting with a lawyer next week to draw up my will. In it I will express my wishes.'

Mark doubted she'd be able to do that without his permission. He'd have to talk to a lawyer himself. More money down the drain. 'Give me time to think about this. It's a lot to take in.'

To her credit she didn't hit back with the retort he deserved. He'd already had plenty of time to think about it. Anything else was putting off the dreadful day. There was nothing else for it. He arranged to go and see Suzanne the following weekend. She wasn't pleased at the delay, but he lied and said he was terribly busy at work.

'Very well, then. I'll see you next Saturday.'

He rang off and went to look for Alex's whisky. Christ, he needed a stiff one.

THIRTY

Glasgow

IN ALL HONESTY, it wasn't a shock that the paternity test was positive. Suzanne was right; you only had to look at Angus to see the resemblance. Mark had read in a magazine article that babies looked like their fathers in the early months of life to ensure that fathers claimed them as their own. Well, Angus was now almost a year old, and damn it, he looked exactly like Mark at the same age. Mark didn't have many photos of himself as a baby, and those he did have were in the attic of the house he had shared with Karen. He recalled one now as he sat in Suzanne's living room with Angus at his feet, playing with a ball. In the photo, Mark had lifted the ball up and was holding it in front of him, mouth open as if he was about to take a bite. And here was Angus doing exactly the same thing! Was that a twinge of affection he felt? Surely not.

'Here you are.' Suzanne appeared in front of him with a cup of coffee. She handed it to him. 'Have you managed to read through the letter yet?'

He put the coffee down on the side table. It was on the

tip of his tongue to say he didn't need to, he knew by looking at him whose child he was, but he stopped himself. No point in giving Suzanne more of an advantage than she already had. 'I was about to,' he lied as he picked up the piece of paper. They sat in silence for the time it took for him to read it. When he'd finished, he handed it back to her. 'What now?'

'I've asked my lawyer to draw up a will stating my wish that in the event of my death, you should be Angus's guardian.'

She'd carried out her threat then. Mark looked at the child in front of him. 'But if you don't die...'

'How many times do I have to say it, Mark. I don't want your money.'

Thank goodness for that. Mark was stretched enough financially as it was. If he had to pay out hundreds in child support he'd be living with Alex Scrimgeour for the rest of his life. Though it wouldn't necessarily be a bad thing. Mark approved of Alex's penchant for neatness and enjoyed it after his time with Karen and the children in a small house that was never tidy. What was he thinking? All the restful surroundings in the world didn't make up for him missing his children. And, if he was honest, Karen. He rubbed at a stain on his trousers. 'But you do want me involved in his life?'

'You have to get to know him.' She held up a hand as he demurred. 'I know, I know. It's going to make things difficult with Karen. But tell me truthfully, Mark. Do you want to go back there? Isn't that a dead relationship?'

'No, I... we've been getting on better lately.'

Suzanne's mouth tightened. 'Good for you.' She got up from the sofa and left the room. Angus started to cry.

Mark didn't know what to do. He was taken aback by Suzanne's reaction. Surely, she wasn't hoping for a relationship with him? Should he go after her? He was half standing when he heard the front door slam. What the fuck!

Three hours later she hadn't returned. Mark was frantic. Angus had calmed down once he'd been fed. Mark had found two Tupperware pots of leftover pasta in the fridge and heated them up. Angus had gobbled them down. He was sleeping now, but that peace wouldn't last for long. And what would he do then? He looked at his watch. Two o'clock. At least the children were ill and not expecting him to come over. Dear God, what if Suzanne stayed away all night? It was the weekend now, but Monday he was back at work and... wait, was that a noise at the door? He ran into the hall. Suzanne was standing there, taking off her jacket to hang it on the coatrack. She was surrounded by carrier bags.

'What the actual fuck?'

'What is it?' She had the gall to look surprised.

'Where have you been?'

'I told you I was going shopping. I took the opportunity while you were here.'

'No, you didn't.'

She frowned. 'Mark, I did. I called to you as I was leaving... said I'd be back by two o'clock.'

Did she? No, of course she hadn't. 'Don't try to gaslight me. You left in a fury because I said I was getting on well with Karen. You didn't want to hear that, so you left. You deserted your child.'

She pushed past him into the kitchen, and he followed.

'What is it, Mark.'

'Suzanne, I won't do this. I won't see you again. And I

won't see Angus either. You always said your sister was a game player. Well, turns out you're one too. Please don't contact me again.'

Her face was pale. 'You can't leave me alone to deal with cancer and with a baby. I told you, Mark. I need support.'

'You have plenty of money, as you keep telling me. Use it to get a nanny.'

'Listen to me, Mark. You will be involved in the upbringing of our child. I am not going to let him be without a father.' Her face twisted as she said the words.

A twinge of unease went through Mark. Perhaps he was being unreasonable. He opened his mouth to speak, but right then Angus let out a piercing scream. Both of them rushed towards him. He was lying on his back in his cot, sick all down his front, his face scarlet.

Suzanne put her hand on his forehead. 'He's burning up. What did you do to him?'

'What do you mean, what did I do? You were the one who left him. I gave him the food there was in the fridge and a bottle, that's all.'

Her voice was shaking. 'Feel him, he's too hot. Tell me he isn't too hot.'

She was right; Angus's face was flushed and sweaty.

'Do you have a thermometer?'

She was already scrabbling in a kitchen drawer. 'There should be one here, one of those ones you point at their heads.' She emerged triumphant. 'Here it is.' She placed it near his head. 'Thirty-eight point three Celsius. Christ, Mark, what are we going to do?'

Phone NHS 24.' Mark already had his mobile phone out. 'What's the number, I can't remember the number. For God's sake, what's wrong with me?'

'111,' said Suzanne.

It seemed like a lifetime before they answered. Mark put it on loudspeaker. 'We are exceptionally busy at this time. Please hold on or go onto our website www.nhs24.scot for further information.'

He turned to Suzanne. 'Take off his clothes and bathe him with a lukewarm face cloth to try and cool him d— Hello? Yes, it's for a baby. He has a temperature of over thirty-eight degrees Celsius and he's been sick. Hold on, I'll put you on to his mother. She'll be able to give you better information.'

To his shame, Mark hadn't known Angus's birthday. What sort of father didn't know that basic fact about his son? He paced the room while Suzanne spoke to the nurse on the phone.

'Yes, he does have a rash. It's not much though.'

The nurse's voice was clear through the loudspeaker. 'I want you to get a glass and press it against the rash.'

Suzanne turned to him. 'Get a glass, a tumbler from the cupboard. That one there.' She pointed.

He rummaged in the cupboard and found a glass, which he gave her, mouth dry. He'd seen the adverts; he knew what it was for. He watched as she placed it on his son's stomach.

The nurse spoke again. 'Does the rash fade when you press down on it?'

'No,' said Suzanne, her voice shaky. 'It's still there.'

'Right,' said the nurse. 'It's likely to be meningitis. We're sending out an ambulance. It should be with you within fifteen minutes.'

It was the longest fifteen minutes of his life. 'I think we should go to the door of the close,' he said. 'That'll waste less time. They should get him to hospital as soon as possible. I'll follow along behind you.'

She shook her head. 'No point. You won't be allowed in. They said one person only and we're luckier it wasn't earlier in the pandemic, because then I might not have been allowed.'

'What shall I do?'

She was rushing around the flat getting clothes and other things together. 'Keep your phone on so I can contact you. Phone the Queen Elizabeth Hospital to cancel my operation. It's due to be done on Monday but that's not going to happen now.'

'But...'

'But, nothing. Surely you realise I can't leave him now.'

'Suzanne, think about this. What if he's fine by Monday? You would have cancelled for nothing. Who knows what'll happen in the next thirty-six hours?'

She continued as if he hadn't spoken. 'And phone the nanny agency. The details are all in there. She handed him a folder. 'Do it, Mark.'

The doorbell rang. 'That'll be the ambulance. We're off now. Spare keys are where they always are, Mark. Keep your phone on.'

Never in his life had Mark felt so powerless. Not when his sister had been reduced to a vegetative state by his violent father, not when Emma had been taken by Suzanne's deranged sister. He sat down with his head in his hands until he was steady enough to drive. Twenty minutes later he was back at Alex's flat. It was a beautiful afternoon; he hoped Alex hadn't decided to go out for a walk. More than anything he needed a sympathetic ear. For once he was in luck.

'Shit,' said Alex after Mark had filled him in. 'Meningitis. Are they sure?'

Mark's shoulders drooped. 'He has the symptoms, rash, vomiting, fever.'

'Look, he's in the right place. They'll be doing everything they can...'

'I have to make some phone calls.' Mark took out the appointment letter Suzanne had given him. There was no answer. Of course, it was a Saturday. He looked for the ward phone number and called them. It was five minutes before a harassed sounding nurse picked it up. 'Yes?'

Mark told her what had happened. 'Thank you for calling,' she said. 'I'll let the surgeon know.'

'Do you have any idea when the operation might be done now?'

'I'm so sorry. I have no idea.' She did indeed sound sorry. 'Poor Ms Yates, and your son too, of course. We have a huge backlog now because of Covid and it's going to take time to arrange another operation, I imagine. But it's very helpful and thoughtful of you to take the time to cancel when you're obviously going through such a difficult period. We should be able to phone someone on the waiting list and get them booked in instead. Try not to worry. I'm sure Ms Yates will be a priority.'

The nanny agency was less sympathetic. 'You do realise the full amount will need to be paid. The terms are clear. We need a week's notice for any refund to be made.'

'Did I ask about a refund?'

'No, but...'

'No. Exactly. I didn't. I have other things to worry about than your sodding fees. But it's interesting to hear that the first thing you think of is your money, with not a word of sympathy for Ms Yates and her son.' He rang off, cursing under his breath. What a piece of work. He leaned back in his seat.

'Why don't you phone the hospital now?' suggested Alex. 'Find out what's what.'

Oh God. How had he gone from saying he was unsure about acknowledging his son to this frantic bag of nerves in the course of an afternoon? He picked up his mobile. Then put it down again. Perhaps it would be better to phone Suzanne. Alex picked up on his hesitation.

'The hospital,' he urged. 'Phone them.'

It was an age before anyone answered the phone. Yet again he felt guilty for disturbing staff who were undoubtedly already busy. He explained who he was and why he was calling.

'Hold on, I'll ask the doctor to speak to you.'

Another age. Then, 'Mr Nicholson, Dr Petrauskas here. It looks as though your son does have meningitis, I'm afraid. We've done a lumbar puncture and should know shortly whether it's viral or bacterial meningitis.'

'What does that mean?'

'Meningitis is caused by either a virus or bacteria. If it's viral then it's not as serious. Bacterial meningitis is treated with antibiotics, but there may be after effects.' He must have guessed what Mark's next question was going to be, because he carried on, 'I'm not going to go into that now. Let's wait and see what the results are. Phone back in an hour. We should have preliminary results by then.'

Mark turned to Alex. 'They're pretty certain it's meningitis. I've to phone back later.' He looked at his phone.

'Mark, don't go there,' warned Alex.

'What do you mean?'

'You're going to google meningitis side effects, aren't you? What's the point? It will only worry you. You'll know the worst in an hour, so leave it.' He held out his hand.

Mark handed over his phone. He went through to the kitchen to make coffee. Alex followed him. 'Tell me what happened. I'm assuming the paternity test was positive. You wouldn't be in such a state otherwise.'

'You know, it's funny. I felt nothing when I read the letter with the results. My only thoughts were, what was I going to do? How was I going to tell Karen? And the children as well. How would they all take it? And now, I'm devastated. I don't understand what's going on.'

'You want to protect your son,' said Alex. 'It's instinctive. Everyone talks about maternal instinct, that need to protect your offspring, but men have it as well.'

'And Suzanne, how must she feel? You know she went off and left me alone with him for three hours. Said she had called out to me as she left the flat to say what she was doing. She's lying, of course. After I said I didn't want to be named as his guardian she stormed off in a huff. It was gaslighting, pure and simple.'

Alex frowned. 'Is it possible you didn't hear her?'

'No. She left me with a baby, no instructions on what he should have to eat. Didn't tell me where the nappies were, where the baby milk was. Nothing.'

'You're right. It does sound suspicious. Look, forget about that for the time being. Plenty of time to quiz Suzanne about it once this crisis is over. Whether you like it or not, you're involved, and frankly you need to be there both for Suzanne and the baby.'

He was right, of course he was. Mark went through to his bedroom, hoping to find something there to occupy his mind until the hour was up. He picked up a book he'd been reading, a bestselling thriller, but the words didn't stick.

He left it for an hour and ten minutes before he phoned again. His heart pounded as he waited for the doctor to come to the phone. At this rate he'd have a stroke or a heart attack.

The doctor's voice was reassuring. 'It's a virus causing it. It might take a while for him to get over it, but he will, hopefully without any lasting side effects.'

'Angus's mother. She has cancer, should be having an operation on Monday.'

'Yes, we know. I understand you cancelled it.'

Mark was defensive. 'She insisted.'

'Yes, she was adamant it shouldn't go ahead and made us phone to check you had cancelled it. To be honest, it would have been better to go ahead with it...'

'Will she get another appointment soon?'

Dr Petrauskas sighed. 'I don't know, I'm sorry. I'd ask you to try to dissuade her from this course of action, but it's too late now. The slot has already been allocated to another patient.'

'Yes, I see. Thank you.' Mark rang off. His feelings were mixed. Relief with a hint of anger at Suzanne and at himself. He should have waited to see how ill Angus was before rushing in to cancel her operation. Nobody was able to tell them when she'd get the operation now. The cancer would continue to spread while she waited. God knows how much time she'd had before. Now? Who knew? Whether he liked it or now, it looked as though he was going to be involved in his son's life.

THIRTY-ONE

Glasgow

MARK HAD ARRANGED to go out and meet friends that evening but called it off. This wasn't the time to socialise. His priority was to speak to Suzanne and find out how Angus was. He picked up his phone to call her, but she rang him first.

'Is he OK?'

'Yes.' Her voice sounded tired. 'He's going to be fine.' She burst into tears.

Mark didn't know how to respond, and after a few seconds she pulled herself together.

'Thank you for cancelling the operation.'

'Doesn't seem to have been necessary after all.'

'No,' she agreed. 'But it was the right thing to do. At least someone else gets the slot now.'

Mark was far from sure it had been the right thing to do. They'd been quick to determine that Angus's condition wasn't life threatening, and surely a day's notice to cancel would have been enough?

'I had to do it, Mark. Me leaving him alone in the

hospital was never an option. What did the nanny agency say?'

'Their only concern was their fee. The first thing they said was, "There won't be a refund you know. The terms were clear, one week's notice." Not a word of care or concern.'

'You sound angry.'

Mark said nothing. Don't get involved, he told himself. But yes, he was angry at the complete lack of concern over a helpless child's illness.

'Perhaps in spite of yourself, you care.' Her voice was soft.

He had to disabuse her of this notion. 'This changes nothing, Suzanne. I can't get involved and I won't.' He cut off the call. Immediately his phone rang. It was Karen. He looked at it for several seconds, finger poised over the reject call button, before he sighed heavily and answered. This was going to be a difficult call; might as well get it over with.

'Karen,' he said. 'Is everything all right?'

'What? Yes, of course. I'm phoning about the paternity test. I assume it's positive.'

Fuck, he'd forgotten. 'Yes,' he said.

After a pause she said, 'So, what happens next?' Her voice was shaky.

'She's got a lawyer and has named me as guardian if she dies.'

'Bloody hell! Is she allowed to do that without your permission?'

'Honestly, I have no idea. I'll try to find out next week. But Karen, there's more.' He told her what had happened earlier.

'That's a lot to take in. And she's cancelled the operation?'

'Yes, I tried to persuade her to wait but she insisted.'

'I can see why. No mother is going to want to leave their child in that situation. Well, well. I've never believed in karma before now, but it seems like I was wrong. Cancer and her baby getting meningitis.' She sounded pleased about it.

Mark wanted to remind her that Angus was his baby too but said nothing. He'd seen this spiteful side to her before and didn't like it. She must have realised, because she apologised.

'That came out all wrong. Poor little soul. I don't think karma – not that I believe in it – would take things out on a baby. Is he going to be OK?'

'They say he'll be fine with no lasting side effects. It's viral meningitis so it's not as bad as it might have been.'

'Mark, we need to talk about this properly. The three of us. This is your child. You have to acknowledge him and you have to plan for what might happen next if she dies.'

'She's not going to die.'

'Isn't she? Ovarian cancer is serious, Mark. One of the worst. Would you allow a child of yours to go into care? Knowing how bad the outcomes of that are?'

'Don't be ridiculous. He'd be adopted, make a childless couple happy. They're desperate for babies in adoption services.'

'And would you be happy with that? Knowing your child was being brought up by complete strangers when his place was with you, his father? What happens when he grows up and decides to look into his background? He'll discover he had a father all along.'

'It won't come to that. She won't die.'

Karen sighed. 'I hope not, and believe me, Mark, I truly mean it, but it's highly possible she will and you can't keep running from it.'

She was right and yet he couldn't bring himself to accept it. At heart he was a selfish bastard.

'I mean it, Mark. Once the children have recovered from Covid, you and I have to have a chat about what comes next. And then we'll speak to Suzanne.' She ended the call before Mark said anything else.

This was a bombshell. What the hell did it mean? It sounded as though – he didn't dare to hope, but it sounded as though she was considering a future with him. He longed more than anything to go back to the days when all he had to worry about was making ends meet. For the millionth time since he'd received the text telling him she was pregnant, Mark wished with all his heart he'd never set eyes on Suzanne Yates.

Sunday brought more positive news of Angus. He was continuing to make a good recovery. Mark was annoyed with himself for being so quick to cancel Suzanne's operation but it was done now. He spent the rest of the day catching up with paperwork. Exhausted after all the drama of the weekend he settled on an early night. To his surprise, Mark slept well. He'd gone to bed sober, reasoning that drinking too much (which was increasingly the case) wouldn't help solve anything. At seven the next morning he woke feeling refreshed and ready to fight the world. The depression that had threatened to overwhelm him over the last few days had gone and he was, well, he could only describe it as relieved. Alex came into the kitchen while he was making his breakfast.

'I've had an email from the PF. We're to charge that pair

of scrotes who conspired to murder an innocent man. Murder for him and conspiracy to murder for her. Oh, and possession of illegal drugs with intent to sell for him as well. I'll let you have the pleasure.'

Mark smiled. It would give him great pleasure to charge Darren Gilmour. He could hardly wait. The wee bastard had taken him for a fool.

The next morning he decided to charge Tracy Daniels first. She looked at him in disbelief. 'You're not serious?'

Had she lost her one remaining brain cell? She'd heard the evidence against her; she must have known she'd be charged.

'Oh, I am. Very serious.'

'But I didn't do anything.'

'The jury will be the judge of that.'

She tried a different approach. 'I told you, I was planning to write a crime novel. I was doing research for it.' Her voice was trembling now. 'It was fantasy, that's all. I didn't think for a second he would actually do it.' Tears spilled over from her large blue eyes. Please, you have to believe me.'

He'd sooner believe in the Loch Ness monster. 'Take her back to her cell.'

Ten minutes later he had Gilmour in front of him. He was defiant. 'I'll get you for this, you'll see.' Mark had heard it all before. He didn't reply but simply read him the charge and left. Gilmour would be a long time in prison.

THIRTY-TWO

Glasgow

MARK LOOKED at his phone to see what time it was. He had to phone Suzanne and find out how Angus was.

'How is he?' he asked as soon as she answered her phone.

'You took your time,' she said, her voice as sour as three-week-old milk.

'I'm sorry. It's been hell here.'

'Yeah, right. You're playing games, Mark. Trying to show you're too busy to look after your child.'

For fuck's sake. 'I'm not going to explain myself to you, Suzanne. I've told you what happened. Now, are you going to tell me how he is?'

'Angus, his name is Angus. Christ, you can't bring yourself to say it, can you? I bet you only just stopped yourself asking how *it* is.'

It was so close to the truth that Mark stalled. It was true; as recently as the weekend he'd been thinking of the baby that way. He went on the attack. 'Are you going to tell me or not?'

'We're home. They discharged him earlier today.'

'And what about your operation? Any word?'

'You know I won't hear anything for weeks. So don't bother asking.'

'You could get a cancellation at any time, surely?'

'I don't have childcare on tap, how's that going to work?'

She was right. Mark cursed himself for his stupidity in bringing it up. He changed the subject. 'I think we should have a meeting about all of this. Once Angus is fully recovered.'

Her voice lightened. 'You'll do it then? You'll agree to be his guardian.'

'That's not what I said. Karen thinks it—'

'What the fuck has it to do with Karen?' She spat out the name. 'This is our child we're talking about. My child.'

'Be reasonable, Suzanne. If I end up being his guardian, then Karen will be involved.'

'You're going back to her.' She sounded defeated.

'If she'll have me.' It was the first time Mark had allowed himself to express this hope to himself. He crossed his fingers, annoyed at himself for the superstition.

'Damn you, Mark.'

What was this? Did she hope there was a chance he'd come and play happy families with her? 'Listen, Suzanne—'

She cut him off. 'We'll talk about this another time. I'll ring you.'

Mark stared at his phone. He hadn't expected this. The last time they'd spoken she'd been reasonable, and yet now... It showed how damaged she was. She had to be, with what had happened. She was eleven when her sister had been abused by their father, and she was fortunate to escape the abuse, but her sister's problems must have had an effect on her. It hit him how much he had lost. His partner, his children, his home, as well as the respect of his colleagues. He should never have got involved with her, and God knows, he was paying for it now.

THIRTY-THREE

Glasgow

THE BODIES in the bungalow case was drawing to a close. Alex instructed Mark to tie up all the loose ends. They knew the name of the deceased from the death certificates of Richard and Doris Cavendish but that was all. 'Who was Dorothy Cavendish?' he said to Mark. 'It should be easy enough to get her date of birth. We need to find that and also where she lived. Someone ought to have reported her missing. But who? Are there any other relatives apart from Edith Drummond?' He tapped his biro on his desk. 'I don't suppose we'll ever know why she was killed, but our main hypothesis has to be that one or both of her children killed her. See what you can find out. At least get her date of birth!'

It sounded easy enough, but not only was there no one of that name who had been reported missing, there was no trace of her on the Scotland's People website. He hit himself on the forehead. What an eejit. He needed her name before she got married. Time to phone Edith Drummond. Perhaps she could shed light on it.

He waited until after five, busying himself with other

reports in the meantime. She answered immediately, suspicion there in her voice.

'We're trying to tie up loose ends in this case,' he said. 'It's about your grandmother. We haven't found any reports of her going missing at the time. But in addition, she's not on the Scotland's People website, or at least not under her married name. Can you help? Do you know what her name was before she got married?' He wasn't expecting great cooperation from her. Since the minute they'd met she'd been obfuscating.

'Well, as she wasn't Scottish, her maiden name won't help you find her in Scotland's People. She was English, as were my mother and uncle.'

'Oh,' Mark was blindsided. He'd been stupid to make that assumption. 'Do you know where she lived?'

'I'm sorry, I don't know for sure. Down south. Richard and Doris came from Devon, I believe.'

'Thank you. We'll start there.'

'She was born in Dartmouth in 1887 and her maiden name was Singleton. I'm sorry I don't remember the exact date but I think it was June. I no longer have the certificates.'

'Thank you, that's very helpful.'

'When will this be over, do you know?'

'The investigation will be stepped down as the suspects are both dead and therefore can't be charged. It's not up to the police to decide to close the investigation; that's for the Crown Office and Procurator Fiscal Service. We'll send all we have to them and they decide whether to close it or not. Whatever happens, all the papers and forensic evidence will be kept in case new evidence ever comes to light.'

'I see. Does that include the remains? What happens to them?'

'If you are the only relative, it's over to you basically. Once the bodies are released, you can make funeral arrangements. I'll be in touch when I know more.'

There was a brief silence broken by a sigh. 'I am more than willing to take on the responsibility of my sibling's funeral, but my grandmother is another thing altogether. Will that be a problem?'

Mark was silenced. He should have foreseen this. The old woman had called Edith an abomination. 'I'm sorry I don't know. I think the estate of the deceased usually has to pay but of course it's so long since she died...'

'And if there is no estate?'

'I think the local authority is responsible. A lawyer would be better placed to tell you.'

'I see. Thank you.'

He could sense the *for nothing* lingering in the air.

It took two days to find out that the older Mrs Cavendish had been reported missing in Devon in 1961 by her daughter. Not Doris, but another one, Joan. Joan Somerville had contacted the police when her mother failed to return from a visit to Glasgow. The case was closed less than a week later when Joan reported she'd received a letter saying her mother had decided to stay in Scotland.

The daughter was alive, based in a care home in Devon. Now at last he might get answers to his questions. Find out what it was Edith Drummond was hiding. He called the care home to see what options they had for face-to-face calling. The manager, Jennifer Cooper, was both helpful and sensible. She listened to his story without interrupting.

'How dreadful. Her mother and a baby? Both of them? Do you know who did it?'

'Yes, we're sure we know who did it, but they're both dead. I'm afraid I can't disclose any more information at this time.'

'Of course,' she murmured. 'I'll do anything to help. Perhaps it would be best if I broke the news. It will be a shock to find out her mother was murdered, but she's resilient. She has a lovely family who are never away from the place now we're allowed visitors again.'

'Is she...?' Mark hesitated, not knowing how to put it. 'Will she understand all right?'

'Yes. She's all there and more. Look, give me a couple of hours to prepare her. It'll be best face to face. Skype? Say six p.m.?'

They exchanged details. 'I'll stay in the room if that's OK in case she gets upset, but I don't think she will. Not too upset anyway. She has a firm belief in God, so that will be a support to her.

'I think you're right. It would be best if someone told her face to face, and the fact you know her well will be helpful, so I'll leave it to you. Well, as I say, I'll be asking about her mother and also about her brother and sister.'

'That's fine. Well, see you at six o'clock.'

The Skype call was answered promptly. Jennifer, the manager, was exactly how Mark had imagined, a pleasant looking woman of about fifty with an air of efficiency about her. She reassured Mark that Joan had taken the news stoically and then went to fetch her. After a short time, an elderly woman sat down in front of the computer screen. Mark was startled. She looked like an older version of Edith Drummond. The same shaped eyes and an upright bearing. Like Edith, she didn't look her age.

'Good evening, Joan. May I call you Joan?' She smiled her agreement and he continued. 'Joan, my name is Mark Nicholson and I'm a detective sergeant with Scottish Police. I believe Jennifer has told you about how a body was found in a house in Glasgow. I'm sorry to say the body is that of your mother, Dorothy Cavendish. I'm very sorry for your loss.' He paused. 'You reported your mother missing in 1961. Is that right?'

Joan straightened herself. 'I'd like a drink of water, please,' she said to the manager. Her voice was firm with only a slight tremor to betray her age. 'Yes, that's right. I reported her missing at the beginning of July 1961. She'd gone to see Richard in Glasgow in June that year. Until then, mother hadn't heard from either Richard or Doris since they left Devon.'

'When was that?'

'I'm not sure what year it was; I think it was about fifteen years before. Not long after the war. Richard left first. Not a word to the rest of us. All he left was a note to say he'd gone looking for work. A couple of months later, Doris went too. Mother got occasional letters from them both. Always different postmarks and never with an address. They didn't want to be contacted, they said. Then she heard from a man in our church who was visiting Glasgow and had bumped into Richard. Richard pretended not to recognise him, but it was him all right. Jeremiah was sure about that.'

'Jeremiah?'

'Yes, he was a lay preacher in the church. I'm sorry but I don't remember his surname.'

Mark smiled. 'I expect he's long dead, so I won't be needing to interview him.'

Joan narrowed her eyes. His puerile attempt at humour hadn't gone down well. 'Quite. Anyway, Jeremiah had made enquiries and found out Richard's address. He sent it to mother.' She adjusted her glasses before carrying on. 'Mother was delighted. She didn't understand why he had left.' She sighed and looked off into the distance as if trying to remember more clearly. 'She decided to visit him. I begged her not to. She wasn't that old, seventy-four, but her health wasn't good. Heart problems. It's a long way to Glasgow and I thought it would be better if I went with her. I was teaching at the time, and it was only a month until the summer holidays, but no, she was determined to go.'

Mark looked at his notes. 'You reported her missing when she didn't come back, am I correct?'

'Did I?' A cloud passed over Joan's eyes. Damn, Mark had hoped she was fully compos mentis. But it cleared almost at once. 'Of course, I did. What happened was, she told me she was going for three days. Well, a week I think it was, passed and she didn't come home. I didn't know what to do so I told the police. My husband wasn't much help – he and my mother didn't get on – and I didn't have Richard's address. Like a fool I hadn't taken a note of it, and Jeremiah had left the church. I had no way of checking up on her.' Her voice quavered. 'Anyway, two days later I received a letter. It was strange.'

'Go on,' urged Mark. 'Do you remember what it said?'

'She said she was going to stay in Glasgow with Richard, that she had written to the council to give up her house and I was to do what I wanted with the contents. "Throw them all in a skip," she wrote. "Except for all my personal papers. You can send them to this address." She didn't give me Richard's address just a PO Box. We had a difficult relationship, my mother and I, but that hurt. I was up at her house every day making her meals, doing her shopping, caring for her, and all when I had a full-time job and four young children to bring up. But then Richard had always been her favourite.' She paused, tears glimmering in her eyes. 'I gathered together all her papers and sent them to the PO Box. It was mainly family stuff you know, birth and death certificates and a couple of bank books.' After a short pause to gather herself, she said, 'The police closed the case then. All they wanted to know was whether it was her writing or not. Oh, and if she had written to the council, which she had.'

'And was it her writing?'

'Yes.'

'Are you sure it wasn't a forgery? Your brother might have written it.'

'Not a chance. My mother had a very distinctive hand, copperplate. She was a beautiful scribe, whereas Richard's writing was as though a swarm of ants had got into an ink bottle. All over the place. Please, tell me everything you know. I need to know what happened.'

Mark hated this part, being the bearer of bad news. He was glad Jennifer was in the room to support Joan. He told her what they had found and what they suspected. 'It seems your mother died or was killed when visiting your siblings and was buried in their cellar.'

Joan gasped. 'Oh dear God. I feared as much when Jennifer told me her body had been found. But, God, I never thought he'd do anything so evil. To kill your own mother.'

Mark waited for her to compose herself. Jennifer had come over to sit beside her and hold her hand. 'I'm very sorry to upset you like this.'

She sniffed. 'You said siblings. Was Doris there, too?'

'Yes, your brother and sister were living together. Your sister had an illegitimate child of whom she was deeply ashamed. They allowed neighbours to think they were married, to prevent any gossip.'

'This is terrible, just terrible. Are you sure my brother and sister killed our mother?'

'That is our hypothesis, yes. No one else had access to the cellar, and your niece was only ten at the time. We think your mother must have been killed not long after she arrived to visit your brother.

She nodded. 'Dear God, what a fool I've been. I thought I'd offended Mother and all this time she was lying dead in their cellar.' She stared into the camera. 'Are you sure it's her? How do you know? Surely Doris and Richard are both dead?'

More bad news to deliver. 'Yes, they died in a car crash in 1991. Doris's daughter is alive though, and we got DNA samples from her. They match with your mother.'

'I don't believe in hell any more. But if I did, I would be glad to think of them rotting there.' She dabbed her eyes. 'You mentioned a child. Are they still alive?'

Mark hesitated, unsure what to say. 'She is, yes. Her relationship with your brother and sister was poor. From the little she's said, I don't think they showed her much affection.'

'Poor lamb. Richard and Doris didn't show me much affection either.'

Mark had to hide a smile at the description of Edith as a lamb. 'She's a teacher too.'

'What's her name?'

Edith Drummond, although she was given the name Enid Cavendish at birth. She changed her name by deed poll after they died.'

'Will you let her know I'd love to meet her? I'm sure the rest of the family would as well.'

'I'll pass the message on,' promised Mark.

The interview continued for another half hour until he had told her the whole story. The most difficult thing had been telling her about the baby's remains. She'd cried for several minutes then became angry. 'I'll be honest with you, Detective Sergeant. I never liked my brother and sister. They were older than me and we never got on. My childhood was a misery because of their bullying and taunting. But double murder? That's a different level altogether. Hell mend them.'

'Are you OK?'

'I've been better. But I'll be fine. Jennifer and the staff here will support me. They're wonderful. And of course I have my family. Four children, ten grandchildren and three great grandchildren. We're very close.'

'Will you be arranging a funeral for your mother? I know your niece is keen to have a service for her sibling.'

'I expect so, though I'll get one of my daughters to do the arrangements. I don't know where to have the service though. My mother was a member of a very strict religious group. We'll contact them to see if they'll do the service.'

'Richard and Doris held their own services and weren't members of a mainstream church.'

'It doesn't surprise me. They left the group after an argument. I don't know what it was about though. An obscure difference about doctrine, I'd think. Richard argued about that all the time.' Joan grimaced. 'I can see him setting up his own church.' She went on, 'It was a hard life being in thrall to that sect. I've never told anyone before, but I was relieved when Mother said she wasn't coming back. She wasn't an easy woman to like. The first thing I did when I was sure she wasn't going to return was to join the Church of England. The sect we belonged to had taken all the worst aspects of Christianity and forgotten the good bits. Mother used to beat us all as children. It got worse after my father died. I was only a baby when he passed but she didn't spare the rod even on me. She was determined to keep us on the straight path. Well, that didn't work with Richard and Doris, did it? I don't understand it. Such evil. That poor baby.'

All of this was said without pausing for breath. Mark listened for a couple more minutes and then broke into her musings to repeat his condolences. He hoped her family would be able to support her through this like she said. She had a lot to say, and in spite of all the years she'd had to get used to being without her mother, it must have been a shock to learn she had been murdered by two of her children. And as for the death of the baby? God knows how that would affect her.

After he signed off, he sat staring at his computer for several minutes trying to gather himself. They now knew more of what had happened. One thing puzzled him though. The letter saying that she wasn't coming back. Joan was adamant it hadn't been a forgery. Perhaps Edith Drummond could help him. He'd phone her tomorrow.

THIRTY-FOUR

Edinburgh

EDITH LISTENED in disbelief to Sergeant Nicholson. 'Say that again, please?' She must have misheard.

'We have found Richard and Doris's sister. She reported your grandmother missing in 1961.'

'They never mentioned any brothers and sisters.' It was true; they'd said nothing of them. All there was in that box was their birth and death certificates, but there hadn't been anything for a Joan. She would have remembered. Presumably Joan had charge of her own birth certificate. 'I don't know what to say. I didn't know about this.'

'Your aunt would like to meet you. She's in a care home in Whimple.'

'Whimple? Where's that?'

'Devon. And she has children, well obviously they're adults now with children of their own. I think there's a fair few of them.'

'How many?'

'She said she had four children and several grandchildren. Ten if I remember rightly. Oh, and three great grand-children, I think it was.'

Over the past three minutes she'd gone from no living relatives to goodness knows how many. A profusion. A surfeit. An aunt, four cousins and ten second cousins or were they third cousins? How she wished she'd known about them when she was a child. That would have shown Jinty McGowan and her silly games. And there were great grand-children too. She had relatives in abundance! She had to ask Sergeant Nicholson to repeat himself.

'There's one thing puzzling me,' he said. 'Your aunt received a letter from your grandmother telling her she was going to stay in Glasgow. She was adamant it wasn't a forgery. Any ideas?'

Edith thought back to the letter she had been forced to write. 'They would have pressurised her to write it. They did the same to me once.' She told him about the aftermath of the social worker's visit.

She'd shocked him into silence. 'Are you there?'

'Yes, yes. Just thinking things over. Why would they have done such a thing?'

Edith bridled. He didn't believe her. 'Do you think I've made this up?'

'What? No, of course not. I'm thinking aloud, that's all. I don't understand why they would have killed their mother. What was their motive?'

'Perhaps they had a fight. I did hear them rowing, as I already told you, or perhaps she fell ill and died and they panicked.'

'It doesn't seem likely, does it?'

She'd tell him about the letter she'd found but not yet. She wasn't ready. 'Money perhaps? I don't know.'

'Mm.' He wasn't convinced. 'Well, if you remember anything else, you know where I am. In the meantime, you should contact your aunt as soon as possible. As I said, she's keen to meet you.' He gave her the phone number of the care home.

She phoned immediately before she lost her nerve. The manager sounded delighted to hear from her. 'Oh, Joan will be thrilled. We can set up a Skype meeting now if you like. She's desperate to meet you.'

Edith wanted to back out. It was too soon; she'd have been better putting it off. But she had to go through with it now. She waited for the Skype call with trepidation. What if Joan reminded her of Doris? She had never wanted to see that face again, had destroyed all the photographs left behind. She trembled thinking about it. This was a mistake. The unmistakable tones of Skype made her jump. While she was ruminating, the care home manager must have set up the call. She stared at the computer screen and pressed accept.

'Edith, my dear. I am so happy to meet you.'

Edith found herself looking at an older version of herself. Joan looked nothing like Doris. She tried a smile. 'Hello,' she managed. 'This is all a bit of a shock.'

'Isn't it? But a lovely one. I've told my family about you. They're all dying to meet you.'

Tears came to Edith's eyes. She never cried. She blinked them back and said, 'I'd love that.'

They talked for over an hour. Edith had never known time to go so fast, and by the end of the call they had arranged to meet during the October school holiday week – if restrictions allowed them to. Half term couldn't come quickly enough. For now they would have to be content with Skype. Soon she'd tell Mark Nicholson why Doris and Richard had killed their mother, but not yet. She wanted to be sure it wouldn't come out in the press. She wanted to give Olivia no excuse to get rid of her, no chance to gloat or worse, sympathise. She didn't want anyone's pity.

Later that week, she'd gone into school feeling jubilant. Things were going her way for once. The police were closing down the investigation into the goings on in her old house and something wonderful had come out of it – meeting her aunt. It was more than she had ever hoped for. So the ambush, when it came, was devastating. She'd gone into her classroom, humming, to find Olivia standing by her desk.

'Miss Drummond,' she said. Her usual fixed smile was missing.

Edith's heart sank. What now? 'Yes, Olivia?' she said, trying to sound as if she didn't care.

She got straight to the point. 'It has come to my attention you have been the subject of a police investigation. A most unsavoury case.'

Edith went on sorting things out in her classroom as if Olivia wasn't there.

'Care to elaborate?'

Edith smiled. 'That is my business, not yours.'

'If it impacts on my school, it certainly is my business. Have a look at these.' She held out a sheet of paper, which Edith ignored. 'I said look at them.'

Edith took the paper and read through it.

xsxsxsxsx

Guys, you'll never guess what I heard! You know that case in

Glasgow – the one with the bodies? Apparently, it's to do with Miss Drummond!!!

xsxsxsxsx
No way! How do you know?

xsxsxsxsx
Little birdie told me. Apparently one of them is a baby. You don't think...?

xsxsxsxsx
What? What are you saying? I know the police came to speak to her a few weeks ago.

xsxsxsxsx
I heard she'd been burgled. Again. It's happened to her before.

xsxsxsxsx
Oh, what a shame. Should we get her flowers?

xsxsxsxsx
What? She might be a criminal.

xsxsxsxsx
I have it on good authority she is. It's to do with when she lived in Glasgow. And we all know what's been going on there. Buried bodies.

xsxsxsxsx
No way is Miss Drummond a Weegie. She's too clean and tidy and speaks too well.

xsxsxsxsx

Is that all you have to say? I'm telling you. They think she had a baby, killed it and buried it in her parents' garden.

With difficulty Edith controlled herself. Now was the time for her best poker face. She waved the sheet of paper in front of Olivia's face. 'Where did you get this?'

'I copied it from a parents' WhatsApp group.'

'I see. And how did you get access to the group?'

'I was shown it by a parent. They said I had a right to know.' Olivia didn't bother to hide her smirk.

'Why have the names been redacted?'

'Well, confidentiality of course.'

Edith took her time to answer. 'Of course. This is libel, you know. All it will take is a simple medical examination to show I have never had a child. And, therefore, have not murdered one.'

Olivia paled. 'Nonsense.'

'Now, what part of what I said is nonsense? That I have never had a child? That I never murdered a child? Or that this is libel?' Edith drew herself up to her full height and peered down at Olivia. 'I can prove the allegations here are false, and believe me, I will sue.'

Olivia made a grab for the paper, but Edith held it out of her reach. 'Oh no, I don't think so. I'll be holding on to this. Evidence, you see. Something you're lacking.' Olivia stomped out of the room. 'Don't forget to close the door behind you,' Edith called after her.

Edith's legs were shaking after the confrontation. She looked at the sheet of paper again. This was terrible. She'd bought herself a little time with her threat of a lawyer, but it wasn't enough. It wouldn't be long before the whole, sorry story was out and what would she do then?

Thank goodness she'd come into school early today. She'd catch up with Tommy to see if he knew anything about who was behind this campaign. Her suspicion was that it was all Olivia's doing, but she had to be sure before taking any further action.

She opened her classroom door and looked up and down the corridor. Good, no sign of her. She went outside to see if he was in the playground. He was at the far gate and looked as though he was trying to fix it. She ran across to see him.

'Yes, Miss Drummond. Can I help you?'

'Tommy, are you still part of the Primary Two WhatsApp group?'

'Yes.'

'Has there been any unusual activity on it recently. Anything about me?'

'Nothing this week. It's all died down now. That woman Greene tried to stir things up a wee while ago, but the rest of the parents were great and shut her down.' He gave her a quizzical look. 'Do you want me to say anything, get more support going?'

Edith was horrified. 'No, please leave it, but I'd like to see the comments, if that's OK?'

Tommy handed over his phone. 'I'd better get on with this or her majesty will be complaining. I'll pop by your classroom before the kids get in and pick up my phone then.'

Edith rushed back to her classroom. She hoped she was right, and it wasn't parents behind it all. She scrolled through the chat. Sure enough Mariella Greene had posted about the fact she'd asked Sophia about what she'd done at the weekend. *Surely this is an invasion of our privacy?* The replies had been succinct. Several laughing emojis with tears. One FFS! And several *Get a grips*. There was nothing else on the chat about Edith and her supposed crimes. She put the phone in the drawer and pondered over what to do. Maybe there was another WhatsApp group that Tommy didn't know about. Were people gossiping behind her back? Time to find out. She went out into the playground where children were beginning to gather. Parents weren't allowed because of social distancing, but several were standing outside on the pavement. She went over to the group of children nearest the railings and spoke softly to them, all the while listening for her name and watching for any guilty glances that might suggest she was being discussed. Nothing. Either she was not being gossiped about or the parents were all brilliant actors. Oh-oh, what was this? One of them was approaching the railings and trying to attract Edith's attention. Edith stood up from her crouching position in front of Jonathon, the youngest child in the class, who had been telling her all about his trip to the seaside that weekend. She smiled at the woman, whose name had fled from her mind. Whose mother was she? Was she a mother? She looked too old, but you never knew these days.

'Miss Drummond? I'm Gilly's nana. You have her for learning support, I believe.'

Relief swept through her. 'Yes, that's right. She's a hard-working little girl and is making excellent progress.'

The woman beamed. 'Isn't she? Her reading has come on so much. I mean it's been hardly any time, yet the difference in her is amazing. And her confidence has grown too..'

'Thank you. She's a delight to teach.'

'No, thank *you*. My daughter asked me to give you this.'

She handed her a card, which Edith took. 'Honestly there's no need...'

'We've been asking for proper support for Gilly since she started school, but... anyway you've no idea how much this means to us.'

Edith waited until she was alone to open the envelope. It was a card drawn by Gilly with a message of thanks from her. *To Miss Drummond. You are the best teacher ever.* There was a letter from her parents as well as a John Lewis voucher for thirty pounds. She'd return the voucher. She couldn't accept that. But the kind words? Those she would savour. They meant more to her than anything.

She put the letter aside. It was lovely to know she'd made such an impact, but the question remained. How was she going to deal with Olivia?

Days later she still had no idea what to do. No whispers of anything reached her ears. There were no sly glances from parents, nothing to show rumours were spreading. But Olivia had got wind of her connection to the house in Glasgow. How had she managed that? Olivia had avoided her since dropping that bombshell, and as yet Edith had not spoken to a lawyer. All she wanted was to be left alone. Although they'd only met she decided to discuss it with her aunt. Joan had been horrified.

'What does she think she's doing?'

'She's trying to get rid of me. She thinks I'm too old to work.'

There was a pause. Edith saw Joan was trying to think of a way to say what she had to, tactfully. 'And you, do you want to continue to work? Are you perhaps trying to spite Olivia by refusing to retire?'

'No.' Edith's tone brooked no discussion. She wasn't ready for retirement and didn't want to talk about it.

Joan took the hint and changed the subject. The call ended without any further awkwardness. Afterwards Edith thought long about her aunt's reaction. And her own. If she was honest, did she not now find herself thinking of retirement with pleasure instead of dread? Especially now she'd found family? But she would not give Olivia the satisfaction.

THIRTY-FIVE

Glasgow

MARK WAS PLEASED to be shot of the bungalow case. Everything they had would be sent to the Crown Office and Procurator Fiscal Service and it was up to them now to decide whether or not the case would be closed. His bet would be yes, but he himself wasn't fully satisfied he'd got the full story from Edith Drummond. There was no denying it; the past few months had been hard. Karen finding out about Angus and giving him the push, Suzanne's ever-increasing demands and of course Angus's illness.

Angus was out of hospital and doing well. Suzanne had refused to meet with him and Karen. 'It's you alone or nothing,' she'd yelled at him.

He dreaded telling Karen, but she took it well, only saying to him he'd better meet Suzanne and sort it out. She was showing a maturity he'd never before seen in her, and it was enough to allow him to hope they'd get back together. If they did, he vowed to himself to never hurt her or his family again. In the meantime, he had agreed to meet with Suzanne.

He was shocked by Suzanne's appearance when she opened the door of her flat. It wasn't that long since he'd seen her, but she'd lost weight. Her face was grey with fatigue and pinched. Her illness made her look years older. And, of course, the fright with Angus wouldn't have been helped. She invited him in.

'Thank you for coming. I'd like to get this sorted out as soon as possible. Have you made a decision?'

For a brief moment, he considered telling her that under no circumstances would he take responsibility for Angus. But the weekend when Angus had meningitis had shown him he wasn't able to walk away. 'Yes, I'll do it. I'll be his guardian if you die.'

'Thank you,' she said. 'You have no idea what a load that is off my mind.'

'Yes, well. You didn't leave me with much choice.' Mark was churlish, but he didn't want her to know he'd had such a change of heart.

'Once I've had the operation, we'll talk about access.'

He was non-committal. Part of him wanted to embrace this with enthusiasm, but the more suspicious part of him was wary of Suzanne and her manipulations. He hadn't forgotten that Saturday when she'd left him in charge without telling him. 'Mm. When is the operation?'

'Next week. I've taken your advice and avoided that nanny agency. But don't worry, I've found another one. It's more expensive, but they do sound better.'

'Right. How long will you be in hospital?'

'Between two and four days. I've booked the agency for four days and have arranged for a woman to come to the flat to look after Angus for around six weeks after as I won't be able to do heavy lifting or housework for a while.'

'Sounds sensible.'

They parted on reasonable terms. Mark wasn't sure what the future would bring, but there was little point in worrying about it now.

It was now over a week later. The operation had taken place and she was due to leave hospital the next day. Visitors were not allowed because of the pandemic, but she had phoned to let him know they had removed the tumour. She didn't know yet how far it had spread, if at all.

Things had continued to improve with Karen. She was talking to him, was civil, and she placed no restrictions on him seeing the children. He was savvy enough to know she was exhausted by having all three at home for so long, first during lockdown and then for the time when they had Covid. It was as well she hadn't caught it. He was on his way there now to pick up the children for a longed-for weekend's access.

The first thing he noticed was that she'd put make-up on. And she'd done something to her hair. Highlights? 'You look lovely,' he said.

She blushed. One of the things he had loved about Karen was her obliviousness to how beautiful she was. 'Thank you,' she said. 'Do you have time for a coffee?'

'I'll make it,' he said.

She laughed. 'Don't trust me, eh?'

'No, no. It's not that.' It was. 'I thought I'd give you a break.'

'Aye right. I can never make it strong enough for you.'

One coffee merged into two. They chatted easily, about the children, school, Karen's job. The children played upstairs while their parents built bridges downstairs. It was a long time since they'd got on that well.

As it was approaching lunchtime, Mark decided it was time to make a move. 'I'd better go,' he said. 'I've promised to take them to Pollok Park this afternoon. We're going to see if we can spot a deer.'

They said their goodbyes and Mark left feeling he'd made a breakthrough with Karen. It was going to be a long steep climb trying to win back her trust, but it was worth it.

***

He was making their tea when his phone rang. It was a number he didn't recognise. He left it, thinking it would be a cold call. A minute later there was a buzzing to indicate a voicemail. It was from the hospital. A nurse from the ward Suzanne was in.

Mark frowned. What had happened? Wasn't she due to get out tomorrow? He rang the number and waited.

'Mr Nicholson? I'm calling you because Suzanne Yates has you down as her contact.'

His heart thumped uncomfortably. Had the operation gone wrong after all? Christ, what if she'd died? He'd have to look after Angus. He hadn't thought for a second it would come to this. 'Yes, that's me.'

'Is Ms Yates with you?'

'What? No, of course she isn't.'

'Oh. Well, she's discharged herself. Against doctor's

advice.' She was outraged, as if no one had ever disputed what the doctor said before.'

'Have you tried her phone?'

'Of course. She's not picking up. Can you try? She ought to be in hospital; there's a danger of infection if her wound isn't properly cared for.'

'Yes, I'll try.'

She didn't pick up for him either. He didn't know what to do, so he phoned the hospital again. 'Why did she discharge herself? Did she say?'

'She left without telling anyone.'

'But how is that possible? Are you sure she's gone? Perhaps she's collapsed. Have you checked the bathrooms?'

Her reply was icy. 'Mr Nicholson, be assured we have checked the whole hospital.'

He rang off, promising he'd get Suzanne to ring the hospital if he managed to contact her. The children were getting restless, so he finished making their dinner and served it to them, all the while with a knot in his stomach as he pondered Suzanne's actions. She was up to something. He'd swear to it.

Once the children were asleep, he rang Karen.

'Mark. Is everything OK?'

'All's well with the kids, yes. It's that bloody woman. She's discharged herself from hospital and disappeared.'

'What?'

'The hospital rang me. She'd put me down as her contact...' He tailed off as he realised how that sounded. 'I never gave my permission,' he hurried to add.

'Never mind. What's she up to?'

'I've no idea. The tumour was taken out. She had an MRI scan a couple of days ago. Is that it? She got bad news?'

'No.' Karen's voice was firm. 'The results won't come through that quickly.'

'Are you sure?'

'Yeah, one of the teachers at school had cancer. It was weeks before she got the results of her scan.'

'God, Karen. What am I going to do?'

Karen said nothing for a few seconds. He didn't blame her. This was his problem, not hers. Eventually she said, 'Let's wait and see what tomorrow brings, shall we? No point in worrying until we have to.'

She was right. His heart had lifted at the use of 'we'. He hoped...? No, he wasn't going to go there. He didn't deserve her support in any way or form. 'I'll bring the children home about five tomorrow, is that OK?'

'Come a little earlier and we'll talk,' she said.

Mark put the phone down feeling a little better.

***

The next day Mark phoned the hospital in case Suzanne had reappeared. She hadn't. He tried her mobile, but it went to voicemail. After the third attempt he left a terse message. 'This isn't funny, Suzanne. Phone me, or preferably, the hospital.' He wouldn't call her again.

He took the children home around four o'clock, stopping on the way to buy a cake. He hoped Karen wasn't on one of her health kicks. She opened the door looking serious. It would take more than a cake to cheer her up.

'Anything?'

He gave her a warning look, not wanting to say anything in front of the children. They ran ahead of him up to their bedrooms, back to their beloved toys.

'Coffee?' said Karen.

'Yes please,' he said and held out the cake to her, a Victoria sponge from Marks and Spencer. She took it from him without a word and went through to the kitchen, returning a few minutes later with two mugs of coffee and two slices of cake. They were silent while they ate and drank.

'What are you going to do?'

Mark closed his eyes. He wanted this to go away but it wasn't going to. 'I don't know,' he admitted. 'Surely she'll turn up tomorrow at her flat. She's got a nanny coming to stay for a few weeks to help her with the baby and a woman to do housework as well.'

'And if she doesn't?'

'I've signed the papers for guardianship, so it'll be up to me, I guess.'

By the time he got back to Alex's flat his mood had flattened. Karen had taken the news of Suzanne's disappearance stoically but had said nothing when he admitted it would be up to him to look after Angus. It was stupid of him to expect anything else. But he hadn't been able to stop himself fantasising that Karen would step in and help him. He opened the door to the flat and stepped inside. Immediately he heard the voices coming from the living room. Damn, he'd hoped to have a quiet chat with Alex. Never mind, he'd ensconce himself in his room with a few bottles of beer and watch a film or two on Netflix. Before he reached his room though, Alex came out waving a bottle of champagne.

'Come and join us, Mark. We're celebrating.'

Damn, socialising was the last thing he wanted. He tried

to signal with his eyes to Alex, but Alex was having none of it. He dragged Mark into the lounge. Kate was there with a young man who Mark had briefly met once before. Her partner, Conor, if he remembered rightly. There was also an older couple who Alex introduced as Conor's parents, Aodhan and Margaret. 'And you already know Kate and Conor. Sit down and let me get you a drink.'

Mark sat down and smiled weakly at the others. They looked much happier than he felt. 'What's the occasion then?' He accepted a glass of champagne from Alex.

'Conor got a distinction in his Master's.'

Mark hadn't a clue what Kate was talking about, but they all looked delighted. He raised his glass in Conor's direction. 'Congratulations.'

'Cheers.'

'And what's more, he's got a job here in the civil service, so he'll be moving back to Glasgow. And Kate too. I can't wait.'

Mark's smile faded. What did this mean for him? Would they want to move in with Alex? Oh God, his stomach writhed with the anxiety. This on top of his worries about Suzanne's disappearance. Shit.

THIRTY-SIX

Edinburgh

FOR THE FIRST time in her life, Edith felt loved. Her aunt was delightful. They spoke on Skype most days, even if only for ten minutes. Only one thing weighed heavy on her mind. Should she tell Joan the truth?

An opportunity came sooner than she expected. Joan brought up the subject of the baby's death. 'You know I've tried and tried to understand why they'd kill a child, a newborn baby. Why would they do such a thing? Mother's death I can almost comprehend. She was a difficult woman, and perhaps if they'd got into an argument with her... Can you think of anything?'

Edith's mouth dried up. This was it; this was her chance to be free. If anyone would understand, it was Joan. She wouldn't judge Edith. It wasn't her fault, though she found it hard to shake off that belief. 'I... I think I know why.'

'What is it, dear? You can tell me anything.'

'You won't judge me?'

Joan frowned. 'You're not going to tell me it was you all along?'

'No, no. Nothing like that. It's... I found a letter from your mother to Richard and Doris.' She stopped.

'Go on,' urged Joan.

Edith took a deep breath and started again. 'I found a letter. From your mother to Richard and Doris. When she visited them in Glasgow, she thought she was only visiting Richard. But, of course, my mother was there, too. It was a small house.' She looked meaningfully at Joan, hoping she didn't have to spell it out, but Joan looked blank. 'It didn't take her long to find out they were sharing a bedroom, sleeping together, fornicating, as she put it.'

Joan had her hands up to her mouth. Edith regretted saying anything, but she had to do this. 'I only met my grandmother the one time. She must have found out by then, because the first thing she said was, 'What's this?' Not who's this, as you might expect. When my parents said nothing and left her to her own conclusions, she turned to me and said, 'You, you are an abomination. The spawn of the devil.''

'Oh, Edith, you poor, poor thing. No child should ever have to hear such a thing.'

Edith gave her a watery smile. 'In the letter she said she was going to report them; they deserved to be punished. They must have killed her because of that.'

'And the baby?'

'I don't know why they killed the baby and allowed me to live. They hated me; that much was clear. I think perhaps they didn't want the expense and burden of another child, or perhaps it was born with a deformity. Or perhaps it was born dead.'

'Dear God. Such wickedness. How evil they were. And you had to live with that?'

'I've never told anyone,' Edith admitted.

'This does not reflect on you, Edith. You are not responsible for their actions.'

Edith wanted to weep with relief. 'Thank you,' she said. 'Thank you.'

'Have you told anyone else?'

'No, never,' said Edith. 'I'll have to tell the policeman who investigated. I think it would help if they knew there was a motive.'

'Yes, I imagine it would. Is there anyone else you want to tell?'

'You're talking about your family?'

'They're your family too.'

Her family too. How good those few words made her feel. 'You can tell them, of course. But please, I don't want to talk about it ever again.'

'I understand, but it's always better to talk about things.'

Edith had never had anyone to talk to about things. She'd kept herself to herself, only talking to Maggie and David all those years ago, never opening up to anyone else. Perhaps she should. She'd think about it, she told Joan, but insisted she would be the one to raise the subject if she wanted to talk.

When the call was over, she had to go and lie down. She had a horrendous headache, as if her secret had manifested itself as a physical presence. After a while she drifted off to sleep, and for once her sleep was dreamless.

The following day she phoned DS Nicholson. She was put through to him immediately, giving her no time to prepare herself. He sounded distracted when he answered, and then when he realised who it was, she'd swear he was irritated.

'Yes,' he said. 'How can I help you?'

'I have more information about Richard and Doris Cavendish.'

'Yes? Perhaps it would be better if we spoke face to face.' He sounded bored.

'I'd rather not. I don't mind you taping this, but it's very personal and it won't be easy to speak about it.'

'Very well,' he said.

Over the next half hour, she revealed what she'd kept hidden for thirty years. The letter from her grandmother that she'd found. The letter that told of the woman's shock when she'd arrived at their house and found her son and daughter living as man and wife with a daughter of their own, Enid. She told him about the half-remembered insults from her grandmother, *retard, monster, unnatural, a sin against God.* At the time she'd been too young to understand, but when she found the letter she understood all too well. All her life she'd known things weren't right in her family. Now she knew what was wrong and it left her with an enduring sense of shame.

DS Nicholson was quiet while she told her story. He didn't interrupt once, as if he understood how difficult it was for her. When she finished he said, 'Thank you for telling me this, Miss Drummond. It explains so much.' There was a pause before he added, 'I'm sorry, but we will have to take a formal statement from you.'

It hit her like a stone in the chest. 'I... this is very hard for me. Do you understand that?'

'I do understand and we will do it as sensitively as possible. Before I hang up I need to ask if you are all right.'

She took a shaky breath. 'I'll live,' she said. 'I'll live.'

THIRTY-SEVEN

Glasgow

MARK PUT his phone down and sighed. The last thing he had expected today was to be told a tale of incest and abuse. That poor woman. His instincts had been right. She had been holding back the truth, and now he understood why. It must have been so hard for her to disclose that. He'd have to go through to Edinburgh to take a proper statement. But not today. Not until he'd found Suzanne. He was going to visit her flat. If he hadn't found her by this evening he'd have to report her as a missing person.

He'd spoken to Alex about it last night after his visitors had gone. Kate and Conor were staying with Conor's parents, to Alex's chagrin. But it wasn't enough to kill his good mood at the news about Kate coming to live in Glasgow. Mark had taken advantage of his mood to ask for time off in the morning to go and see whether Suzanne was at her flat.

He waved over to Alex on his way out. 'Back in an hour, I hope.' He crossed his fingers as he said this. It would take more than an hour, but he didn't want to push Scrimgeour too far.

It took him ten minutes to find a parking place. And another five to walk to her flat. Christ, the Southside was bad for parking... but this was another level entirely. Once outside her flat he rang the buzzer and stepped back, so she'd be able to see him from her window. He was sure she'd be there, and if she was, she'd be very careful about who she'd answer the door to. A few seconds later he heard the buzz of the intercom. Result.

The door to her flat was open. Suzanne was nowhere to be seen. He stepped inside and looked for her. She was lying on a sofa in the living room. She raised a feeble hand in greeting.

'Thanks for standing where I could see you. I didn't want to let on I was here. The hospital has been phoning me nonstop.'

'What the hell do you think you're doing? Discharging yourself.'

'I wanted to be at home. Surely you understand? It was as hot as hell in there so I couldn't sleep, and there was Covid. I kept hearing of people getting Covid. I'm not going to risk that in my state.'

'But...' Mark gave up. There was no point in arguing with her. 'When does the help get here?'

'I have a full-time nanny to look after Angus. He's out with her at the moment. I've also arranged for someone to come and do household things as I've already told you, so you don't need to worry. I'll be fine.'

She looked terrible. He doubted she'd be fine, but what could he do? Drag her back to hospital? Mark stayed for another hour, making sure she had everything she needed before going back to his work.

The next evening, when he was about to serve out food to Alex, Kate and Conor, the doorbell rang. 'Will somebody get that?' called Mark. 'I'm juggling three pans and four plates right now.' Moments later Kate appeared at the kitchen door. 'Mark, you'd better get out here, now.' Mark put down the pan he was holding and went out into the hall. There, in a pushchair, was Angus, laughing away as though he hadn't a care in the world.

'Where is she?' said Mark.

Kate swept her hair back from her face. 'There was no one there but the baby. Conor's gone downstairs to see if he can catch her.'

Alex joined them. 'She'll be long gone. I bet she buzzed another flat to let her in, left the pram at our front door, hoofed it back downstairs and then rang our buzzer.'

The baby, sensing the tension in the flat, began to grizzle. Mark unstrapped him and picked him up. There was a letter and a set of keys underneath him.

Conor came panting into the hallway. 'She's gone. At least I think it was her. Forties, blonde hair, blue car? She was getting into it as I came out of the close, but I was too far behind to catch her.'

'That's her,' said Mark. He handed the baby to Kate. 'Take him for a second, will you please? Do you mind?'

'Not at all.' Kate and Conor disappeared into the living room, both cooing at Angus, who laughed happily in return, leaving Mark and Alex staring at one another. 'What does she say?' asked Alex.

Mark tore open the envelope and read the letter aloud. 'Dear Mark, I've left you the keys to my flat. You have my permission to stay there if you like. I don't suppose your boss will be too happy to have a baby staying. I need to concentrate on myself and my health. So, I'm going away for a while. I hope it won't inconvenience you too much to have to look after Angus. All his things are in the nursery along with a list detailing his routine, what he likes to eat, when he naps, that sort of thing. I've also left money. It's in the top left-hand drawer of my desk. I hope you understand why I'm doing this.' He flung it to the floor. 'I don't fucking believe this. She's mad, she has to be.'

'What are you going to do?'

'What can I do? Report her to the police, to social work? I've signed papers saying I'll be his guardian if anything happens to her so...'

'Look, let's eat and we'll talk about it later. We can go over to her flat and pick up whatever's needed.'

'I don't have a car seat that will fit him. Emma's is too big.'

'I'm sure Kate and Conor won't mind looking after him for an hour or two while you sort yourself out. They're naturals, judging by the sounds of what's going on in the living room.' Angus was giggling and so were they.

'You're not chucking me out, then?'

'Not yet, no.'

Tears came to Mark's eyes. 'You're a good man, Alex. Thank you.'

'Try any more of that sentimental stuff and you'll be down those stairs faster than a beer goes down my throat on a Friday night.'

They drove Alex's car over to the west end and picked up the baby stuff. It was all neatly laid out, and as promised there was a list of instructions. 'What about the money?' asked Alex.

'I don't want her money.'

'Don't be a fool, man. You'll need to hire a childminder. You can't take a wean to work.'

He was right. This was a nightmare. How would Karen take it; how would his children cope? And as for finding a childminder or a nursery place at such short notice, forget it.

Mark opened the drawer. There were ten bundles of notes stacked together. He picked up one of the bundles and counted it. Fifties, twenty of them. 'Bloody hell, Alex. There's ten grand here. How long is she planning to stay away?'

THIRTY-EIGHT

Edinburgh

Now EDITH HAD LET GO of the secret that had shamed her for most of her life, she felt much better. Life would be perfect if it wasn't for Olivia's campaign against her. Olivia hadn't said anything else about the WhatsApp group, making Edith surer than ever that Olivia had invented it. But how she'd heard about Edith's involvement with the case in Glasgow was a mystery. Edith's name had never been published in any reports about it in the media, and no one knew about her change of name. Was David behind it? Had he recognised her after all and put two and two together? She didn't think so. Who had told Olivia?

Olivia had been avoiding her at school. That suited Edith fine, but it couldn't go on like this. Talking to her aunt about retirement had unsettled her, and she found herself thinking about it more and more. This particular evening, she was restless. Edith lived right beside Holyrood Park, and she left her flat intending to make her way up Arthur's Seat. It was a walk she often did. One of the attractions of Edinburgh was the extinct volcano that was accessible from the city centre.

Thousands of tourists climbed it every year, often ill-prepared. She'd seen hen parties up there in stiletto heels, giggling and clinging on to each other on the rocky path. Fools. It wasn't a hard climb; she'd be up and down again in less than an hour. Nonetheless people had died up there.

It wasn't busy like it was on a summer's day. It was a dreich evening and the haar from the North Sea had lingered all day, casting a cloak of grey mist over the city. But she needed fresh air to clear her head and help her think through her problems. She wasn't taking any notice of the few people who were also mad enough to be out in such weather, but gradually she became aware of a woman's voice, penetrating and shrill. Olivia Waring. Her unmistakable nasal tones drifted down the hill towards her. She was with a man, all cooried up to him. Edith peered at the couple through the haar. He looked familiar. They were several metres ahead of her, walking slowly. Edith slowed down as she didn't want to bump into them. It would be better to take one of the other paths. She was about to turn back when she realised who the man was. Sophia Greene's father. This must be why Olivia was reluctant to call social work. They were having an affair. That poor child. Self-preservation stopped her from challenging them. She had to be cannier than that. Looking back for one last glimpse, she saw they were kissing passionately right in the middle of the path, oblivious to everything.

She made her way back down the path, fuming. All she could think about was their deceitfulness and how it was impacting on an innocent child.

THIRTY-NINE

Edinburgh

DAVID HAD FORGOTTEN his conversation with Edith about the child she was worried about. There were never ending changes to deal with regarding what to do about coronavirus. Olivia had given him the lead on that, which didn't best please him, but he made the best of it. Parents were the main problem, especially the requirement to wear face coverings when dropping off and picking up children. Fuck! The reactions he got. You'd think they'd been asked to sacrifice their first born. And it was up to David to police that. It was only a minority who complained. One of the fathers, another David (except he was called Dave and insisted on calling David Dave too) was a conspiracy theorist who didn't believe in the 'so-called virus'. 'It's a bad case of flu, Dave,' he intoned in the middle of an argument. David almost lost it then. His father had been one of the first to die from it. He squared up to Dave, but before it got out of hand, Edith, of all people, smoothed it over.

'What's going on here?' she said in a school-marmish voice. She was late for once. You could set the clock by Edith.

Every day she arrived an hour before the bell rang, went straight to her classroom and got on with work. She wasn't one of those teachers who came in early to hang around the staffroom or stayed on late to show they were allegedly working, all the while chatting with their friends and drinking coffee and tea other people had paid for. But this particular day she was much later than usual and arrived at five minutes to nine, pushing her bike, not sailing in on it as she usually did. She had a punctured tyre.

She stopped beside them and looked at Dave. 'Mr Prendergast. Why are you not wearing a mask?'

David braced himself. He'd asked that question two minutes before she arrived and had been subjected to a torrent of abuse. But perhaps because she was a woman, Dave held off on the swearing and instead muttered about not needing any protection.

'I'm not expecting it to protect *you*,' she said. 'The point is to protect other people. Now,' she reached into her rucksack and pulled out a disposable mask in a plastic bag. 'Put this on.'

He ignored her offering, grumbling beneath his breath, 'I've got one, thanks. He turned away and walked off, pulling out a grubby looking mask from his pocket as he did so. David was glad to see him go. The atmosphere between them had been worsening over the past few days and they were both spoiling for a fight. David was short-tempered at the best of times. And this was not the best of times. He turned to Edith.

'What's your secret?'

She tensed. What was that about? 'I'm sorry, I don't understand.'

'He was scared of you.'

Immediately her whole body relaxed. 'Oh, that. I used to

teach him. He was a wee bugger then and he hasn't changed. But for whatever reason, he toes the line when I'm around. I don't think you'll have any more trouble with him. Now, if you'll excuse me, I'd like to get to my classroom before the children do.'

David stared after her, wondering about her reaction to his question. She definitely had a secret. It was time to prise it out of her.

———

It was several days before he saw her again. Not to speak to at least. Olivia kept him hard at it. She was a difficult woman to work for, and he began to see why staff didn't like her. Not that they said anything to him. As far as they were concerned, he was every bit as bad. Fair enough, it wasn't that long ago he'd been on the wrong side of management. No, it was obvious from the little glances that passed between them, the sighs that he heard during staff meetings. They were weary of her slavish devotion to finding new ways of making them work harder than they already were. If social distancing hadn't been in place there would have been nudges and notes passed between them. David sat apart from it all and watched. He wasn't going to take sides. Edith, of course, behaved impeccably. She was always professional during these staff meetings, eyes downcast, taking notes. She arrived the moment the meeting was due to begin and left as soon as it was over. Any attempt to engage her in conversation was met with a half-smile and a murmured, 'I must be off now.' Once David heard one of the younger teachers mutter behind her back, 'What's the hurry? You've got nothing to go home to, you sad old sack of bones.' She was a probationer and David fumed at her lack of respect. She was surprised when he called her in to his office the next day and subdued by the time she left. She'd be more careful with her bitchy comments in future. Edith was an enigma, but he remembered her from that week long summer school in Stirling all those years ago. She was worth ten of any uppity little madam from Morningside.

When David had seen Maggie and Enid together for the first time at the summer school, his first thought was how different they were. Maggie, with her wild hair and her outrageous statements, was the dominant one of the two. Enid, as she was then, was quieter – at least to begin with. He had joined them at the bar. Enid was suspicious but Maggie welcomed male company, and as the night went on and the drink flowed, Enid relaxed and became almost flirtatious. But then it all went a little weird.

Enid announced she was a virgin. Maggie's mouth gaped. Enid added that she would be forty soon. David was twenty-five, and at that age, anyone over the age of thirty might as well be dead. He was genuinely shocked. She had an old-fashioned air about her even with her fashionable clothes, which it turned out she had bought with money stolen from her mother. She had an air of being from a different era. But she didn't seem old. If anything, she seemed younger than Maggie, who she had ten years on.

Over the course of the week David had grown fond of Enid. She was bright and funny in spite of the difficult circumstances she'd found herself in. How many people could have put up with the vagaries of her parents' weird religion? He certainly wouldn't have. He'd have been out of there, money or no money, and he and Maggie had spent hours trying to persuade her to leave.

He hoped it hadn't been too long. She'd made a thorough job of it anyway by moving to another city, changing her name and getting herself a job where the salary was paid to her and not her parents. He'd never heard of such a thing, parents taking control of their adult child's wages. Perhaps they'd died. Well of course, they must be dead by now. She was nearly seventy after all.

David found himself more and more intrigued by her. He asked one or two of the longer serving teachers about her, but they were as much in the dark as he was. 'Keeps herself to herself,' he was told. He put her to the back of his mind and got on with trying to keep up with Olivia's demands.

———

Then one day Edith was late for school. Proper late. The children had gone into class. When David saw Olivia, he winced. She was furious. She'd had a hellish two weeks with the primary two parents. Kieran Winter had been off, and against David's advice she'd decided to let Edith take them full time and to put the supply teacher in to do learning support. He'd warned her what would happen. You might have thought that move would satisfy the primary two parents who'd been campaigning for such a thing since the children's return to school in August, but you would be wrong. It added fuel to their campaign, and she was inundated with emails telling her she had to keep things as they were. On the other hand, the parents of the children who needed support were less than happy Edith was no longer taking their children for half the week. Their children might need support, but they were no less eloquent in their emails than any other parent.

'Where the hell is she?' she hissed at David, as if he had insider knowledge.

'I don't know,' he said.

'Get her records from my secretary and phone her.'

He raised an eyebrow. Head teachers didn't have secretaries; the school had clerical support, but Olivia imagined it made her sound better if she talked about her 'assistant' or 'secretary'. She used the term persistently in front of parents, even when one of them said, 'You must be very important, Ms Waring, to have a personal assistant. At Julie's last school the head teacher had to do with a clerical support worker.' David was embarrassed for her, but he could have spared his blushes. Olivia hadn't picked up on the sarcasm of that remark. Instead, she smirked and said nothing. Christ, that woman was so far up her own arse, she was coming out of her mouth.

There was no reply when he phoned Edith. It worried him. She lived alone. It was possible she'd been taken ill or maybe she'd fallen off her bike on her way to school. Either way it didn't look good. He didn't think she had pulled a sickie as other members of staff did from time to time. According to Ann, Olivia's 'secretary', Edith had never been off once in the twenty-five years she'd worked there. David was sitting at his desk wondering what to do next when he spotted her coming through the school gates. It was ten o'clock. From a distance he saw she wasn't herself. There was an air of belligerence about her. She wasn't walking into school, she was marching, her back ramrod straight, her bicycle beside her. This didn't look good. He needed to get to her before Olivia did. He caught her at the school door.

'Edith, what's wrong?'

'Wrong? What do you mean, Mr Cameron? I'm fine. That head teacher of ours though. Lying bitch.'

He stared at her. 'No, you're not fine. You're an hour late for work. Two hours really as you're always in by eight o'clock. You haven't combed your hair, your blouse is buttoned up wrongly and you're not wearing a mask.' He wanted to add *and you're spoiling for a fight* but refrained.

She looked down at herself and hastily corrected the misbuttoning. Then she reached into her rucksack, pulled out a mask and put it on. 'Satisfied?'

'Why are you late?'

'I couldn't sleep. Awake until five in the morning and then I overslept. Now if that's all?'

'No, I think I should take you home. I'll tell Olivia you fell off your bike and I'm taking you for an x-ray.'

'No, I'm fine—'

He held up his hand. 'Believe me, Edith, you don't want her to see you like this. And you do not want to be calling her a lying bitch. Do it my way.'

'She is a lying bitch though.'

David didn't ask what she meant. That could wait. The main thing was to get her out of the school. He steered her towards the door to the car park. Thank God, she acquiesced, making him more certain than ever something was seriously wrong. David pulled down the back seats of his car and hefted Edith's bike into the space left. Once they were in his car, he texted Olivia with his story. She answered with a terse *get back here asap*.

Nothing was said on the way to Edith's house other than for David to ask and for her to give him her postcode for the satnav. When they pulled up outside her apartment block in

Newington, David got out of the car to get her bike before escorting her to her door. 'Where shall I put your bike?'

'The bike shed's over there. I'll come with you. You need a code.'

David helped her deal with the bike and then followed her into her flat. To his shame, he'd expected a stereotype of an elderly spinster with chintzy upholstery and oatmeal carpets. Instead, the floor was reclaimed oak, likely from an old school gymnasium. It hadn't been sanded to within an inch of its life as they habitually were. The pock marks and stains remained, though it was waxed and polished. There were no flowery curtains at the windows. She'd had wooden slatted shutters installed and they were folded back to let the sunlight stream in. The walls were painted white, not brilliant white but a shade darker. No doubt it was a posh emulsion number called Chalk white #04 Dover cliffs or some such pretentious name. Off white, in other words. Whatever it was, it made a perfect backdrop for the modern and original paintings that hung there.

She spotted him looking round and said, 'I didn't want anything dark in here, not after the upbringing I had.'

'Of course,' David said without thinking. 'You'd want to leave all that behind you.'

She sat down on the teal blue sofa. 'How long have you known?'

'I recognised you immediately.'

'I thought I was too old and withered to be recognisable.' Her gaze was wary.

'No. And you obviously recognised me,' said David.

'You've aged,' she said. 'And put on weight. But as soon as I heard your voice I realised who you were.'

Fuck, who was she to talk about *him* ageing? But this

wasn't the time to take offence. 'You changed your name, why?'

She looked away. 'I wanted to put my past behind me. Surely you understand, after what I told you?'

David wasn't sure. 'Were you trying to get away from your parents, make sure they couldn't find you?'

She was non-committal. 'Mm.' She pointed to a two-seater sofa that matched the one she was sitting on. 'Sit down, won't you? You're making me nervous looming over me.'

David took a seat. His mouth was dry. He had missed his mid-morning cup of coffee, and the truth was he desperately needed it, for once again he had drunk too much the night before. Since this time last year his alcohol consumption had doubled. The pandemic and now working with Olivia Waring were to blame. His head was pounding.

'Can I have a drink of water, please?'

She stood up. 'Of course. Or would you prefer tea? Coffee? I seem to remember you were a coffee fiend.'

What a relief. 'Coffee please. Black and strong.'

'I remember,' she called over her shoulder.

The coffee when it came was good, definitely not a super-market blend. It had a nutty taste that David associated with freshly roasted coffee of the sort sold in one of the roasting houses that were beginning to appear in the city. He hoped the pandemic didn't mean they'd disappear.

He put his cup down. 'What's the story, then?'

'What do you mean?'

'You turn up late at school for the first time ever in all the years you've worked there. You look like shit, as if you've not slept for a month. And what on earth are you wearing?' Her outfit was bizarre to say the least. Red tartan trousers with a purple blouse and a green parka jacket.

She looked down at herself. 'It's not my best choice, is it?'

'No. Tell me what's going on?'

'I'm not sure I trust you. I hardly know you after all, and more to the point, you're sidekick to the devil herself.'

'If by the devil you mean Olivia, let me assure you there's no love lost there, and as for not knowing me, didn't we get to know each other well during that week?'

She stared at him as if she didn't understand. She hadn't forgotten, surely?

'It was a long time ago. I may have got to know you a little during that week but...'

'I promise you I won't say a word.'

'Oh, very well then. I've been interviewed by the police several times recently.'

He was not expecting this. 'Go on.'

'There's been a story in the news recently. The remains of two people, one of them a baby, were found in a house in Glasgow that was being renovated. I expect you've heard about it.'

He had but only in passing. His wife had mentioned it to him, but he hadn't paid too much attention to it. 'I have, yes.'

'The house was the one I was brought up in. My parents murdered two people. She gazed at him, trying to gauge his reaction, he thought. He kept his face impassive, knowing if he allowed his horror to show, he would have lost her.

It took her the best part of an hour to tell him. All the time she was speaking, he was remembering the things she'd mentioned at summer school all those years ago, the hints about unspeakable things her parents had done. He and Maggie had discussed it behind her back but dismissed it as nothing. 'She probably heard them having sex and couldn't deal with it,' said Maggie. 'Her being a forty-year-old virgin and everything.' He'd frowned at her, not liking the fact that she sounded spiteful. They'd never imagined anything like this.

'The thing is,' she said. 'Olivia knows and she's trying to spread a rumour that the baby was mine.'

'I've heard nothing,' he hastened to reassure her.

'No, I think I put a spoke in her wheel. It wasn't mine. I was—'

'Yes, I remember. You were a virgin.'

Not only that. I was thirteen and my periods didn't start until I was much older. My medical records will show that and I told her. She soon shut up after that.'

'It sounds as though you've got it all sorted.'

'Yes, but how did she find out? How did she make the link? You're the only person who knows I was ever called Cavendish. It must have come from the police.'

'I don't know,' he said. 'It certainly wasn't me who told her about your change of name and I hadn't made the connection with the case in Glasgow.'

'Anyway, that's not all. Last night I saw her on Arthur's Seat. She was with a man and they were kissing passionately. The man was Sophia Greene's father.'

'Michael Greene? The lawyer? Are you sure?'

'Positive. They were all over each other.'

He tutted. 'Well, mystery solved. I know where the leak has come from. His brother Lewis is high up in the police. He works in Glasgow. That's where the information must have come from. Right, this is what we're going to do. We note down all the concerns we have and then when we have enough we go to social work. We'll go over her head. It'll be easy enough. We'll pick a day when she's out and has left me in charge. And if you're worried about anything about Sophia then question her.' He looked at his watch. 'Shit, I'd better get back to school. Olivia will...' He tailed off. 'You sure you're not going to tackle her? We will get her if we're patient.'

'I hope that's the case, but in the meantime poor Sophia is going through God knows what.'

'We'll keep a close eye on her. Here's my number. Phone me back later so I have your number too.' David scribbled down his number and passed it to her.

Edith took it. Already she felt calmer knowing someone had listened to her concerns. She was going to get Olivia she could feel it in her bones.

FORTY

Edinburgh

SHE DIDN'T NEED to confront Olivia after all. The resolution came sooner than either David or Edith expected. That very weekend in fact.

Edith was all set to relax in front of the television. It was a miserable day, and although she liked to go for a walk at the weekend she decided to stay at home. There was a series on Netflix she wanted to watch. She poured herself a large gin and tonic and switched on the television. When the doorbell rang, she wasn't best pleased. She rarely had visitors.

It was Sophia Greene and her brother. Both were soaked through. This was a trap, surely. Olivia must have found out she knew about her and Mr Greene and had set this up to accuse her of child abduction, but she dismissed the idea when she saw how upset they both were.

'What are you doing here?' she managed to say.

'Please, Miss, we're hungry,' said Sophia's brother, Oliver. 'Soph said you gave her food in school one day.'

What was this, the nineteenth century? Edith looked to see if anyone was watching. 'Come in,' she said.

Once inside, the first thing she did was set up her phone to record. She didn't want anyone accusing her of wrongdoing. 'When did you last eat anything?'

The two children looked at each other. 'Yesterday evening.'

'OK. I'll make you a sandwich and then I'll take you home.'

'Mummy's not there,' said Sophia. 'She went out this morning and didn't come back.'

'What about Daddy?'

'Daddy's never at home,' said Oliver. It's why Mummy cries all the time.'

First things first. She had to get food into these children. Edith gave them each a towel, switched on the gas fire and told them to dry themselves. Within minutes they were sitting at the table eating the sandwiches she'd made and looking much happier. When they'd finished eating, she sat down beside them with a plate of biscuits.

'How did you know where to find me?'

The children looked at each other. 'Please Miss, you won't be angry?'

'Of course not. I'm just interested.'

'Last year we were up at the loch and we saw you there. Mummy said she wanted to see where you lived. When you left, we followed you.'

'We were being detectives,' said Sophia.

'Shut up, Soph!'

'But that's what daddy said!' Sophia started to cry.

'Children, children. It doesn't matter. It's good because it meant you knew where to come today.' She offered them a biscuit and Sophia calmed down. 'How did you get here?'

Oliver spoke through a mouthful of crumbs. 'We walked. It took a long time.'

'Where do you live?'

'In Duddingston.' He named the street. Edith knew it at once. It was near the Sheep Heid Inn in the heart of the village. Duddingston was nearer to her flat than the school was but it was a long way for two young children to walk. Sophia's voice interrupted her thoughts.

'Can I have another drink, please?'

Of course you can.' Edith went in to the kitchen and poured them each a glass of water. She put it down in front of them and said, 'Now, you mustn't be frightened, but I'm going to call the police.'

Sophia's bottom lip quivered. Edith took her hand.

'I'm worried your mummy and daddy aren't at home. We have to ask the police to help to find them.' She picked up her phone and dialled. It was several minutes before it was answered. 'My name is Edith Drummond,' she said. 'I am a teacher and one of my pupils has turned up at my flat with her brother.'

She listened for a moment. 'Sophia and Oliver Greene. Sophia is in my class, she's six, and her brother is – hold on a second – how old are you, Oliver?'

'Nine,' he said. His face had misery written all over it.

Over the next few minutes, she answered all their questions to the best of her ability. The police said they'd be there within the hour, but first they were going to the children's house to check on their parents. Edith got up to search for a game for them to play. She found a pack of cards and taught them how to play Rummy and then when they got fed up with that, Cheat. The game had them in fits of giggles as

Edith played to the gallery, putting down six cards at a time and pretending she'd only put down two.

At last, the police arrived. There were two of them. They introduced themselves as PC Amina Sharif and PC Imogen Warrington and said a social worker was on their way. Edith settled the children down with paper and coloured pencils and took the police into the kitchen to allow them to speak in private.

'Are the parents back home now?' she asked.

Her question was ignored. 'Tell us in your own words what happened,' said the older of the two women, PC Sharif.

As Edith went through the story, she noticed the glances between them. 'What is it?' she said. 'What are you not telling me?'

'Please, continue with your statement.'

Edith bowed to her request. When she'd finished her statement, she left the room to pick up her phone. 'I've recorded what the children said.'

They listened to the recording, frowning. When it finished, PC Sharif said, 'This is extremely helpful, Miss Drummond. We'll have to take a copy as evidence.'

'That's fine.' The doorbell rang and she got up to answer it. The social worker was there, looking harassed. Edith showed him into the flat.

He introduced himself as Stefan. 'I'm the duty social worker. I'm going to have to ask both you and the children some questions. Could I start with you please? Edith, is it?'

The police officers went through to speak to the children while the social worker spoke to Edith. Once all the questioning was over and the children were settled with their drawing, Edith asked what would happen next.

Stefan spoke first. 'We'll need to find emergency foster

care for the children, interview the parents and report to the Children's Panel. They will make the ultimate decision on the children's future.'

'I see. And will the parents be charged?' She directed her question at PC Sharif.

'That will be up to the Procurator Fiscal. I should warn you though, the parents are claiming you abducted the children from their garden.'

So, this was why there had been all those glances while she had been giving her statement. 'I've been here all afternoon,' she said. 'I didn't know where they lived until I asked them this afternoon.'

The younger police officer, PC Warrington leaned across the table. 'You must have access to their address on the register at school?'

'Yes, of course. Sophia's address and twenty-three others. However, I have no reason to memorise or know any of them.'

'And how did the children know where you live, for that matter? It's a long way for them to walk.' PC Warrington sounded suspicious and Edith was pleased to see PC Sharif give her a warning frown. At least one of them seemed to believe her.

'It's a little over a mile and very straightforward, perfectly doable for two healthy children. And as to knowing where I live?' She nodded towards her phone. 'You heard it on the recording.'

'Yes, of course.' The police officer smiled. 'Well, it will all be investigated thoroughly. There are police officers in their street at this moment asking neighbours if they saw anything. I wouldn't worry too much. The recording you made is vital evidence.'

Edith sighed. She checked to see whether the children

were listening but they were engrossed in their drawings. Nonetheless she lowered her voice. 'There's one more thing you should know. Mr Greene is having an affair with the head teacher of the children's school.'

'How do you know this?'

'I saw them together walking on Arthur's Seat. They were kissing.'

Stefan shrugged. 'Mm. Well that's not a crime.'

'No, of course not, Stefan. But it might mean Ms Waring is less than truthful when you talk to her about how the children are in school. I reported issues regarding Sophia to her twice and she didn't act on them. Or at least, not to my satisfaction.'

'Do you have proof of this?'

Thank goodness she'd kept copies of the emails she'd sent to Olivia. 'Yes,' she said. 'Yes, I do.'

The children had been reluctant to leave. Edith noticed PC Warrington making notes and thought this was a good thing. It helped corroborate all she had said. She breathed a sigh of relief. The Netflix series would have to wait. No way could she concentrate on it now. She decided to phone David to tell him what had happened.

'You must be psychic,' he said. 'I was about to phone you with an update on our mutual friend.'

'Me too,' said Edith. 'That's why I was phoning you. But you go first.'

'I've heard Mariella Greene has discovered her husband is playing around. She walked out on him this morning.'

'I was just about to tell you the same thing. And more.'

Edith went on to tell him the day's happenings. 'You don't think they'll believe the Greenes' story that I abducted the children? I mean they have powerful friends.' He was as supportive as she'd hoped.

'Not a chance. It's all over Duddingston and Portobello as well. The whole town knows what's been going on between them.'

'But why would they neglect their children? It doesn't add up.'

'Too absorbed in their work and their personal lives, I suppose.'

'But to feed a child a chicken nugget the cat had licked?'

'I'm sure social work will get to the bottom of it.'

Edith hoped so. She hoped the children were going to be safe. That was the important thing.

FORTY-ONE

Glasgow

MARK WAS delighted when Kate and Conor said they'd look after Angus while he tried to find a childminder. It was an ideal solution. Angus already loved them, and they were crazy about him.

'Are you sure?'

'Yes, it's no problem. Mum and Dad will lend a hand and Alex has said he'll help too,' said Conor.

'Alex?' Mark stared at his boss, who was looking shifty over by the window.

'What?' said Scrimgeour. 'It'll be fine. I have some leave due. Where's the problem? Now you do your part and find a childminder. A good one, mind. Can't have this little fellow being neglected, can we?' He smiled at Angus, who beamed back at him. He was a charmer, that child. 'Oh, and don't forget to speak to Karen while you're at it.'

Mark was dreading updating Karen. They'd been getting on so well this last couple of weeks. But to throw another woman's baby in the mix? What would that do to their relationship? 'I'll speak to her later today,' he promised.

'Best leave Angus here with us, then,' said Kate. 'Go now and we'll hold the fort.'

He arrived at his old house sooner than he wanted. He hadn't thought through what he was going to say yet. He got out of his car feeling like a teenager on his first date. Sophie opened the door to him. 'Mummy's out in the back garden. She's building us a castle.'

'Oh? Sounds intriguing.' Mark followed her through to the garden where Karen was putting the final touches to a complicated play structure taking up half the garden.

'Hold this beam here, would you?' She pointed to where she needed help. 'You've come at the right moment. Any news of Suzanne?' She mouthed the last word so the children didn't hear.

'I'll tell you when we've done with this.'

They worked on for another ten minutes. 'Right, I think that's it,' said Karen. 'Children, why don't you come and play on this magnificent castle I've built for you?'

'Well done,' said Mark. 'Puts me to shame.'

Karen sniffed. 'Nothing to it. Follow the instructions, that's all. Tea?'

They went inside. 'OK, spill the beans,' said Karen as she put on the kettle.

To give her credit, she let him speak without interrupting. When he'd finished, she was glowering at him. 'She doesn't deserve a baby.'

'She's ill, frightened. I don't think she knows what she's doing.'

'Mm. You know what I think? She's planned all this. Oh,

not the cancer.' She waved away Mark's protests. 'But the rest; 'bumping' into you in town, getting pregnant... Don't you remember the letter she sent to me claiming she was going to have a baby? She might have been lying then, but...'

'I don't know what to say. I'm sorry.'

'She'll leave the baby with you long enough for you to get attached to him and then she'll be back. I don't think I can take much more of this, Mark. I've been trying to be understanding, trying to forgive you, but this is too much.' Tears were streaming down her face.

'I'm sorry,' he repeated.

'Please go. I need to think this through. She's fucking with your mind, Mark, and you don't see it. I'll phone you when I've calmed down. If I calm down.'

Mark drove back to Alex's flat feeling worse than he ever had. What had he expected? It was one thing to know your partner had a child with another woman. He saw now she'd been on the verge of accepting this. But how could he mend his relationship with her if he was trying to build one with his son?

Kate and Conor had gone by the time he got back. 'How did it go?' said Alex.

'Terrible. She says Suzanne's got a plan.' Mark went over their conversation with him.

'She's got a point, but what can you do? I think you'll have to sit this one out. But Mark, whatever you do, don't be tempted to take up Suzanne's offer of going to live in her flat. You and the baby are welcome here for as long as you like.'

'Are you sure? I was going to look for a flat.'

'Aye. It'll be good practice for me.' Alex gave an embarrassed grin. They're trying for a baby. Kate and Conor.'

The last few months had been hard. Mark had been chucked out of his home for what was admittedly a very good reason. He was self-aware enough to see how badly he had behaved over the past two years. Now he had another son to care for and little hope of returning to his family. Work had been challenging too with the bodies in the bungalow case and the sorry story of Edith Drummond, not to speak of how he had been duped into believing that Darren Gilmour happened to be in the wrong place at the wrong time. It didn't look as though things were letting up though. This morning reports had come in of a stabbing in Shawlands. A night out at the pub had ended badly for one poor sod. He was on his way out to the scene when Scrimgeour stopped him. 'You're not going to like this,' he said. 'Another young lad's been killed. Priesthill this time. Word on the street is the two murders are linked. We might have some sort of gang warfare going on.'

So much for his hope of things quietening down. Thank goodness he'd been able to find a decent childminder. Conor had given him the name of a friend's mother who was able to take on Angus, and after meeting her a couple of times and seeing how well she got on with the baby, he snapped her up. There had been nothing from Suzanne. He'd tried phoning the hospital, but it was a waste of time. There was no way they were giving out any information. Karen too remained remote. The only good thing to happen to him was Angus. Perhaps Karen was right. He was becoming very attached to the child, who was the most placid delightful baby he'd ever met. But he'd be damned if he ever became involved with Suzanne again. That boat had truly sailed. Unfortunately, Karen didn't believe him.

On the way out of the building he checked his dookit. His payslip was there and there was a handwritten letter too. He picked them up and put them in his pocket. He'd check them both later. For now, he had work to do.

FORTY-TWO

Edinburgh

EDITH SAT BACK in her seat in the first-class compartment and sipped her gin and tonic. For once she was at peace. Olivia was under investigation for unprofessional conduct and was suspended for the time being. David was acting head. She'd been offered the role of acting depute but refused. Since meeting her aunt, work didn't seem as important. She'd see this year out and then retire. It was enough that Olivia hadn't got her way. She hoped the Greene children were all right. Mariella was in hospital with depression, and Edith's heart went out to her despite Mariella's meanness to both Edith and her own children. Depression was a hard state to cope with. The children were living with a relative meantime.

Since revealing her past, she had been thinking a lot. DS Nicholson would have received her letter by now. What would he do once he read it? She'd been relieved to tell her secret first to her aunt and then to the police. DS Nicholson had come to the house to take her statement with that nice young police officer, Morven was it? No, Megan. He'd sent her on ahead to the car so he could speak to Edith alone.

'I'm sorry I gave you such a hard time during the investigation. If I'd known what you'd been through...'

'It wasn't your fault. I should have been more open with you.'

'I always sensed you weren't being completely honest with us. Child abuse is a terrible thing.' He hesitated. 'I've experienced it myself. My father was brutal. He went to prison for what he did to my sister. Throwing her down the stairs so she was left—' He stopped himself from saying more. 'Please accept my apologies. I don't know why I'm telling you this, it's unprofessional.'

She put her hand on his arm. 'That must have been awful for you.'

'It's the anger I can't deal with. If I'd been older, I think I might have killed him.'

That was the sentence that made her mind up. She had to tell someone, and if anyone would understand it would be him. They'd parted on excellent terms. Any dislike she'd had for him had disappeared. He was a good guy.

Her mind went back to the day she'd killed her parents. After she found the letter, she'd been devastated. For days she'd been unable to speak to her parents. They hadn't liked that; they were losing control of her. She'd hated herself too. All those years of trying to win their approval. The emotional blackmail, the emotional abuse, the physical abuse. She made plans to get away from them.

Killing them had never really been an option. How would she do it, for one thing? Poison? She had no knowledge of that. Staging a burglary and stabbing them? How would she explain her own escape? Pushing them under a bus? It had a certain appeal, but a busy street harboured potential witnesses. No, she had to leave. She was more than halfway through her Open University degree. Once she'd finished, she'd be able to get another job where the salary was paid to her, not her parents. She'd move cities, perhaps to London. She was only thirty-nine: she had years ahead of her.

It was only when she met David and Maggie at summer school that she began to seriously consider she might get away with murder. After she'd revealed her miserable life to them and made a silly joke about killing her parents, they spent at least part of each day dreaming up 'dreadful demises' for Richard and Doris. Talking and laughing about it made her feel better. The scenarios were ludicrous and unattainable until the day David talked about cars.

He was a mechanic. She didn't press him about how to fix up a car so it would crash, but Maggie did.

'What about fiddling with the brakes?' she'd said.

'It's too obvious. Sure, you can cut the brake cables, but any accident investigator would be on to that at once.'

'There must be a way of doing it undetected.'

He'd shaken his head. 'You sound as though you'd actually do it.'

Maggie laughed then. 'Come on. You know it's fantasy, and it's helping Enid.'

Enid had joined in. 'Damn right it is. I may never be able to do it, but oh what bliss just to dream of it.'

'All right. I read an article in a motoring magazine once. It was about the dangers of slow punctures. This bloke was injured when he drove off in his car, which had had one of its tyres ripped. He hadn't noticed anything. His journey had involved a trip on the motorway, and the tyre's deflation and subsequent blow out led to him crashing. Apparently, he was very lucky not to have been killed. Lots of people are.'

Enid tucked away that piece of information. It had possibility. She'd have preferred a guarantee of death, but it wasn't easy.

It took a few months to perfect her plan. The first thing she did was slash all the tyres on one of their neighbour's cars. It created a flurry of unease in the street. Neighbours gossiped about it for a week or two then forgot it. All except for the victim. Then she did the same in the adjacent street, targeting two cars this time. Once again there was an initial outrage that faded after a couple of days. She waited two more months before deciding the time was right.

Her parents were going away for a weekend. They were going to leave early in the morning and frost was forecast. It was ideal. With the other cars she'd tampered with she'd done it overnight, to give the tyres plenty of time to deflate before morning. She wasn't a psychopath; it was only her parents she wanted dead. After they'd gone to bed she slipped out of the house and tore into the tyres of a car parked at the top of their street. Her plan was to make it seem like a random act of violence. She set her alarm for six a.m. so as to be sure to be awake when they were leaving.

As it turned out she didn't need the alarm. She was awake by five and lay there for an hour, her heart beating wildly as she contemplated what she was about to do. At one minute past six, when she was sure her parents were awake, she got out of bed and had a shower before getting dressed. She had to get the timing right.

They'd said they were leaving at six thirty. When she heard them in the hall she sat on the edge of her bed, poised for action. Once she heard the door slam she ran along the hallway, grabbed a scarf from the coat stand and stood at the front door listening for the car engine to start up. As soon as it did, she opened the door and rushed out.

'Wait,' she said, waving the scarf in front of them. It dropped to the ground right beside the passenger door and she dropped with it, taking the chance to slide the knife out of her sleeve and rip into the tyre. Not hard enough for it to immediately deflate. That was not what she wanted. Knife back inside her right sleeve, scarf in her left hand, she knocked on the window.

'Don't you need this?'

'What for?' huffed her mother.

'Well... it's cold. I thought...'

'Oh, give it here.' Her mother grabbed it from her. The car was already moving.

Enid waited until the car was out of sight before going inside. Anyone watching would think her the dutiful daughter, up before dawn, wishing her parents a safe journey. When it turned the corner at the bottom of the street she went inside, washed the knife thoroughly – she didn't think it would be of interest to the police, but who could be sure? – and placed it with the others in the knife rack. Once she had done this she went back to her room, lay on her bed and read for a while before drifting back to sleep.

She was dreaming of being attacked by wasps when she awoke with a start to the noise of the doorbell buzzing. She looked at her watch – was this it? – and made her way to the front door.

'Enid.' It was Mrs Donnelly from next door. 'Did you hear or see anything last night? The McLeods have had all four tyres slashed on their car.'

Enid put a hand up to her mouth. 'How awful. Do they have any idea who did it?'

'Not a clue, no. It's happened a couple of times now. Better say to your mum and dad. I can't see their car anywhere.'

'Oh, they were off first thing this morning.'

'Never mind. I'm sure they would have noticed if they had a flat tyre! You're sure you didn't see anything? Mary across the road said you were out late last night.'

Damn this place. Full of nosy people. Enid pretended to think for a second or two. 'Sorry, no. I can't think of anything out of the ordinary and I didn't see anyone either. I can't imagine who could have done such an awful thing.'

Back inside she leaned against the wall in the hallway. Whoever it was who had seen her, hadn't seen her slash the tyres. They'd have said, surely. Called the police. Her mouth was dry with nerves. She was wide awake now in spite of her near sleepless night. She went through to the kitchen and filled the kettle. But when the water boiled, she left it. Her stomach was churning. This waiting about was awful. She had no guilt. They deserved what was coming to them, but what if her plan failed, what if she'd been seen? She hadn't spotted anyone last night or this morning, but anyone might be looking out of their window. How many years might she get? It would be a prison sentence without any doubt. Christ, she was going to be sick; she had to get out of here. Go for a walk; that always calmed her down. She grabbed her coat from the coat rack and went outside.

She went to Ross Hall Park, one of Glasgow's many green spaces. It was a small park, but she liked it, especially the rock garden. After about an hour her nerves were calmer and she was ravenously hungry. It was time to go home.

She saw the police car as soon as she turned the corner into her street. No flashing blue lights, just a quiet presence in front of her house. She tried not to look at it as she went into the garden but noted there was a male and a female police officer. They got out of the car immediately and came over to greet her. This was going to take all of her acting skills.

'Is this about the tyre slashings? I heard another car was targeted last night.' She kept her voice light and unflustered.

'Do you live in this house?' asked the woman.

'Yes, I do. Why?'

She ignored Enid's question. 'What is your name, please?'

'Enid Cavendish. What is this about?'

'Who lives with you here?'

Enid frowned; a frown was appropriate here, she believed. 'Richard and Doris Cavendish.'

'Shall we go inside?'

Enid drew herself up to her full height. 'Why?'

The police officer reddened. 'Please, inside.'

For a moment she considered making a fuss, drawing out their obvious discomfort. But that would be cruel. 'Fine,' she said. 'Come in.'

The living room was gloomy and she turned on the lights. 'Please, take a seat.' She indicated the two armchairs, which were faded from years of use.

They remained standing, only sitting once she herself had taken a seat. They exchanged a look and the man gave a slight nod to the woman. Permission to speak.

'Miss Cavendish, my name is Police Constable Victoria Shields and this is Police Sergeant Paul O'Donnell. We're very sorry to have to tell you your parents were involved in a serious car crash on the M8 earlier today.'

It had worked. 'I... what happened? Are they all right?'

A pause and another exchange of glances between the police officers. *Get on with it*, thought Enid.

'I'm afraid both of your parents sustained injuries that are incompatible with life.' It was the man talking. Pompous ass.

'I don't understand.'

PC Shields frowned. 'Your parents died at the scene of the crash.'

'No.'

'I'm afraid so.' PC Shields voice was gentle. She sounded as if she cared.

Enid brought the beatings she'd had to mind, and sure enough tears came to her eyes. 'But they were here. A matter of hours ago. Looking forward to their break.' She had no idea whether they were looking forward to it or not, but it was the sort of thing people said. Wasn't it? She had no idea.

'I know. I'm so sorry for your loss. Can I get you a cup of tea, Miss Cavendish?

'Please, call me Enid.'

'And I'm Vicky. No, don't get up. I'll find my own way to the kitchen.'

Enid was dumbstruck. It had worked. She was free. 'Do you know how it happened? Was there anyone else involved?' God, what if she'd killed someone else, a child perhaps? What had she been thinking? More tears ran down her face.

But Sergeant O'Donnell was shaking his head. 'They were in the outside lane, overtaking. We don't know for sure, but a woman in the car who was overtaken thinks a tyre blew out. The car began to shake and they ploughed into the central reservation.'

Enid said nothing. She put her head in her hands. She was beginning to enjoy this acting lark. Vicky came back into the room with tea for all of them.

'Here you are. I've put sugar in it, for the shock.'

So, people actually did that then. Amazing. Enid took a sip. It was too hot and she put it on the table beside her. She began to shake.

Vicky put an arm round her. It took all Enid's willpower not to shrug it off. 'Can you put on the fire, please?' She indicated the gas fire.

Paul leaped up, glad to have something to do. 'It's the shock,' he said. 'It makes you shake.'

The three of them sat in silence for a few minutes. At last Enid broke the silence. 'What now? Do I have to go to identify them?'

The silence intensified. 'I'm afraid that won't be possible.'

Here it was then. They'd been stringing her along. 'Why not?' she managed.

Another look. She was sick of them. 'What aren't you telling me?'

'The car crashed at speed. There was a fire. It was... destructive.'

'Oh.'

'Are you all right?'

'You mean they were burned?'

'Yes. And there's little left of the car too.'

She had to say it. 'So, we won't know what caused the blowout, if that's what caused the crash?'

'No.'

347

'There's been a spate of tyre slashing round here. Is it possible they had one of theirs slashed?' It was risky asking them, but it would be more suspicious if she didn't mention what was the hot topic for the street.

Paul shook his head. 'I wouldn't think that's what's caused it. They'd have noticed a flat tyre pretty early on. It's more likely to have been underinflated. That's the usual cause of a blowout. Did they keep an eye on tyre pressure?'

'I'm not sure,' lied Enid. Her father was obsessional about his car and checked the pressure every time he filled up with petrol, but why make trouble for herself? 'Please excuse me. I'm finding all of this a little hard. Is there anything else you need from me?'

There was no mistaking the look of surprise that crossed both their faces. Had she sounded too abrupt? Said the wrong thing? She hid her face in her hands and allowed a sob to escape. She didn't dare look at them.

'I'm not sure you should be left alone,' said Vicky. 'You've had such a shock. Is there anyone we could phone? A relative or a friend.'

Enid took a tissue from her pocket and blew her nose noisily. 'I'd rather be on my own if you don't mind.' She didn't admit she had no real friends.

'Well, if you're sure.' There was no hiding the relief in Vicky's voice. Enid didn't blame her. It must be shit telling people their loved ones had died. For a moment she allowed herself to think of what it must be like to lose a loved one. If only her parents had loved her. She would have loved them back. But as it was, they'd never shown her any real affection, only feigned it when they were being watched.

Vicky and Paul stood up to go. They were more relaxed now. 'Someone will be in touch to tell you what happens next. There will be post-mortems of course, but the morgue will be in touch to let you know when the funeral parlour can pick them up.'

Enid followed them to the door, hoping her face didn't betray anything. She hadn't realised there would be a post-mortem. Surely it was obvious the car crash had killed them? Thank God she hadn't followed through on her plan to put a sleeping pill in her father's early morning tea as back up in case the tyre plan didn't work. She had nothing to fear. She crossed her fingers as she saw the two police officers out. All she had to do was keep her nerve.

The following days were the worst of her life. Every visit, no matter who it was from, made her jumpy. Neighbours called with cards and condolences and their speculations about what had happened.

'If they catch that tyre slasher, they should hang the bastard.'

In a flat tone, Enid repeated what the police had said. 'The police think the tyres were underinflated. That's the usual reason for a blowout.'

She continued to be jumpy for some weeks. It was during this time she decided to change her name. Move to another city. Give herself a fresh start. With the money from the sale of the bungalow and the money in her father's savings account, she would be comfortably off. Richer than she'd ever dreamed.

Edith forced her thoughts back to the present day. She was on her way to see her aunt, to meet her and her cousins and other relatives. Well, not all of them; there were restrictions in place and no more than six people were allowed to meet indoors. They were lucky to live in Devon, which had been put on a medium alert. Her heart beat faster at the thought of meeting all these new people. She wouldn't tell them about what she'd done though. It might put them off her.

Had Sergeant Nicholson read the letter yet? She wasn't sure she'd done the right thing in writing to him. It was a risk telling all this to a police officer, but he'd understand. Wouldn't he?

The End

Acknowledgments

First of all, I'd like to express my gratitude to Rebecca Collins and Adrian Hobart at Hobeck Books. Their professionalism and expertise is second to none. Rebecca and Adrian nurture their writers. They talk about being a family and this is evident in the way their authors all support each other. I love being part of the Hobeck family. Thank you to all of you.

Thanks are also due to Sue Davison who copyedited this book. Sue is a superb editor with a fastidious eye for detail. I am in complete awe of her talent. Jayne Mapp designed the cover and as always, did a fantastic job.

I am a member of two writing groups and I would like to thank them for their continuing support. The Glasgow University editorial group are now far flung (from Orkney to Hebden Bridge) and we rarely get to meet in person but we do manage (almost) monthly Zoom meetings. Thank you to Ailsa Crum, Alison Miller, Ann Mackinnon, Clare Morrison, Griz Gordon and Heather Mackay for your friendship and support. The Glad group is more local and their support is also invaluable. Thank you to Ailsa Crum, Alison Irvine, Bert Thomson, Emily Munro, Emma Lennox Miller, Les Wood, and Natalie Whittle.

I must also thank my friend, Geraldine Smyth, who has been a tireless and enthusiastic advocate of my books as well as a most excellent friend.

Finally, my husband Martin and our three grown up children, Katherine, Kevin and Peter have been very supportive since I started writing. They have been beyond patient with me as I've grumped and groused about the writing process.

MAUREEN MYANT

About the Author

Maureen worked for over 25 years as an educational psychologist but has also worked as a teacher and an Open University Associate Lecturer. She is a graduate of the prestigious University of Glasgow MLitt in Creative Writing course where she was taught by Janice Galloway, Liz Lochhead, James Kelman, Alasdair Gray and Tom Leonard among others. She also has a PhD in Creative Writing. Her first novel *The Search* was published by Alma Books and was translated into Spanish, Dutch and Turkish. It was longlisted for the Waverton Good Read Award and was one of the books chosen to be read for the Festival du premier roman de Chambéry. Her second novel, *The Confession*, was published by Hobeck Books in 2022 and introduces DI Alex Scrimgeour and DS Mark Nicholson. In an earlier incarnation it was shortlisted for a Crime Writers' Association Debut Dagger.

Maureen has been a voracious reader since the age of six when, fed up with her mum reading Noddy stories to her, she picked up her older brother's copy of Enid Blyton's The Valley of Adventure and devoured it in an evening. She hasn't stopped reading since and loves literary fiction, historical fiction, crime fiction, psychological thrillers and contemporary fiction but not necessarily in that order. Her favourite book is *The Secret History* by Donna Tartt and go-to comfort read is *Anne of Green Gables*.

Maureen lives in Glasgow with her husband. She has three grownup children and six grandchildren who love to beat her at Bananagrams.

Hobeck Books - the home of great stories

We hope you've enjoyed reading this novel by Maureen Myant. To keep up to date on Maureen's fiction writing please do follow her on Twitter.

Hobeck Books offers a number of short stories and novellas, including *You Can't Trust Anyone These Days* by Maureen Myant, free for subscribers in the compilation *Crime Bites*.

- *Echo Rock* by Robert Daws
- *Old Dogs, Old Tricks* by AB Morgan
- *The Silence of the Rabbit* by Wendy Turbin
- *Never Mind the Baubles: An Anthology of Twisted Winter Tales* by the Hobeck Team (including many of the Hobeck authors and Hobeck's two publishers)
- *The Clarice Cliff Vase* by Linda Huber
- *Here She Lies* by Kerena Swan
- *The Macnab Principle* by R.D. Nixon
- *Fatal Beginnings* by Brian Price
- *A Defining Moment* by Lin Le Versha
- *Saviour* by Jennie Ensor
- *You Can't Trust Anyone These Days* by Maureen Myant

Also please visit the Hobeck Books website for details of our other superb authors and their books, and if you would like to get in touch, we would love to hear from you.

Hobeck Books also presents a weekly podcast, the Hobcast, where founders Adrian Hobart and Rebecca Collins discuss all things book related, key issues from each week, including the ups and downs of running a creative business. Each episode includes an interview with one of the people who make Hobeck possible: the editors, the authors, the cover designers. These are the people who help Hobeck bring great stories to life. Without them, Hobeck wouldn't exist. The Hobcast can be listened to from all the usual platforms but it can also be found on the Hobeck website: **www. hobeck.net/hobcast**.

The Glasgow Southside Crime Series

The Confession

2001 SHORTLIST TITLE FOR A CRIME WRITERS' ASSOCIATION DEBUT DAGGER

'Superb. Fast-paced and intense. *The Confession* is a rollercoaster of a read that kept me nailed to the sofa. A truly original premise and an addictively intense plot.' Linda Huber

The Deception

'Wow, what a gripping book – I couldn't put it down yet didn't want it to end.' Gillian Jackson

Both books available to buy from Amazon or Hobeck Books.

The Search

In Czechoslovakia, 1942, Jan's father has been summarily executed by the Nazis. His mother and his older sister Maria have disappeared, and his younger sister Lena has been removed to a remote farm in the German countryside. With Europe in the throes of war, the ten-year-old boy embarks on a personal journey to reunite the family he has been violently torn from. The experiences he goes through and the horror he faces during this desperate quest will change his life for ever. While examining the devastating effects of war on ordinary families, *The Search* provides an exploration of fear and loss, and of the bond between parents and children. Riveting, moving, at times disturbing, Maureen Myant's debut novel will haunt its readers for a long time after they have put it down.

Available from Amazon.